The Oyster Girl

Margaret Pemberton is the bestselling author of over thirty novels in many different genres, some of which are contemporary in setting and some historical.

She has served as Chairman of the Romantic Novelists' Association and has three times served as a committee member of the Crime Writers' Association. Born in Bradford, she is married to a Londoner, has five children and two dogs, and lives in Whitstable, Kent. Apart from writing, her passions are tango, travel, English history and the English countryside.

By Margaret Pemberton

Rendezvous with Danger ❋ The Mystery of Saligo Bay
Vengeance in the Sun ❋ The Guilty Secret
Tapestry of Fear

African Enchantment ❋ Flight to Verechenko
A Many-Splendoured Thing ❋ Moonflower Madness
Forget-Me-Not Bride ❋ Party in Peking
Devil's Palace ❋ Lion of Languedoc
The Far Morning ❋ Forever

Yorkshire Rose ❋ The Flower Garden
Silver Shadows, Golden Dreams ❋ Never Leave Me
A Multitude of Sins ❋ White Christmas in Saigon
An Embarrassment of Riches ❋ Zadruga
The Four of Us ❋ The Londoners
Magnolia Square ❋ Coronation Summer
A Season of Secrets ❋ Beneath the Cypress Tree
The Summer Queen ❋ The Oyster Girl

Writing as Rebecca Dean
Enemies of the Heart ❋ Palace Circle
The Golden Prince ❋ Wallis

Writing as Maggie Hudson
Fast Women ❋ Tell Me No Secrets
Nowhere to Run ❋ Looking for Mr Big

The
Oyster Girl

MARGARET
PEMBERTON

PAN BOOKS

First published 2025 by Pan Books
an imprint of Pan Macmillan
The Smithson, 6 Briset Street, London ECIM 5NR
EU representative: Macmillan Publishers Ireland Ltd, 1st Floor,
The Liffey Trust Centre, 117–126 Sheriff Street Upper,
Dublin 1, DO1 YC43
Associated companies throughout the world
www.panmacmillan.com

ISBN 978-1-5098-4181-3

1 3 5 7 9 8 6 4 2

A CIP catalogue record for this book is available from the British Library.

Typeset in Ehrhardt MT Std by Palimpsest Book Production Ltd, Falkirk, Stirlingshire
Printed and bound by CPI Group (UK) Ltd, Croydon, CR0 4YY

Visit **www.panmacmillan.com** to read more about all our books
and to buy them. You will also find features, author interviews and
news of any author events, and you can sign up for e-newsletters
so that you're always first to hear about our new releases.

To my children:
Amanda
Rebecca
Polly
Michael
Natasha
and not forgetting Henry

Chapter One

7 May 1910

'The King is dead!' Tilly Shilling shouted as she ran over the cobbles towards the little harbour-side cottage that was home to her, and to her niece and nephew. Her niece, seventeen-year-old Janna, was seated in the doorway, a large sack at either side of her as she cleaned the last batch of that season's oysters ready for market.

'He died last night!' Tilly, who was only ten years older than Janna, came to a breathless halt, a mane of blue-black hair tumbling down her back in untamed waves and curls. 'Billy Gann saw it on the front page of the paper, so it must be true, and the news is now all over town.'

The harbour served as the centre of Oystertown and people were beginning to throng the quayside, relaying the news to each other in shocked disbelief. King Edward, or Bertie, as he was affectionately referred to, had been a man of the people. Unlike his late mother, Queen Victoria, he hadn't hidden himself away at Windsor or Balmoral, fraternizing only with close family and a few intimate courtiers. He'd strolled the world's stage, his bulky figure as well known in Paris, Biarritz and the fashionable spa towns of Germany as it was in London. No major race meeting had been complete without his presence, a homburg hat tilted at a rakish angle, a cigar in hand

and Caesar, his little fox terrier, at his heels. He had been king for only a little over nine years – no time at all compared to his mother's sixty-three-year reign – but it was instantly obvious that the world would be a duller place without him.

'According to the *Oystertown Gazette*, he returned from a visit to Biarritz only a few days ago.' Dazedly Janna pushed the sacks of oysters aside and rose to her feet. 'I can't take this news in without a cup of strong tea. Have you time to join me? Or do you need to get back to the Duke?'

The Duke of Connaught was Oystertown's most popular public house and Tilly, with her hour-glass figure, was far and away its most popular barmaid.

'I need to get back,' she said regretfully, 'and when I do, I'll be run off my feet. Every man with a good arm will be raising a pint in memory of King Edward.'

She turned to go and stubbed her toe on one of the sacks. 'Are these what is left of Jasper's last catch until dredging starts again in September?'

'Yes.' Janna was still thinking about King Edward's shockingly unexpected death. 'Do you think Queen Alexandra will allow Alice Keppel to attend the King's funeral?'

'I shouldn't think so. Would you allow a woman who had been your husband's mistress for the last twelve years to upstage you at his funeral? I know I wouldn't. From now on Alice Keppel will have to sing elsewhere for her supper.'

And well aware that the respectable matrons of Oystertown regarded her in exactly the same light as they regarded Alice Keppel – and not giving a fig about it – Tilly hitched up her ankle-skimming skirt and set off at a run in the direction of the high street and the Duke of Connaught public house.

Struggling to come to terms with the enormity of the change that had suddenly taken place in England and ignoring the oysters that were still waiting to be cleaned, Janna filled a kettle with water and put it on the hob. Then, tears streaming down her face, she put a scoopful of tea into a brown glazed teapot and took a cup and saucer from the dresser and set them on the table. What was life going to be like now their colourful, larger-than-life king was dead and his successor, his eldest surviving son, George, was king?

Unlike his father – whose exuberant love of life had always been blazingly obvious – there was nothing genial or hail-fellow-well-met about George. On every newspaper photograph she had ever seen of him he had looked glum, and as for him ever having had a mistress – the idea was beyond her imagination.

As she waited for the kettle to boil she looked around the small, cosy room. Her father, an oysterman like Jasper, had drowned twelve years ago in one of the biggest storms of the last century and her mother had died of consumption two years later. It was then that her father's young sister had come to her and Jasper's rescue, saving them from an orphanage.

'I'll take care of them,' she had said fiercely as, stunned and bewildered with grief, they had clung to her skirt.

The kettle began to sing and she took it off the hob and filled the teapot. Tilly's method of earning enough money for the three of them to live on was one ages-old, but none of the local men who paid for her company ever stepped foot across the cottage threshold. Tilly had had her standards and their home had been sacrosanct.

Janna poured milk into her cup, remembering the winter evenings when the two of them had sat before the fire making the gaily coloured rag rugs that now took the chill off the stone flooring. The kitchen range – an iron oven on one side of its hob grate where a fire burned throughout the day, an iron tank with a constant supply of hot water on the other side of it – was scrupulously black-leaded every week. The deal table in the centre of the room was scoured so regularly the wood was nearly white. In spring and summer wild flowers in a spare milk jug graced the centre of the table. In winter she and Tilly bought tubes of coloured wax from the local stationer's and made small half-moons that, when curled around twigs, gave the appearance of a flower. Beneath a muslin-curtained window was a stone sink with a bucket underneath so that the dirty water could be carried into the yard and thrown over the flagstones.

The family's laundry was taken care of in a lean-to outhouse where there was a large coal-fired copper for boiling clothes, a dolly-tub and a head-high mangle. Janna could remember how carefully Tilly had shown her how to fold clothes that had buttons on so that the buttons lay over the edge of the mangle's two heavy rollers and didn't get crushed. Also in the outhouse and hanging on a large hook was a tin bath that was hauled in front of the kitchen-range every Friday night so they could take turns at having what Tilly called 'a good wash and a soak'. Across a small paved yard there was an outside privy and a water pump. Upstairs she and Tilly shared one bedroom, Jasper had the other and Wellington, a ginger tomcat, kept their little home mouse and rat free.

On the day Jasper had been old enough to take his late father's fishing smack, the *Pearl*, out onto the oyster beds and put his earnings on the deal table, Tilly had abandoned the occupation that until then had kept food in their larder and coal in the grate. Her becoming a barmaid – and nothing but a barmaid – hadn't, however, changed the way she was thought of and when it came to marriage, Oystertown's working men steered clear of a woman with a reputation such as Tilly's, not wanting a bride their mates most probably knew a little too well. Oystertown's young women were usually married before they were twenty-one, but at twenty-seven, Tilly was still a spinster and Janna had no idea whether Tilly cared, or whether she was carelessly indifferent.

She had just poured scalding tea into the cup when there came the sound of Jasper's booted feet on the harbour-side cobbles and moments later he strode through the open doorway, ducking his head as he did so because of his height.

Whenever she saw her brother unexpectedly, as now, Janna couldn't help thinking that he could more easily be taken for Tilly's brother than her nephew, for they both had the same unruly hair, gold-flecked brown eyes and the same careless, almost insolent attitude towards life.

At the sight of her sitting idle when there were oysters still waiting to be cleaned, he said dryly, 'The King may be dead, Janna, and those oysters may be all that is left of the last batch of the season, but I've a customer waiting for them.'

'I'm sorry. Tilly told me about the King. I just can't get my head around his not being there anymore. How can England feel like England without him? Do you want some tea?'

'England will always feel like England, but you're right in that dull and boring George won't be able to fill his father's boots and yes, Janna, I will have a pot of tea.' He lifted a pint mug down from the dresser, set it on the table and then straddled a chair, folding his arms across the back of it, his shirt open at the neck, his sleeves rolled up. 'I've not come home mid-morning because of the news about Bertie. I've come because there's something I need to tell you before anyone else does.'

She paused in the act of pouring his tea, filled with apprehension. Jasper had been seeing an awful lot of Moody Gibbs's wife. Had Moody found out? Unlike Jasper – who thrived on trouble – she hated it.

'Don't look like that, Janna,' he said, reading her mind. 'It's nothing to do with Rosie. Do you remember when the Easter Fair came to town and I won three sovereigns getting into the ring and flooring what the fairground barker had trumpeted as being their "Unbeaten Bare-Knuckle Boxing Champion"? Well, I'm going to do it professionally.'

'What? Knock out their bare-knuckle champion?'

His strong-boned face split into a wide grin. 'No, silly goose. Do some bare-knuckle boxing. I've had a word with Ozzie at the Duke and he's all for having matches take place in a room at the back of the pub. It would be something to bring extra money in – especially during the summer months.'

She stared at him, appalled.

She and Tilly had been with him when, to roars of encouragement from the crowd, he had yanked off his shirt revealing chest muscles that were whipcord hard and had stepped into a makeshift boxing ring and taken on a massively built fairground thug. The thug hadn't given him the chance to square up to him before he'd fisted Jasper a blow that had sent Jasper reeling back against the ropes.

'Don't let him get away with that, Jas!' Tilly had shouted, clutching his shirt to her chest as the crowd had cheered and booed in equal measure and sobs had risen in Janna's throat.

And Jasper hadn't let his formidable-looking opponent get away with it. As the thug had borne down on him, leering from ear-to-ear, Jasper had dodged him and landed a powerful low blow to his exposed midriff. The unbeaten champion had doubled up, gasping for air. Lightning fast, Jasper had fisted a solid right hook to the side of his opponent's head and followed it up with a solid left hook to the other side of it. The thug had fallen to his knees, swayed, struggled to his feet, then tottered. To jeers and boos from the crowd, he had slumped to his knees again and, showing no signs of a quick recovery or of wanting to continue with the match, he had been counted out.

Jasper had raised his arms in victory, had very reluctantly been given three sovereigns, and had been told by the fairground barker that he never wanted to see him again. Although the fight had been short and, for Jasper, successful, it had never occurred to Janna that it would set a precedent and yet now here he was, announcing that he intended fighting bare-knuckle on a regular basis in the back room of the Duke.

She was about to say that when Tilly heard she would put a stop to it by threatening to quit as a barmaid there – and if it came to a choice between having Tilly as a barmaid or bare-knuckle boxing in the back room, Ozzie, in his late thirties and balding, would surely opt for retaining Tilly as a barmaid – but she remembered Tilly's shouted encouragement when Jasper had fought at the fair and she didn't think Tilly would threaten to quit. She thought Tilly might take the attitude that Jasper was old enough to make his own decisions about how he made a living – and that his chances of death on entering a boxing ring would be far less than when he skippered the town's lifeboat in horrendous winter seas.

Knowing it would cause an argument if she put her thoughts into words, she bit back what she had been on the point of saying and poured herself a second cup of tea.

Jasper pushed his barely touched pint pot to one side. 'Something else before I go. A family new to town have moved into the mill.'

'The mill?' There were no mills in, or even close to, Oystertown. 'Do you mean the windmill?'

He nodded and her eyes widened. Oystertown lay huddled at the bottom of a steep hill known as The Heights and the distinctively white windmill standing high on the top of The Heights was a landmark for miles around – and served as an especially vital landmark for boats out at sea. It hadn't been a working mill for over a decade and although Oystertown children often played inside it, no one before had made any attempt to try and make a home in it.

'How do you know?' she asked. 'Who told you?'

'Smelly Bell.'

Smelly was a tramp who passed through Oystertown several times a year.

'He said there was a horse and cart outside it and that the cart was full of odds and ends of furniture and lots of pictures painted on bits of board and a man was taking the pictures into the mill first.'

'Pictures?' The teapot was now empty and, intrigued and wanting to hear more, Janna refilled the kettle and pushed it back on the red-hot hob. 'What kind of pictures?'

'Hell, Janna! How do I know?' Jasper pushed a tumble of night-black curls away from his forehead. 'I'm just telling you what Smelly told me.'

Not many Oystertown homes had pictures on their walls and, when they did, the pictures were mostly of Bertie and Queen Alexandra. Wondering if these would now be taken down and replaced by pictures of the new king and his wife, she said, 'He seems a strange kind of person to be coming to live at Oystertown, Jasper. Will he fit in?'

'As he's clearly not an oysterman, I shouldn't think so. And even if he was an oysterman, he couldn't dredge here. Only Oystermen born and bred can harvest Oystertown oysters.'

He rose to his feet and she said quickly, having one last question before he left the house, 'What about his family? Was it just the man and his wife moving in, or were there children helping to carry in pictures?'

'There was no wife – or none that Smelly could see. He said there was a bearded, heavily built, foreign-looking man who was dressed like something out of a circus in purple trousers, a yellow shirt and a short black cape; a young bloke about my age who was dressed quite normally; and a girl a little younger with hair the colour of burnt marmalade.

Don't get any ideas about seeking them out, Janna. From Smelly's description of them, they're probably tinkers and best given a wide berth. Keep something hot for me tonight, I'm going to be late in.'

And in a couple of strides he was ducking beneath the head of the door and striding out onto the cobbles, Wellington shooting out of the cottage ahead of him.

Janna moved the kettle off the hob. Having had a second cup of tea she didn't want a third cup. A new family in the town – for although the windmill was a little over a mile and a half away it was still counted as being part of the town – and a family who thought moving pictures into their new home came before moving furniture into it. It was all very interesting and she decided that when she had finished cleaning the oysters she would take a walk up the Heights and see if she could catch a glimpse of the odd-sounding newcomers for herself.

It was midday before she had enough free time to be able to do so. Oystertown's only fully cobbled street ran all the way from the harbour to the foot of the Heights and when she turned into it she came to a sudden halt, sucking in her breath, for from end to end it was a sea of Union Jacks. Last used for Bertie's coronation they had been hastily retrieved from lofts and lumber rooms and fluttered from the upper windows of shops and pubs. Halfway down the high street the town's Anglican church was flying one at half-mast, as was the Methodist church which abutted the Fox and Firkin, the last public house before the high street petered out. From then on the road began a steep climb up the Heights with nothing but open country on either side of it and, at the top, the windmill.

The high street was just as thronged as the harbour-side had been with everyone having an opinion on why the King had died so unexpectedly.

'It was that nasty Frenchy air that did for him,' Gertie Dadd, Ozzie's mother, said to everyone who passed her as she leaned against the door jamb of her tobacconist's shop, beefy arms folded across her chest. 'He should have stuck to going to Balmoral or the Isle of Wight like his mother did, then he'd still be with us.'

Other opinions Janna heard as she weaved her way between knots of people was that instead of sticking to English oysters, and more importantly oysters from Oystertown, the King had eaten a foreign oyster and died of food poisoning; that he had caught a chill whilst romancing a potential new mistress in the open air; that he had choked on a chicken bone.

As she began nearing the bottom end of the high street, she heard Mrs Pettman, the Methodist minister's wife, say to the local coal merchant, 'You don't think the King's death could be anything to do with the number of cigars he smoked in a day and the amount of champagne and brandy that he's said to have drunk, do you, Harry?'

Janna never heard what Harry's reply was, for from the alley next to the Fox and Firkin came shouts and screams and the sound of galloping hooves. Seconds later a terrified horse with no one at its reins erupted out of the alley, dragging a wildly rocking cart behind it.

As the horse swerved around the corner into the high street everyone who had been walking across the high street, or standing in the middle of it gossiping about the King's death, made a panic-stricken run for the pavement, grabbing their children's hands as they did so, or hoisting them into their arms.

A toddler remained unclaimed. Wearing nothing but a short filthy vest, he was sitting directly in the path of the horse, rolling a marble from one hand to the other.

For Janna, there wasn't time for thought, only for instant action. Afterwards she didn't remember sprinting across the cobbles.

She didn't remember scooping the toddler up as the horse thundered towards them, eyes rolling, nostrils flaring. All she remembered was the animal's terrifying size; the smell of its sweat and its fear; the certainty that she and the child were about to be trampled to death.

And then it was galloping past her, so close she could feel the heat of its body. Her relief was so colossal it made her dizzy. Still running, she neared the edge of the pavement while people ran into the road to meet her. As the now screaming toddler was taken out of her arms, she tripped, falling full length on the cobbles. For several seconds she was too stunned to move, aware only of people crowding around her and of their concern.

Harry was asking urgently, 'Are you badly hurt, pet? Have you broken anything?'

Her skirt was torn, her knees were bleeding, her legs felt like jelly and the side of her body that had taken her full weight was throbbing with pain, but she was alive when she could so easily have been trampled to death.

She knew something else, as well. No way could she continue with her walk up the Heights in order to satisfy her curiosity about the newcomers. Catching sight of them would have to wait until another day.

Dazedly she realized that Harry was helping her to her feet, his hands caked with coal-dust. 'Come on. If you like, I'll give you a lift home on the back of the coal cart.'

Undignified as it was, it was an offer she accepted.

Chapter Two

'This is not one of your better ideas, Papa.'

Exasperatedly eighteen-year-old Marietta Picard lifted back the thick braid of red hair that had fallen forward over her shoulder and surveyed the filthy ground floor of what was to be their new home. 'How can we live here? There are fox droppings, owl droppings . . .'

'All of which can be swept up, my treasure,' her father said complacently, 'and you have not yet seen the other floors; there are five of them. Five! Just think of the quality of light! Just think of what a magnificent studio I will have!'

Marietta appreciated the importance of a studio with splendid light, but there were other considerations. 'And what about a kitchen?' she demanded, looking around at the huge octagonal-shaped space they were standing in. 'Is there one? What am I to use for an oven? For a sink?'

Pascal Picard frowned. Ovens and sinks were not things that had been at the forefront of his mind when, in London, he had been introduced to Mrs Eames, the elderly widow of Oystertown's last miller. All he had thought about was the light and the peppercorn rent Mrs Eames was asking for the windmill. Coming at a time when he had been threatened with eviction from their rented flat in London's Rotherhithe, the prospect of a five-floor windmill overlooking the sea had been one his bohemian heart had leapt at.

'I'll soon find a wood-burning stove and a sink from some-where,' Marietta's brother said, propping the iron bedhead he was carrying against one of the octagonal walls. 'And until the windmill is liveable in we could probably rent a cottage in the nearby fishing town.'

His father's complacency vanished. 'Never, Daniel! Never will I rent a cottage when I can live in a windmill! A windmill that still has its sails! A windmill God has put across my path!'

His cape had fallen forward over his shoulder and theatri-cally he flung it back, striding across to the fixed iron ladder that led up to the first floor. 'And now, *mes enfants*,' he said, recovering his temper as fast as he had lost it. 'I will climb to the top of the windmill and look at the view. My fellow artist and countryman, Monsieur Monet, has painted the same haystack a dozen times, always when the light is a little different and casts different shadows. I, Pascal Picard, will paint the view from the top of my windmill countless times in countless different kinds of light. I am embarking on a new path as an artist. I am poised on the edge of artistic greatness; I can feel it in my blood and in my bones!'

And with surprising agility for a man of his girth he took the rungs of the ladder two at a time.

'Look on the bright side of things,' Daniel said encour-agingly as their father disappeared from view. 'Pa is no longer in London. There is no longer a public house only a minute away from where we are living. True, the mill is only a hundred yards or so away from the road and he could walk down the hill to the town easy enough, but coming back up the hill, worse for drink, will utterly defeat him. I doubt there will be any gaming clubs in Oystertown and so he won't, on the throw of a dice, be losing the little money he sometimes earns.'

'Maybe not, but he won't be earning *any* money unless I continue hawking his work around London galleries, and to do that I'm going to have to take his work up to London and that means train fares. Before, when things were sticky, the money you earned at Selfridges enabled us to manage, but there are no stores like Selfridges outside of London and in a small fishing town there won't be a department store for you to apply to for a job. There may be a draper's shop, but I wouldn't count on it!'

'I'll find work of some kind.' Daniel was always unflappably positive and, unlike their father, blessedly practical. 'Take that worried look off your face and let's get to grips with the mill. With five floors there must be a couple that can be made liveable.'

Doubting it very much, Marietta followed him across to the ladder.

When, one after the other, they stepped out onto the first floor, they were both immediately aware of how quickly the rooms in the windmill tapered off in size.

'Although it isn't as big as the ground floor it has more possibilities,' Daniel said, ignoring the stale, musty air and the mice their presence had sent fleeing for cover.

Reluctantly, Marietta admitted that he was right. Four of the octagonal walls had windows. All of them were thick with years of grime but Marietta knew that when they were cleaned, two of them would give views over open countryside, the other two would give views of the town and, beyond the town, the sea. More importantly still, windows meant the room would be full of light and would make a perfect studio for their father.

'Let's see what the second floor has to offer,' Daniel said. 'The railed wooden staging –' the windmill's balcony – 'that runs around the outside of the mill is at second-floor height and there must be doors leading out on to it.'

With more interest than she had started off with Marietta followed him up the second ladder, stepped off it and came to a stunned, horrified halt. The entire floor was filled with machinery. There was a head-high wheel with giant cogs. A wooden vat encased two enormous millstones. Above the millstones a chute led down from the third floor coming to a halt above a massive wooden tray with high-sided, inward-sloping sides. There was a hoist. There were pulleys. There was lots of belting. Below a jumbo-sized sieve there was a sinister-looking vertical machine and a much smaller pair of millstones.

'Hell's bells!' Daniel, too, came to a sudden halt. 'How are we going to get rid of this lot? It would take a squad of army engineers to shift it.'

'Well, we certainly can't.' The brief flood of optimism she had felt on seeing the first floor had vanished. 'Let's look at the remaining floors. If they are the same as this one, then with or without you and Pa, and despite the floor below being suitable for a studio, I'm going back to London. I mean it, Daniel. So help me, I truly mean it.'

Knowing how capable she was of carrying out her threat, he followed her with rising concern to where the next ladder led upwards.

Marietta climbed it first, not knowing whether she was relieved or disappointed when she stepped from it into a room a couple of feet smaller again than the one they had just left and one that was empty apart from two trap doors, a hoist, and a chute that led down to the high-sided tray on the floor below.

'I can dismantle the hoist and get rid of the chute,' Daniel said encouragingly. 'It means that so far, counting the ground floor, we have three floors that can be made liveable in and we still haven't seen the state of the fourth floor.'

'We can't live on the first floor, Daniel.' Her attitude that the windmill was yet another of their father's impractical, hare-brained enthusiasms wasn't one she was willing to abandon.

'It's the only floor we've seen so far that Pa could use for a studio. As for the ground floor . . .' The tone of her voice showed him what her opinion of the ground floor was.

'Then a lot depends on the floor above us,' he said, unruffled.

This time he went up the ladder first – and when he reached the top, he didn't even step from it.

'What's the matter?' she called up to him. 'Is it no use?'

'None at all. The entire space is taken up by the machinery that turns the sails.'

She was silent for a moment, and then she said: 'Any sign of Pa?'

'Yes. I can see him through the rafters in what was described as the fifth floor, but is actually the odd-shaped, cap-like top of the windmill. It couldn't possibly be used for living in. It's far too small and it's open to the air.'

'And what is he doing?'

'Doing?' Despite his disappointment at what he'd found there was wry amusement in Daniel's voice. 'He's sitting on the shaft that connects with the sails, admiring what I imagine is one of the best views in England.'

As he came back down the ladder she said, 'Well, that's it, then. We have to go back to London. Pa won't like it. He'll be as obstinate as a mule, but you'll have to make him see sense. We can't possibly live here.'

Daniel made a noise in his throat that could have meant anything and that she hoped was agreement. They climbed down the ladders to the third and then the second floor and he said impulsively, 'Let's go out onto the staging.'

Marietta didn't care what they did as long as they didn't continue bringing more furniture into the mill.

To reach the door leading to the staging they had to skirt around the machinery and the door, when they reached it, was so stiff Daniel had to put his shoulder to it to open it.

The rush of air that met them was heavenly – warm and fresh and sweet. And the view they hadn't been able to see from any of the mill's filthy windows was breathtaking.

'Oh!' she gasped as they stepped onto wooden decking broad enough for them to walk on side by side and made safe by a waist-high wooden railing, 'This is lovely!'

They had stepped out onto the north side of the mill and could see that, instead of dropping away steeply, as the land to the south did, the ground shelved gradually in undulating waves. Poppies dangled scarlet heads. Dazzling-white marguerites grew in thick swathes. There were so many buttercups that parts of the hillside seemed to be a gently moving, golden sea.

'It's a very paintable view, don't you think?' Daniel said, lighting a cigarette.

'Oh, yes!' Her agreement was unhesitating. For her, the staging had changed everything. As mercurial in her moods as her father, her feelings about the mill had undergone a dramatic change. Of course she wasn't going to return to Rotherhithe when she could live with a staging, and a view, like this. She wasn't a complete lunatic.

'Pa is right about the mill.' She hugged his arm. 'This is the perfect place for him to paint. His subject matter is all around him. He can paint *en plein air* on the staging, and at other times he can paint in the studio we will make for him on the first floor. It's perfect. I don't know why I didn't realize it before.'

Beneath a thatch of russet hair Daniel's face broke into a wide, relieved smile. 'Better late than never, Sis. What do you think of our making the ground floor our main living area? I can make it habitable. Trust me. And I can divide the third floor into two bedrooms, one for you and one for me and Pa.'

She didn't doubt his ability to do so. Daniel was both clever and, like their father, creative, although unlike their father his creativity found its outlet not in painting, but in designing and making things.

'And the mill has another couple of advantages that you probably haven't realized yet.' He blew a plume of blue smoke upwards.

'It has a water supply – I haven't yet managed to turn it on, but I will – and there's a horse trough.'

'But no stable?'

'No. A drawback, I must admit, but Hector is accustomed to sleeping out of doors. As soon as we've moved in, I'll make building a stable for him my first priority.'

She hugged his arm. 'It's all going to be absolutely wonderful, Daniel. Is the ground fertile enough for us to be able to grow vegetables?'

'With a bit of loving care, I think it will be. If I could get vegetables to grow in our London allotment, I don't see why I shouldn't get them to grow here.'

'And we could begin keeping hens for eggs. We could even,' she added as an afterthought, 'have a goat.'

'A goat?' His sandy eyebrows rose nearly into his hair.

'For milk.'

He took a deep, steadying breath. Until now they had only ever lived in huge cities – Paris and London – and their knowledge of livestock was nil. At a pinch he thought common sense would enable them to look after a cockerel and some hens, but a goat was surely a step too far.

He said hesitantly, 'If you want milk from a goat, I think you'll find it has to be pregnant first. Which means having another goat. A male one.'

'Then I'll get one.' She tucked her hand into the crook of his arm. 'Let's take a look at the view over the town.'

Moments later as they looked out over the town and the glorious, glittering expanse of estuary and open sea, she said,

'It's smaller than I had imagined it would be and I love the way it huddles around its harbour. It reminds me of something out of a child's story book.'

Daniel knew what she meant. The town nestled at the foot of the hill as if challenging anyone to find it, and grassy slopes rose on its outskirts hemming it in even further.

As well as the tang of the sea, there was a scent of wild marjoram in the air. Bees buzzed. On the horizon a three-masted ship was making its way eastward. A scattering of small boats with dark red sails were heading towards the harbour.

The scene was idyllic, and then Marietta noticed the flags. 'I wonder why there are so many flags flying? I thought at first it was just the two church spires that were flying them, but it isn't. What looks to be laundry hanging out of windows isn't laundry. It's Union Jacks.'

Daniel shielded his eyes and squinted into the sun. The two flags flying from flagpoles were at half-mast and now that he realized, as Marietta had, that it wasn't laundry hanging from the windows of the town's closely packed houses, he frowned.

It was highly unlikely that such a display of public mourning was for a local councillor or similar local worthy. Union Jacks only flew at half-mast on public buildings when a senior member of the royal family died, or perhaps, although he wasn't sure, when a prime minister died.

Reading his thoughts and suddenly concerned, she said, 'Do you think King Edward has died?'

'I hope not. He's the most popular king we've ever had.'

While they had been standing on the staging there had been quite a lot of movement up and down the nearby road, all of which they had ignored, but Daniel was now anxious to attract someone's attention.

'*Hello there, sir!*' he shouted through cupped hands at an elderly man who had just reached the point in the road where the short lane to the mill led into it. '*Why all the flags in town?*'

Billy Gann came to a halt. In all of his sixty-three years he had been addressed as a lot of things, but never before as sir. Pleasure surged through him. He knew a family had arrived that morning at the mill with a horse and a cart full of furniture because Smelly Bell had told him so, but Smelly had said the newcomers were tinkers. He, Billy, now knew they weren't. Tinkers were a lot of things, but none he had ever met had spoken to him politely, or had called him sir.

Aware he was now being given a brilliant opportunity to be the first person in town to have close contact with the interesting-sounding newcomers, he turned into the lane.

'*Why all the flags?*' Daniel shouted again as Billy drew nearer.

'*The King has died, God bless 'im!*' Billy shouted back, and he headed towards the windmill with all the speed he could summon.

'So, you're the folk who be moving in,' he said a couple of minutes later, as he came to a halt below the staging. It was a statement not a question. 'I know this mill like the back o' my 'and. The last miller were a cousin o' mine. You'll have a job on your 'ands if you want rid o' its machinery. Corn mill machinery was made to last until the Second Coming.'

'I believe you.' There was deep feeling in Daniel's voice. A sudden thought occurred to him. 'You wouldn't happen to know anyone who could give me a hand dismantling some of it, would you?'

Billy's dirt-ingrained face split into a grin, revealing very few teeth. 'O' course I do. I could give you a hand. I'm Billy. Billy Gann.'

'Daniel Picard,' Daniel said, aware that with luck a whole weight of worry was about to be lifted from his shoulders. 'Stay there, Billy, I'm coming down to you.'

'I'm Marietta,' Marietta said as Daniel headed to the nearest of the staging's two doors. 'If you know all about mills, Mr Gann, can you tell me if they all have staging like this one?'

'Aye, I reckon all corn mills have stagin'.' Billy hadn't enjoyed himself so much in years. The girl was a smasher. There was something exotically foreign-looking about her. Her thick-lashed, cat-green eyes were set at a slight slant and there was a lack of shyness about her that should have been brazen, and yet wasn't.

Marietta leaned over the railing, her braid swinging down over her shoulder like a glossy, fire-red rope. 'But why do they have staging, Mr Gann? What was it used for?'

Billy grinned. As the few teeth he had were stained brown by his habit of chewing tobacco, it wasn't a pretty sight.

'It's fer the miller to walk out on and judge the weather and feel the power o' the wind – somethin' he'd need to be aware of almost 'ourly, as it's the wind that's responsible for the speed o' the sails, and it's the speed o' the sails that's responsible for the speed at which the corn is ground.'

There came the sudden sound of her father clattering down the ladders that led from the windmill's cap to the ground floor.

Marietta could read her father like a book. His moving at such speed meant he'd seen Billy from his bird's-eye viewpoint and had judged from the look of him that he would know where the nearest public house was.

Moments later he burst out of the windmill, a beam of delight on his face, his arms open wide as if greeting a long-lost relative.

'*Un voisin!*' he cried, throwing his arms around a startled Billy in a bear hug that nearly lifted him from his feet. 'A neighbour! This deserves a celebration! You don't by any chance have something in your pocket we can toast the moment with, do you?'

Regrettably, Billy hadn't.

Well aware where this was heading Daniel tried to regain control of the situation. 'Mr Gann is going to help me dismantle some of the machinery, Pa.'

'*Bien sûr qu'il est!* Of course he is!' The upturned ends of Pascal's magnificently waxed moustache quivered with the force of his emotion. 'But all in good time, Daniel. For the moment, what is important is that my friendship with . . . with . . . ?'

'Billy,' Billy said obligingly.

'. . . with Billy is celebrated in proper style in the nearest hostelry, which is . . . ?'

'The Fox and Firkin at the bottom o' the hill,' Billy said even more obligingly.

Knowing exactly what was now about to happen, Marietta watched in amusement as Daniel tried yet again to retrieve the situation.

'The Fox and Firkin will have to wait until another day, Pa,' he was saying through gritted teeth. 'We haven't finished unloading the furniture yet.'

'As to that, Marietta will help you,' his father said genially, and then, to Billy, 'She's a strong girl. Shall we be off, then?'

And then, as if the matter was satisfactorily settled and as if he and Billy had known each other for years, he tucked his arm through his new friend's and began propelling the mesmerized Billy at a brisk pace in the direction of the lane.

'Bloody, bloody *hell*!' Daniel ran his hands exasperatedly through his hair. 'We've only been here five sodding minutes and already he's found a drinking buddy and is off to the nearest pub!'

Reluctantly Marietta knew it was time she said goodbye to the staging and its stunning view and went and gave him some much-needed sisterly support.

'Look on the bright side,' she said to him a couple of minutes later, as he had said to her not so very long ago. 'Pa is no use even when he's here. And a drinking buddy who knows the mill like the back of his hand and can help dismantle the machinery is worth his weight in gold. So it isn't all bad news, is it?'

He gave a rueful grin. 'No. I suppose it isn't.'

'We're on the brink of an entirely new lifestyle.' She closed her eyes and raised her face to the sun, 'A lifestyle of beautiful views and hens and goats and new friends and, like Pa, I am absolutely certain his paintings of Oystertown will be paintings that will make him famous.'

'I certainly hope so. God knows his work is good enough. And what about you, Marietta? What are you going to do now we're living on the coast?'

'Me?' She opened her eyes. 'I'll do what I've always done. I'll look after Pa and I'll take his paintings up to London art dealers.'

She turned away from him, heading back into the windmill, saying impishly over her shoulder, 'And in my spare time I'll do something I could never have done in Rotherhithe. I'll find myself a handsome young oysterman to have a romance with!'

Chapter Three

When, in an imposing Belgrave Square mansion, an early morning telephone call from Buckingham Place informed Lord Robert Layard that King Edward had died at 11.45 the previous evening, the news was not unexpected. Lord Layard had been a close friend of Bertie's for over forty years and had visited him only days ago when Bertie had returned from Biarritz suffering from a severe bout of bronchitis.

Still in his paisley-silk dressing gown, Lord Layard had woken his wife and his daughter with the news. Lady Layard had collapsed in grief. His only child, twenty-year-old Claudia, had been too stunned for tears. For as long as she could remember she had regarded the King almost as an uncle. When she was a small child, he had encouraged her to race slices of buttered toast down his immaculately trousered legs. He had played ping-pong with her. On her last birthday he had given her an exquisite pearl necklace with matching earrings.

And now he was dead and, because he was dead, there seemed to Claudia to be a great void in the world. With passionate intensity she wished her cousin Kim had been at home when her father had received his dreadful early morning telephone call. Just as the King had not been her uncle, but she had always thought of him as an uncle, so Kim, who was four years her senior, was not her brother, but she had grown up thinking of him as being her brother.

Kim's father, her father's youngest sibling, was a tea planter in Ceylon and when Kim was eight, he had been sent on a steamer to England to begin his education, first at a prep school in Berkshire, and then at Eton. His school vacations had all been spent with Claudia and her parents either in Belgrave Square, or Rose Mount, their country mansion on the outskirts of the little town of Oystertown. He was a high-flyer and after university he took up a position in Portsmouth as part of a design team working on the development of a submarine capable of a far greater operating depth than anything the Merchant Navy or, just as importantly, the Imperial German Navy yet had.

Her thoughts were disturbed by her mother entering the room. She was dressed entirely in black and was also dressed to leave the house. 'I've sent for the carriage so that I can leave a condolence card at the palace,' she said, 'and Harrods are sending round two waist-length mourning veils for the funeral.' Her voice was unsteady, thick with grief. 'Knollys has told Papa that when poor darling Alexandra is finally able to part with the King's body – apparently at the moment she is refusing to allow it to be moved – it will be placed in a sealed coffin on a purple-draped catafalque in the Throne Room. From there it will be taken to Westminster Hall where it will lie in state for three days in order that members of the public can file past and pay their respects. He also told Papa that the funeral will be held at St George's Chapel at Windsor, where he is to be buried.'

It was an awful lot of information – all of which was still to be made public – but Knollys had been King Edward's private secretary and so there was no doubting its accuracy.

'Whether Alice Keppel will be allowed to pay her respects in private at Westminster Hall, or have the dignity of being invited to the funeral, heaven only knows,' her mother continued, 'and the same goes for Daisy Warwick. I don't envy the person doing the funeral seating plan.'

'But neither of them will be at the funeral, Mama. The Queen will not want to be reminded of them at a time like this.'

'That will certainly be the case where Daisy Warwick is concerned, but not, I think, with Alice. According to Knollys, when it became obvious Bertie was on his death bed, Alexandra had Alice sent for in order for her to say goodbye to him. If ever a woman deserves to be called a saint, it is Alexandra.'

All the time she had been talking she had been fiddling with her black net gloves. Now she pulled them on. 'One last thing, Claudia. All your social engagements for the next few weeks will, of course, be cancelled and as soon as the funeral is over, we shall be leaving for the peace and quiet of Rose Mount.' And lowering the net veiling on a wide black hat lavishly decorated with glossy-black ostrich feathers, she left the room.

Claudia loved going down to Rose Mount. It was situated in lonely splendour a little less than two miles from Oystertown's harbour and had uninterrupted glorious sea views. At the end of its long, sloping and well-tended garden, wrought-iron gates led out on to a private stretch of shoreline backed by marram grass. In the summer delicate yellow sea poppies, sturdy clumps of rosy-pink valerian and deep-blue viper's bugloss grew in the shingle. There was a small beach hut so that members of the family who wished to swim could conveniently change into their bathing costumes.

Her father greatly enjoyed a morning swim, but his real passion was yachting and the family yacht, the *Sprite*, had a permanent mooring in the town's busy little harbour.

Sometimes, with a couple of local men acting as crew, he sailed the *Sprite* across to France and often her mother accompanied him.

King Edward, too, had loved to sail. For both the King and her father, Cowes week in August had been sacrosanct. It was at Cowes that she and her mother had been introduced to Kaiser Wilhelm of Germany, who every year pitted his yacht *Meteor* against King Edward's racing yacht, *Britannia*.

Privately Claudia had thought that for a man well into middle age the Kaiser was still rather good-looking. There was a vigour about him that appealed to her. Her mother hadn't thought him attractive in the slightest.

'He was wearing several rings with vulgarly large stones,' she had said afterwards with a shudder of distaste, 'and before he shook hands with me he turned them around and then gripped my hand so tightly the stones cut into the flesh of my palms. When I gasped with pain he *leered* at me and said, "The Teutonic mailed fist, Lady Layard! What? What?" '

It suddenly occurred to Claudia that there had been very little difference in age between the King and her father and the prospect of her father dying filled her with panic. Overcome by the need to feel the reassurance of his arms around her she ran from the room and down the curving sweep of balustraded stairs in the direction of his study where he had been closeted making telephone calls ever since he had received the news of the King's death.

'Papa, it's me.' She gave an urgent knock on the door. 'May I come in?'

There came the sound of his chair being scraped back from his desk and then his footsteps as he crossed the room and opened the door.

'I suddenly thought . . .' she said, her face streaked with tears as he put his arms around her, 'I suddenly thought . . .'

'I think I know what you thought,' he said gruffly, almost as emotional as she was, 'and you can put your mind at rest. Bertie smoked twelve cigars and twenty cigarettes a day and drank champagne and brandy morning, noon and night. I have never indulged in tobacco or alcohol to excess and as a consequence I'm fit and healthy and, God willing, I have decades of life still in front of me.'

Her anxiety ebbed. What he had said was as good as a promise, and her beloved Papa had never broken any promise he had made to her.

'I'll have tea sent in while we spend a little time together.' He sat down again at his desk. 'I've been thinking of how different Europe is going to be without Bertie at its helm, keeping the political situation from getting out of hand.'

He took a packet of Garibaldi biscuits out of his desk drawer, offered her one and took one for himself.

'The problem is,' he continued, 'that while Bertie was alive, peace in Europe was assured. Without him there is no other monarch capable of holding Kaiser Wilhelm in check. And the Kaiser,' he added, 'is a loose cannon. He says whatever comes into his head, no matter what political trouble it causes.'

The tea was brought in and when the footman had left the room, he said, 'All through Bertie's reign the Kaiser tried to stir up trouble between England and Russia by filling the Tsar's head with nonsense. Nonsense which, because the Tsar isn't quite the fool the Kaiser takes him for, fortunately came to nothing.'

He bit into a biscuit, brushing crumbs from his immaculately tailored waistcoat.

'It has been Bertie, a born negotiator and peacemaker, who has kept Europe stable this last nine years and George will not be able to pick up where his father left off. George,' he added, 'is capable of nothing other than shooting birds at Sandringham, bringing down stags at Balmoral and sticking stamps into albums.'

That her father should speak of the man who was now their king in such off-hand terms shocked her. It had long been accepted by those who knew him that although he had a cultured and intelligent wife, George was a dullard. And now the dullard was King of the United Kingdom and Emperor of India.

Reading her thoughts her father patted her hand. 'Don't worry, sweetheart. England has had its share of not very bright monarchs and we are still the mightiest country in the world. George has inherited an excellent Private Secretary in Francis Knollys. Knollys will keep him on the right track and give him all the advice he needs and, who knows, George might surprise us. And now I must get on with my telephone calls. The Duke of Norfolk has responsibility for organizing the King's funeral in St George's Chapel and he's in a quandary over what to do about Caesar.'

Seeing her bewilderment he said, 'At the Queen's request Caesar is to walk immediately behind the King's coffin in the funeral procession through the streets of London. Can you imagine how the crowned heads of Europe are going to feel, walking in solemn procession behind a dog? The Kaiser is going to have an apoplectic fit. And Norfolk's dilemma is how he is to accommodate Caesar when it comes to the public lying-in-state. He's left a message asking for my advice.'

'And what will your advice be, Papa?'

'That it would be highly improper for Caesar to be seen sitting beside the coffin in Westminster Hall. What if he were to cock his leg up against it?'

As she re-entered the drawing room, she caught sight of herself in the ornate mirror that hung above the fireplace and came to a sudden, shocked halt. Never before had she worn unrelieved black. She was fair-haired and pale-skinned and the black gown that her mother had speedily had delivered earlier that morning from Madame Lucile's drained her of what little colour she had.

Her mother would, she knew, be wearing black from now until long after the funeral was over, and would expect her to do the same. And all the May balls and country house parties she had been so looking forward to would be cancelled. A cloud of dejection as black as her gown descended on her and then she heard a motor car rattle to a halt outside the house.

Knowing how unlikely it was that anyone would be paying house calls on a morning such as this she walked swiftly over to the wide windows that looked out over the square.

At what she saw, despondency vanished. Her cousin, as tall, slim and fair-haired as she was, was vaulting out of a yellow, open-topped Wolseley.

'*Kim!*' she shouted elatedly, knocking on the window to attract his attention.

He looked up, a wide grin on his handsome Layard face, gave her an acknowledging wave and then, in long easy strides, he crossed the pavement, stepped beneath the pillared portico and rang for admittance.

She rushed out of the first-floor drawing room, down the curving staircase and across the Italian tiled hall to greet him, saying effusively as a footman relieved him of his coat, driving gloves and goggles, 'Oh, I'm so glad you're here, Kim, and not still in Portsmouth! Are you home because King Edward has died? Will you be going to the funeral with Mama and Papa?'

'I'm not sure whether the funeral invitation will include me, but I certainly want to be in London when it takes place.' He gave her a huge bear hug. 'Where are the folks? Are they at home?'

'Mama isn't. She's gone to the palace to leave a condolence card. Papa is in his study making telephone calls.'

'Then I won't disturb him. I must say black makes you look very sophisticated, Claudia, although if you top the all-black look with a waist-length mourning veil you're also going to look extremely nun-like.'

'Becoming a nun has always been a secret ambition of mine,' she said teasingly, tucking her hand in the crook of his arm as they by-passed a *jardinière* of ferns and white lilies and made their way up the stairs. 'How are things coming along in Portsmouth? Are you any nearer to designing a Royal Navy submarine that will have the Kaiser gnashing his teeth in despair?'

'We're getting there, but we're not yet so far ahead of the Germans that we can rest on our laurels. Royal Navy policy has always been to have twice as many ships as any other country, but thanks to the Kaiser's determination to outmatch us – and especially when it comes to submarine production – that is no longer the case, which is why it is so urgently necessary that our future submarines are capable of far faster speeds than anything Germany is yet capable of building.'

'But why all the urgency?' she asked as they entered the drawing room. 'It isn't as if we're ever likely to be at war with Germany. The Kaiser is King Edward's eldest nephew and when the King's funeral takes place, he will be a very prominent mourner.'

'His being a prominent mourner is one thing. His being a genuine friend of England is quite another.'

He sat down on one of two facing, velvet-covered sofas. Resting an arm along its deeply buttoned back he said with an apologetic grin, 'Sorry, Claudia. The King having died is bad enough without me being a prophet of doom and gloom into the bargain. I promise I won't bring up the naval race subject again. Bring me up to date on your love-life. Is Toby Calverley still in the picture? As he's heir to a dukedom and a Scottish estate the size of two English counties, I'm hoping he is.'

'He isn't.' She perched on the arm of the opposite sofa. 'I've become a very passionate supporter of Mrs Pankhurst. Toby stuffily said he couldn't possibly have his name linked with the name of a girl who believed women should have the right to vote and I said I certainly wouldn't want my name linked to a man who had no sympathy at all in what the Women's Social and Political Union were trying to achieve.'

'And have you become a fully paid-up member of Mrs P's fighting force?' he asked, trying not to show how concerned he suddenly felt. There were two branches in the Suffragette movement. The Women's Social and Political Union, known for short as the WSPU, who took militant action such as chaining themselves to the railings outside Downing Street, heckling politicians, setting fire to public property and generally making God-awful nuisances of themselves which resulted in them being carted off to police stations and facing unpleasant jail sentences, and the more respectable NUWSS, the National Union of Women's Suffrage Societies, which took a far more law-abiding approach in the Votes for Women struggle.

'Yes, I have, but I haven't yet told Mama and Papa. Wonderful as the King was, he was always deeply opposed to women's suffrage and, in loyalty to him, it is the stance Papa has always taken. You won't say anything to him, will you? Not when the King's death has distressed him so deeply.'

'No,' he said, unhappy with the situation. 'Just promise me you won't do anything silly like chaining yourself to the railings in Downing Street, or publicly heckling the Prime Minister.'

'Of course I won't,' she said, smoothing a crease from a skirt that ended a modest three inches above her ankles in order to avoid his eyes.

It wasn't an outright lie, but considering that only two days ago she had taken part in a WSPU demonstration in Downing Street in which a stone had been thrown through one of Number 10's windows, it wasn't exactly the truth either.

* * *

Dinner in the Layard home was usually a jolly occasion, especially when Kim was with them, but that evening the King's death weighed heavily on everyone and the usual gentle family teasing was absent.

'What was the reaction among your fellow design engineers when the news came early this morning of the King's death?' her father asked Kim as pudding was served. 'I take it for granted they were grief-stricken, but what was their opinion of what will now happen politically?'

Kim hesitated, and then said bluntly, 'The immediate talk was of how, without the King's stabilizing influence, war between Britain and Germany is now inevitable. Not immediately,' he added, 'but certainly in five or six years' time.'

His uncle pushed his untouched pudding dish to one side. 'And what are your thoughts, Kim? Are you in agreement with them?'

'No. I think it will be sooner – and when it comes it will be the first war where submarines will play a major part. They are going to bring an entirely new dimension to naval warfare, which is why it is so essential that their speed capacity will always outstrip Kaisermarine speed capacity.'

No one spoke and then Robert Layard said heavily, 'I always knew your work at Portsmouth was of vital national importance, my boy. Until now, though, I had never realized quite how important.'

Celia Layard looked around the dinner table, saw that no one was showing any inclination to embark on their dishes of champagne and primrose jelly and was just about to ring for the dishes to be cleared away and port, cheese and biscuits to be brought in, when there came the faint sound of the doorbell being rung.

'Now who on earth can that be at half past eight in the evening?' she said, looking across at her husband. 'You weren't expecting anyone, were you, Robert?'

'No. It's possibly a late delivery of some kind. Perhaps one of your women friends is sharing the grief of the day by sending flowers.'

A few minutes later Beamish, the butler, entered the room. His face was, as always, impassive, but his voice was highly nervous as he said, 'Excuse me, sir. There are two policemen at the door.'

Robert Layard's eyebrows rose nearly into his hair. 'Policemen? What the devil can they possibly want?' In deep irritation he scrunched up his napkin, threw it down on the table and rose to his feet.

Beamish cleared his throat. 'It is Miss Claudia with whom they wish to speak, sir.' Taking a deep breath and praying he would survive the moment, he added, 'They have come with a warrant for her arrest, sir.'

Robert stared at him stupefied. *'A warrant for her arrest? Are you drunk, Beamish? Have you completely lost your mind?'*

'No, sir. They were quite explicit. They are here to take her to Bow Street police station where she is to be charged with malicious damage.'

'How utterly ridiculous!' Lady Layard's sapphire-blue eyes flashed fire. 'The men are quite obviously not genuine policemen. It is an ugly and cruel practical joke. Robert, please go downstairs and put an end to this nonsense immediately.'

Kim, whose eyes since Beamish had made his announcement had never left Claudia's face, was certain it was far from being a practical joke. He was also certain that when Claudia had promised him she wouldn't chain herself to the railings in Downing Street, or publicly heckle the Prime Minister, it had only been because she had already earned her WSPU spurs.

He said to her tautly, 'If there is any truth in the allegation, Claudia, it would be best to say so now.'

'Good God, Kim!' His uncle rounded on him violently. 'How can you even begin to believe that there's truth in such a preposterous allegation?'

Claudia rose to her feet. 'But there is, Papa.' Her voice was only slightly unsteady. 'Two days ago, I was one of half a dozen suffragettes who entered Downing Street in order to make a protest that Prime Minister Asquith wouldn't be able to ignore and, as was planned, a stone was thrown through one of Number Ten's windows. Four of my friends were arrested. Two of us got away.'

Her mother rose unsteadily to her feet, her face drained of blood.

Her father stared at her in dazed incredulity.

'I'm sorry for causing you hurt, Papa. And you too, Mama. But I can't – and won't – passively accept that women are no more capable of being able to vote than a baby or . . . or a dog. And now, before the police enter the house to take me by force, I think I should go down and face them.'

'So that you can be arrested and charged with breaking the windows of Number Ten Downing Street?' Celia Layard's fine-boned face was ashen. 'You will be sent to prison and suffragettes are treated abominably in prison.' Her voice cracked and broke. 'You have never experienced harshness and filthy conditions, Claudia. You can have no idea of what imprisonment will be like. When Lady Howard's daughter went on hunger strike, she was force-fed! How could you possibly cope with an abomination such as that?'

'I don't know. I think I would try and find escape by thinking of nice things; things such as joining you at Rose Mount when I'm released. And now, Mama and Papa, please do one thing for me. Don't come downstairs with me. I'd rather you didn't see me being put into a Black Maria.'

Her mother blanched.

Her father breathed in so hard his nostrils were white.

Grim-faced and aware, with admiration, that Claudia was far, far tougher than he had ever thought possible, Kim said, 'I'll escort you downstairs and I'll come with you to Bow Street.'

Gratefully she rose to her feet and tucked her hand into the crook of his arm. To her parents she said, 'I won't have to serve a long prison sentence for a first offence, perhaps only a few days. I'll be back home before you know it.'

'Back home?' Her father was trying to think which of his influential friends was best placed to have her name removed from the Bow Street charge sheet. 'You won't be back home in Belgrave Square, Claudia! You'll be at Rose Mount – and as there won't be any foolish suffragette activity in Oystertown for you to become involved in, for the rest of the year, Oystertown is where you are jolly well going to stay!'

Chapter Four

21 May

It was the day after King Edward's funeral and in Oystertown the queue for newspapers led all the way from the newsagent's, in the middle of the high street, to the harbour.

Tilly, always up with the birds, had been one of the first in the queue and she was now back home with a fresh pot of tea on the table and the *Daily Mail*, with its several pages of photographs of the funeral, spread out in front of her.

She skipped through some of the headlines above the photographs: *Nation mourns death of Edward VII*; *Nine kings and heads of state follow the coffin*; *Crowds estimated at 500,000 line processional route*; *King George V rides alongside Kaiser Wilhelm*; *Caesar says goodbye to his master*; *Former President Theodore Roosevelt represents America.*

Wearing only trousers, Jasper stepped in from the yard where he had been having his morning wash at the pump and looked over her shoulder, drops of water gleaming on his strongly muscled chest.

'Caesar? Who the Blue Blazes is Caesar?' he asked, dragging a kitchen chair up to the table and straddling it.

'The King's little pet dog. Just look, Jasper. Have you ever seen anything more heartbreaking?'

The photograph she drew his attention to showed a kilted

Highlander leading a dispirited-looking white wire-haired fox terrier on a lead. They were walking immediately behind the gun carriage on which the King's coffin was being transported from Westminster Hall to Paddington Station for its onward journey by train to Windsor. Behind them in the photograph rode the new king, King George, and, beside him, his late father's nephew, the Kaiser.

'The Kaiser looks as if he rides well considering he has a crippled left arm,' Jasper said, giving credit where it was due.

Tilly read the newsprint beneath the photograph aloud. '*Caesar, King Edward's beloved constant companion, leads nine kings in his master's funeral procession. Immediately behind Caesar ride our new king, George V, and his cousin, Kaiser Wilhelm of Germany. Behind them ride King George of the Hellenes and two other kings, King Haakon of Norway and King Alfonso of Spain. The next three sovereigns seen riding abreast in the photograph are Tsar Ferdinand of Bulgaria, King Manoel of Portugal and King Frederick of Denmark. King Albert of the Belgians is behind them.*'

Janna stepped into the house, a pint-sized metal jug in either hand. 'Sorry I took so long. The milk cart was late getting down to this end of the high street. Is that today's paper? Are those photographs of the late king's funeral procession?'

She put the jugs of milk on a shelf in what served as their larder and then joined them at the table. She pointed to a photograph lower down on the page. 'It says royalty from all over the world took part in the procession and paid their respects. Wouldn't it have been wonderful to have been in London and seen it all? Nine kings! Seeing nine kings all together might never happen again, Tilly. Are there photographs on other pages as well? I expect queens were further behind in the procession in carriages drawn by black horses.'

'Does it say how many queens there were in the procession apart, of course, from our own poor, dear, widowed queen?'

'No. There's mention of there being seven in attendance, but only the Dowager Empress of Russia, the Queen of Norway, and our new queen, Queen Mary, are mentioned by name.'

Jasper turned the page to more photographs. 'You need to look at this bird's-eye view photograph, Tilly. It must have been taken from a high building and it shows a huge stretch of the procession all at once. Have you ever seen such a sea of white-plumed helmets? I rather fancy wearing something similar myself when I walk into the back of the Duke of Connaught for a bare-knuckle fight. If word gets around, it's bound to draw a crowd, don't you think?'

'I think you're barmy. I'm only glad it's taking Ozzie a while to get it all arranged. Do you want a slice of bread and dripping?'

'Please – and with plenty of salt on it.' Losing interest in the photographs he took a drink of his tea and then said, 'According to Smelly Bell, Lord and Lady Layard arrived back in town late yesterday.'

'Then they must have left London immediately after the funeral. Was their daughter with them?'

'I've no idea. Smelly didn't say.'

She handed him his slice of bread and drip. 'If she isn't, it's a bit odd.' It was an oddity she easily dismissed. The aristocracy were a law unto themselves and nothing they did was capable of surprising her.

Making short work of his bread and dripping Jasper rose to his feet. 'I'm going to make a start white-liming the bottom of the *Pearl* this morning and then I'm going to catch up with Jonah.' Jonah Goldfinch was a deep-sea diver and Jasper's closest mate. 'And if Rosie comes round crying her eyes out because I'm no longer seeing her, tell her she's better off without me.'

He pulled a collarless shirt on, rammed the tails of it beneath the broad leather belt which held his trousers up and, ducking beneath the head of the door, walked out on to the harbour-side in long, easy strides.

Removing the newspaper from the table, Tilly said, 'You'd best be getting a move on, Janna, otherwise you're going to be late for work.'

Until September, when oyster dredging began again, Janna was working at Keam's baker's shop in the high street.

'You'll keep the paper, won't you, Tilly?' she asked, rising to her feet. 'You won't throw it away?'

'I'll put it in a frame and hang it on the wall, if that's what you want,' Tilly said cheerfully. 'Now off you go or you'll be losing your job.'

Janna liked working at Keam's. Mr Keam, who did all the baking in the bakery at the back of the shop, was a heavily built, ruddy-faced man and in the time she had been working for him she had never seen him without his long white apron and baker's hat. His wife, who took care of the shop, was short, stout, well-corseted and mostly even-tempered. To Janna, accustomed to long days working Jasper's oyster perches – the large stone divisions just beneath the sea's surface which every oysterman had and where his daily catch of oysters was tipped – and, when not working the perches, cleaning, selling and sometimes pickling oysters, life behind the broad counter of Keam's Baker's was a haven of leisure.

The main thing Mr Keam baked was bread, for bread was the staple diet of all Oystertown families. From early morning onwards he would regularly emerge from the bakery at the back of the shop with a tray of loaves fresh from the oven which she and Mrs Keam then stacked on the shelves. Bread left over at the day's end was either made into bread pudding, which was then sold cold in handy-sized squares, perfect for a working man to slip into the pocket of his jacket, or sold to the high street's butcher, who used it to bulk out his sausages.

As well as bread, Mr Keam baked shortbread and rice cakes, decorating each shortbread slice with a glacé cherry and sprinkling the rice cakes with crystallized sugar.

There were always queues outside Keam's until long after lunchtime and the minute Janna had put on the wrap-around overall Mrs Keam provided her with every day, she was on her feet, a bright smile on her face and a few cheery words for every customer she served.

The shop closed at four, and today, at five to four, a girl Janna had never seen before came in.

She knew, the minute she set eyes on her, who she was. Hair that Smelly Bell had described as 'burnt marmalade', but was actually a fiery fox-red, hung in a heavy waist-length braid over one shoulder. Tall and slender, she was wearing a shabby green linen skirt that ended just above her ankles and a shiny mustard-coloured blouse which was open at the throat and which had clearly seen better days.

With effortless grace and easy confidence, she stepped up to the counter and Janna felt her mouth go dry with sudden shyness.

The girl said pleasantly in a voice that had a faint accent Janna couldn't place, 'Are you Janna Shilling? I'm told you sell oysters. Do you sell them from here, or do I have to go somewhere else?'

'The oyster season is over,' Janna said apologetically. 'There won't be any oysters for sale until September.'

Marietta frowned, 'But why on earth . . . ?' she began, and was cut short by Mrs Keam, who had quickly bustled up to stand alongside Janna.

'Are you buying bread, or not?' she said in a manner which was, for her, unusually sharp. 'Because if you aren't, it's five to four and we're closing.'

'I'm not,' Marietta said with a careless shrug and then, as she turned to leave the shop, she said over her shoulder to Janna, 'I'll wait for you outside. I want to know why there are no more oysters until September.'

And taking her time about it in a manner which Mrs Keam later described to her husband as being blatantly insolent, she strolled out of the shop.

'And there,' Mrs Keam said to Janna as she began clearing away the few items that were left on the shelves, 'is a young madam a nice girl like you should have nothing to do with!'

Janna didn't answer her and, mercifully, Mrs Keam was too busy lowering the inside blind of the shop's window, to notice.

Half an hour later, after wiping down all the shelves and sweeping the floor Janna took her overall off, handed it to Mrs Keam and stepped out of the shop, her heart beating fast and light. Would the windmill girl have kept her word and be waiting for her?

There was no sign of her. The high street was as busy as usual, but there was no glimpse of blazing-red hair or a satiny-shiny mustard-coloured blouse. Disappointment flooded through her. Of course the windmill girl hadn't waited for her. Why should she? If she went to the harbour, she would easily have her question answered as to why there were no oysters.

A child bowling a hoop ran past her. Two Shire horses clip-clopped slowly down the centre of the cobbled street taking a waggon-load of beer barrels from the local brewery to the Duke of Connaught. A farm cart piled high with sacks of potatoes was at a halt outside the greengrocer's directly across the street.

Overcome with disappointment she bit her lip and then, just as she was about to turn dejectedly for home, the windmill girl stepped out of the shop next to the greengrocer's.

'I thought the old witch was going to keep you in there for ever,' she called out, crossing the road towards her, a paper cone of sweets in her hand.

'Do you want a sherbet lemon?' She held the paper cone out so that Janna could take one. 'My name is Marietta. Where shall we go while we chat about the lack of oysters in Oystertown? The harbour? I won't be able to hang around for long as my papa frets if I don't get home at the time I've said I will.'

'Then I'll walk with you up the Heights.'

Marietta tucked her hand through the crook of Janna's arm as if the two of them had been friends since childhood.

It was an action that put paid to the last of Janna's shyness. She said, 'On the day you moved into the windmill, I set off to walk up to it, but outside the Fox and Firkin I was nearly trampled by a runaway horse. Afterwards my legs were so wobbly that Harry, the local coal-man, gave me a lift home on his coal cart.'

Marietta shot her a wide, curving smile. 'That was nice of him. I like the sound of Harry. My papa has made friends with someone called Billy Gann. Do you know him?'

'Yes. Everyone knows everyone else in Oystertown. Nine families out of ten are related to each other.'

'And so what is it about the town having no oysters between May and September?' Marietta said, getting down to the question that was puzzling her.

'The summer months are when oysters spawn. By the end of September spawning is over and that is when dredging starts again.'

'You may as well be speaking Chinese.' Marietta offered her another sherbet lemon and took one for herself. 'What does the word spawn mean?'

'It means when oysters breed.'

'Breed? *Grand Dieu!*' Marietta tottered in mock disbelief. 'I thought oysters were a kind of sea vegetable! Are you telling me they have a sex life?'

Janna giggled. 'I'd hardly call it that, but they make something called spat, and the spat finds a nice place to settle, such as a bit of rocky seafloor, and if it is left undisturbed, it slowly grows a shell and becomes a baby oyster.'

They had passed the Fox and Firkin and had begun climbing up the Heights and Marietta changed the subject. 'Daniel says it's a wonder anyone living in Oystertown ever attempts to leave it when there is always this steep hill to climb.'

'When you have been here a little longer, you'll climb it without even thinking about it. Who is Daniel? Is he your brother?'

'Yes. He's a little on the quiet side, but you'll like him. Everyone likes Daniel.'

'And is your family just Daniel, your father and you?'

'Yes. *Maman* died a long time ago.'

As they walked Janna plucked a long blade of grass from one of the waist-high clumps growing by the roadside and began pushing its seeds off between her thumb and forefinger, saying as she did so, 'Both my parents are dead. My father drowned at sea when I was five and then, two years later, our mother was ill and then she died. Our aunt – who is more like an elder sister – moved in with us and took care of bringing us up and so we are a family of three, just as you, Daniel and your papa are.'

'And who is the third member of your family?' Marietta shared the last two sherbet lemons between the two of them. 'Is it a sister, or a brother?'

'A brother. His name is Jasper and he's an oysterman.'

'An oysterman?' Marietta's interest was instant. 'How old is he?'

'Almost twenty.'

'And is he handsome?'

'Tilly – that's our aunt – says he's too handsome for his own good. He has black curly hair, brown eyes and he's six foot four.'

'*Parfait!* I can't wait to meet him!'

They were beginning to draw nearer and nearer to the crown of the hill and a thrill of excitement ran along Janna's nerve ends. When they reached the windmill would Marietta invite her inside it? And why did she keep using foreign words? Even her name sounded foreign. Not only had she never met anyone called Marietta before but she had never even heard of the name.

'What does *paafay* mean?' she asked. 'And that other foreign expression you used when I told you the meaning of spawn?'

'*Parfait* is French for perfect and *Grand Dieu* is French for good heavens. My *maman* was English, but Papa is French. He has lived so long in England that he rarely lapses into French now and Daniel and I have been brought up speaking English, but sometimes French words come out without thinking.'

'Have Daniel and your papa found work in Oystertown?' Janna asked, almost certain they hadn't because, if they had, it would have been the subject of local gossip.

'Daniel has found a position at the local draper's. He starts next Monday. Papa is an artist.'

Once again Janna was aware of how strange and different her new-found friend was. No one else she knew would have used the word 'position' when they meant job. 'Position' was the sort of word someone posh – someone like Oystertown's only doctor or the vicar of the Anglican church – might use.

As for Marietta's father, being an artist – painting pictures such as the ones Smelly Bell said he had seen being carried into the mill – surely wasn't a job? She wondered if it was another posh word for his being a painter like Sparky Holden, who made a living slapping distemper onto the inside walls of Oystertown cottages and whitewash on the outside walls. But posh people didn't live in abandoned windmills. They lived in double-fronted terrace houses or, if they were posh on the scale Lord and Lady Layard were posh, in a mansion that stood in its own grounds.

They turned off the road and on to the unmade track that led the short distance to the mill.

'Daniel shouldn't be working in a shop,' Marietta said suddenly with passionate fierceness. 'He's creative like Papa, but in a different way.'

'In what kind of different way?'

'It's hard to explain. He likes inventing things.'

It was an answer that left Janna more puzzled than ever, but she didn't have the chance to ask any more questions because they had reached the mill and the most extraordinary figure she had ever seen was standing in the doorway.

He was of medium height and stout. He had a mass of white hair that reached his shoulders, an equally white beard and a magnificent upturned white moustache. His clothes were of such clashing colours that Janna wasn't surprised Smelly Bell had said he'd looked like something out of a circus, and as if the colours – scarlet trousers, turquoise braces and peacock-blue shirt – weren't enough, purple paint spattered his boots from toe to knee.

'My papa, Pascal,' Marietta said unnecessarily and without the least trace of embarrassment. 'Papa, meet my new friend, Janna Shilling. Her brother is an oysterman.'

'An oysterman!' Pascal couldn't have looked and sounded more impressed if Marietta had said Jasper was High Sheriff of the county. 'A man with a trade as old as time! A harvester of the pearls of the sea! Do you think he would sit for me?'

Janna blinked, not understanding.

'Papa means would your brother like to have his portrait painted?' Marietta said, leading the way into the mill.

Janna was just about to say as politely as she could that she doubted it very much, when her mouth fell open in wonder, for the large, octagonal-shaped room they had stepped into resembled a vast Aladdin's cave. Colourful shawls were draped over shabby, battered sofas. There was a rocking chair, its padded back covered in scarlet wool embroidery. The shelves of a kitchen dresser were full of pretty, mismatched china. There was an ottoman, its long lid covered in vivid Oriental-looking fabric and two pouffes, their amber-coloured leather tooled with the outlines of elephants. There were gilt and glass candle-sconces on the walls and in a corner of the room an iron ladder with dried flowers wound around its supports led up to the floor above.

It was the paintings, though, that had her sucking in her breath. There were three of them hanging on the walls, and all three were portraits of Marietta.

Marietta, with her braid of hair wound in a plaited crown on the top of her head and standing on the windmill's staging, leaning against its waist-high railing and with nothing behind her but a distant view of the sea and a cloud-filled sky. Marietta wearing a shimmering white dress and walking through a field of waist-high marguerites, her hair parted in the centre and falling thigh-length in a glorious red-gold curtain of tight, crinkly waves. Marietta in a chemise and seated at a dressing table, looking into the mirror and brushing her torrent of beautiful hair.

The intimacy of the third painting shocked her profoundly. Why would Marietta's father have painted her in such a state of undress? How could Marietta have been happy to let him do so? And how could either of them have thought it appropriate to hang such a painting on the wall of the mill's only downstairs room, where any friends and acquaintances were bound to see it?

There came the sound of someone climbing down distant ladders.

'That's Daniel,' Marietta said. 'His den is on the fifth floor.'

Mentally Janna counted him down four separate ladders and then he began climbing down the ladder that led into the ground-floor room.

As he came into view he had his back to them and Janna saw a pair of corduroy trousers which were not a world removed from the kind Jasper wore. Unlike Jasper he wasn't wearing a belt to keep them up, but braces, and his flannel shirt looked a lot more respectable than the shirt Jasper had been wearing when he had left the house that morning.

When, slim-hipped and supple, he reached the bottom of the ladder and turned around, Janna's heart seemed almost to cease to beat.

He wasn't handsome in the way Jasper was, and he certainly wouldn't turn heads walking down the street as Marietta did, and yet she had never seen anyone like him. Nor had she ever felt an emotion as strong as this.

His russet-red hair was swept back poker-straight from his forehead. His eyes were a golden hazel and very clear and light. He had a sprinkling of freckles. All in all, there was absolutely nothing exceptional about his looks and yet Janna instinctively knew it was a face she would never tire of looking at.

How could she have woken up this morning thinking the day in front of her would be as unexceptional as always? How could she not have known how special it was going to turn out to be?

'Daniel,' Marietta said, 'meet my new friend, Janna Shilling. She's working in a baker's at the moment because the oysters are spawning, but she's really an oyster girl.'

'Nice to meet you, Janna,' he said with a friendly smile.

His voice was pleasantly deep and as nice as his face, but then she had known it would be.

'It's nice to meet you, too,' she said, wondering how long it would take for him to feel about her, the way she already felt about him.

Chapter Five

June

It was early evening and Jasper, Jonah and Harry were sitting with Ozzie in the snug of the otherwise nearly deserted Duke of Connaught. Tilly was minding the public bar and from where they were sitting in the snug, Ozzie could see her and, if there was a sudden rush of customers, could quickly join her if she needed a hand.

'Problem is,' Jonah was saying, 'I can only go down to a hundred and twenty feet. And even then, only with difficulty and the wreck under discussion is a good hundred and forty feet deep. I know, because I've already had a go at trying to reach it and it's simply not possible.'

'Well, if you can't reach it, you can't reach it,' Harry said glumly, his hands wrapped around a pint of pale ale, 'but there's an advantage to that, because it means no other diver can reach it either.'

'And how do we know it's worth reaching?' Jasper asked, lighting up a cigarette. 'When a wreck is out of reach and the cargo is unknown it's always rumoured to be brandy or bullion when probably all it's got on board are empty beer casks.'

'Too true,' Jonah said with deep feeling, adding, 'At least this Thursday's dive won't come with any problems.' He drained his pint glass and wiped his mouth with the back of his hand.

'Tunny Boardman's boat wasn't carrying cargo. Just a metal box he's desperate to retrieve. And he swears the boat came to rest well within my hundred-and-twenty-foot diving limit.'

Harry was also sitting over an empty glass and Ozzie shouted in a voice loud enough for Tilly to hear, 'Same again in here, Tilly love!'

Minutes later Tilly, her riotous mane of hair anchored away from her face by two tortoiseshell combs, brought in four pints of beer on a tray. 'Janna's friend's brother is in the public bar,' she said, setting the glasses down on the table her boss, her brother, Harry and Jonah were sitting around. 'He's on his own and reading a book.'

Jasper snorted with amusement.

Harry raised his eyes to heaven.

'I hope he's realized the Duke is a pub and not a bloody library,' Ozzie said, not wanting his pub to get a bad name.

'I'll say this for him,' Harry said magnanimously, 'if he's a fairy, at least he doesn't mince.'

'Just because he works in a draper's doesn't mean he's a fairy,' Jasper said.

'And I'm not.'

All eyes swung to the snug's doorway.

Daniel, wearing the same suit for his new job in the high street's draper's that he had when working at Selfridges, looked startlingly out of place compared to Ozzie, Jasper, Jonah and Harry, all of whom were in their working clothes of shabby corduroy trousers, broad belts, flannel shirts and boots.

Jasper looked at him with interest. He'd heard a lot about Daniel Picard from Janna. Nothing she'd told him had, though, conjured up a picture of someone who had the bottle to face four extremely fit blokes – one of them the landlord of the pub he was in and another a bare-knuckle fighter – and take them to task for having spoken deridingly about him.

'Not what?' Harry asked blandly.

'Not a fairy,' Daniel said, equally unperturbed. 'And that's not why I've walked in on the four of you. I'd like to be on the boat when Saturday's dive takes place.'

Jonah cracked with laughter. 'Why? Are you hoping to see me sink beneath the waves never to be seen again?'

'No, but I would like a close-up look at what you wear when you dive.'

'What? Like one of the kids who are always asking if they can come aboard when I go out diving? I'm not a circus act. I don't give free shows.'

Daniel ignored the rebuff. 'Do you wear a Siebe Gorman?'

'And what the hell is a Siebe Gorman when it's at home?' Ozzie asked, tired of Daniel's unasked-for interruption of the matey conversation the four of them had been having.

With a different tone in his voice, Jonah said, 'Siebe is the name of the bloke who designed the full-length watertight canvas suit and massive windowed metal helmet I, and every other diver I know, dives in. And my answer to your question,' he said to Daniel, 'is yes, I do. Why do you want to know?'

'Because I'd like to see if I could improve on it.'

'Merciful God,' Harry said devoutly. 'We have a lunatic in our midst.'

Jonah, impressed both by Daniel's familiarity with the Siebe Gorman name, and by his manner, reached for a spare chair and pulled it up to the table. 'Sit down,' he said, ignoring the disbelieving expression on Ozzie's face, 'and tell me what you have in mind.'

Daniel sat. 'I don't have anything in mind at the moment, apart from thinking how wonderful something less bulky and clumsy would be. Especially if a less bulky and clumsy diving suit still enabled Jonah to dive just as deep as he does at present. I couldn't help overhearing what you were talking about and as the shop where I work has Thursday as its half-day closure, I wondered if I could come along when you do your dive?'

For a quiet-looking bloke there was something oddly impressive about Daniel and after a moment's hesitation Jonah said, 'I guess I have no objections, just as long as you keep out of everyone's way.'

Left to his own devices Ozzie would have sent Daniel packing with instructions to do his future drinking in the Fox and Firkin, but as Jonah was happy to have him on Thursday's dive, he felt it wasn't up to him to object.

'Another pint in here, love,' he said to Tilly, who was still in the snug, looking forward to when she would be able to tell Janna all about Daniel seamlessly integrating himself into the little, almost sacred, clique that was Ozzie, Jasper, Harry and Jonah.

And then to Daniel, Ozzie said, 'And for the love of God, don't come dressed like that on Thursday. You stick out like a sore thumb. You need a pair of cords and waterproof boots.'

'And then,' Tilly said to Janna much later that night as they were having nightcaps of cocoa before going to bed, 'Ozzie called Daniel a Copper Knob and Daniel said, "My name is Daniel. I don't do nicknames," at which point, knowing Ozzie, I thought everything was going to go belly-up, but Jasper made everything okay by cracking with laughter and saying that neither he, nor Jonah nor Harry were known by a nickname, but that if Daniel found himself after today being referred to as "Lion's Den Picard" it was something he would have to take in his stride.'

At the mention of Daniel, a flush of colour touched Janna's cheeks. 'Daniel is nice, isn't he?' she said, a warm feeling flooding through her just by saying his name. 'He's very clever.

He likes designing things. Marietta says he's wasted behind the counter of a high street draper's.'

'From what I've seen of him, I think Marietta is probably right. He certainly had Ozzie, Harry, Jonah and Jasper eating out of the palm of his hand and I've been around a long time and never seen that trick pulled before. To look at him you'd think he was too polite to swat a fly, but anyone making that mistake would get short shrift. He's not the sort of young man who could be bullied, and that's for sure.'

'And is he now friends with Jasper, Jonah, Harry and Ozzie?'

Tilly rose to her feet and closed the kitchen range dampener to prevent cold air from entering the house overnight.

'I think it's safe to say he's made friends with Jasper, Jonah and Harry. I'm not sure about Ozzie. Ozzie,' she added, 'is a law unto himself.'

'Is he still living in hope?'

'Where I'm concerned? Yes. But he's my boss and I've learned from long experience that work and pleasure don't mix very well. One lover's tiff and I'd be out of a job.'

And then, feeling she had said quite enough where she and Ozzie were concerned, Tilly kissed Janna on the cheek, said, 'Goodnight, sweetheart, pleasant dreams,' and went up to bed, well aware that with thoughts of Ozzie on her mind, sleep would be a long time in coming.

'You're going to do *what*?' Marietta asked Daniel disbelievingly as he prepared to leave the windmill early on Thursday morning.

'I'm going out with the local diver, Jonah Goldfinch. A boat has sunk with something aboard its owner dearly wants retrieving and Jonah is going to retrieve it for him. Janna's brother, Jasper, is going along as well, and so is a bloke called Harry who is—'

'Oystertown's coal-man,' Marietta finished for him as he put a packet of sandwiches he'd made for himself into one of his jacket's two large front pockets, 'and Jonah is a bad-luck name for anyone who makes their living on, and in, the sea. If I were him, I'd change it.'

It was something that had also occurred to Daniel although, unlike Marietta, he hadn't put it into words.

Marietta chewed the corner of her lip. After several attempts she had still not managed to meet Jasper Shilling, but here, surely, was an opportunity.

'I need to go to Keam's for bread,' she lied glibly, 'and so I might as well walk down with you. I'll let Pa know, but he's so engrossed in the landscape he's working on, I won't be missed.'

Minutes later they were heading down the Heights at a fast pace; so fast they were in the high street before any of the shops had opened.

'I'll come with you to the harbour and wave you off,' she said, hoping that the reality of Jasper Shilling wasn't going to be a disappointment.

Although oyster dredging was now at an end, the harbour was still busy with boats, for through the summer lots of oystermen turned to fishing of a different kind. As well as fishing smacks jostling next to each other, full lobster-pots were being brought ashore. An elegant-looking yacht with the name *Sprite* across its prow was being loaded with provisions. A shabby-looking cutter was being loaded with bulky objects.

'The yacht belongs to Lord Layard,' Daniel said, having picked up a lot of local information from his new friends. 'He has a seaside retreat a mile or so out of town. Jasper says Layard is a good yachtsman. Apparently, he sailed with the late king at Cowes.'

A tousle-haired, cheery-faced young man stepped out of

the cutter's cabin and onto the deck and then, seeing Daniel, waved energetically, shouting as he did so, 'If that's your girl-friend Lion, you're a lucky dog! If it's your sister, you're still a lucky dog, but she can't come aboard – age-old diving super-stition and all that.'

'Lion?' Marietta looked at Daniel disbelievingly.

'It's a nickname. Most men in Oystertown have a nickname.'

'Harry doesn't seem to have one. And Janna hasn't mentioned that Jasper has one.'

'Actually, Jasper has lots of nicknames, but they are nearly all to do with his being a bare-knuckle boxer, but as Ozzie, Harry and Jonah never refer to him by any of them, I don't either. I did say I didn't do nicknames – especially when Ozzie called me Copper-Knob – but because of my name and the way I faced them in the snug, Jasper came up with Lion's Den Picard – and to be honest, now it's been shortened to Lion, I can live with it.'

Marietta didn't know if she could live with it, but decided that now wasn't the time to say so. 'And is that Jasper?' she asked as they drew nearer to the boat.

'Lord, no. That's Jonah.'

Marietta was relieved. From a distance Jonah appeared to be reasonably good-looking, but he wasn't heart-stoppingly so, and she had got the impression from Janna that her brother was. Would Janna have been impartial about the matter, though? She would hardly have said her brother was a no-hoper in the looks department.

Jonah ducked down into the cabin again and Daniel turned to say goodbye to her. As he did so she saw a tall, broad-shouldered young man about Daniel's age turn the corner from the high street and stroll onto the quay. His unruly black hair was as thick and curly as a ram's fleece. One ear was pierced with a small gold ring and his thumbs were hooked nonchalantly into the belt that sat satisfyingly low on his hips. He looked for all the world like a Barbary pirate and, knowing immediately who he was, a slow smile spread over her face.

'Here's Jasper,' Daniel said unnecessarily, 'and the man with him must be Tunny Boardman, the businessman who wants a metal box retrieving.'

Marietta had been too taken with Jasper to take any notice of the short, fat, anxious-looking middle-aged man who was wearing an ill-fitting suit totally inadequate for going to sea in, and who was struggling breathlessly to keep up with Jasper's long, easy strides.

'Any sign of Harry?' Jasper asked Daniel as he and his unhappy-looking companion walked up to them.

'No, not yet.'

'Bugger the coal-man,' Tunny Boardman said impatiently. 'Let's get aboard the boat and be off.'

'Mind your language in front of who, I take it, is Lion's sister, or you won't be going anywhere.' There was an edge to Jasper's voice that only a very foolish man would have ignored. His black-lashed brown eyes met Marietta's. With a half-smile on his very attractive mouth, he said, 'When Tunny's been reunited with his ill-gotten gains and we're back on dry land, I reckon I'll need a walk up the Heights.'

'And about what time do you think that will be?' she said unblushingly, uncaring of Daniel's discomfiture and Tunny Boardman's rising impatience.

'About four o'clock?'

She smiled assent. Somehow – and only with difficulty – she would live through the time until then.

Jonah emerged from the cabin of the nearby boat. 'We're ready to cast-off,' he shouted to Jasper. 'Harry isn't here, but I'm not hanging around for him.'

'Don't leave Pa on his own for too long,' Daniel said

to Marietta and then, side-stepping a coil of oiled rope and an empty lobster pot, he walked across the cobbles and jumped aboard the cutter as if it was something he did every day.

Tunny boarded eagerly and clumsily, helped by the two men who had been loading the boat with equipment.

Jasper unhooked the bow-line and then the stern-line from their bollards, looked towards Marietta, gave her a wink that set her heart pounding and, as the boat began edging slowly away from the quay, jumped aboard her.

At the same time there came the sound of heavily booted, running feet and then Harry – Marietta knew it could be no one else – hurtled past her and she clapped in applause as he took an awe-inspiring leap for the moving cutter, landing on its deck only by the skin of his teeth.

On her way back home, she called in at Keam's for bread and, ignoring Mrs Keam's icy glare, told Janna that Daniel had just sailed out of the harbour with Jasper and Harry aboard Jonah's cutter. What she didn't tell her was that Jasper had asked her to meet him on the top of the Heights at four o'clock. She sang softly but delightedly to herself as she made her way back to the windmill.

'You're never here!' Pascal complained forty minutes later, emerging out of his studio, a streak of blue paint in his shock of white hair and a paintbrush in his hand. 'How can I work properly when you're never here?'

'I'm nearly always here and if you want bread and cheese at lunchtime – or bread at any time, because making it is not my favourite occupation – I have to go down to the high street. Would you like a mug of tea?'

'Tea? *Tea?*' Pascal waved his arms in exasperation. 'Would Monet, would Degas, drink tea while they created great masterpieces? *C'est impossible!*' He looked at her filled with sudden doubt. She was looking very pleased with herself; almost radiant. 'What is it I do not know?' he asked suspiciously. 'What is it you are keeping from me? Me! Your loving papa!'

'Nothing, other than that you have done a very good job this morning of painting your hair blue. If you don't want a mug of tea, what would you like instead?'

'Absinthe,' he said unhesitatingly, 'but we have none. However, there is a bottle of beer in the pocket of my coat.' He waved in the general direction of a hook on one of the studio's octagonal walls and then said, his mood changing with its usual swiftness, 'What a good girl you are to your poor old papa. What a lucky, lucky man I am to have a daughter so beautiful, so caring and *merveilleuse!*'

As the painting he was working on didn't need her to act as a life model for him the respite gave her a chance to catch up on household tasks. Until a little after three o'clock she spent the day washing clothes, sweeping floors, hanging bedlinen from upper windows in order for it to air, feeding the hens and collecting their eggs, milking Hortense, their bad-tempered nanny-goat, and making a hearty French onion soup. And all the time she was doing so her thoughts were full of Jasper Shilling, broad-shouldered, lean-hipped and dark-haired and – just as importantly – possessing a nature she sensed was just as reckless as her own. It made her sing aloud with anticipation.

At a few minutes past four and with her hair unbraided and falling down her back in an untamed riot of waves and curls, she stepped out of the windmill.

Jasper was a couple of hundred yards away on the crown of the hill smoking a cigarette and looking down to where Oystertown lay huddled between the foot of the Heights and the sea. At her approach he turned his head and as their eyes met, he tossed his half-smoked cigarette away and strode swiftly towards her.

She entered his arms like an arrow entering the gold and his hair was coarse beneath her fingers, his hands hard on her body and his mouth dry as her tongue slipped past his.

Chapter Six

It was seven o'clock in the evening and a storm was in the air as Jasper, Jonah and Harry huddled around the Shillings' kitchen table, impatiently waiting for Daniel to spread the drawings he had brought with him on its well-scrubbed surface.

'This is only a theory,' he said, putting the first drawing on the table as Janna entered the room and put the kettle on the hob to make everyone a mug of tea. 'I just want to know if Jonah thinks it is viable – if it is, the next stage would be for me to build a prototype and for Jonah to do a trial dive.'

There was no sign of a Siebe canvas diving suit and a heavy, windowed, all-encompassing metal helmet. Instead, the drawing showed a stick figure with what looked to be a long tube of rubber connecting the diver's mouth to what Daniel had labelled was an air intake on the surface supported by a float.

Jonah stared at the drawing, riveted.

Daniel slid a second drawing onto the table. It was of a T-shaped mouthpiece. 'One side will connect to an air hose through a one-way, non-return valve, the other side to an exhaust with a check valve.'

'And what does that mean in plain English?' Harry asked.

It was Jonah who answered him. 'It means when I breathe in, I draw air down the tube through the one-way valve, and when I breathe out, the air is expelled through the exhaust.'

'That, anyhow, is the theory.' Daniel's eyes held Jonah's. 'If you're willing to give a prototype a try, I'll begin making one.'

'Of course I'm willing.' There was no doubt in Jonah's voice. 'And the sooner you have the prototype ready, the better.'

Keeping her eyes off Daniel only with difficulty, Janna said, 'Would you all like tea? I've just brewed a fresh pot.'

'No thanks, Janna. We're off to the Duke.' Jasper rose to his feet and everyone else hurriedly pushed their chairs away from the table, Daniel stuffing his drawings into the inside pocket of his jacket as he did so.

' 'Night, Janna pet,' Harry said, cramming a thick woollen cap on his head as he followed Jasper out of the cottage.

Jonah, who, for a good-looking young man with a highly dangerous occupation was extraordinarily shy with girls, said, ' 'Night, Janna,' and hurried in Jasper's footsteps before she should see that he had begun to blush.

Daniel, thinking of the prototype he was about to embark on, merely smiled towards her, said a polite, 'Goodnight,' and closed the door behind him as he left.

Janna drew in a deep, unsteady breath, poured herself a lonely cup of tea and wondered why it was that Jonah, who she wasn't remotely interested in, was, she suspected, interested in her, while Daniel, who she was very romantically interested in, showed not the slightest spark of romantic interest in her. Like a lot of things in life, it simply wasn't fair.

As Jasper, Jonah, Daniel and Harry walked the short distance to the Duke, there was a rumble of distant thunder. On their bit of coastline summer storms could be fierce and Jonah, who along with Harry was a member of Jasper's lifeboat crew, shot Jasper a swift glance. Meeting it, Jasper shrugged his shoulders. If they got called out to a boat in distress, they got called out. Ozzie was also a crew member and, as at this time in the evening the other men on call were nearly always to be found drinking in the Duke, if the lifeboat crew had to be mustered it would only take seconds to muster it.

Once in the pub Daniel shouldered his way to the bar in order to get the drinks in and Jasper, Jonah and Harry made for a table in a relatively quiet corner where their conversation was unlikely to be overheard.

'Do you seriously think this barmpot idea of Lion's will work, Jonah?' Harry asked, shrugging himself out of his heavy coal-man's jacket.

Jonah grinned. 'I'll soon find out when I give it a try.'

'And if it doesn't work?' Jasper asked.

Jonah raised his eyebrows. 'Then I'll most likely be dead man's bones.'

Harry was just about to ask him if he was joking, or if he really meant what he'd said when a man slammed open the pub door and barged in, shouting, 'There's a yacht in distress and it looks as if it's Lord Layard's!'

Even as he was shouting there came the sound of alarm rockets being fired and Jasper, with Jonah, Harry, Ozzie, and every other member of the lifeboat crew who had been drinking with them, sprinted full pelt for the door, Daniel hard on their heels.

The lifeboat station was only a hundred yards away and as their booted feet pounded over the cobbles the threatened storm broke with a vengeance. Lightning knifed the near-black sky, the heavens opened and in gale-force wind rain began lashing down like stair-rods.

Jasper reached the station in seconds, aware that ten of the lifeboat's crew were with him – which meant that as coxswain he was a man short.

'Where the hell is Shanty Porter?' he shouted over the noise of a wind that was fast reaching hurricane force and as the lifeboat was being hauled down its slipway.

No one knew and before Jasper could ask for a volunteer from the crowd that had gathered to see the lifeboat launched, Daniel said to him fiercely, 'I can pull a heavy oar in rhythm. I'll take his place.'

Jasper would have rejected any other novice volunteer out of hand, but he knew enough about Daniel to know he would never claim to be able to do something he couldn't.

'You're on the left side of the boat, oar six!' he yelled back to him, throwing him an oilskin and a cork and balsa life-vest. 'Harry's on your right!'

The boat shot into the water and everyone jumped on board, scrambling into their designated positions. They dared not risk using the sails, as the wind was wild and unpredictable. Out beyond the harbour fresh lightning illuminated ferocious-looking waves and a glimpse of the crippled yacht tossing as helplessly as if it was in a whirlpool.

To Daniel the next forty minutes seemed like forty hours. As the wind shrieked, the lifeboat rose almost vertically high on one wave and then plummeted down into an abyss of seething water before rising high again on the next wave. Spray and rain leaked into his oilskin, saturating him to the bone. Fiercely he concentrated every atom of his being on pulling the oar in unison with everyone else; in praying they would reach the yacht in time to save the lives of its crew and passengers; in vowing he would never step into any boat ever again.

'It's no use trying to rig up a tow rope!' Jasper shouted as, in what seemed to be an eternity of wind and waves coming from all angles, they neared the disabled yacht. 'We'd never get a line to her!'

There was another flash of lightning. It illuminated four men on the yacht's suicidally tilting deck, all of them gripping the *Sprite*'s rails for dear life.

'Are we going in broadside on?' Jasper's helmsman, Ozzie's younger brother, shouted to him.

'We'll have to!' Jasper shouted back over the unearthly caterwauling of the wind and the thunderous pounding of the waves. 'I can't see any other way of taking them off!'

Someone in the lifeboat – Daniel thought it was Sparky Holden – shouted at the top of his voice, 'If we go broadside on, we'll roll over!'

Through the howling wind and the roar of the waves Jasper's reply was almost unintelligible, but everyone caught the gist of it, which was that it was a risk they were just going to have to take.

'Don't worry, Lion!' Harry shouted across to him as, under Jasper's directions, the lifeboat moved near enough to the *Sprite* for a rescue attempt of her crew to be made. 'A man born to hang never drowns!'

Daniel tried to shoot him a grin, but the muscles on his face were too frozen by the vicious winds, driving rain and the crashing spray from waves the size of a house and all he managed was a clenched-teeth grimace.

Attempt after attempt was made by Ozzie to throw a coiled rope from the lifeboat to the stricken yacht, but the gale-force wind whipped it away each time. Finally, on the fourth attempt, one of the *Sprite*'s crew successfully caught hold of it and, through the spray of mountainous waves and as the two boats pitched and rolled, Daniel saw the man secure it.

With the two boats linked together, Jasper bellowed to the

men on the *Sprite*, 'If we wait until the boats are pitching in unison can Lord Layard make the leap across?'

'*Yes!*' Lord Layard roared back before anyone could answer for him.

Daniel bit his lip so hard he tasted blood. He had no idea how old Lord Layard was, or how agile he was, but with both the yacht and the lifeboat being tossed around like corks, Layard was quite obviously going to have to make the jump of his life.

As everyone held their breath he did so, landing into Ozzie's steadying arms, his crew following after him.

Jasper's relief that Layard and his crew were aboard the lifeboat was shattered as Layard grasped hold of his arm, saying dementedly, '*My wife is still aboard, below deck!*'

As he spoke the *Sprite*'s broken mast crashed down on top of its cabin and the yacht began keeling over into the waves.

'*My wife!*' Robert Layard shouted frantically, seizing hold of Jasper's arm. '*We have to save my wife!*'

'*Sweet Christ, man!*' It took a lot to horrify Jasper, but he was steeped in horror now. 'You should have had her on deck when you saw us coming!'

Knowing that with the weight of a broken mast lying across the cabin's door, and with the yacht about to sink at any second, saving Lady Layard was an impossibility, all eyes of the lifeboat's crew were on Jasper; they were aware that the only rational action was to head back to the harbour before more lives were lost.

Instead, over the roar of the wind and the crashing waves he shouted to Ozzie, 'Take over!' and, the next second, he took a death-defying leap from the lifeboat onto the sinking yacht.

For the rest of his life Daniel had nightmares about the next few minutes. He saw, or thought he saw – for through a deluge that was biblical it was impossible to be sure of anything – Jasper wrench the mast away from the cabin's door. Through a wall of water, he saw the cabin door swing wide and then, with a great shudder, the *Sprite* disappeared beneath the merciless waves, taking Jasper and Lady Layard with her.

He heard Ozzie shouting orders, although what those orders were he was too shocked to take in. Although there was no sign of Jasper and Lady Layard, ropes were being thrown and then suddenly Jonah shouted, 'Give me another rope! I can see them!'

Daniel's relief was so all-engulfing he thought he was going to pass out.

'I told you,' he heard Harry shout euphorically as the rope was thrown. 'A man born to hang never drowns!'

Lady Layard was only semi-conscious when she was hauled from the seething sea into the lifeboat. Jonah and Ozzie hauled an exhausted, half-dead Jasper aboard. Lightning knifed the sky again, but this time it didn't do so directly over their heads and when thunder followed it was no longer deafening, but a merciful distant rumble.

'It's peaked!' Harry shouted across to Daniel as the lifeboat began heading back to land and instead of the sea being a maelstrom of forty-to-fifty-foot-high waves, it began rolling, white with foam.

In pitch-black darkness Daniel and the rest of the crew began the long, arduous, sodden, bone-weary pull for the distant harbour. Through the slackening rain scores of hand-held lanterns glimmered on the quayside.

They were nearly home.

And never in his life had Daniel been so grateful.

Chapter Seven

A week after the *Sprite* had disappeared beneath the hungry waves the Shillings received an invitation to take tea at Rose Mount.

'All of us?' Janna said, staring at the embossed cream invitation card with as much reverence as if it had come from King George himself. 'Not just Jasper, but you and me as well, Tilly?'

'It says to Mr Jasper Shilling and family,' Tilly said, reading the card over Jasper's shoulder, 'and so unless Jasper has a secret family that you, me and Smelly Bell the self-appointed town crier don't know about, that's you and me, Janna.'

Jasper flicked a corner of the stiff card with his finger. 'I'm not happy about it,' he said bluntly. 'If Layard wants to thank anyone for having saved his life, his wife's life, and his yacht's crew's lives, he should be thanking the entire lifeboat crew, not just me.'

'He can't have the entire lifeboat crew traipsing out to Rose Mount and tramping over his best Turkey carpets,' Tilly said in a voice of sweet reason. 'This way whatever he gives you in the way of thanks is bound to be something you can share equally with the crew. And can I point out that the invitation extends to me and Janna as well, and there is no way – no earthly way at all – that I am turning down the experience of chatting over the teacups with Lord and Lady

Layard. So the next question that has to be settled is: what on earth are Janna and I going to wear when we hobnob with our betters?'

'I have a ruby-red silk afternoon-dress that was my mama's,' Marietta said helpfully to Janna. 'Even though it fits me perfectly I've only worn it once. A ruby-red dress with fox-red hair is the worst colour clash in the world, but with your brown hair it will look sensational – and as it fits me, it will fit you.'

And the dress did fit her. It fitted her like a glove. Tilly's and Jasper's riotous curls had passed her by and she always thought of herself as the plain Jane of the family. In a dress that had been made by a French seamstress for Marietta's late mama and in a pair of lace-up ankle-length boots that Tilly had polished until she could see her face in them, she didn't look a plain Jane. She looked like someone she barely knew. She wished that Daniel could see her now, for if he did, she was sure there would be an expression in his eyes far different to the casual friendliness she usually met with.

Tilly's wild waist-length hair had been tamed by fierce brushing. Coiled in a heavy knot in the nape of her neck it was topped by a dainty straw hat which she had decorated with a cluster of red poppies. Her Sunday-best blouse, usually worn with its top few buttons undone to give a glimpse of her magnificent cleavage, was now demurely buttoned up to the throat, her jewellery a glass bead necklace that had once belonged to her mother.

Introductions were made as if it was quite commonplace for Lord and Lady Layard and their daughter to be receiving an oysterman and his family as guests. Janna was so over-whelmed at being introduced to the Layards and their daughter in the intimacy of their home that she would have bobbed into a curtsey if Tilly hadn't restrained her.

Lord Layard took Jasper's hand in a firm clasp. 'As a family we owe you and your lifeboat crew the deepest and most profound thanks, Mr Shilling. The bravery of you, and your men, was outstanding.'

'It is what lifeboat-men do, your lordship,' Jasper responded, not remotely intimidated by his surroundings, or on receiving thanks from a member of the House of Lords. 'In a storm so violent and life-threatening we would have done the same for any poor devil.'

Hearing her husband referred to, however obliquely, as a 'poor devil', Lady Layard sucked in her breath. Claudia pressed a hand to the back of her mouth to stifle a giggle. Tilly's generously curved mouth twitched in amusement and Janna closed her eyes, wishing herself a million miles away.

The only person completely unperturbed was Lord Layard.

'Well, Mr Shilling,' he said good-humouredly, 'this particular poor devil would like to express his gratitude to you and your crew by donating a new lifeboat to Oystertown. One that as well as having sails and oars, is petrol-driven.'

Tilly gasped. A petrol-driven lifeboat! She knew there were such things, but not many fishing towns as small as Oystertown possessed one. A petrol-driven lifeboat would be able to reach people in danger of drowning far faster than Oystertown's present oar and sail lifeboat could and it would give Jasper and his crew an extra edge of safety whenever they launched into gale-force winds and a ferociously heavy sea.

'Thank you, your lordship.' There was a slight unsteadiness in Jasper's voice. Whatever he had expected when he had received the invitation to Rose Mount, it wasn't that he was going to come away with the promise of a new, up-to-the-minute lifeboat. It would have to be the right size, though, and would Lord Layard know what size that was?

'She would need to be forty-three feet in length and twelve

feet, six inches in the beam,' he said as, from behind him, there came the sound of the drawing-room's double doors being opened.

A young man wearing the uniform of an officer in the Royal Navy entered the room. 'In that case,' the newcomer said in a cultured, upper-class voice, 'as I assume you'll need her to achieve at least seven knots an hour, she'll need a forty-boiler horsepower engine.'

'My nephew, Lieutenant Kim Layard,' Robert Layard said as, with a cry of pleasure, Claudia ran towards her cousin and slid her arm through his, hugging it tightly. 'Kim is well aware of what we, as a family, owe to you and your crew, Mr Shilling.'

'I certainly am,' Kim Layard said as Claudia released her hold of him long enough for him to shake hands with Jasper and be introduced to Tilly and Janna.

As far as Tilly was concerned the day was getting better and better. In her opinion, however good-looking a man might be, he always looked even more eye-catching in uniform, and in naval uniform, two bands of gold braid encircling the cuffs of his jacket, Lieutenant Layard – tall, blue-eyed and fair-haired – was head-turningly handsome.

'I hope you don't have to dash off anywhere, Mr Shilling,' Kim said, returning his attention to Jasper. 'I'd enjoy a chat if you have the time.'

Mindful that he had Tilly and Janna with him, Jasper hesitated.

Lady Layard solved the problem by saying, 'Kim and Mr Shilling having a chat will give you an opportunity to show Miss Shilling and Janna around the garden, Claudia.'

Claudia rose eagerly to her feet. She had already made up her mind that she wanted to know this family better – especially Janna, who she judged was the same age as herself, or very close to it, and who she was determined to make a friend of – and now her mother was unwittingly giving her the opportunity to do so.

'Whereabouts in Oystertown do the two of you live?' she asked in friendly curiosity as they stepped from the house and into a garden so long that it ended only where the shoreline began.

'We're an oyster family,' Tilly said, warming to Claudia's utter lack of pretentiousness. 'Our cottage faces the harbour.'

'How lovely! It must be wonderful to be able to see all the fishing boats coming in with their catch.'

Janna giggled. 'I don't think you would like the constant smell of fish, Claudia.'

Claudia giggled with her. 'No, perhaps not. Is Mr Shilling a fisherman when he isn't being a lifeboatman?'

'Jasper is an oysterman.' There was pride in Tilly's voice.

'And are you and Janna oyster girls?'

'Janna is. I'm not.'

Tilly waited for Claudia's next question, knowing very well what it would be, and wondering what Claudia's reaction was going to be when she told her.

'And what about you, Tilly?' Claudia asked. 'What do you do?'

The immaculate tidiness of rose beds close to the house was giving way to roses that had been left to run riot. They brushed past a head-high bush of Roseraie de l'Hay and as Tilly said, 'I'm a barmaid,' were deluged in a scattering of deep crimson petals.

Claudia came to an abrupt halt and, as their arms were still linked, forced Tilly and Janna to come to a halt with her. 'A barmaid? Do you really mean it? You're not teasing me?'

'I'm not teasing you. I enjoy being a barmaid. It's a far easier job than working oyster perches in freezing winter weather, which is what most women in Oystertown do, and as Janna does for Jasper.'

'Oyster perches?' Claudia said, happily accepting that she was now not only friends with an oyster girl, but with a barmaid as well. 'What are oyster perches?'

'They are man-made stone divisions just beneath the surface of the sea. All oystermen have their own perches and tip their daily catch of oysters into them to keep them fresh.'

'And then what happens to them?'

'Oyster girls like Janna pick them from the perches before the tide comes in and sort and clean them and sometimes sell them as well.'

They began walking again until eventually the garden came to an end and only pebbles, sand and sea were in front of them.

'I think we make a very interesting trio,' Claudia said as they came to a halt, 'An oyster girl, a barmaid and a suffragette.'

'A suffragette?' Tilly's eyebrows shot nearly into her hairline.

Satisfaction shone in Claudia's eyes at the way she had caught Tilly's attention. 'I believe that women should have the same voting rights as men and I'm a member of the WSPU, the Women's Social and Political Union. It's why I'm at Rose Mount. I was on a WSPU protest in Downing Street when a stone was thrown through a window of Number Ten. Many of my friends were arrested then and there. I managed to get away, but not before I had been recognized. Then two policemen came to the house with a warrant for my arrest and Papa infuriatingly contacted one of his government minister friends. Within hours my name was removed from the Bow Street charge sheet – something I had *not* wanted to happen – and Mama and Papa decided I was to spend the rest of the summer down here, at Rose Mount, well away from any further WSPU activity.'

Tilly, a fierce supporter of votes for women, regarded Claudia admiringly.

Janna said, 'I can't wait to tell Marietta and Daniel that there was once a warrant out for your arrest!'

'Who are Marietta and Daniel?' The sea breeze tugged strands of corn-coloured hair from the heavy knot of curls in the nape of Claudia's neck and she tucked them back in place. 'Are they oyster people too?'

'No. Marietta is my friend and Daniel is her brother. He's a shop assistant in the high street draper's, although what he likes doing best is inventing things. At the moment he's working on a way to enable a diving friend to extend the length of time he can remain underwater.'

'Then one of these days we must introduce him to Kim. Kim is part of a Royal Navy design team. I don't know exactly what the team is designing, but I think it has to do with submarines.'

'And Daniel was also part of the lifeboat crew that rescued your mama and papa.' Now that she had begun talking about Daniel, Janna didn't want to stop. 'He's not a regular member of the lifeboat crew, but they were a man short the night your papa's yacht capsized and Daniel took his place.'

'In that case I must meet him. Where do he and Marietta live? Do they live near the harbour, close to you and Jasper?'

'No.' At the thought of Claudia meeting Marietta and Daniel, excitement flooded through Janna. 'They live in the windmill at the top of the Heights.'

'Then that clinches it! I absolutely *have* to meet them. I can't do it while Mama and Papa are still at Rose Mount, but they will be returning to London at the end of the week and then, apart from Rose Mount's housekeeper, I'll be on my own again.'

'When you are, come into town. As the oyster season is over until September, I'm working at the baker's in the high street, but Thursday is half-day closing, both for me and for Daniel. I could meet you by the Fox and Firkin and we can walk up the Heights together and you can meet Marietta, Daniel and Pascal.'

'Pascal?'

'Pascal is Marietta's and Daniel's father. He's French, and an artist. Marietta says he's such a good artist he will one day be as famous as a friend of his, Claude Monet.'

Claudia's eyes widened. She was far from being a snob, but she hadn't expected an oyster girl like Janna to be familiar with the name Claude Monet – or that there was an artist in Oystertown able to claim Monet as a friend.

'Why would I want to make friends with a stuck-up member of the aristocracy?' Marietta said crossly when, at the windmill, Janna told her of her visit to Rose Mount and of how Claudia had said she would like to meet Daniel and thank him for the part he had played in saving her parents' lives. 'And Daniel isn't going to want to be thanked simply for having been part of Jasper's lifeboat crew the night the Layards' yacht capsized. You know how reserved he is. He doesn't like drawing attention to himself.'

'Claudia's very nice. She isn't at all stuck-up. How could she be when she's a suffragette – especially when she's a militant suffragette. If her parents hadn't packed her off to Rose Mount, she would be in a prison cell having been found guilty of taking part in malicious damage to Number Ten Downing Street! And as for Daniel—'

She paused. No one knew better than she how reserved Daniel could be. 'Daniel being thanked for having taken part in the rescue of Lord and Lady Layard and their crew isn't drawing attention to himself,' she continued firmly. 'And if he avoids Claudia so that she can't thank him he'll only succeed in drawing even more attention to himself!'

As this was so true Marietta didn't bother denying it. 'Well, she can't thank him when he's behind the counter at the draper's,' she said bad-temperedly. 'His embarrassment would be so total he'd never get over it. And being who she is, she certainly can't waylay him in the Duke. The only place she can thank him where it wouldn't cause comment is here, at the windmill. And as girls like her never go anywhere un-accompanied, you will have to accompany her.'

'Then I will.' Janna thought Marietta was being unneces-sarily churlish about meeting Claudia, but then Marietta didn't yet know how likeable Claudia was. As it happened, it all fitted with the plan she'd made anyway, and so it was most clearly meant to be.

The next Thursday afternoon she and Claudia walked arm-in-arm up the Heights together.

'I know this is silly,' Claudia said when, at the top, they took the short track leading to the mill, 'but I'm feeling so shy my tummy is in knots.'

'Shy of meeting Daniel?' Janna was incredulous. 'But you've no reason to be.'

'I know. It's just that as Daniel isn't a lifeboatman – or a sailor of any kind – he must be a very special person to have volunteered to make up the numbers on a lifeboat that was about to head out into one of the worst storms at sea Papa, an experienced yachtsman, says he's ever experienced, or ever wants to experience.'

A warm feeling flooded through Janna at hearing Daniel being spoken of so admiringly. Daniel *was* special. She loved him with all her heart and her secret hope was that he would one day feel the same about her.

As they neared the mill Marietta stepped out of it. For a few seconds Janna held her breath, fervently hoping Marietta wasn't still holding on to her crossness about Claudia's visit. With vast relief she saw that Marietta's mood was one of sunshine and light as she came running towards them, a brilliant smile of welcome on her face.

'Claudia! I've been looking forward to meeting you for simply ages.' She ran up to her, taking Claudia's hands in hers. 'I do hope you are going to like the mill and the goats and the hens!'

'I can tell already that I'm going to adore the mill,' Claudia said as Marietta let go of her hands in order to link arms with her. 'And although I can't promise to adore the goats, I think I will find it quite easy to be on good terms with the hens.'

'Hens are silly creatures. All mine have names, but none of them ever respond to them.'

'And do the goats have names as well?' Claudia asked, laughter in her voice.

'*Mais oui!* But of course! The billy-goat is Henri and the nanny-goat is Hortense.'

Pleasure flooded through Janna at the way Marietta and Claudia had so instantly taken to each other. It meant there was going to be no problem at all in the three of them becoming firm friends. And then her heart slammed against her breastbone as Daniel stepped into view.

He didn't walk towards them. He simply remained in the open doorway of the mill, the sun glinting on his fiery-red hair, his hands hooked into his trouser pockets.

And then he recognized who the third girl with Marietta and Janna was and his jaw tightened. He was a supporter of the newly formed Labour Party and the last thing he wanted was to be introduced to a member of the aristocracy. Exasperatedly he took his hands out of his pockets, bracing himself for the encounter.

'Claudia has come to say how grateful to you she is,' Marietta said as, with Janna and Claudia at either side of her, she walked up to him.

At the expression on Daniel's face Janna realized she had been taking things far too much for granted in imagining he was going to be pleased at Claudia thanking him in person for his part in saving her parents' lives. Instead of his being pleased she was now certain it was an embarrassment Daniel was never going to forgive and forget – and she was the one he would quite rightly blame for his embarrassment.

'My brother, Daniel,' Marietta said to Claudia.

The blood drummed in Janna's ears. Why had she thought this a good idea? Was Daniel ever going to speak to her again? Had she scuppered even the faintest chance of his beginning to care for her in the way she longed for him to do?

'I'm very pleased to meet you, Daniel,' Claudia said shyly as he shook her hand.

Janna dug her nails deep into her palms, praying that embarrassment wasn't going to make Daniel respond clumsily.

It didn't.

With a hesitation in his voice she had never heard before, he said, 'The pleasure is all mine.'

Janna stared at him, and at the expression on his face felt as if the ground was shelving beneath her feet for Daniel wasn't at all embarrassed at being so unexpectedly introduced to Claudia.

Instead, and far, far worse, he seemed absolutely dazzled by her.

Perhaps she was mistaken, her longing for him making her see something that wasn't there. But the fact remained, he'd never looked at her like that, however much she wanted him to.

Chapter Eight

Jonah Goldfinch was a quiet young man, but lately he had become quieter than ever. It was Harry's opinion that something was worrying Jonah and that he and Jasper should try and find out what it was.

'We can't have his thoughts being on other things when he's doing a dive scores of feet deep,' he'd said when he and Jasper were enjoying an early evening drink together in the Duke. 'I think we should ask him outright what it is he has on his mind.'

'OK.' Jasper was easy with the suggestion. 'Ask him.'

He could see immediately from Harry's soot-grimed face that Harry had no intention of asking him.

'I think it would be best coming from you, Jasper. I don't think he'd take much notice of me. There's a bit too much of an age difference between him and me.'

'What? Ten years? It isn't as if you're old enough to be his father. Are you ready for another pint?'

'Yes, I am. And I still think it's you who should ask what's bothering him. He's more likely to tell you than he is to tell me.'

Suspecting this was true Jasper drained his pint of best bitter, said that he'd have a word with Jonah, and suggested they have a game of darts.

* * *

'Harry thinks something is troubling you,' he said a couple of days later to Jonah.

They were on Jonah's boat, the *Neptune*, and Jonah was cleaning the heavy, copper and brass three-windowed helmet that, when he was diving, attached with screws to the metal breastplate of his canvas diving suit.

Jonah stopped what he was doing. 'Nothing is troubling me,' he said, 'but there is something I'd like to talk to you about.'

'And that is?' Jasper ran a hand through his hair, wondering if Jonah was having problems with the new breathing apparatus Daniel had made for him. He'd tried it a few times but they weren't yet happy with it.

'It's Janna. I've been sweet on her for ages, but I've never had the courage to take it any further. I wondered – if you didn't mind and if I asked her to walk out with me – if you have any idea what her response might be? I don't want to make a fool of myself.'

Jasper, who had never in his life doubted what a girl's response would be when he suggested they spend time together, was mystified. How could someone like Jonah, so fearless in his day-to-day occupation, be so backward in coming forward where girls were concerned?

'I have no idea what her response might be,' he said truthfully, 'but up to now I've never known Janna show any interest in having a boyfriend and if she's still not interested in having one it's something you'll have to take in your stride. It won't mean she doesn't like you, so if she doesn't leap at the idea, don't take it personally.'

'I won't,' Jonah said, knowing full well that if Janna rejected his suggestion, he would be so mortified he would never be able to face her again.

* * *

It was a late, stiflingly hot afternoon and Janna had just come home after finishing work at Keam's when Jonah's shadow fell across the open doorway.

'If you're looking for Jasper, I've no idea where he is,' she said, filling the kettle for the cup of tea she always made on coming home from work.

'I'm not looking for Jasper.' He was blushing like a girl and, what was worse, he knew it.

She put the kettle on the hob and turned towards him. She had known him all her life and so knew how shy he was with girls, but thought his being shy with her was pushing shyness to the limits.

'Would you like a mug of tea? The kettle won't take long to boil.'

'No. Yes. Thank you.' He stepped into the welcome shade and took a deep, steadying breath. 'I wanted to ask you something, Janna.'

She took a bag of biscuits from a shelf and offered him one.

He shook his head, not wanting to be distracted from what it was he'd come to ask.

'Well?' she prompted.

'I wondered . . . I thought . . .' he said, overcome with nerves, and then said in a sudden rush: 'If I were to ask you, would you walk out with me?'

At first Janna wondered if she had misheard him. She had guessed he might be sweet on her but had never really imagined he would say anything.

The expression on his face showed her she hadn't.

The kettle had begun to steam. She ignored it as several thoughts raced through her head. The first was that much as she liked him, and fond as she was of him, she had never daydreamed about him, as she daydreamed about Daniel. Her second thought was that Daniel had never given the slightest indication of one day asking her to walk out with him, and she didn't believe he ever would. And her third thought was that if she was ever to have a boyfriend other than Daniel, then there was no reason why that person should not be Jonah Goldfinch.

'If you were to ask me,' she said unsteadily, 'and I would very much like you to ask me, then my answer would be yes.'

Relief flooded through him and he said, blushing more furiously than ever, 'Then I would very much like to kiss you, Janna,' and, as she made not the slightest objection to the idea, he drew her towards him and lowered his head to hers.

It was Janna's first kiss, and she was always to remember it as being the most tender kiss imaginable.

Marietta disentangled her legs from Jasper's, fastened the buttons of her blouse that earlier she had shamelessly allowed him to undo, and sat up. They were in a small dell not far from the windmill and shielded from view by a thicket of five-foot-high yellow-flowering furze.

'I'm going to London tomorrow.' She swatted a bee away as Jasper remained where he was, shirtless in the hot sunshine and lying propped up on one elbow, a gleam of perspiration from the heat on his strongly muscled chest.

'London?' He was suddenly all attention.

'Yes. Why are you so surprised?' She rose to her feet and stretched languorously, like a cat. 'I'm only going for the day. Pascal has finished a painting he thinks the Gilroy Gallery in Bond Street will be interested in – they specialize in Post-Impressionist works – and he thinks this painting is the finest he has ever done.'

He didn't ask what the subject matter of the painting was and, as she had sat for it naked but for a wisp of chiffon, a sixth sense told her it was best if he didn't know. And it was certainly best he didn't know that a week earlier Claudia's cousin, Kim Layard, had accompanied Claudia when she had been visiting the mill and that the attraction between her and Kim had been instant.

Tomorrow, in London, Kim would be meeting her at the gallery and he had said that after her business there was concluded he would take her to a cafe for afternoon tea. When she had told Claudia, Claudia had insisted that she must be dressed appropriately for such a special occasion and had brought to the windmill one of her own London outfits, a tailored, very narrow bronze-coloured skirt that cleared the ground by a daring three inches, a high-throated cream lace blouse and a wide straw hat decorated with clusters of orange roses which, as soon as she saw it, Marietta knew she would wear tipped provocatively low, towards her nose.

'And please wear my French pocket watch,' Claudia had said. 'With that pinned to your breast, you will look business-like as well as elegant.'

At the prospect of entering a cafe in Piccadilly, or The Strand, in such fashionable clothes and on the arm of a hand-some uniformed naval officer, Marietta's blood sang along her veins. Other than Jasper she hadn't had an amorous adventure for a long, long time, and the prospect of being faithless to Jasper was one that didn't trouble her in the slightest.

By the end of the summer, everyone in Oystertown had accepted that Janna and Jonah were a courting couple.

'When is he going to put a ring on your finger and make an honest woman of you?' Ozzie's mother, Gertie Dadd, demanded as they neared the open door of her shop on the way to their favourite walk on the lower slopes of the Heights.

'It's not for the want of my asking,' Jonah responded, wishing Gertie would mind her own business.

Gertie gave a cackle of laughter. 'Then you need a girl a bit more enthusiastic. Try Rosie Gibbs. She's not shy of coming forward as another member of the Shilling family once found out.'

'I'm sorry, Janna,' Jonah said as they quickened their pace so as to be out of earshot of what Gertie regarded as being friendly banter. 'I wish Gertie would keep her opinions to herself.'

'But think how boring that would be for her.' Her arm was linked through his and she gave it a loving squeeze. 'Watching the world go by from her shop doorway is the only entertainment Gertie gets.'

It was very seldom they met with anyone else when walking on the more distant parts of the slopes. Sometimes they came across Pascal's chief drinking companion, Billy Gann, happily stumbling along from his isolated cottage on his way to the high street and the Fox and Firkin, or, a little more ambitiously, the Duke of Connaught. Today, though, Billy was nowhere to be seen and if they wanted to stop and kiss, they could.

'How many times have I asked you to marry me?' he said as they came to a halt in the middle of a swathe of knee-high ox-eye daisies.

'I don't know.' She was well aware that by now both of them had lost count. 'But if you're going to ask me again, my answer is still the same. I'm not ready for marriage yet.'

'But why?' He was baffled. 'You're seventeen. Half the girls of Oystertown are married by the time they're seventeen. I've got a cottage of my own. We wouldn't have to live with other people as most young couples have to do. And I'm only human, Janna. I can't be content with nothing more than kisses and cuddles for ever. Is it because, though you say you love me, you don't truly love me? Is that why you won't marry me?'

'No. I do love you, Jonah.' And it was true. She did.

'Then what is it? What's stopping me from putting a ring on your finger now? Today?'

It was impossible to give him the reason. It was impossible to say that although she loved him, it was not so long ago that she had also loved someone else as well; someone who didn't love her; someone who regarded her only as a friend.

'I'm simply not ready for marriage yet,' she said again, praying he would continue to be patient. 'Perhaps next year, Jonah. When I'm eighteen.'

He wanted to tell her that he had run out of patience, but he couldn't, not only because it wasn't true, but because he knew how devastated she would be if he were to do so.

They began walking again and he said, aware it was time he changed the subject, 'I've got an interesting dive coming up next week. It's going to mean being away a couple of days as it's near Dover. It's a wreck that sank over sixty years ago and until now it's been too deep for anyone to reach it, but I reckon I could if I was wearing Daniel's new breathing apparatus. And there's no need to worry,' he added as she sucked in her breath and gripped his hand more tightly, 'I'll have a couple of diving friends from Dover with me for backup and, when I tell them about it, no doubt Jasper and Harry will be along to give me their usual noisy encouragement before I do the dive, and to celebrate with pints of Guinness after it.'

In the late afternoon of the day of the dive, Janna handed in her notice at Keam's.

'The oyster season has begun,' she said, stating what was obvious to everyone in town other than Mrs Keam. 'It's time for me to begin working my family's oyster perches again.'

'Perches?' Mrs Keam was appalled at the thought of losing a shop assistant as popular with her customers as Janna. 'Why do oysters need perches? They're not budgerigars! And don't think you can walk back in here any time you want and that I'll take you on again, Janna, because I won't!'

It wasn't true and both she and Janna knew it.

'I'll bring you some of Jasper's oysters,' she said placatingly from the doorway, seeing no reason why she should be unpleasant just because Mrs Keam was being unpleasant, and before Mrs Keam could make a response, she stepped out into the street, shutting the door firmly behind her.

Almost immediately she became aware that something was very wrong. People were gathering in small groups and no one was meeting her eyes; no one was saying a cheery 'hello' and stopping her for a friendly chat. There was the same kind of bad news atmosphere as when the lifeboat was called out in heavy seas, but the maroon hadn't gone off and the sea was as calm as a mill pond.

She became aware of a familiar aroma and, seconds later, Smelly Bell was at her elbow. 'You've 'eard, then?' he said, hurrying along at her side. 'A death at sea is a terrible thing, a most terrible, terrible thing. The boat with 'is body on 'as just sailed into 'arbour. I couldn't believe it – no one can believe it – and when I did believe it, I was on my way to Keam's to tell you.'

Janna came to such a sudden halt she fell against him, sending him rocking back on his heels. 'Boat? Which boat?' Her heart slammed against her breastbone. And then with raw urgency: 'Whose body?'

'The *Neptune*.' As he answered her first question Smelly struggled to regain his balance. 'I'm sorry for your loss, Janna, for they broke the mould when 'e was made. Unlike everyone else in town, 'e always had time for me. Whenever 'e saw me, 'e'd always put 'is 'and in 'is pocket and give me whatever 'e could spare . . .'

She didn't wait to hear what else it was Jasper had always done. With fear roaring along every nerve in her body, her heart pounding, she caught up the length of her skirt and broke into a run, running faster than she had ever run before in her life. With a prayer on her lips she sprinted past Gertie's sweet shop; past the grocer's; the greengrocer's; the ship chandler's; the Duke.

Narrowly avoiding knocking down a small child she raced out of the high street and onto the quayside.

Usually, it was a hive of activity, but now there were no fishermen bringing their catches ashore; no fishermen mending nets or carrying out other familiar tasks on their boats. Instead, they were gathered in a stunned, silent crowd, looking down grim-faced to where the *Neptune* lay at anchor.

'Let me through!' she sobbed, pummelling brawny backs with her fists, terrified of what she was about to see. 'Please let me through!'

And then she was at the front of the crowd and looking down at the body lying on the *Neptune*'s deck and the blood drummed in her ears, the world tilting on its axis, for it wasn't Jasper.

It was Jonah.

Chapter Nine

Everyone was very kind to her. For the first couple of days, when all she wanted to do was lie on her bed in a darkened room and sob herself into exhaustion, Tilly fended off all callers.

'Gertie Dadd has left you a bunch of flowers,' she later remembered Tilly saying as she sat by the side of the bed, holding her hand. 'Rosie Gibbs says if there is anything at all she can do, you have only to ask. Mrs Keam says that if you want a funeral cake baking, Mr Keam will bake one for you.'

Jasper said to her, his handsome face gaunt with grief, 'Jonah may not have had any immediate family, but his funeral is going to be the biggest Oystertown has ever had. Divers are coming from as far away as London and Dover to pay their respects. Both the vicar and the Methodist minister have asked for the privilege of burying Jonah in their respective church-yards, but I told them that as the sea was Jonah's natural element he wouldn't want to be laid to rest in the earth; that he would want to be laid to rest in the sea.'

On the day that Jonah was taken aboard the *Neptune* for the last time an entire fleet of fishing boats set sail with her. On the deck, on a board lying on a trestle, was Jonah's body, sewn into a weighted sailcloth shroud. Facing each other on either side of the trestle, standing two by two, were Jasper and Harry, Ozzie and Daniel.

Also on the boat was a dazed, barely comprehending Janna flanked by Tilly and Smelly Bell, Smelly having insisted that Jonah would have wanted him to be there. With them, in order to commit Jonah's body to the deep in a Christian manner, was Reverend Samuel Pettman, Oystertown's Methodist minister.

Daniel's face was ashen. He had wanted to make further improvements to the new breathing apparatus he had made for Jonah and which Jonah had been wearing on his dives since early summer. Consequently, when Jonah had run into difficulties deep below the surface of the sea, he had been wearing his old breathing apparatus, and the old breathing apparatus had failed him.

'It wasn't your fault,' a grief-stricken Janna had said to him time and time again. 'You mustn't blame yourself, Daniel. Please don't. It's the last thing Jonah would have wanted.'

But Daniel was blaming himself and beneath his scattering of freckles his face was sheet-white as, with all the other boats that had sailed out of harbour with them, the *Neptune*'s sails were lowered and, together with Jasper, Harry and Ozzie, he stood ready to slide Jonah's body into the sea.

Reverend Pettman adjusted his stole, the two ends that fell to the hem of his cassock fluttering in the strong sea breeze.

The hymn 'Abide with me' was sung, but Janna's throat was too choked with grief for her to be able to join in the singing.

And then Reverend Pettman led them in the Lord's Prayer and she was dimly aware of Ozzie – big, burly Ozzie – stumbling over the words, tears rolling down his cheeks.

Waves slapped rhythmically against the *Neptune*'s hull. 'Amen's were said.

'We have gathered here to praise God,' Reverend Pettman's voice continued in a rich baritone, 'and to witness to our faith as we celebrate the life of our friend, Jonah Saul Goldfinch. We come together in grief, acknowledging our human loss.

May God grant us grace that in pain we may find comfort, in sorrow hope, in death resurrection.'

The blood pounded in Janna's ears as she struggled to come to terms with the reality of what was happening; struggled to comprehend that Jonah was truly dead and was about to be buried in the sea and that she was never going to see him again; that they would never again walk hand-in-hand on the slopes; that she would never again know the bliss of being held in his arms and of being kissed by him; of hearing him say how beautiful he thought her; how precious she was to him; how she had made him the happiest man on earth.

It was an enormity that until now had been too terrible for her to fully grasp; an enormity it was now impossible to evade. Why hadn't she said she would marry Jonah the very first time he had asked her? Why had she been so certain they had years and years of life ahead of them? Years in which they would be married; years in which they would have had children; children who would have had Jonah's unruly hair and his gentle, loving nature.

As if from a far distance she heard Reverend Pettman say, 'In the New Testament it is written that neither death, nor life, nor angels, nor principalities, nor powers, nor things present, nor things to come, nor height, nor depth, nor any other creature, shall be able to separate us from the love of God, which is Christ Jesus our Lord.'

He laid a hand on the sailcloth shroud.

Aware of what was about to happen, Janna made a low choking sound.

A pulse throbbed at the corner of Ozzie's clenched jaw.

Tilly whispered a private prayer.

In a nightmare it was impossible to wake from Janna saw Jasper, Harry, Daniel and Ozzie brace themselves for the task that lay ahead of them.

She saw Reverend Pettman bow his head, heard him say, 'Unto Almighty God, we commend the soul of our brother, Jonah Saul Goldfinch. And we commit his body to the deep in the sure and certain hope of the Resurrection unto eternal life, through our Lord Jesus Christ, at whose coming in glorious majesty to judge the world, the sea shall give up her dead, and the corruptible bodies of those who sleep in him shall be changed and made like his glorious body, according to the mighty working whereby he is able to subdue all things unto himself, Amen.'

In perfect unison Jasper, Harry, Daniel and Ozzie lifted the board with Jonah's body on so that within his shroud Jonah's feet rested on the *Neptune*'s rails and then, as Janna gave a gasping sob, her heart hurting so much she thought it was going to split into two, they gently tilted it and Jonah's body slid for the last time into what had always been his natural home, sinking deep below the waves, lost to her for ever.

Hours later, while the men of Oystertown paid their respects to Jonah in time-honoured fashion in the Duke, Tilly made a brew of tea in the cottage. 'I never knew Jonah's middle name was Saul,' she said, putting milk and sugar on the table. 'His mother must have had the Old Testament in her hand when she gave birth.'

'She died when Jonah was very young, but he grew up knowing she had been a Methodist and that was why Jasper asked Reverend Pettman to conduct Jonah's burial service.'

They fell silent again, Tilly wondering how best she could help Janna cope with her terrible loss and Janna thinking of how she had not allowed Jonah to put an engagement ring on her finger, and of how she would now give anything in the world for him to be doing so.

Bleakly she rose to her feet. 'I need a walk and fresh air and to be with someone who didn't know Jonah, and so who isn't grieving for him and whose grief isn't adding to my grief.'

'Marietta?'

Janna nodded, knowing that Daniel wouldn't be at the windmill; knowing that Daniel would be in the Duke with Jasper and Harry and the rest of Jonah's many, many friends and that for today at least she wouldn't have to cope with Daniel's grief as well as her own.

Not wanting Janna to be walking up the Heights unaccompanied when she was in such a state of dazed distress, Tilly pushed her barely touched cup of tea to one side, saying, 'Then if you're set on going to the mill, I'm coming with you.'

Although she had ejected a drunken Pascal from the Duke more times than she could remember – often for him to fall into the horse trough that stood outside it – it would be her first visit to the windmill for Marietta was Janna's friend, not hers, and she had never had any previous reason for turning left at the top of the Heights.

She was just wondering what kind of a reception they might get from Pascal, whose rage, when disturbed while working, was legendary, when Janna said as they passed the Fox and Firkin, 'Jonah wasn't afraid of dying, Tilly. It was a risk he knew he ran with every diving job he took. He wouldn't have wanted to leave me, though. He would have done everything possible not to let that happen.'

'You were his one and only love, Janna. He could have taken his pick of local girls, but he never walked out with anyone before walking out with you. The two of you may have only been together for a short time, but the love you shared was something very, very special. It was something that everyone would like to experience and that not many people do.'

Tears glittered in Janna's eyes. She knew how fortunate she had been to have been loved by Jonah. And she was certain she would never again love, or be loved, so deeply and so sincerely ever again.

It was late afternoon and the late September sun was still hot on their backs as they reached the top of the Heights and began walking towards the windmill, their skirts brushing against knee-high buttercups and stray scarlet poppies.

From a distance they could see the bear-like figure of Pascal standing at his easel on the staging that ran all the way around the mill, but it wasn't until they were fifteen yards or so away that, out of the tail-end of his eye, he became conscious of their approach.

He immediately put down his paintbrush, aware he couldn't give in to a surge of rage at being disturbed; not when Jonah had been buried at sea that morning and his visitors were a deeply grieving Tilly and Janna. At a fast trot he made for the staging's door, shouting, 'Marietta! Tilly and Janna are on their way! Get out glasses, a jug of water and what is left of the Pernod!'

His booming voice carried clearly and Tilly rolled her eyes. 'Pernod? That man's liver must be as pickled as a Christmas walnut.'

'It helps that he never gets drunk when he's working,' Janna said, surprised that Tilly hadn't known and then, realizing that Tilly couldn't possibly know when she had never been to the mill before and so aware of Pascal's working habits, she added, 'He's a different person when he's sober.'

'Truly?' Tilly arched an eyebrow, her voice doubtful.

Minutes later, as they walked up to the mill, Pascal stepped out of it to meet them.

'*Ma pauvre enfant!*' he said, opening his arms wide and folding Janna against his mammoth bulk. 'To lose a man as kind and brave as Jonah! For Jonah to die so young! It is a catastrophe! *C'est une tragédie monstreuse!*'

The sobs Janna had valiantly been holding in check broke free, making her gasp for breath and Pascal's big, generous heart went out to her. Hugging her close to his side he stepped back into the windmill's large, ground-floor room, Tilly following close behind them.

'Grief, dear child,' she heard him say with extraordinary gentleness as Marietta joined them, 'is the price we poor mortals pay for love.'

The first thing Tilly had realized when he had opened the door to them was that Pascal wasn't drunk and wasn't even squiffy. A sober, compassionate Pascal was a Pascal she had no previous experience of, and it came as something of a revelation.

The room they had stepped into was also a revelation. She had expected the interior of the mill to be like its owner, chaotic and untidy. It wasn't, although it was certainly furnished differently to any other room she had ever been in. Instead of stone, the flooring was cinnamon-coloured wood which she later learned Daniel had foraged from an abandoned cottage. There was an exotically patterned carpet in faded reds and purples that looked as if it had come out of an Eastern bazaar. There was a mish-mash of battered furniture, including an ottoman and two well-worn green-and-yellow leather-tasselled pouffes. A Chinese-looking three-panelled screen painted with butterflies and flowers partially hid the kitchen area. The octagonal walls were thickly hung with paintings, some done in oils; some in watercolour.

'You have memories *ma petite*, and you must treasure them,' Pascal was saying, one arm still holding Janna close as, with his free hand, he dragged a huge, blessedly clean handkerchief from beneath his painting smock and handed it to her. 'Would a little Pernod steady you?'

Janna shook her head and, taking a deep breath, slowly brought her sobs to a shuddering halt. 'I would prefer a cup of tea,' she said shakily when she could trust herself to speak.

'Tea?' Pascal looked around him in the manner of a man not familiar with the word.

'Tea,' Marietta said firmly as Janna began wiping her tears away with Pascal's handkerchief. 'I'll make a pot of it and because I'd like a little time on my own with Janna, why don't you show Tilly around the mill? I'm sure she'd like to see the views from the staging and perhaps the views from the top of the mill as well.'

When drinking heavily in the Duke, Pascal had always found Tilly's curvaceous bosom, handspan waist and torrent of coal-black curls deeply arousing. Now, in stone-cold sobriety, he found her earthy, gypsy quality so paintable his fingers throbbed with the urge to start work, capturing her essence first on paper, and then on canvas.

Wondering why on earth he had never previously thought of painting her and wondering if he could persuade her to stay at the mill long enough for him to be able to make a preliminary sketch of her, he said, 'If you would like to see around our humble abode, Miss Shilling, nothing would give me greater pleasure than to give you a tour of it.'

'Since when have I become Miss Shilling, and not Tilly?' she said, playing for time before answering him. There was nothing she would have liked more than to be shown around the rest of the windmill, but that wasn't the reason she was there. She was there to be with Janna.

'You are Miss Shilling because you are not, at the moment, behind the bar at the Duke.' He lowered his voice and said with what passed for him as a whisper, 'And if you look around the mill with me, it will give Janna and Marietta much needed time together on their own.'

She looked across to where Marietta had her arms comfortingly around Janna, and knew that he was right.

'Thank you,' she said. 'I'd very much like to see the rest of the windmill.'

A man whose mood could always change lightning-fast, he shot her a broad, beaming smile. 'Then be prepared to climb several ladders, Miss Shilling, because windmills do not have stairs.'

'Please drop the "Miss Shilling". It makes me feel as if I'm in my dotage. And why is it that windmills don't have stairs when they have so many floors?'

'Stairs take up space. Ladders don't.'

She wondered if he would climb the ladder first, or if he would think it better manners for her to climb up first. If she did and he followed up behind her, his face would be disconcertingly close to her skirt-covered bottom, a pleasure she didn't want to give him.

At the foot of the ladder he gave a theatrical bow, 'Ladies first, Tilly.'

Tilly gritted her teeth, although why she was mentally making such a fuss about things she couldn't imagine. At the Duke, she ran up and down the ladder from the bar to the cellars without a thought and why someone with her racy past was worrying about Pascal being indecently close behind her as she climbed a ladder was ridiculous.

Resolutely she put a foot on the bottom rung and then, just as if she was in the cellars of the Duke, mounted the ladder as confidently and speedily as Marietta always did.

'Bravo!' It was Pascal's opinion that there weren't many women like Tilly Shilling in the world.

He clambered up the ladder behind her. 'This,' he said expansively with a large, all-encompassing gesture of a paint-daubed smocked arm, 'is my studio!'

Not for one minute had Tilly thought it could be anything else.

Light flooded in unimpeded from windows that Daniel had enlarged. The wide-open door that led to the staging Pascal had been standing on as they had approached the windmill let in even more sunlight and what the sunlight revealed was a room cluttered and chaotic and messy beyond imagination.

A large paint-stained table stood in the middle of the room. On it were a dozen or more brown-glazed jugs crammed with brushes of different sizes. There was a chipped china pot full of pencils, and other pots held a variety of well-used crayons. There were small metal implements scattered on the table, some with wide, blunt ends, others with ends as finely pointed as a needle. An open box of watercolour paints vied for space with a bottle of turpentine, a bottle of linseed oil and a tub of varnish; a tray held an enormous number of soft aluminium tubes of paint and a cardboard box beneath the table was overflowing with paint-daubed rags. Easels with their struts down were propped against two of the walls. All the other walls had finished and half-finished paintings propped against them and there was an upright easel with a work in progress resting on it and a wooden stool in front of it.

For the first time Tilly began to appreciate that when Pascal was painting – and she knew from Janna that he was nearly always painting – he wasn't merely passing the time, but he was painting because that was what he had been born to do, just as Jonah had been born to be a diver. It was a compulsion he couldn't have denied, even if he had wanted to.

She ran a fingertip over the tubes of paint, looking at the names on them. Manganese violet. Cobalt blue, cerulean blue, chromium green oxide, chrome orange, emerald green, India yellow, cadmium yellow, zinc white, rose madder.

He noted her interest with satisfaction. As she touched one

of the many small metal tools, he said: 'That is my sgraffito knife. I use it to scratch into a surface layer of paint when I want to reveal a different colour beneath it.'

'And this?' She picked up a knife that had a curious bend in its handle, reminding her of a garden trowel.

'That's a painting knife. The bend keeps my knuckles clear of paint I've already applied and that is still wet.'

Through the open door she could see where he had been standing at an easel as she and Janna had approached the mill.

'Our arrival interrupted you in what you were doing on the balcony and I'm sorry that is what happened, but it just couldn't be helped. Were you painting a view of the town?'

'Of the sea. And what I was standing on isn't referred to as a balcony. The correct name for it is staging.'

She committed the word to memory and said tentatively: 'I've never seen an artwork in progress.'

'And other than Marietta I've never allowed anyone to see what I am working on. Never before have I allowed anyone into my studio other than Daniel and Marietta, but for you, Tilly, I made an exception – and I will now make another exception.'

The light was behind him and his great shock of white hair shone silver. The ends of his flamboyant moustache were immaculately waxed into twirls. Beneath his strongly marked eyebrows his eyes were flecked with tawny shades of brown and amber and for the first time she was aware of regarding his bulky build not as being ungainly and cumbersome, but instead as being magnificently broad-chested and reassuring.

She said: 'Why the exception where I'm concerned?'

With laughter rumbling up from deep in his chest, he said, 'Because you have a very well-shaped *derrière* to follow up a ladder, Tilly Shilling!'

And he led her out onto the staging, feeling ten years younger than when he had woken up that morning.

Chapter Ten

It was November and Claudia and Kim were seated opposite each other at the breakfast table in the Layards' London home. Lord Layard had already breakfasted and, chauffeured in his Wolseley-Siddeley motor car, had left for an early morning meeting in the House of Lords. As was her usual habit, Lady Layard was having breakfast in bed.

Kim was on a Thursday-to-Monday leave from Portsmouth and staying in Belgrave Square as he did every leave he had.

'So what are your plans for today, Coz?' Kim asked, taking advantage of their privacy and spearing a mushroom with his fork. 'Is it going to be shopping and art galleries?'

'It is. I shall be shopping at Fortnum and Mason – my favourite store in the whole of London – and then crossing the road to visit the Royal Academy gallery – and although I won't say that you will be accompanying me, I'm hoping that if we leave the house at the same time, Mama will make that assumption and so not worry unnecessarily.'

Kim's own deceits – all of which concerned Marietta – were of such a scale that, although he knew he should be telling her she shouldn't lead her mother into wrong assumptions, he couldn't bring himself to commit such hypocrisy. Especially not when Marietta always arranged her trips to London with Pascal's paintings so that they coincided with a date when he, Kim, was in London also.

'Would you like me to drop you off at Fortnum's?' Kim had only days ago changed his open-topped Wolseley for a two-seater Rover tourer capable of whizzing along at twelve miles an hour and he was eager to show it off.

'Yes please.' She desperately wanted a motor car of her own. Lady Clifford's daughter, who was a fellow member of the WSPU, had one and Claudia couldn't think of anything more delicious than having the freedom that a motor car would bring her.

Twenty minutes later, after Claudia had said a fond goodbye to her mama, she was seated next to Kim in his new, spiffy-looking scarlet motor car heading the short distance to Piccadilly via Hyde Park Corner. It was typical November weather, cold and damp, and she was wrapped up well, a thick beaver collar on her ankle-length coat, her gloved hands tucked into a matching beaver muff, a chiffon scarf tied over her hat to hold it in place while she was in the car.

'The thing I hate most about winter,' she said, 'is not being at Rose Mount. Mama is very strict about when it is suitable to leave London for the coast. In her eyes April to the end of September are when visits to Rose Mount are appropriate, and even then they must come second to the Season. October to March are for London and London's winter entertainments.'

'And what is it you miss most about Oystertown?' he asked as he approached the chaos of horse-drawn carriages, omnibuses, motor cars and bicycles all vying for space as they negotiated Hyde Park Corner.

She didn't hesitate. 'It isn't so much what, as whom. I miss Marietta and Janna the most, but I also miss Tilly. I received a postcard from her just the other day saying that even though it is now the season for oyster-catching and Jasper is out on his boat for long hours every day, he and Marietta are still as inseparable as ever and she's hoping that before next year is out there will be a wedding and—'

She broke off with a scream as Kim swerved and, in doing so, nearly drove into the back of a Fortnum & Mason delivery van.

'Marietta and Jasper? *Jasper?* Tilly's raving! I've never heard anything so ridiculous in all my life!' A pulse was pounding at the corner of his jawline and the blood had drained from his face.

'But why does it matter?' she was mystified. 'It will mean Marietta and Janna will be sisters-in-law, and they are as close as sisters already. The person who will be most inconvenienced is Pascal, because if Jasper and Marietta marry, Jasper can't move into the windmill, not when he's skipper of the lifeboat, and so that means Marietta moving into the Shillings' cottage and how Pascal will manage without her I can't imagine as he relies on her for everything. She even takes his finished paintings to the few London galleries who are happy to try and sell them for him.'

Breathing in so hard his nostrils were white, Kim brought the car to a shuddering halt opposite Green Park. 'It matters, Claudia, because first of all I refuse to believe it. Don't forget that I have met Marietta and I can't believe she would ever consider hitching herself for life to a womanizing Lothario like Jasper Shilling! Someone who fights in the back rooms of pubs! What I can easily believe is that he has made a pass at her and has been told in no uncertain terms that she isn't interested in him, and his pride is so hurt he's making out that she's yet another of his conquests so as not to lose face!'

Claudia gasped, looking at him as if he was a stranger. 'I can't believe you are saying all these ugly things about Jasper, Kim! How can you? How *dare* you, when Jasper risked his life in the worst storm at sea for a decade in order to save my parents' lives and the lives of the *Sprite*'s crew?'

Kim groaned and thumped the dashboard of the Rover in overwhelming frustration as a horse-drawn cart loaded with cabbages clattered past so near it was a miracle it didn't scrape the Rover's immaculate bodywork. Incredibly, he had forgotten that side of Jasper; the reckless, but undoubtedly courageous side and what the Layard family owed to him. Jealousy at even the thought of Marietta being unfaithful to him had driven him into behaving like an idiot. And he had behaved like an idiot because, from the little he knew about Tilly Shilling, he was certain she wasn't the kind of woman to spread untrue salacious gossip about her nephew and her niece's best friend.

He was twenty-five, a member of the aristocracy, a naval lieutenant with a glittering naval career in front of him. Tall and slim-hipped, fair-haired and blue-eyed, he knew that he was extremely attractive to women and that in another ten years' time, when he would no doubt begin thinking of marriage, he would not have the slightest difficulty in finding a beautiful and aristocratic young bride. Until that time came, he had, like other young men in the same station and position in life, satisfied his carnal urges with young women who, though young and beautiful, were far from being aristocratic, but were always obliging and, after they had been obliging, were swiftly forgotten. That was until he had met Marietta. And he would defy any virile male to make love to Marietta and then swiftly forget the experience.

He certainly hadn't been able to. And what added greatly to her allure was her 'Frenchness'. He knew she could speak without a French accent and usually did so, but that she also knew how arousing he found it when she spoke with an accent and peppered her speech with French words. The other great difference between her and what he thought of as being other girls of her class, was that as Claudia had given her several chic outfits that she herself had tired of, Marietta was always appropriately dressed when he took her to places such as the Café Royal at the bottom end of Regent Street and Kettner's, a very elegant French restaurant in Soho that had an enjoyably *risqué* reputation.

He remembered how amused Marietta had been when he had told her that the late king had courted the actress Lillie Langtry in one of Kettner's private dining rooms and of her delight when he, Kim, had wined and dined her in the same private dining room. And then he thought of her in the arms of Jasper Shilling and something twisted so hard and sharp in his gut that he groaned.

'Are you all right, Kim?' Claudia's indignant anger at the way he had spoken about Jasper had turned to concern. There were beads of sweat on his forehead and he looked most unwell.

'Yes. Fine.' Somehow he wrenched himself back into the present moment; became aware of the traffic surging past and of how he owed Claudia some sort of explanation for his angry outburst about Jasper.

'I keep getting occasional nasty stomach pains,' he fibbed. 'Incipient appendicitis, probably. I'll see the quack about them when I get back to Portsmouth. And I didn't mean to speak so vilely about Jasper, although I do think Tilly has got it wrong about him and Marietta.'

All that Claudia registered was the terrible word 'appendicitis'. People died of appendicitis and although Kim now seemed back to being his usual affable self, he had, for a few moments, behaved totally out of character and had looked awfully ill.

'You must tell my father about the nasty pain you keep having. I'm sure naval doctors are very good, but my father will want to make a Harley Street appointment for you.'

'Yes, well, I will if I get another such nasty attack again. For now, though, I'm going to drop you off at Fortnum's.'

He had left the engine running and so there was no need to re-crank it and five minutes later he drew up outside

Fortnum & Mason. A uniformed doorman opened the car door for Claudia and, after giving Kim a cousinly kiss goodbye on his cheek, she stepped out of the car and walked across the pavement into the deliciously enticing interior of Fortnum's ground-floor food department where she intended buying a box of stem ginger chocolates for her mother.

Two hours later, after a leisurely wander around all four floors and after buying the chocolates and a bottle of eau de cologne she crossed the road and spent a further hour in the Royal Academy, which, as the artist Robert Walker Macbeth had recently died, had a hastily assembled collection of his work on display. There were several of Macbeth's etchings and watercolours, and then there was an oil painting that took her breath away. It was titled *The Lass that a Sailor Loves*, and, if she hadn't known any better, she would have said it had been painted by Pascal, and that the fisher-girl depicted was Janna.

She stood looking at it for several minutes and then walked back out into Piccadilly and flagged a horse-drawn hackney down.

'Four Clement's Inn, The Strand, please,' she said, stepping into its carriage.

This was the moment of the day she had been most looking forward to. Number 4 Clement's Inn was the address of WSPU headquarters. Always a bustling hive of activity, it was where, under the direction of Mrs Emmeline Pankhurst, her daughters, Christobel and Sylvia and a committee of WSPU members, WSPU strategy was hammered out and where demonstrations, marches and direct action were planned. It was where she loved to be. It was where she was quite certain that, in her own small way, she was helping to change the world.

'Good,' Annie Kenny, a Lancastrian by birth, said the minute Claudia entered the main office. 'We need as many people manning the telephones as possible. Tomorrow's march on the

Houses of Parliament is going to be the biggest demonstration by far that we have ever mounted. Suffragettes from all over the country are already heading into London for it. That devil of a Yorkshireman, Asquith, is going to learn he can't promise to introduce a Conciliation Bill to allow a measure of Women's suffrage in national elections and then renege on it.'

Annie was small and skinny and a human tornado. A former mill girl she had been imprisoned many times for suffragette activity and Claudia was in awe of her.

Taking off her coat and hat and cramming them on an already full coat hook, she seated herself at a table and began answering one of the constantly ringing telephones.

'Yes. The march will start after a rally at Caxton Hall, Westminster, tomorrow,' she said over and over again.

'Tell callers we will be handing out white silk badges with the words "Deputation 1910" on them!' Christobel Pankhurst shouted over the general din and Claudia nodded to show that she had heard her.

The next morning, Claudia dressed in WSPU colours: her purple skirt representing loyalty and dignity, her green coat representing hope and the white cockade in her hat representing purity. She didn't bother with breakfast because she didn't want a breakfast-table interrogation about what her plans were for the day. Instead, she took an apple from the nearest fruit bowl and five minutes later was in a hansom cab on her way to Clement's Inn, from where, much later on in the morning, she would march with all the other Clement's Inn suffragettes to Caxton Hall.

'Have you ever been in a head-to-head with the police, Claudia?' Flora Drummond, an early member of the WSPU, asked her. Flora was a hefty girl who liked to wear an officer's cap and epaulettes.

'Once, after I was at a demonstration when something was thrown through one of the windows in Downing Street.'

Flora lit up a cigarette. 'Well, you'll very probably be arrested a second time today. The coppers are going to be out in full strength and it's going to be a no-holds-barred confrontation once our march reaches the Houses of Parliament.' Flora sounded as if she was looking forward to it. 'If you get arrested, don't go quietly. Knee them in the nuts if you can, and if you have a hat-pin, use it.'

Claudia's narrow ankle-length skirt wouldn't have enabled her to knee anyone, policeman or otherwise, in what Flora so graphically described as being their nuts, and even if it hadn't been narrow, she couldn't ever imagine herself taking such action.

She wondered what Kim would have said if he'd heard the advice she had been given and, despite the seriousness of the situation, a giggle rose in her throat. Kim would be as horrified as her parents would be if they knew how she intended to spend her afternoon.

At Caxton Hall and under Flora's diligent direction, over three hundred women formed themselves into military-style groups of twelve and, led by Mrs Pankhurst, the hugely respected Dr Elizabeth Garrett Anderson and Princess Sophia Duleep Singh, a god-daughter of Queen Victoria's, they set off along Victoria Street with a police escort.

Claudia's heart was full of passionate certainty that what she was doing was right; that it was something she would always be able to be proud of, for to her it was a matter of simple justice. As men had the vote, so women should have it also – and on exactly the same basis as men.

The crowds lining the route, made up mainly of women, cheered them on, so that the atmosphere was almost holiday-like. She was in the same group of twelve as Annie Kenny and when she saw someone from the group behind Mrs Pankhurst run back down the line in order to walk alongside Annie for a little way, engaging her in urgent conversation, her tummy muscles tightened.

With her message to Annie passed on, the woman ran to the group of women marching directly behind them, and passed her message on to them as well.

'What is it?' Claudia asked Annie urgently. 'Are we not going to be allowed to continue?'

'We're going to continue, but it's not going to be the usual police force we shall be dealing with. Policemen from Whitechapel and the East End have been drafted in to bulk up the numbers.'

'And is that going to be a bad thing?'

'I imagine so. They'll be used to dealing with East End thugs and the way they treat them is probably the way they are going to treat us.'

Soon they were approaching Parliament Square and she could see that it was a seething mass of people, the greater part of them helmeted London bobbies. Supportive women bystanders had now given way to men, both working-men and men in city suits, who pressed in on either side of them, shouting out lewd comments and trying to grab hold of them by their arms and to kick at their legs.

To Claudia's amazement the police did nothing to try and stop such attacks. Worse, as they entered Parliament Square, they began taking part in the assaults, hauling women from their orderly groups and instead of arresting them, squeezing and wrenching their breasts, dragging them by their hair and knocking them to the ground, kicking and punching them.

'Link arms!' Claudia heard a fellow suffragette shout over the din of screams and shouts as what had been a disciplined march broke up into terrifying mayhem. 'If we link arms, we won't be such easy targets!'

The advice came far too late. Claudia saw an elderly suffragette being sexually manhandled and then she, too, became a victim as a policeman seized hold of her by her arms, twisting them agonizingly high behind her back, calling her a vile name as he did so. Her hat was wrenched from her head and her hair pulled so savagely that it tumbled from its pins and then she was thrown like a sack against iron railings.

As she slithered to the pavement, she glimpsed Flora being dragged along the ground by two policemen, saw the trail of blood she was leaving behind her; saw a fellow suffragette being hurled from one policeman to another like a rag doll; saw a suffragette she didn't know lying unmoving on the ground, jeering policemen standing in a ring around her.

And then she felt blood trickling down the side of her face and knew that those who weren't there to witness what was happening would never believe it when they were told of it; that they especially wouldn't believe there was no one in authority trying to bring such unleashed violence against defenceless women to a halt.

The mayhem continued for six hours and there were so many scores of badly injured women that Caxton Hall was turned into a makeshift hospital. Helped by fellow suffragettes, all of whom had their own injuries, Claudia managed to reach the hall and her arm was put into a hastily improvised sling and the cut high on her cheekbone was swabbed and salve put on it to help coagulate the bleeding.

Looking around at some of the other injured women – and there were scores of them with dozens more arriving every minute – she knew she had come off lightly. Her arm wasn't broken and she hadn't been sexually molested as so many others had been. She knew something else as well. She also knew that along with her fellow suffragettes she had entered into a war – a war that wouldn't be won until, at whatever the cost, women were given the same voting rights as men.

Chapter Eleven

It was 23 December and the saloon bar of the Duke was strung with colourful paper-chains that, helped by a pair of scissors and a pot of glue, Tilly had made with Janna. Despite the paper-chains there was, though, something a little off-key about the atmosphere in the Duke and, as far as the regular drinkers were concerned, there had been for several weeks. Ozzie, for instance, had stopped making any attempt to be a genial land-lord and the usual saucy repartee between him and Tilly had become strained. Even stranger was that Billy Gann's drinking companion, Pascal Picard, was now only completely legless at closing time four nights out of seven, instead of seven nights out of seven. This was regarded as being a shame as it meant that hauling Pascal out of the horse trough at the end of the evening was something that could no longer be confidently looked forward to.

It was still early evening when the general run of things was altered by a stranger walking into the saloon bar and the usual hubbub of conversation died instantly. Strangers were a rarity in Oystertown. The last strangers to put in an appear-ance had been the Picards and, considering how outlandish Pascal was, the Picards had slotted into Oystertown life rela-tively smoothly. The stranger didn't even have the air of being an oyster man, or, indeed, a fisherman of any kind. He was dressed like a working man, in a reefer jacket and trousers and boots that had seen better days, but he wasn't built like a working man. He was of only average height and narrow shouldered.

'A breath of wind would blow him over,' Moody Gibbs said scathingly to Sparky Holden. 'D'you think he's going to ask for a glass of milk?'

The stranger didn't. He asked for a pint of Guinness.

Despite his slight height and unprepossessing appearance there was an easy confidence in his voice. Several pairs of eyebrows rose, not because he'd asked for Guinness, but because he had a distinct Northern accent. Oystertown was far closer to France than it was to the north of England. And the only reason any of the Duke's regulars could think of for a stranger turning up in Oystertown was that he was looking for work farming oysters – in which case, he would be out of luck, because no one in Oystertown would employ a stranger, not when there were always plenty of family members for them to call on.

Tilly pulled him his pint, saying as she did so, 'Are you here looking for work?'

'I could do with some work, but that's not why I'm here. I'm here because I'm looking for someone, or anyone really, just as long as their surname is Shilling.'

Behind him a pin could have been heard to drop.

Tilly sucked in her breath, her first thought being that he had some kind of an issue with Jasper, although if he had, for a man of his build he was taking a lot on seeking Jasper out.

Ozzie, who had been at the far end of the bar changing the pumps, stopped what he was doing. He didn't think trouble was brewing, but you could never tell. In a public house trouble could come from the most unlikely sources.

'And can I ask why?' Tilly asked, not about to admit to the name until she knew what a total stranger wanted with a member of her family.

He didn't look like a troublemaker, just the opposite, for he had one of the most pleasant, friendly faces she had ever seen.

His eyes held hers. 'I'm family,' he said. 'Long lost family and I'd like to make myself known to them.'

She sucked in her breath, and then said, 'The Shillings are an oyster family. If you're hoping to find they have money, then you're wasting your time.'

He grinned. 'I'm not after money, pretty lady. I'm after trying to find people I'm related to.'

Even though there was no veiled threat in the stranger's voice Ozzie closed the short distance between himself and Tilly and stood beside her, polishing a glass with a tea towel as he did so. Harry, who had been having a drink with Tunny Boardman, left his drink on the table and strolled up to the bar so that he, too, would have the pleasure of helping the stranger out into the street if Tilly indicated she thought such action was necessary.

'Then you must be related to old man Jumbo Shilling,' Tilly said, trying to catch him out by plucking a nickname out of nowhere.

The stranger shook his head. 'No, I never heard my mother speak of a Jumbo Shilling. She said my father's name was John Herbert Shilling.'

The blood left Tilly's face and the atmosphere in the bar became electric with tension, for everyone knew that John Herbert Shilling was not only Tilly's late brother, but Jasper and Janna's father.

'A public bar is no place for this conversation,' she said, when she could trust herself to speak. 'I'll meet up with you when I finish work.'

'You can meet up with him now, and for as long as it takes,' Ozzie said, still with the tea towel in his hand. 'Harry will cover for you behind the bar, won't you, Harry?'

Harry nodded.

'Thanks, mate.' The stranger shook Ozzie's free hand. 'Much appreciated. My name is Archie. Archie Wilkinson.'

Snow was beginning to fall as Tilly left the Duke with Archie Wilkinson. 'It's too cold for talking in the street,' she said as he turned his jacket collar up and she noticed how thin the jacket was. 'I live in one of the harbour-side cottages. I think it's best we talk there.'

As she began walking, he fell into step beside her.

'My niece, Janna Shilling, will be home,' Tilly said, 'Her young man recently died in a diving accident, so please excuse her if she isn't full of Christmas cheer. And my nephew, Jasper, won't be home. He's fighting tonight in the back room of the Fox and Firkin.'

'Fighting?' Archie came to an abrupt halt, his eyebrows shooting high.

'Jasper is an oysterman, but he's also a bare-knuckle boxer. And a lifeboatman,' she added for good measure.

Whatever else Archie had thought he might find when coming south to look up his late father's family, a bare-knuckle boxer who was also a lifeboatman hadn't been on the list.

'And so what is the relationship between my father, whom I never knew as he never troubled to marry my mother, and you and your niece and nephew?'

'If your father was John Herbert Shilling, and if he came from Oystertown, then he was my much older brother which, incredible as it might seem, makes me your aunt and it makes Jasper and Janna your half-brother and half-sister. As for your father . . .' She paused, suddenly aware that he might have expected to find his father in Oystertown, alive and well. 'As for your father,' she said again, 'John Herbert died a little over twelve years ago.'

She saw what a blow the news was. He was silent for a little while and then he squared his shoulders and said, 'Well, I may

113

not have found my dad, but I have found family. I now have an aunt and a half-brother and a half-sister and that's riches compared to having been without any family at all.'

As they turned into the row of cottages facing the harbour he stopped for a moment, drawing in a deep breath of air. 'Even in the depths of winter there's nothing as good as sea air. I was born in Whitby. It's a small Yorkshire fishing town and until now I've never lived anywhere else. Like Oystertown, it's famous for its oysters, which perhaps explains why John Herbert was visiting it in the summer of 1886. He stayed long enough to tell my mother his name and where he was from and then he headed back down south, never to be seen again.'

'So he may not have known he'd left your mother in the family way?'

'No. I don't suppose he did. My mother only told me his name and where he was from shortly before she died, and here I am – and even though I'm here a good twelve years too late, by meeting you I've still reconnected with family, haven't I?'

There was something so hopeful in his voice that Tilly's heart went out to him and as the snow began coating her head and shoulders, she knew what it was her late brother would have wanted her to say and do.

'Yes,' she said gently. 'Yes. You have reconnected with your family, and as you apparently have no other family but me, Jasper and Janna, perhaps you would like to spend Christmas with us?'

'That'd be grand,' he said, his voice suspiciously thick, as if he was choking back tears.

Three minutes later she opened the door of the home that was so important to her and to Janna and Jasper and that, no matter how crowded it would then become, she already knew was going to become a home to Archie as well.

Stepping straight from the street into the cosy living room-cum-kitchen, she said cheerily, 'Prepare for a surprise to end all surprises, Janna. Not only has Ozzie given me an early night off, but the Shilling family has just increased in number by one.'

By the cosy light of an oil lamp and candles Archie had a quick impression of a neat and tidy, warm and comfortable home. There was a roaring coal fire in the grate of a black-leaded kitchen-range. There were colourful tab rugs on a scoured stone floor. There was the enticing smell of recent baking.

Seated at a well-scrubbed deal table, staring at him with a look of shocked surprise on her face, was someone who, even in a crowd, he would have picked out instantly as being his half-sister, for they shared the same ash-brown hair colouring and her eyes were light green, flecked with amber, as his were. He found her hair and eye colouring infinitely reassuring, for Tilly's abundant glossy black curls and flashing dark eyes were so different to his own colouring that he'd been finding it hard to believe she was a blood relation.

With the help of a darning egg his new-found half-sister had been mending a man's thick woollen sock; a sock that was presumably Jasper's.

Very slowly she put the mushroom-shaped wooden tool down with the sock still stretched over it.

'I don't understand,' she said slowly, rising to her feet and looking bewilderedly from Tilly to the pleasant-faced young man standing next to her, and then back to Tilly again, 'What do you mean our family has increased by one?'

'Before I go into an explanation – or let Archie go into an explanation – I'm going to put the kettle on for some tea. Sit down at the table, Archie.'

As she took a kettle from its hook on the kitchen range and crossed to the stone sink to fill it, Archie obediently sat down.

After hesitating slightly Janna sat down again, doing so opposite him.

Tilly didn't seem about to launch into the very necessary explanation and Archie decided it was up to him to do so.

Giving Janna what he hoped was a reassuring smile and seeing no sense in going round the houses before he got to the point, he said, 'I'm a Yorkshire tyke from Whitby and I'm a—' He was about to say 'a bastard' but thought better of it. 'I'm illegitimate. My full name is Archie Wilkinson, Wilkinson being my mother's surname. My mother never spoke about my father, but a few weeks ago, just before she died, she told me his name was John Herbert Shilling and that he was an oysterman from somewhere down south called Oystertown. Whitby is an oyster town too, so that is perhaps why he had fetched up there. She couldn't tell me anything else, because she didn't know anything else – and before you think it was pretty shabby of him to have left my mother in the lurch when she was having his baby, she didn't know she was pregnant until after he had left for the south.'

Janna opened her mouth to speak, but no words came.

She tried again. 'And so you are . . . you are . . .'

She couldn't finish the sentence. A few short minutes ago she had been darning one of Jasper's socks and fighting back tears as she thought of Jonah as she darned, and then, the next, she was facing an amiable-looking, but otherwise nondescript-looking young man who, if she had understood him correctly, was her half-brother.

Another realization slammed home. What was Jasper's reaction going to be when he was told? Especially as he was nothing at all like Jasper in appearance. Hard on the heels of that thought came another, which was that she, Janna, was nothing like Jasper – or Tilly, come to that – in appearance. The young man seated opposite her – and who looked to be in need of a few good square meals – did, though, have her colouring and her slender build.

She wondered how old he was and quickly did some mental arithmetic. Jasper had been twenty in August and her parents had married six months before he had been born. For Archie to have been conceived before her parents had married it would mean her father's trip to Whitby would have had to have taken place at the very latest before March 1890. And so for her father not to have been unfaithful to her mother meant Archie had to be at least twenty years old.

As if reading her mind, he said: 'I'm twenty-three. How old is Jasper?'

'He was twenty in August. I will be eighteen next April.'

As she waited for the kettle to boil Tilly breathed a sigh of relief. It meant that her late brother hadn't been fooling around in Whitby when he'd been married to Janna's and Jasper's mother.

'It's a little early, but I suggest we have a bite of supper,' she said, certain the suggestion would be very welcome to their new family member. 'There's a hard end of cheese in the larder. How about we have it melted hot on toast?'

Janna was just about to say that the cheese was for Jasper to take with him when he went off to work in the morning, but Tilly flashed her a look that made her change her mind.

'That'd be grand.' Archie couldn't remember the last time he'd had something as tasty as cheese on toast and he certainly couldn't remember ever having eaten anything as good as cheese on toast in front of a roaring fire and with such wonderfully likeable kith and kin.

'And so what do you do for a living, Archie?' Tilly asked, setting about making their pot-luck supper.

'Anything that comes my way. I'm not toughly built, but I'm very wiry. There's not much I can't turn my hand to.'

Tilly believed him. He was also very amiable, which, in Tilly's experience, was a big help when it came to job hunting.

'And where do you live?' Janna asked. 'Do you still live in Whitby?'

'Not now. Now I've come down south, I'm going to stay here.'

'And so where . . . ?' Tilly left her question hanging in the air, fairly certain of the answer.

He hesitated and Tilly could see anxiety at the back of his eyes.

'I rather thought . . . now that I've come to know yourself and Janna and, hopefully, will soon be getting to know Jasper as well . . . that I'd try and find work here, in Oystertown. That is if my doing so won't cause embarrassment to any of you.'

Tilly thought of when she had been younger and had earned herself the reputation of being the town's lady of the night. A reputation which, although no longer applicable, she had never managed to live down.

'No,' she said, keeping a straight face only with difficulty. 'It would take a lot more to cause this family embarrassment than my having a nephew turn up out of the blue, and for Jasper and Janna having a half-brother turn up.'

There came the sound of Jasper's fast, familiar booted tread on the harbour cobbles and, seconds later, the door was flung open, letting in not only Jasper, but bitter cold air and a flurry of falling snow.

'Harry left the Duke immediately after you left it,' he said to Tilly, letting the door bang shut behind him. 'He gave me some story about a bloke having turned up claiming to be related to us. I'm assuming this is him?'

Archie had risen to his feet and both Tilly and Janna gave him full marks for not appearing at all fazed at facing six-foot-four of slim-hipped hard muscle, and hard muscle that showed

Jasper had come fresh from a fight, for he had a cut high on one of his cheekbones.

'Archie Wilkinson,' Archie said, holding his hand out. 'My father was John Herbert Shilling. He was never married to my mother – in fact, I think he barely knew her and he'd left town – the town being Whitby – long before my mother knew she was having me. She died a few weeks ago and before she died, she finally gave me all the information she had about him, which was that his name was John Herbert Shilling and that his home town was Oystertown on one of the south coast estuaries.'

It was quite a long speech and had been said with straight-forward sincerity.

Like Tilly and Janna, Jasper didn't doubt that Archie Wilkinson was telling him the truth. Until now his fists had been clenched. Slowly he unclenched them.

'Hell's bells,' he said graphically, taking off his snow-covered woollen cap and shrugging himself out of his wet jacket. 'And if you're from Whitby, are you an oysterman?'

'No. I'm afraid not. I am, though, very adaptable.'

Looking at him, Jasper didn't doubt it. He sat down at the table and Tilly took his pint pot down from the dresser.

'So is the long and short of it that we're related?' he asked as Archie sat down again.

'Yes. As far as I'm concerned that's good news because I don't have any other family, but I'm well aware you may have a different outlook on it.'

Jasper laughed. He was already beginning to like his new half-brother. 'So now that you've no doubt learned our father died several years ago, are you going back to Whitby, Archie?'

'No. I'm not going back up North.' He grinned. 'It's too full of northerners,' he added, making Jasper laugh.

'And so what are you going to do?'

'If no one has any objection, I thought I'd stay on in Oystertown for a bit. Find myself a job and some lodgings.'

There was a pregnant pause around the table and then Tilly said, 'Have you ever done any bar work?'

'Oh aye, plenty of times. I can pull a pint and I'm honest at a till.'

'Then I'll have a word with Ozzie. Ozzie is the landlord of the Duke.'

'In which case, a job at the Duke is already yours as Ozzie has never been known to refuse Tilly anything,' Jasper added.

'And you won't have to worry about accommodation,' Tilly said with certainty in her voice. 'The Duke has unused upstairs rooms. None of them will be ready for instant occupation, though, and so until one of them is, which is something I will see to myself tomorrow, you'll have to bed down for another day or two wherever it is you've arranged to bed down.'

'Yes.' There was deep relief in Archie's s voice. 'That sounds a grand plan. I'm very grateful to you, Tilly.'

Jasper's eyes had narrowed. 'And just where are you bedding down tonight?'

Oystertown wasn't a tourist town and, like the Duke, the Fox and Firkin, didn't rent out rooms.

'I can't remember the street name, but I know my way there. What I'd like to know now, though, is how the boxing match went tonight. Did you win?'

Jasper grinned. 'Of course I won. If I'd been matched against your fellow Yorkshireman, "Iron" James Hague, I'd still have won.'

'Iron' James Hague was the current British heavyweight champion.

'Now there's a match I'd like to see.' Archie grinned. 'I expect you know Hague won his latest title against Jim Moir with a knockout punch in the first round?'

Tilly raised her eyes to heaven, knowing that for the rest of the evening the conversation was not going to move far away from a boxing ring and, because Archie and Jasper were getting on so well together, not caring.

When, two hours later and not wanting to run the risk of outstaying his welcome, Archie rose to his feet and said thank you to Tilly for the cheese on toast and the warmth of welcome she had given him, Jasper walked with him to the door. Outside the snow was still falling and was now several inches deep.

'How far away are your lodgings?' he asked, suddenly aware that the soles of Archie's boots were probably as thin as his jacket.

'Not too far.' For the first time his usual ring of truth was absent.

Suddenly suspicious, Jasper frowned. 'Just whereabouts are your lodgings, Archie?'

'Somewhere in the high street. Don't worry. I'll find them easy enough.'

'No, you won't, because you're the most hopeless liar I've ever come across. Get back in the house. You can sleep in a chair for tonight and if tomorrow Tilly can drum up a camp bed you can stay for as long as you want. I've never had a brother before, and now I finally have one, I've no intention of losing you to frostbite!'

Chapter Twelve

April 1911

As Easter approached no one could remember a time when Archie Wilkinson hadn't been part and parcel of Oystertown. The day after his arrival Ozzie had set him on as a barman at the Duke, something that had put him on friendly terms with everyone capable of lifting a pint which, where the men of Oystertown were concerned, was practically everyone other than Reverend Pettman who, being a Methodist minister, was a teetotaller.

The early plan, that he should rent one of the Duke's empty upstairs rooms, came to nothing, because Archie fitted into the Shilling family so seamlessly the idea was never mentioned again. Instead, Tilly asked Gertie Dadd if she still had Ozzie's old iron bedstead. Gertie's response was that she had, and that she would dearly like to be rid of it as it took up precious room that she could use for other things. So Archie and Jasper had dismantled it and carried it down the street to its new home in Harbour Row. And just as Archie had been able to effortlessly make friends with Jasper, so he had been able to speedily make friends not only with Daniel, but also, thanks to Janna, with Marietta and Claudia as well.

He never flirted with them. He never flirted with anyone. He was simply always affable and if he could do a kindness for anyone, then he did.

'He's even won over Mrs Keam,' Janna once said to Claudia. 'If he goes into the baker's for Tilly, he always comes away with whatever it was Tilly had asked him to bring back, plus a bun or a jam tart given him free for himself.'

He began acting as Jasper's second whenever Jasper had a bare-knuckle fight at the Duke or the Fox and Firkin, pouring a jug of cold water down Jasper's sweat-soaked neck between bouts and kneading his legs, fanning his face and, on the rare occasions when it was necessary, putting salve on any cuts to stop the bleeding. Instead of this close relationship adversely affecting Jasper's long-standing friendships with Harry and Daniel, the four of them merely became a close-knit quartet – a quartet that no one with any sense ever interfered with.

The second of April was Census Day and Archie was tickled pink at the prospect of being officially included in it as a Shillings family member. In London, in Belgrave Square, Claudia was taut with excitement for her suffragette friend, Emily Davison, planned to hide in the House of Commons that night in order to avoid being counted as a citizen by a government that didn't recognize her right to vote. Emily's intention was to emerge from her hiding place in the morning when the cleaners arrived, knowing she would then be arrested and that her action would make newspaper headlines and be grist to the mill for what she and her fellow suffragettes referred to as 'The Cause'.

'But *where* in the House of Commons?' Claudia had asked her when Emily had told her of what she planned to do.

'I don't know yet,' Emily had said, 'but the House of Commons is so vast there must be somewhere I can hide. A store room, perhaps. Or a large cupboard.'

* * *

'Promise me, *promise me*, that you are not going to join her in such a reckless action,' Kim said through gritted teeth when she told him of where Emily intended spending census night. 'I don't know what position her parents hold socially . . .'

'They are very respectable and middle-class.'

'Then they must be appalled at her actions, but at least her actions are unlikely to ruin her parents' lives. Your father is one of Mr Asquith's cabinet ministers, but he won't be one for much longer if your name and photograph are emblazoned on the front sheet of every newspaper in the country!'

'As I am *not* going to hide in the House of Commons overnight, or engage in any other kind of suffragette demonstration this evening, that is not going to happen, and as you seem to see fit to interfere in my life, allow me to do the same in yours. Marietta is quite open about the fact that you and she meet up in town if you are on leave when she is delivering her father's paintings to London galleries and I hate the thought of you leading her on when nothing can ever come of it.'

'I'm not leading her on.' Kim's face was as grim as his voice. 'Far from it. If anyone is playing fast and loose, it's Marietta. You're close enough to the Shilling family to know that whenever my leave comes to an end Marietta is once again back with Jasper. Or at least she used to be.'

'What do you mean "used to be"?'

'I mean she will soon be doing so no longer, because I'm going to ask her to marry me.'

Claudia gaped at him. 'Marry her? Marry Marietta?' She tried to imagine what her parents' reaction to Kim marrying Marietta would be, but the effort was beyond her.

'Why not?' Kim lit up a cigarette and blew a wreath of blue smoke into the air. 'When she is in elegant clothes – and thank, you, Claudia, for ensuring that when I meet up with her in London she is always head-turningly elegant – she is very passable; even her speech doesn't let her down, for she has no working-class accent, only a delightful French accent. My parents are dead and so can't be mortified that I'm marrying the daughter of a near-to-penniless French artist, and although your parents will be shocked to the core, I know Marietta's social capabilities and your parents will be thinking her absolutely wonderful in no time at all.'

'My father might be, but I can't envisage my mother ever doing so.'

'Then that will be a disappointment to me, but not so much that it will make me change my mind.'

It occurred to Claudia that Kim was taking it far too much for granted that when he proposed to Marietta, Marietta would instantly accept him and, knowing Marietta as she did, she thought he might be in for a quite devastating surprise.

Her conversation with Kim wasn't the only unsettling conversation she had that day. Later on in the morning, she was unexpectedly summoned to her mother's boudoir.

'I would like,' her mother said, 'to have a long overdue conversation with you, Claudia.'

Her mother was seated at her dressing table and Claudia's immediate assumption was that Kim had wasted no time in appraising her of his intention of asking Marietta to marry him and that her mother was about to ask her to inform Marietta that due to class differences such a marriage was unlikely ever to take place.

Instead, her mother said: 'The London Season is nearly upon us, Claudia. It is three years since you were presented at court and the fact that you are still unmarried has become something of an embarrassing talking-point. This time last year Papa and I had high hopes that you would marry Toby Calverley. He very correctly asked Papa's permission to propose to you, which Papa naturally gave, and then, when he did propose, you turned him down. If you hadn't – and since his father died six months ago – you would now be a duchess. Instead of which you are still unspoken for and have the handicap of very openly being friends with suffragettes.'

There was a wobble of genuine distress in her mother's voice and Claudia said gently, 'I'm not only friends with suffragettes, Mama. I *am* a suffragette.'

As her mother had been speaking, she had been arranging and rearranging the cut-glass bottles of perfume that stood on her dressing table.

'And that you are – and that you draw attention to yourself by wearing suffragette colours – causes both me and your papa considerable concern.' Her mother moved a bottle of Penhaligon's English Fern so that it stood between Coty's Chypre and Guerlain's L'Heure Bleu. 'It gives me nightmares when I think of how close you came to severe injury when you demonstrated outside the House of Commons.'

For a moment Claudia thought her mother had forgotten all about the original subject of their conversation, and then her mother returned to it, saying: 'How are you to find a suitable husband when every year you are a year older and every year there is a fresh clutch of young debutantes for eligible bachelors to snap up? Papa and I always hoped for a match between you and Kim. In our class of society cousins have always married cousins and it would have been such a *satisfactory* arrangement. Perhaps . . .'

She stopped rearranging her perfume bottles and looked through one of the dressing table's triple mirrors, her eyes meeting and holding Claudia's eyes. 'Perhaps, if you gave up your suffragette activity, it still could be?'

Claudia knelt by the side of her mother's dressing table stool and took hold of one of her mother's hands. 'Dear Mama,

I hate being such a disappointment to you. I've always been aware that you would have liked to have seen me married to Kim, but close as Kim and I have always been, we neither of us have wanted our relationship to become even closer.'

It was on the tip of her tongue to say that anyway it was too late for such an arrangement as Kim already had a very firm idea of who it was he was going to propose to, but as that person was Marietta, she knew that it was up to Kim to break that particular piece of earth-shattering news to her parents, not her.

'And there will be few trips down to Rose Mount while the Season is on,' her mother added, changing tack once again. 'If I am ever to have a son-in-law and grandchildren you will have to throw yourself heart and soul into all the events of the Season, which means the Derby, Ascot, Cowes, the May Exhibition at the Royal Academy and accepting every party and weekend house invitation that comes along.'

'I can't just fall in love to order, Mama.'

'One doesn't have to fall in love to be suitably married. Even without being in love a couple can have a very close and understanding relationship and time is going by. Soon you will be spoken of as being on the shelf . . .' She broke off, her voice wobbling again, this time dangerously so. 'At your Coming-Out you were spoken of as being the most beautiful debutante of the year and to hear you spoken of as being – as being—' She broke off, unable to say the hideous words 'on the shelf' for a second time.

To Claudia's horror she saw that her mother's eyes were brimming with tears. She was so overcome with guilt – even though she felt the guilt was unjustified – that she said urgently, 'Please don't cry, Mama. I can't bear to see you crying. I promise I'll accept every invitation that comes my way and I'll go to every event of the Season, and I'll do my very best to attract the attention of someone who pleases me and who meets with your approval, but please don't cry, Mama, I truly can't bear it.'

There was a surprise guest for dinner that evening. 'His name is Xan Keller,' her father said to her when he arrived home from Downing Street at an unusually early hour. 'He's a friend of Kim's from Kim's university days at Oxford. He's Swiss,' he added. 'Works for their embassy, apparently. His parents lost their lives in a motor car accident some years ago. Kim thinks very highly of him. '

Claudia didn't doubt it. And she didn't for a moment doubt that her mother's earlier tête-à-tête with her had been triggered by her mother's knowledge that, thanks to Kim, an eligible young man was to be their guest at dinner that evening. Even if he was Swiss and not part of their immediate aristocratic circle.

As she had more or less made her mother a promise to begin thinking of young men in terms of whether they were, or were not, good prospective husband material, she wasn't very much looking forward to being under her mother's eye that evening, for to keep her mother happy she would have to spend as much time in conversation with Kim's friend as she did with Kim. Having grown up with Kim as if he was her brother, she had long experience of having to suffer his friends, all of whom rarely disguised the effect her blonde hair, sapphire-blue eyes and very kissable mouth had on them.

With a heavy sigh she mentally prepared herself for a stultifying evening of having to be pleasantly polite to Kim's old college friend without, while doing so, giving him the slightest hint of encouragement. To please her mother she did, though, have her maid take extra care when combing her hair into a softly swirled, Grecian-style chignon and, instead of wearing a gown that had come from Madame Lucile's, wearing one the colour of her eyes that had been made in Paris in the very latest neoclassical style. Fashionably low at the bosom and worn without the uncomfortable constraint of a corset, it seductively skimmed the pleasing curves of her body before falling sinuously straight to her feet. With it she wore a three-strand pearl choker that earlier in the year had been her parents' birthday gift to her and, on an upper arm, a silver snake-bracelet that had been Kim's birthday gift to her.

Before leaving the room, she looked at herself in her full-length mirror and was quite certain that no one could accuse her of not having made an effort and, minutes later, when she met their dinner guest, she was very glad that she had done so.

For some illogical reason she had expected that being Swiss, Xan Keller would wear spectacles and be as boring as one of his country's famous cuckoo clocks. The minute she set eyes on him she knew she had been doing him a great disservice.

In many respects he and Kim could be mistaken for brothers, for they were both tall and fair haired, but unlike Kim's hair, which was so springy he had to use Macassar oil to subdue it, Xan's was naturally poker-straight and he wore it brushed sleekly back without a parting and, unlike Kim, who was clean-shaven, he sported a very trim and very attractive blond moustache.

His handshake was pleasantly dry and firm and as their eyes met, she saw that his were an unusual shade of grey and that they were intelligent as well as admiring.

The usual courtesies were exchanged and then he asked her if she would be attending Covent Garden in June when Diaghilev's famous Russian dancers would be appearing.

Overhearing him, and before she could make a reply for herself, her mother said swiftly, 'The Russian Ballet's official debut, Mr Keller, is on Wednesday, the twenty-first of June, and, in fact, we have already secured our tickets.'

'How very fortunate,' Xan replied, and Claudia could have sworn there was a very heavy hint in the way he said the words.

It would have been very ungracious for her mother to fail to pick up on the unspoken request.

With only the slightest of hesitations, Celia Layard smiled at their guest. 'I am sure we can easily add another to our party.'

Without missing a beat, Xan said, 'That would be very kind, Lady Layard. It is an invitation I much appreciate.'

It was on the tip of Claudia's tongue to say that as the Coronation was taking place the day after the ballet, and as she and her parents would be in attendance at it, she was crying off Covent Garden in order to be well rested for the long service the next morning in Westminster Abbey. Her intention never became action. Xan Keller was too divinely attractive for her to want to avoid being in his company.

At dinner that evening the conversation moved on to King George and Queen Mary's Coronation and of how, in contrast to his late father, George often cut an insignificant figure.

'It isn't his lack of height,' Robert Layard said to Xan. 'His father wasn't tall but he had presence, and although King George has many commendable qualities, presence is unfortunately not one of them.'

'It may be one of them after he has been crowned,' Celia Layard said charitably. 'And there isn't a queen, past or present, able to outshine our dear Queen Mary for stateliness and grandeur.'

It was a statement too true to be argued with and Robert Layard changed the subject, saying to Xan, 'What is the Swiss attitude to the King's cousin's persistent build-up of his navy?'

'The Kaiser?' A wry smile touched the corners of Xan Keller's mouth. 'As we Swiss are a landlocked nation, Lord Robert, and as we consequently do not have a navy, we are not too perturbed by it. However, it is a little unnerving that the German Navy now outnumbers the British Navy where warships are concerned.'

'Good gracious, where did you get that idea from?' Abandoning his poached salmon Robert Layard laid down his fish knife and fork. 'The true statistics are that the British Government has commissioned eight new dreadnoughts. And just like Britain's original dreadnought, which is now five or six years old, their armoury is massive. If Switzerland thinks Germany has the upper hand over Britain where the naval race is concerned, then I can only say that Switzerland is in for a surprise.'

'I'm relieved to hear it. It would be good to see Kaiser Wilhelm taken down a peg or two.'

'By which I take it that Kaiser Wilhelm is no more popular in Switzerland than he is in England?'

Xan laughed. 'Probably not. He is a hard man to like and not, I think, very trustworthy.'

Celia Layard had had enough of the Kaiser for one evening. Not wanting any further reminders of Germany's unlikeable emperor, she decided it was time she took control of the conversation and said pleasantly, but firmly, 'Enough, for now, of disagreeable subjects. Papa and I have an announcement to make and, as he shows no sign of making it, I shall do so. I'm sure you all know that the biggest ship in the world is about to be launched on the thirty-first of May and that after her interior is fitted out, she will sail on her maiden voyage sometime in April next year. Papa's friend, Lord Ismay, who is chairman and managing director of the White Star Line, says she will not only be unsinkable but the most luxurious ship ever built. Papa has been able to reserve first-class staterooms and Papa and I will be aboard when, next year, she sails from Southampton to New York.'

At the thought of such an adventurous trip Claudia sucked in her breath, her eyes widening. She would not be averse to joining them herself. Xan was visibly impressed, if not downright envious, she thought, and no wonder.

He said to Robert, managing to keep the longing from his voice, 'May I ask if there is a proposed name for the ship?'

'Ismay tells me she is to be named *Titanic*.'

Celia frowned. 'I can't say I care for it. If it was a warship it might be different. I like female-sounding pretty names for liners. Names such as Cunard's *Mauretania* and *Lusitania*.'

Robert Layard regarded his wife lovingly. 'So you would have preferred *Titania*, would you, Celia?'

'Yes,' she said, knowing she was being teased and not minding a bit.

'*Titanic*,' Kim said as one of the Layard's footmen topped up his wine glass. 'I like it. It's the kind of name that once heard is unforgettable and who would not want to sail on the largest ship in the world? At some point in the near future, I may even book a return passage on her myself.'

Chapter Thirteen

May

'Marry you?' Marietta said quizzically, a throb of laughter in her voice. '*Mon Dieu*, Kim! Why would I want to marry you?'

It wasn't the response Kim had so confidently been expecting because, as far as he was concerned, there were a hundred-and-one reasons why. For one thing, marriage to him would elevate her to a position that socially she could only otherwise dream of; for another, there would be no more living in a windmill that, according to Marietta, didn't even have piped water and a gas supply, deficiencies which, to his incredulity, didn't seem to trouble her in the slightest.

It was late afternoon and in a discreet Soho restaurant they were seated across from one another at a table for two, a bottle of champagne nestling in an ice bucket beside them. She had just delivered two of Pascal's paintings to the Gilroy Gallery and had received payment for the two paintings she had left with them on her last visit, which they had successfully sold.

'It isn't a tease, Marietta. I've never been more serious in my life.'

She tilted her head a little to one side. 'Then I think it is very sweet of you to wish to marry me,' she said, amusement still thick in her voice, 'but I do not wish to marry anyone. For me, *mon amour*, being single means being free. And,' she

133

added with a Gallic shrug of her shoulders, 'I very much like being free. '

His disappointment at her reaction was so total that before he could stop himself, he said tightly, 'So that you can play fast and loose with whomsoever takes your fancy? Is that what you do with me, Marietta? Am I just for the occasional weekend when I have navy leave and you are in town trying to place your father's paintings in Bond Street galleries? And when you return to Oystertown do you also play fast and loose with Jasper Shilling?'

Again she gave an indifferent, infuriating shrug of her shoulders. 'And if I do, why does it matter so much? When you are on leave and I am not in town, do you not pick up an agreeable girl to spend the evening with? Because if you do, I do not blame you. There is an English saying, is there not, that what is good for the goose is good for the gander?'

It was all so far away from the kind of conversation he had anticipated they would be having that he was beginning to feel as if he had been transported to another planet. For the first time it occurred to him that, incredible as the possibility was, it was Marietta who was in control of their relationship, and not him. The realization that he was in competition for her favours with a rough, tough oysterman brought bile into his throat, but what was the alternative? If he gave her the ultimatum that she was to break off all relationship with Jasper Shilling, she would either acquiesce – and not mean a word of it – or refuse. Either way it would come to the same thing.

For as long as she wanted to have a relationship with Jasper at the same time as she was having a relationship with him, she would do so, because Marietta always did exactly as she pleased without giving a fig for other people's feelings. With a tightening of his gut he knew that even if she had accepted his proposal of marriage, being married would make no difference to her. As her husband he would never know which of his friends knew her just as intimately as he did. And now he had finally accepted this truth the only sane thing to do was to end his relationship with her with the same suddenness with which he had embarked on it.

He looked across the table at her. She was wearing a hobble-skirted emerald-green silk *tailleur*, the jacket nipped in at a waist that he knew from personal experience was no bigger than a handspan. It wasn't a high-fashion outfit that had been bought for her by him – infuriatingly she never allowed him to buy anything for her other than perfume and flowers – but it was an outfit he had seen before because it was one Claudia had worn on her birthday the previous summer.

On Claudia the outfit had looked expensive and elegant. On Marietta, it also looked expensive and elegant, but more than that it sizzled, turning heads, both male and female, wherever they went.

They were turning now and he knew that in such a public place he couldn't risk provoking her volatile temper. He was also aware of another certainty which was that, whether she was or wasn't in a relationship with Jasper at the same time as she was in a relationship with him, he couldn't demand that she end that relationship, for to do so would be to run the risk of losing her.

He took hold of one of her hands across the table, trapping it between both of his. 'If you are returning to Oystertown on the seven o'clock train, then it's time we began making our way to Albany.'

Albany was a nearby eighteenth-century Piccadilly mansion that had been remodelled into sets of rooms for aristocratic men about town and almost immediately after embarking on his affair with Marietta, Kim had rented one of the sets.

Marietta took a last sip of her champagne and then pushed the glass away from her, indicating that if he was ready to leave, then so was she. He rose to his feet, weak at the knees as he thought of the physical pleasure the next couple of hours would bring. He knew himself to be an experienced, sophisticated, aristocratic young man. How, then, could he have fallen so wildly and senselessly in love with a girl who, tomorrow, would be collecting eggs from her hens and milking a goat that went by the name of Hortense?

At the same moment in time that Marietta was rejecting Kim's proposal of marriage, her father had been proposing to Tilly, and although his proposal wasn't being rejected out of hand, it was still not being accepted in quite the way he had anticipated.

'You say you cannot marry me?' He tottered backwards and was steadied by coming into contact with a convenient wall in the otherwise empty saloon bar of the Duke. 'Me? Pascal Picard! *Mais pourquoi pas?*'

'Because in the past I earned the reputation of being what, in English, is referred to as "a lady of the night". And a lady of the night – even if she is one no longer – is not the kind of lady that men marry.'

He was genuinely perplexed, his bushy white eyebrows meeting above a nose as large and magnificent as that of a Bourbon king's. 'As a lady of the night you are a woman who is vastly experienced in the bedroom! What red-blooded Frenchman would not want such a wife?'

At the simplicity and sincerity of his thinking tears choked Tilly's throat and he rocked her in his arms, holding her tightly against his massive chest. 'And so you will marry me, my lovely Tilly? Yes?'

She shook her head. 'No, Pascal. How can we marry? Your windmill isn't large enough for two strong-willed women such as myself and Marietta to live in it together and my Harbour Row home is not big enough for you to have a studio there and, even if it was, the light would not be the right light for you to paint in.'

'*Mon Dieu!* I would not expect you to move into the windmill! And I would under no circumstances move into Harbour Row!'

The very idea made him grateful for the wall that was still supporting him.

'We would live as we live now. You would live in Harbour Row with Jasper and Janna and Archie; I would live in the windmill with Marietta and Daniel. Nothing would change except that we would be married – and our being married would make me very happy and would please me very much. And so you will marry me. Yes?'

With incredulity she realized he was serious and, with even more incredulity, she realized that such a scenario was entirely possible. Slowly, not trusting herself to speak, she nodded her head, a whole new future opening up in front of her.

'*Très bien.* Then as I am a widower and you have never been married before, we will marry in a church and I will have Daniel as my best man and you will have Janna and Marietta as bridesmaids and because your papa is long dead, Jasper will walk you down the aisle and give you away. It will be a splendid occasion, my love. Our wedding breakfast will take place in the windmill and the windmill will be *en fête*. What we must do now, my beautiful bride-to-be, is break this stupendous news to Jasper, Janna and Archie, and of course to Daniel and Marietta. Think how pleased they will be for us! Think of what a family we soon will be!'

* * *

Jasper's reaction to the news that Tilly and Pascal were going to marry was to give Pascal a hearty slap on the back and to say that of course he would walk his aunt down the aisle.

'And Billy Gann, not Daniel, is to be my best man,' Pascal said to him. 'And that's because Daniel *refused absolument* to wear the kilt and sporran left over from a painting I once did of Bonnie Prince Charlie. Billy will look *merveilleux* in a kilt, especially if I can find him some knee-high tartan socks.'

That toothless, habitually unwashed, sixty-four year-old Billy would look *merveilleux* in anything, let alone a kilt and a sporran, was too hard for Jasper to imagine and he didn't make the attempt. He was simply grateful that Pascal hadn't tracked down a second kilt and sporran for him, Jasper, to wear.

When Tilly told Janna that she and Pascal were going to marry, Janna flung her arms around her and was as happy for the two of them as Tilly had known she would be. In his quiet manner Daniel was also genuinely pleased about Tilly becoming not only a friend, but also family.

'If Tilly is going to continue living in Harbour Row as she says she is, nothing much will change,' he said to Marietta. 'And let's face it, it could be worse. Ozzie's mother is a widow. It could be Gertie Dadd Pa is about to walk down the aisle with, that is if Methodist churches have aisles.'

Marietta didn't know whether they did or not, and didn't care either way. What she did care about was no longer being sure of coming first in her father's affections. Although she had always been on friendly terms with Tilly, she now began avoiding her and, on the occasions when avoiding her was impossible, she treated her with hurtful, icy coolness. And Marietta wasn't the only person who was giving Tilly a hard time.

* * *

'You're going to do *what*?' Ozzie demanded when, before opening time at the Duke, Tilly told him she had accepted a proposal of marriage from Pascal. 'You're going to marry *who*?'

'Pascal,' Tilly said again. 'Other than Janna and Jasper, and Marietta and Daniel, you are the first person to know.'

Ozzie whipped off the tea towel that, serving as an apron, had been tucked down the front of his trousers. 'I should bloody well think I am the first other person to know!' He threw the tea towel into the bar's sink. 'Hell's bells, Tilly! We've had an understanding for years! Why would you suddenly decide to bring it to an end in order to marry a drunk like Pascal?'

His bewilderment was deep and genuine and she said gently, 'Because not only does he love me, but he thinks enough of me to want to marry me. And he may have a quick temper – although it never lasts for long – and he may have to be hauled out of the horse-trough after an evening in the Duke and regularly have to be helped up the Heights, but no one has ever known him to be nasty in drink. He's kind and loving and incredibly talented and I count myself fortunate that he wants me to be his wife.'

'And so when do you move into the windmill? When do I have to begin looking for a new barmaid?'

'You don't have to look for a new barmaid because I'm not moving into the windmill. I'm going to remain living in Harbour Row.'

The situation was now completely beyond Ozzie and he clapped the flat of his hand against his forehead. 'For mercy's sake, Tilly, what kind of a marriage will that be?'

'It will be our kind of marriage, Ozzie. Mine and Pascal's.'

There wasn't a shadow of doubt in Tilly's voice and Ozzie's thick-set shoulders sagged as he belatedly realized all that he had lost by not making an honest woman of her years ago.

Chapter Fourteen

June

King George's and Queen Mary's coronation was to take place on the twenty-second of the month and in the run-up to it, the excitement in Oystertown was at fever-pitch. Barrels of beer rolled seemingly endlessly into the cellars of the Duke in anticipation of the celebratory heavy drinking that would soon be taking place. Red, white and blue streamers were strung across the high street all the way from where it began at the harbour to where it came to an end at the foot of the Heights. The town's schoolchildren all received a commemorative coronation mug decorated with a likeness of King George, Queen Mary, the Union Jack, the Royal Standard and a lion and a unicorn standing rampant with a banner beneath them bearing the words *Dieu et mon droit*.

'Which means "God and my right",' Marietta said when Archie asked her for a translation.

Archie was still perplexed. 'Then why the 'eck doesn't it say so in plain English?'

They were seated companionably on the harbour wall, Archie doing so because he he'd arranged to meet Daniel at the harbour and Daniel hadn't yet arrived, and Marietta because she was waiting for Jasper to finish checking his oyster beds.

'Because it's a French motto that the English have stolen,' she said.

It wasn't something Archie had a reply for and he took a half-empty packet of Woodbines out of his pocket and offered her one.

She shook her head. 'No. You know I don't smoke. Although sometimes I wish I did because I would use a cigarette-holder, and I think cigarette-holders for women are *très élègante*.'

He cracked with laughter. Marietta always amused him and there was a platonic rapport between the two of them that both of them found pleasantly agreeable.

'Where,' he asked, 'have you ever seen a woman with a cigarette-holder in Oystertown?'

'Nowhere, but I have seen ladies using them in London.'

'London?' For a moment he was taken by surprise and then he remembered her trips to London taking her father's paintings to Bond Street galleries. But did women smoke in art galleries? He couldn't imagine them doing so. And would the kind of women who shopped in the most expensive street in London smoke in the street? For the life of him, he couldn't imagine that either. The only place he could imagine a woman smoking outside of her home was in a restaurant or a public house, but who would Marietta have been with in a London restaurant or public house?

Deciding it was absolutely none of his business whom she might, or might not, have been with, he changed the subject, saying, 'Will you be flying the Union Jack from the top of the windmill on the twenty-second? Ozzie wants the bar staff togged out in red, white and blue and he says he's going to wear a cardboard crown all day.'

'And is he going to have you wearing one as well?'

'Nah.' Archie blew a smoke ring. 'I'm a Republican, and Republicans don't hold wi' kings and queens.'

It was this kind of remark that made Archie such a stimulating companion and Marietta looked at him with interest.

'Because Pascal is French, and Daniel and I are half-French, we, too, are Republicans, but Pascal likes anything theatrical and so he flies the Union Jack whenever there is the slightest excuse to do so, and on Bastille Day he very properly flies the Tricolore.'

Archie gave a laugh. 'And why not? You can bet your life that when Yorkshire declares independence, I'll be back up North wearing a white rose and manning the barricades.'

'Do you mean you are actually going to be in Westminster Abbey when King George and Queen Mary are crowned?'

Claudia and Janna were walking barefoot on the beach at the end of Rose Mount's long, sloping garden and enjoying the icy pleasure of the ripples breaking rhythmically over their feet.

'Yes. Papa is a peer of the realm, which makes Mama a peeress. All peers and peeresses are invited to coronations and, as their only daughter, I have received an invitation as well.'

There was no showing off in Claudia's voice, but then there never was.

'And what will you wear? Will your dress be like a bridesmaid's dress?'

'I won't be wearing anything as frilly as a bridesmaid's dress, but I will be wearing a new evening gown and,' she added as an afterthought, 'a tiara.'

Janna had never possessed an evening gown and wasn't sure what a tiara was. Seeing her confusion, Claudia said, 'A tiara is a kind of fancy bejewelled headband.'

Janna gave a rapturous sigh. 'You're going to look like a princess, Claudia.'

'I'm going to look like a very bored princess. Coronation ceremonies go on for ever and ever and you can't just get up and go to the lavatory whenever you want. It's all right for the men. They can manage with a bottle beneath their robes, but there's no such easy option for ladies.'

It was a side of the religious majesty of the crowning in the abbey that had never previously occurred to Janna and she wished Claudia hadn't enlightened her, for it took the edge off the magic.

The outskirts of Oystertown and the harbour were now only five hundred yards or so away and Claudia came to a halt. 'I've something to tell you, Janna. Something that is far more exciting than talking about tiaras.'

Janna couldn't imagine anything more exciting than talking about tiaras, but then Claudia proved her wrong by saying in a rush, 'I've fallen in love. His name is Xan Keller and he's absolutely wonderful. He's Swiss and he's handsome and clever and he's a diplomat, and I'm almost certain he's going to ask me to marry him and, when he does, I'm going to accept him.'

Janna had been friends with Claudia long enough to have a good idea of what Claudia's parents' expectations were when it came to their future son-in-law and was certain that someone non-British was not among them.

Reading her thoughts, Claudia said, 'That I will not be marrying someone heir to a dukedom – someone like my ex-beau Toby Calverley – will be a crashing disappointment to Mama and Papa, but it will be a disappointment they will get over, given time.'

Linking arms, they turned and began strolling back the way they had come.

'And another thing,' Claudia continued, 'Xan fully supports my suffragette activities, something Toby would never dream of doing.'

Claudia's suffragette activities were something Janna deeply admired and she said wistfully, 'I do envy you. Because you have a home in London as well as having a home here, it means you can attend all the major suffragette meetings and take part in all the London marches and demonstrations.'

'So could you now the oyster season is at an end until September. All you have to do is tell Mrs Keam you are taking some time off and come with me when I return to London. Mama would be very happy for you to do so. She's never forgotten that when the *Sprite* sank she and Papa would have drowned if it hadn't been for Jasper's bravery, and the bravery of his lifeboat crew. The two of us could then march together in the Women's Suffrage Coronation Procession which takes place this Friday, five days before the actual coronation in Westminster Abbey.'

Janna opened her mouth to protest that she couldn't possibly come to London and stay in a posh Belgrave Square mansion and Claudia swiftly cut her off, saying firmly, 'And before you make the excuse that you haven't got any clothes suitable for London, you can borrow some of mine. It's what Marietta does when she comes up to London with Pascal's paintings. And if you are coming up to London for the Suffragette Coronation Procession, you may as well stay on for the King's Coronation Procession, and so you will speak to Mrs Keam, won't you?'

'Yes.' Any doubts Janna may have had, had faded. Of course she would accept Claudia's invitation, and of course she would stay on for King George's Coronation Procession. She wouldn't be in Westminster Abbey, of course, like Claudia and her family, but she would make sure she was somewhere on the processional route from Buckingham Palace to the abbey, one of the crowd of hundreds of thousands waving a paper flag and cheering herself hoarse. It was a spectacle she was quite certain she would remember until the day she died.

* * *

Ozzie, Jasper, Harry, Daniel and Archie were having a companionable after-hours late-night drinking session in the snug of the Duke.

'So, do you reckon Kaiser Bill is going to turn up for the Coronation?' Harry asked as Ozzie got another round in on the house. 'He is the King's cousin after all.'

'And not only a cousin, a *first* cousin,' Archie said, wiping a moustache of beer foam away with the back of his hand.

'And how do you know that?' Archie's ability to always be so well-informed irritated the hell out of Ozzie.

'Because where I come from in Yorkshire there are so many German square-heads living there a whole area is known as Little Germany. I grew up in a street called Stuttgart Street. So that's 'ow I know so much about Germany. It's because when I was a kid nearly all my friends were Krauts.'

'All right, all right, we get the picture.' Ozzie's patience was wearing thin. 'I'd stop now Archie, otherwise we'll be beginning to think you're a square-head as well.'

The remark was so ridiculous Archie didn't even bother rising to it. Instead, he said, 'Kaiser Bill wants a war. He's always sabre-rattling. Give it another couple of years and, trust me, we'll all be in khaki and heading for Berlin.'

Daniel stubbed out the cigarette he'd been smoking, saying, 'Then you'll all be doing so without me.'

'Rubbish.' As always, Harry put his twopenn'orth in. 'What if they were to bring in conscription, Lion?'

'I still wouldn't put on an army uniform. I'd be a conscientious objector.'

'And I'd be a sugar-plum fairy,' Ozzie said, not believing him. 'What say we have another hand of three-card brag before we call it a night?'

* * *

Although until now the summer had been one of the hottest on record, the weather on Coronation Day opened dull and cloudy.

'Oh dear.' For the first time in living memory Celia Layard was up by six o'clock in order to make sure that she, her husband and her daughter, were all dressed and seated in the abbey by eight, 'There's a threat of rain in the air. The entire procession will be spoiled if it rains.'

Ignoring the fact that it had already started to drizzle, Robert Layard said emphatically, 'It won't rain, although I wish it would. Wearing a heavy fur-edged velvet cloak and an uncomfortable coronet on a day that is obviously going to be hot is going to be a nightmare. A bit of rain would cool things down.'

'Stop complaining, darling.' She kissed him on his cheek. 'It's an historic occasion.'

'You said that when we endured the marathon of Bertie's crowning.'

At the memory of King Edward VII, Celia Layard's face softened. Bertie had been a magnificent king as well as being a dear friend. George was a very different kind of king, unsocial except when he was with a very small group of people – a group of which she and Robert could, thank goodness, count themselves members.

Janna left the Belgrave Square house even earlier than the Layards, knowing that thousands of people would have camped out overnight on the processional route in order to have a good viewing position and that finding a similar position for herself was going to be difficult.

The streets had been crowded enough for the procession a few days earlier, in which Janna had been thrilled to take part. Suffragettes and Suffragists had marched together, or ridden on floats, in costumes, carrying garlands and banners. It had been like nothing she'd ever seen before, and to walk alongside

Claudia had opened her eyes to what might be possible. They'd arrived back at Belgrave Square elated and exhausted, Janna unable to imagine the capital could offer anything more dramatic.

Yet now every street on the short distance from Belgrave Square to The Mall was thronged with eager, happy royalists. Even though there were another three hours before the procession from Buckingham Palace to Westminster Abbey was due to start, Union Jacks waved and whistles blew, the atmosphere was one of good spirits and the noisy jollity was deafening.

Once in The Mall, Janna realized with dismay that the stands which had been erected were already full to capacity and the crowds on The Mall's broad tree-lined pavements were so many feet deep she didn't see how she would ever be able to push a way to the front of them.

A hefty East End woman came to her aid. 'Wanting to get to the front, are you, dearie? So am I, and if you tuck yourself in close behind me, you'll soon be so far in front you'll think yourself part of the procession.'

Her new-found friend hadn't been exaggerating. With arms as beefy as a blacksmith's she elbowed a way through the crowd in front of them with all the ease of Moses parting the Red Sea.

'You need a bit o' weight on you when it comes to crowds like this,' she shouted over her shoulder to Janna, who had tight hold of the back of the belt surrounding her new friend's enormous girth. 'It's no use being polite and poncing around saying "excuse me, please". That'll get you nowhere. I can tell you're not a Londoner,' she continued as she successfully forged a way through to where policemen were lining the route. 'Up from Kent, are you?'

'I'm from Oystertown. It's on the coast.'

Her new-found friend wasn't listening. She was digging the policeman standing immediately in front of her in the back.

'You make a better door than a window,' she said when his head whipped round and he glared down at her. 'If you could edge to the right six inches or so, me and my friend would have a lovely view.'

Janna wondered if the dig in his ribs would count as assault and, if it did, if the policeman would arrest her and if she, Janna, would be arrested for aiding and abetting.

Realizing at a glance that entering into an altercation with his assailant would be taking on more than he wanted to trouble himself with, the policeman obligingly shifted his weight six inches to the right.

'There now,' Janna's new friend said appreciatively. 'That's lovely.' And then, to Janna, 'My name's Nellie. Would you like to share a pork pie? I've got one tucked away somewhere on my person. I never believe in going hungry if I can help it.'

Xan Keller would very much have liked to have been in the abbey for King George's official crowning as King of Great Britain and Ireland and all her Dominions over the Sea, but every seat in the abbey had a reserved name on the back of it and security at the abbey was so tight even peers and peeresses were being vetted before being allowed to enter.

Having no intention of joining the flag-waving throng lining every inch of the processional route, he made for Soho and the Bavarian pub where he had arranged to meet his regular contact, a high-ranking German Embassy official, trying to decide, as he did so, if the time had yet come for making a proposal of marriage to Claudia Layard.

Making such a proposal – and being accepted – had always been his long-term aim, ever since he'd managed to persuade his old Oxford acquaintance to invite him for dinner. The prospect was irresistible for, as Lord Robert Layard's son-in-law, his social circle would, at a stroke, include nearly every person of political influence in British government. Although most of the British seemed happily unaware of it, war between Germany and Britain was, Xan knew, growing closer and closer every day and every scrap of information he gleaned from Kim about British submarine construction was vital, as was any glimpse he could get of the Cabinet papers in Robert Layard's briefcase. A briefcase that, when Layard was at home, was sometimes negligently left unlocked.

He could tell that Claudia's parents were wary of him, even if they had been impeccably polite to him at the ballet. Claudia herself, though, was a different matter. It had taken no time to ensure that she was completely smitten, and Xan was certain that all he had to do was to pick his moment. Then his future would be gloriously secure.

Chapter Fifteen

February 1912

Ever since Christmas, the weather had been bitterly cold. Shielded by the steep hill at its back Oystertown was often spared the worst of Britain's winter weather, but even Oystertown was now deep in snow and glittering slivers of ice floated on the water in the harbour. All work on the oyster beds had come to a halt and, as a result, money in the town was short and tempers were even shorter.

The road leading from the end of the high street to the top of the Heights was too treacherous for all but the heaviest of cart horses and so there was none of the usual busy horse-and-cart traffic. Tilly, who prided herself on never being caught out on the food front no matter what the circumstances, had a reassuring supply of basic necessities in her Harbour Row store cupboard and, in the few short months since her marriage to Pascal, she had seen to it that there was a similarly well-stocked cupboard at the windmill.

She suggested to Daniel that with the snow so thick on the Heights it would be easier for him to get to and from the draper's he was now manager of if he was to move temporarily into the Shilling family home on Harbour Row.

'Although if you do,' she warned, 'you will have to sleep

on the sofa. The room Archie shares with Jasper isn't big enough for a third person.'

Even though it would, while the snow lasted, make life a lot easier for him, Daniel hesitated. 'Won't it look a bit strange, Tilly? You being newly married to my father, but not living with him, and me moving in here with you and Janna when your Harbour Row cottage is already packed to the rafters?'

Tilly's generously full mouth quirked in amusement. 'Where the Shilling family and the Picard family are concerned, strangeness is something people got accustomed to a long time ago, which is something I don't mind, because while they are gossiping about us, they are leaving other people alone. And Pascal won't mind,' she added. 'I doubt if he'll even notice. As you know, the Gilroy Gallery have agreed that in April they will give a month-long exhibition of his paintings and he's working like a dervish in order to have enough paintings of suitable quality ready to be put on show.'

'Daniel?' Janna looked at Tilly, certain she must have misheard her. 'Lodging here until the snow clears? But where is he going to sleep? With Archie sharing a room with Jasper we don't have an inch of spare space.'

'He's going to sleep on the sofa. It's an arrangement he's quite happy with. It isn't as if it's going to be for long, only until a thaw sets in and the Heights become walkable again.'

It was obvious to Janna that Tilly had no idea of how, only a little over eighteen months ago, she had believed herself to be in love with Daniel. That, of course, was before she had experienced real love – the kind of love she had felt for Jonah. Now what she felt for Daniel was loving friendship, but knowing how she had once wished it could be so very different was, she knew, going to make her feel awkward once the two of them were living – for however short a space of time – beneath the same small roof.

It wasn't as if she could even give vent to her feelings to Marietta or Claudia, for Marietta was snowed in at the windmill and Claudia was in London and would presumably have no choice but to remain there until a thaw set in. And when a thaw did set in Janna knew it would make no difference to her frozen heart, for how could she love again when she still loved Jonah, and always would love Jonah?

She felt tears on her cheeks; tears that weren't caused by the bitter cold weather, but by grief. It was at times like this she fervently wished Jonah was buried in the Methodist graveyard in a grave she could regularly visit and carefully look after and lay flowers on. As it was, his body was fathoms deep beneath the sea and she had no tangible memorial of him. All she had were memories, and no gold in the world could have been treasured more.

As an only child, Claudia had previously never had to battle with her parents over anything, but she was having to battle with them now for Xan had asked her to marry him and, when he had, she had flung herself into his arms believing herself to be the happiest young woman in the world. What was threatening to destroy that happiness was that Xan hadn't first asked her father's permission if he could propose to her – as she was over twenty-one, there had been no reason why he should have done so – and to her stunned surprise when, as a courtesy, Xan asked her father for her hand in marriage, her father hadn't instantly given them both his blessing. Instead, he had asked them to wait a year before an engagement was announced.

'Apart from his being Swiss, his having been at Balliol with Kim and his parents having died in a motor car accident, neither I nor Mama know anything about him,' he had said to her. 'You can't blame us for being cautious.'

She didn't, but at twenty-one she was already older than most girls were when they became engaged and she didn't want a twelve-month wait before having Xan's ring on the third finger of her left hand.

Only after a great deal of pleading were her parents persuaded to agree to an engagement date only four months away.

'It can't be any sooner, Claudia,' her mother had said, not happy at the thought of acquiring a son-in-law she barely knew and one who appeared to have no family whatsoever. 'As a family, we sail to New York on the *Titanic* in April, returning on the *Mauretania* in mid-May. I hope you realize how fortunate you are to be able to accompany us on this trip of a lifetime. It would be very odd for your engagement announcement to be made when we are either at sea or in America, and so June is the very soonest an engagement can be announced.'

'And then a wedding at Christmas, Mama?'

'Absolutely not.' Her mother's voice had been implacably firm. According to her husband, a war with Germany was growing increasingly likely and if the emotionally and, in her view, mentally unstable Kaiser declared war on Britain, she didn't want her daughter being regarded as an enemy alien because of Xan's German-sounding Swiss surname. With a year-long engagement there would at least be a hope of the present uncertain relationship between Britain and Germany stabilizing, or of either Claudia or Xan voluntarily breaking off their engagement.

Not for the first time Celia wished that marriages between first cousins weren't so frowned upon and that Claudia was in love with Kim and he with her. It was what she and Robert had always hoped for and it was Kim who had unintentionally scuppered those hopes by introducing Claudia to Xan.

She chewed the corner of her lip, reminding herself that there was a four-month breathing space before Claudia and

Xan's engagement was to be announced and that a lot could happen in four months. Something that was definitely happening in April was their long-arranged family trip to America aboard the *Titanic*. There were bound to be lots of exceedingly rich and well-bred American bachelors among their fellow passengers and it was quite possible one of them might change Claudia's mind about becoming engaged to someone as unsuitable as Xan Keller.

Optimism flooded through her. She would ask Robert to obtain an early copy of the *Titanic*'s passenger list. Where Claudia was concerned, she wouldn't leave anything to chance. She, Celia, would orchestrate suitable introductions as deftly as an army general and, with luck, by the time they arrived back in England, Claudia would be in love with someone else – someone socially acceptable and suitable – and Xan Keller would be consigned to history.

Marietta made an infinitesimal movement in order to alleviate the crick in her neck that was the result of holding the same position for too long.

'*Merde!*' Pascal erupted exasperatedly. 'How can I capture Helen of Troy's look of tragic wistfulness if you keep fidgeting?'

With great restraint Marietta managed not to give an indifferent shrug of her shoulders. Instead, she said, 'I do not think tragic wistfulness is an expression Helen would have worn. I think that in the Greek myth, after she was abducted by Prince Paris of Troy, she wouldn't want to be reunited with her aged husband. I know that I wouldn't. As well as painting her as the most beautiful woman in the world, I think you should also paint her as being one of the most treacherous.'

Pascal's shaggy silver eyebrows met over his nose in a deep frown. '*Traîtresse?*' he said queryingly. '*Une femme dangereuse?*'

'But of course she was a traitress and a dangerous woman!'

Sometimes her father exasperated Marietta beyond all endurance. 'Didn't she take part in Bacchic rites and exult in all the havoc she caused? The Gilroy will find it far harder to find a buyer for a chocolate-box depiction of Helen than they will one charged with lust.'

Pascal chewed the corner of his lip and then slowly nodded his head. As she always was about these things, Marietta was right. 'Yes,' he said. 'Yes. That is exactly how I will paint her. And although there have been many, many images of Helen of Troy, she will never before have been depicted as I, Pascal Picard, will depict her!'

Satisfied that she had once more successfully acted as a muse to her father's creativity, Marietta again took up her pose as Helen, but her thoughts weren't of Helen, or of Paris, or Troy. They were of her last trip to London which had been taken before the snow had fallen and when, in the Gilroy Gallery, she had been approached by a fat, flamboyantly dressed, bald-headed little man.

'Excuse me, young lady,' he had said, taking a business card out of his waistcoat pocket and handing it to her, 'I wonder if I could introduce myself and have a few words that will, I am sure, be to your advantage? The manager of the Gilroy will vouch for my respectability.'

Indifferent as to whether he was respectable or not she had looked down at the card. It stated that his name was Mr Adolphus Cuthbertson and that he was a Theatrical Manager and Music Hall Agent.

Mildly interested, she had quirked an eyebrow.

'I see you are a young lady who is not easily surprised,' he had said. 'I understand from the manager of the gallery we are in that your papa is the artist Monsieur Pascal Picard and that you regularly negotiate on his behalf?'

'And?' she had said, wondering if Mr Cuthbertson was about to buy one of Pascal's paintings.

'And in deep sincerity,' he had said, 'I wish to ask if you have thought of embracing the stage as a career? Your beauty and stunning vibrancy cry out to be seen on the stages of major cities.' With a flourish of his hand he had added, 'Cities such as Leeds and Manchester and Edinburgh.'

She had remained unimpressed.

'And Paris, Berlin, St Petersburg,' he had added swiftly.

Her eyes had narrowed speculatively as she had said: 'And what is it you have in mind for me to do on the stages of Paris, Berlin and St Petersburg?'

'I want you to dance,' he had said, 'for I am certain that you can dance. Can you also sing?'

She had given a careless shrug of her shoulders and had told him that of course she could sing – and that she could sing in French as well as in English.

His response had been to say that he could see her name on billboards and handbills already. 'Direct from Paris!' he had said with a theatrically expressive wave of a stubby-fingered hand. 'Mademoiselle Marietta Picard, songbird extraordinaire!'

Without looking at the card, she had tucked it inside the chinchilla muff which, along with the chinchilla-collared coat she was wearing, had been borrowed from Claudia. Then she had turned her back on him and unhurriedly and with hip-swaying seductiveness had walked out of the gallery.

Now, posing immobile for Pascal, her thoughts returned to Mr Adolphus Cuthbertson.

There had been a time when she would never have considered any other way of life but the one she was presently living, but that had been before her father had married Tilly. Now, although Tilly divided her time almost equally between the windmill and Harbour Row, she was at the windmill too often for comfort – and when she wasn't at the windmill several of her possessions were, and Marietta found the sight of them infuriatingly invasive.

Making matters worse was the fact that the situation was unlikely to change and, if it did change, the change might not be for the better, for Tilly could well take it into her head to move into the windmill permanently.

If she did, Marietta knew she would have to move out of it. Where, though, could she go? In theory she could, of course, move into the Harbour Row cottage Tilly would have vacated. She knew instinctively that she could easily live with Janna without falling out with her, but living at Harbour Row wouldn't only mean living with Janna. It would mean living alongside Archie and Jasper as well – and her relationship with Jasper was far too volatile for them to live amicably beneath the same roof.

She thought of the way music hall artists were constantly on the move, living in digs as they travelled from town to town, and knew that such an itinerant lifestyle would suit her restless nature. She also knew she could easily create mesmerizing dance routines for herself and she had a huskily distinctive singing voice. Becoming a music hall artist was definitely a possibility, especially as Kim was getting irritatingly possessive, Jasper was as faithless as she was and, since his marriage to Tilly, her father no longer relied on her in the way that had once made her feel so necessary to him.

While Pascal mixed cadmium yellow deep with chrome red on his palette, she came to a decision. As soon as the snow cleared, she would contact Adolphus Cuthbertson. The novelty of the windmill and Oystertown had worn off and she was going to leave Pascal, Hortense and the hens in Tilly's care and embrace a way of life far more suited to her talents.

Chapter Sixteen

It was the evening of 9 April and everyone in the Layard household, apart from Claudia, was in a fever of excitement. Early in the morning, the family would be departing on the boat train for Southampton in order to board the biggest liner in the world on her maiden voyage. It was something their household staff hadn't stopped talking about for days and all their conversations, from the butler down to the boot-boy, were peppered with the name *Titanic* in a way that gave everyone the feeling that they, too, had a connection with the greatest ship ever built.

Only Claudia was uninterested in how luxuriously furnished the *Titanic* was said to be, or if she would prove to be the fastest liner ever to cross the Atlantic, or whether the number of passengers she could take really was 3,547. And the reason she wasn't interested was because when a week's stay in New York and a return voyage on a different ship was taken into account, it would mean her not seeing Xan for at least three weeks. Her parents, however, were adamant that she should accompany them.

'It will be your last trip with us before you become officially engaged,' her father had said with loving firmness when she had suggested they travel without her, 'and your mother and I are greatly looking forward to spending time with you in the relaxing atmosphere of the ship. Selfishness has never been a part of your nature, Claudia. Don't let it become a part of it now.'

Remorsefully she had entered his arms as if she was still a little girl and had hugged him tightly. 'I'm sorry, Papa,' she had said sincerely. 'Of course I want to spend time with you and Mama. Xan will miss me, but I know he will understand.'

'Three weeks without you – the thought is unbearable!' Xan hadn't had to fake sadness. Three weeks without the opportunity of a peek into Robert Layard's briefcase would, for him, be three weeks too long. 'Dear heavens, Claudia! An entire ocean separating the two of us? How are we to endure it?'

'It will be dreadful,' she had said, her heart already hurting at the thought, 'and all I will think about to make the time pass more quickly is that when we return to England you will be waiting for me and our engagement will be nearer by three weeks.'

They had been snatching a few moments of delicious privacy amidst the exotic plants in the Layards' conservatory. Not letting the matter rest and playing the part of distraught lover to the hilt, he had said, 'And what if an American billionaire sweeps you off your feet?'

'Don't be such a silly.' Her hands had slid up the back of his neck, her fingers hooking into his sleek blond hair. 'If an American billionaire crosses my path I promise I will pay him no attention whatsoever.'

His mouth had been very close to hers and she had closed her eyes, her breath coming fast and light.

'Just as long as you don't,' he had said, this time with passionate sincerity, for he didn't want to find himself suddenly no longer welcome in the Layard family home and without access to Lord Robert Layard's briefcase and British cabinet secrets.

His mouth had closed on hers and her senses had reeled. If he had demanded it of her, she would have given herself to him then and there, uncaring of the danger of someone walking in on them.

The next morning, on the boat train speeding down from Waterloo to Southampton, she reflected on how fortunate she was in being able to look forward to becoming engaged to someone she was so deeply in love with, especially when that someone possessed no aristocratic lineage and was a foreigner.

'Although I have never really regarded the Swiss as being foreigners,' she had once overheard her mother say to their family friend Sir Edward Grey, the Foreign Secretary, and his rather startled reply had been that as a nation, the Swiss were, indeed, very hard to find fault with.

The *Titanic* was very hard to fault and, within seconds of boarding her, Claudia was certain that she was impossible to fault. The grand staircase they descended when being escorted by brass-buttoned stewards to their adjoining First-Class staterooms was worthy of a Florentine palace and when her parents entered their stateroom – a suite with two bedrooms, a sitting room and a bathroom lavishly decorated and furnished in the period of Louis XVI – even her mother was overcome by its splendour and attention to detail.

'I never imagined a ship could be so royally furnished,' Celia said, adding with a sigh of satisfaction, 'and I am now going to ring for a steward and ask for a pot of Ceylon tea and some Garibaldi biscuits.'

Robert Layard's eyebrows lifted. 'Are you not returning to the deck in order to wave goodbye to England as we set sail, Celia?'

'No. I will have plenty of time to sit out on deck and enjoy the sea air once we are under way.'

'And you don't mind if I return to the deck with Claudia?'

'No, darling. Of course I don't mind.'

'Then in that case . . .' Robert Layard crooked his arm so that Claudia could slide a kid-gloved hand through it. 'We'll go back on deck and leave your mama to have a little rest. I'm curious to see how such an enormous vessel smoothly leaves the dockside and gains the open sea.'

A few minutes later, as they stepped onto the deck, a five-piece orchestra in the ship's stern began vying to be heard with a brass band that was playing on the dockside.

'She's scheduled to sail at noon and it's five to twelve now, which is why there is so much activity,' her father said, having to raise his voice to be heard as, not without difficulty, they found a place at one of the crowded deck rails. 'I've never seen so many people come to see a ship off! There must be thousands of people on the dockside – and all of them are waving!'

'This is the greatest fun, Papa.' Claudia hugged his arm, wishing that Janna and Marietta were sharing the experience with her and that Xan was on the waterfront lovingly waving her goodbye.

'Have you noticed that all the gangways have been withdrawn?' Her father took out his pocket-watch. 'There are only a couple of minutes to go now.'

All around them fellow passengers were looking at their watches and, as they did so, a chant went up: 'One minute fifty seconds! One minute forty-nine seconds! One minute forty-eight seconds!' Then, in increasing excitement, 'Thirty seconds! Twenty seconds! Ten seconds!'

Precisely on time, the *Titanic*'s whistle blasted the air piercingly and Claudia clapped her hands over her ears.

'This is it!' her father shouted as, to a deafening roar of farewells from the dockside, the liner slowly and majestically began easing away from her moorings and into the narrow channel that led downstream towards the Solent and the open sea. 'We're off!'

Slowly the ship began picking up speed.

Ahead of them were berthed two much smaller liners, one with the name *New York* on her prow, and the other bearing the name *Oceanic*. With a note of apprehension in her voice, Claudia said, 'We look as though we're heading perilously close to those two ships, Papa.'

'Nonsense.' Robert's voice was reassuring. 'There's no need to be nervous, Claudia. The pilots on the tugs guiding us into the Solent know what they are doing.'

He spoke seconds too soon for the suction of the *Titanic*'s gigantic propellers pulled the *New York* from her mooring. To shouts and screams of horror there came the terrifying sound of hawsers snapping and the stern of the *New York* scraped the side of the *Oceanic* and began swinging directly in front of the *Titanic*'s bow.

'There's going to be a collision!' Claudia grasped tightly hold of her father's arm. 'The *Titanic* is so big it's going to crush that little ship!'

Robert would have liked to have said such a thing was impossible, but he couldn't bring himself to do so, for even to him it looked as if the ships were about to collide. Then, to his vast relief, the *Titanic*'s engines ceased to throb and he knew that the *Titanic*'s captain was in full control of the incident. He saw, too, that a tug had got a line to the *New York*'s stern and was pulling her to safety.

'Dear God,' he said with vast relief as the thousand or so passengers who had been on deck throughout the incident leaned over the deck rails to applaud and give the pilot of the tug a rousing cheer. 'That could have turned very nasty. The pilot of that tug deserves a medal.'

'Thank goodness Mama wasn't on deck to see what nearly happened.'

'Hear, hear, to that.' There was devout sincerity in his voice. 'An experience like that, before we had even made open sea, would have had your mama disembarking the minute we docked in Queenstown.'

'And do we do that tomorrow, Papa?'

He nodded. 'Today we sail to Cherbourg, where this evening we will take on more passengers and then we sail through the night to Ireland, docking overnight at Queenstown, where the ship will take on the last passengers to board – all of whom will most likely be emigrants travelling steerage to seek a new life in America.'

Now they were too far away to wave to people who had come to see them off. The drama of the near-collision was at an end and the crowds at the ship's rails had thinned.

'How about we have a gentle stroll and familiarize ourselves with all the ship's many amenities?' Robert suggested, having no immediate desire to return to his luxurious stateroom where he was quite certain Celia was now making up for their early start that morning by having a restorative afternoon nap. 'There is a Verandah Cafe and Palm Court – places where I know your mama is going to enjoy socializing. There is also a swimming pool, a rackets court, a gymnasium—'

He broke off abruptly, distracted from his description of all the *Titanic* had to offer by a boy of about six or seven hurtling towards them, bowling a hoop.

'Algy!' a female voice cried out in extreme agitation. 'Algy, please be careful not to run into that lady and gentleman!'

'Too late came the cry,' Robert said good-naturedly as he and Claudia smartly stepped out of the way, but not before the hoop had toppled over and come to rest against his immaculately tailored trouser-leg.

'Sorry, sir,' the child said apologetically, 'but the deck has a very slight tilt to it. It's not noticeable when you are just walking on it, but it is when you try and bowl a hoop.'

'I imagine it is.' Robert's mouth twitched in amusement. He had already become aware of the *Titanic*'s barely noticeable slight list to port and had assumed it to be caused by the huge amount of coal the ship must be carrying. He didn't know how many coal-fired boilers there were aboard her, but for a ship of the *Titanic*'s colossal size it had to be at least twenty and quite possibly thirty, which meant she must be carrying at least five or six thousand tons of coal.

He was still deep in thought about the mechanics of the *Titanic*'s construction when the hoop had been righted, Algy's mother had been assured that no harm had been done to his Savile Row-tailored trousers, and he and Claudia's pleasant stroll had continued.

Claudia didn't mind their companionable silence for she had plenty that she, too, wished to think about and, for a change, Xan wasn't top of her list. It was Janna who was at the top of her list, for just as Marietta's way of life had changed drastically over the last couple of months, so had Janna's.

In late February, when the last of the snow had disappeared, Janna had stayed overnight at Belgrave Square in order to attend a WSPU meeting with her at which Mrs Pankhurst had been present. Janna no longer felt nervous in such company; her having been in the office so often last summer had reassured her that she had just as much right to be there as anyone else. Even so, she was surprised when at the meeting Mrs Pankhurst had approached her and asked her if she would be interested in joining the WSPU's small full-time office staff at their new address in Lincoln's Inn House, just off The Strand, in Kingsway.

Janna had flushed crimson at being singled out in such a way and had begun to say that she would love to join the

WSPU's full-time staff, but that she lived too far away to be able to do so, when she, Claudia, had interrupted her. 'Not if you accept Mama's long-standing invitation for you to make Belgrave Square your second home,' she had said. 'The least you can do is to give it a try.'

And so that had been exactly what Janna had been doing. She could hardly believe she was missing the final few weeks of the oyster season, but she could not turn down this chance. A hard worker and quick on the uptake, she had been put in charge of the WSPU's Ticket Department.

Claudia suddenly became aware of her father coming to a halt. 'Now there's an odd thing,' he said, surprise in his voice. 'We've just walked the length of the deck and I've only counted eight lifeboats. Going by the lifeboat I bought for Oystertown – and these boats look to be identical to that one – each boat can hold sixty people, sixty-five at a pinch. Now, as I am assuming that there are the same number of lifeboats on the other side of the ship, the total number of places in lifeboats is only . . .' He broke off to do a quick sum in his head. 'Good God! It's only nine hundred and sixty! Which surely can't be right? Not for a ship this size.'

Claudia giggled. 'You really are being very pedantic, Papa. The *Titanic* is unsinkable. She doesn't need lifeboats.'

A ship's officer was standing close by and Robert approached him. 'Excuse me, officer,' he said pleasantly. 'I am in a discussion with my daughter about the number of lifeboats aboard the ship. I am surprised by the apparent small number of them, and my daughter says that as the ship is unsinkable there is no need for a larger number. Is she correct in thinking that?'

The officer gave him an indulgent smile. 'Yes, sir. *Titanic* has sixteen water-tight compartments. It is impossible for her to sink. But just to put your mind at rest, the ship is also carrying four collapsible lifeboats.'

'Which is perhaps just as well,' Robert said to Claudia as they continued with their stroll, 'for if she was to sink, can you imagine the panic on a ship able to carry well over three thousand passengers? It would be mayhem. We're just approaching the Palm Court. Would you like a glass of champagne before we return to Mama?'

Chapter Seventeen

Janna felt very strange being a guest in the Layards' Belgrave Square house when the Layard family were hundreds and hundreds of miles away somewhere in the mid-Atlantic. Claudia's mother had, however, been very firm that she was just as welcome there when Claudia was away as when she was in residence.

'And when many months ago I asked you to regard our house in Belgrave Square as your second home, I truly meant it,' Celia had said to her with her usual kindness. 'You will no doubt miss Claudia not being here to keep you company, but three weeks isn't very long. We'll be back before you know it.'

Three days after the Layards had left for America, and just as she was about to leave her room and set off for The Strand where she had arranged to meet Marietta in a Lyons Corner House, a maid knocked on her door.

'Excuse me, miss,' she said when Janna opened it, 'but Beamish says to tell you Mr Keller is in the entrance hall. He says he mislaid his pocket-watch when he was here the evening before the family left for America. Beamish is supervising a search for it.'

Janna felt a flutter of panic. What was the correct way to react? Had Xan been left standing in the hall? And if he had, surely that bordered on rudeness when she knew from Claudia that she and Xan would be announcing their engagement once she returned from America?

Good manners meant she should go downstairs and at least say hello to him. It was what the Layards – and possibly even Beamish, the butler – would expect of her.

'Would you tell Xan – Mr Keller – that I am on my way down?'

Pausing only long enough for the message to be delivered she took in a deep steadying breath and then headed out of the room in the direction of the wide staircase. On the first-floor landing the door to the drawing room was open and she caught a glimpse of Beamish and the maid searching down the sides of chairs and sofas for the pocket-watch.

Turning the last bend in the stairs she expected to see Xan standing in the hall, waiting for Beamish's return, but to her consternation it was empty. For a horrified moment she wondered if he had left in a huff at being kept waiting, although the only way she could have come downstairs any quicker would have been if she had taken them at a run.

The room to the left of the hall was Robert Layard's study and the door was slightly ajar; ajar enough for Janna to see that far from having left the house, Xan was rifling through the drawers of Lord Robert's enormous Beidermeier desk.

In shocked indignation she took the last of the stairs at high speed, running across the marble-floored hall and pushing the door wide open.

'What *do* you think you are doing?' she demanded in a voice so authoritative she scarcely recognized it as her own. 'No one is allowed into Lord Layard's study unless he is also present! Absolutely no one!'

'And no oyster girl speaks to me as you just have!' He breathed in hard, aware that much as he hated having to do so to a nonentity such as Janna Shilling, an explanation for his actions would have to be given. He gave her a tight smile, forcing himself to say conciliatingly, 'I'm looking for my pocket-watch, Janna. I put it down somewhere when I came to wish Claudia *bon voyage*. If it had been found, Lord Layard may have thought his desk the safest place to keep it until, on his return from America, he was able to personally hand it back to me.'

She was far from sure that she believed him, but there was no way she could say so. She said, forcing her voice to be steady, 'If a pocket-watch had been found by any of the household staff they would have handed it to Beamish for safe-keeping.'

'Ah! Of course! I should have thought of that for myself. I'll pop along and have a word with him now.'

Janna stood to one side so that he could stroll past her out of the room and then she very pointedly closed the study door. She would ask Beamish to have the door locked until the Layards returned. And when they returned, she wouldn't say anything to Lord Layard about the incident. It would only put her in the position of being a sneak and a tell-tale and, after all, no harm had been done.

As she left the house she did, though, wish most passionately that Claudia wasn't in love with Xan and wouldn't, on her return from America, be announcing her engagement to him.

'Have you already been to the Gilroy Gallery?' Janna asked as she seated herself at the table in the Corner House that Marietta was already seated at, noticing that there was no brown-wrapped painting propped by the side of Marietta's chair.

'No. I'm not in London today on Pascal's behalf.'

Not for the first time Janna wondered how her friend could transform herself with such ease from the carelessly dressed Marietta of Oystertown's windmill, a girl who wore her torrent of hair loose and who, by choice, was often to be found barefoot, singing loudly as she went about her chores, into someone who not only appeared to be well-bred, but who also effortlessly adopted the manners of someone who *was* well-bred. Long-term friendship with Claudia and her relationship with Kim had obviously been a great influence on her, but even so, Marietta's ability to take on a completely different persona whenever she wanted to never ceased to amaze her. On one of her previous trips to attend a meeting of the WSPU with Claudia, Kim had been in town and he had met them afterwards and taken them to a picture-house to see America's Mary Pickford in a silent movie.

It had been the first silent movie she had ever seen and she had been mesmerized by it. Afterwards it had occurred to her that Marietta would look glorious on the silver screen – although not in the kind of roles Mary Pickford apparently always played. Crimped hair, a demure expression and a bee-stung mouth were light years away from Marietta's tempestuous, siren-like qualities.

'When I leave here, I'm meeting up with a theatrical agent at the London Pavilion in Piccadilly,' Marietta said carelessly, as if her doing so was a quite commonplace occurrence. 'Dolly – Adolphus Cuthbertson, my agent – wants to see what I look like on stage and if my singing voice is strong enough to reach to the back of the stalls.'

Janna's jaw dropped. 'But you can't become a music hall artist! They have terrible reputations! People will think you are a . . . a . . .' She couldn't bring herself to finish her sentence.

Marietta had no such scruples. 'A lady of the night?' she said, not bothering to keep her voice down. 'Jasper told me Tilly was once known as Oystertown's lady of the night – although I don't think it was a reputation she deserved,' she added, seeing the expression on Janna's face.

Two elderly ladies seated at a nearby table had by now heard more than enough to convince them that their favourite Lyons Corner House was no longer the respectable establishment it had once been and hurriedly they rose to their feet and headed for the door, leaving behind them a pot of tea that was still hot and a plate of untouched toasted and buttered crumpets.

When, forty-five minutes earlier, Janna had taken her leave of Xan, believing him to be seeking out Beamish in order to ask if Beamish had his pocket-watch in safe keeping, Xan – his pocket-watch in the pocket it had never left – had followed her. His intention was to catch up with her, fall into step beside her and charm her into changing her very cool attitude towards him for something much warmer, and so less potentially dangerous.

He could have done so several times as she left Belgravia and walked at a swift pace in the direction of The Strand, but instinct – the instinct that seldom let him down – ensured he merely kept her in sight.

Thirty minutes later she had made straight for the Lyons Corner House on the corner of The Strand and Craven Street, a teashop so large it seated well over a hundred people. He had hesitated, giving her time to be safely seated before he, too, entered it, finding a table that offered him a rear view of her and the woman friend she had come to meet, without allowing her a view of him.

For a stunned moment he had thought the young woman she had come to meet was Claudia, for she was wearing a fashionable nip-waisted two-piece *tailleur* he had often seen Claudia wear. Claudia, however, was now aboard the *Titanic* and halfway to America and, even if she hadn't been, the luxuriantly heavy chignon in the nape of Janna's friend's neck wasn't Claudia's corn-gold hair; it was a fiery fox-red and he had never seen Claudia wear a hat tilted at such a tantalizingly saucy angle.

She was mesmerizing and the more he looked at her, the more he wanted to be up close to her. He wanted to see the colour of her eyes, smell the fragrance of her perfume. He wanted to know who she was, how it was that she was wearing clothes he had last seen being worn by Claudia, and how it was that an unexceptional-looking girl like Janna Shilling was on such obviously close terms with her.

Most of all he wanted to be introduced to her. He *had* to be introduced to her. If he went across to their table Janna would know his being in the same cafe she was in was no coincidence. He chewed the corner of his lip, wondering what reason he could possibly give for having followed her there and then realized that all he had to do was to tell her that he wanted to apologize for his earlier churlish behaviour. Good manners would then ensure she introduced her mesmerizingly beautiful friend to him and the rest would be up to him. Where women were concerned, his athletic physique, blond hair and startlingly blue eyes had never let him down yet and he was certain they wouldn't let him down now.

He was also certain that he now had leverage over Janna, for in the Layards' absence she was quite obviously allowing her companion to make free with Claudia's wardrobe.

As he approached their table, he saw Janna's eyes widen in shocked incredulity and then manners that had been polished by friendship with the Layards came to her aid.

'Marietta,' she said, trying not to let her feelings show in her voice, 'Mr Xan Keller. Xan is a friend of Kim's.'

Marietta eyed Xan with interest. And then, to Janna's rising despair, Marietta said in the French accent she rarely lapsed into, but when she did, always to devastating effect, 'Would you care to join us, Monsieur Keller?'

'I'd be delighted,' he said, aware of Janna's hostility and ignoring it.

The waitresses in Lyons' Corner Houses were known as 'Nippies', and a Nippy scooted up to their table, laying an extra place on it for Xan and taking his order for a pot of Earl Grey tea.

Without being offensively rude there was nothing Janna could say. All she could do was to grit her teeth and endure.

When Xan courteously asked Marietta if she lived in London and she told him she lived in a south-coast fishing village, he hid his shocked surprise. She then told him her father was an artist and that she regularly came up to London to deliver his work to various galleries and art dealers.

'And is that your reason for being in London today?' he asked, entranced and intrigued by her slight French accent.

'No. I am here to meet with my theatrical agent at the London Pavilion.'

He heard Janna's quick intake of breath and for a moment he wondered if his leg was being pulled.

Janna was wondering how she could indicate to Marietta that it was time for them to be making an exit for alarm was now adding to her already deep sense of unease. Xan was the last person in the world she wanted Marietta to begin flirting with. It was bad enough Marietta being in a romantic relationship with Kim at the same time that she was in a romantic relationship with Jasper and that both men had been forced to tolerate the existence of each other in her life, but Xan Keller was a different matter.

She hadn't yet allowed herself to wonder just why he had been rifling through the drawers of Lord Layard's desk, but she suspected it hadn't been because he believed his pocket-watch to be in one of them. Even though he was a friend of Kim's – and she was certain that Kim was quite unaware of the side of Xan's character that she was now aware of – Xan Keller was someone Marietta should be avoiding, not encouraging.

She became aware of Marietta picking up her beaded purse – or, to be more exact, Claudia's beaded purse – and preparing to leave. Hastily and with vast relief she picked up the dolly-bag that held all she needed for an afternoon working behind a desk at the WSPU offices and the three of them stepped out of the cafe and onto the crowded pavement to say their goodbyes.

It was after they had said them that, as far as Janna was concerned, disaster struck.

'Did you say you had an appointment at the London Pavilion?' Xan asked Marietta. 'I'm going in that direction. If you have no objection perhaps you would allow me to walk with you part of the way?'

From beneath her luxuriantly thick lashes Marietta gave him a look that was blatantly flirtatious. '*Mais oui*. That would be very nice indeed.'

Janna's route to WSPU Headquarters lay in completely the opposite direction and she watched in rising concern as they walked away from her and as Marietta, with easy and intimate familiarity, tucked her hand into the crook of Xan's arm and leaned her body into his.

Chapter Eighteen

Aboard the *Titanic* Claudia was enjoying herself far more than she had thought possible when Xan wasn't there to share the pleasure with her. All the First-Class passengers she met with were delightful and although the general age group was middle-aged to elderly there were enough eligible young bachelors – both British and American – whose attentions to her, even though she didn't encourage them, she couldn't help but find flattering.

On the fifth night of the six-day crossing she kissed her parents goodnight and went to bed early, taking with her a book she had borrowed from the ship's library. What time it was when she fell asleep, the book still in her hands, she didn't know, but she did know what had woken her. It had been a jolt so jarring she thought it must have reverberated throughout the entire ship.

And then something else impinged on her consciousness. For the first time since leaving Queenstown the ship's engines had stopped. She looked at her watch. It was 11.45 p.m. Puzzled, she swung her feet to the floor and reached for her dressing gown.

At the same moment that she opened her stateroom door, her father opened the door of the stateroom he and her mother were sharing. Other doors all along the broad, first-class corridor were also being opened, and there were cries of, 'What the devil was that?' and calls for the night steward who, when he speedily appeared, attempted to be reassuring.

'It's nothing,' he said as ladies, too, now stepped out into the corridor, wrapping silk dressing gowns tightly around them. 'Only a little hiccup. We'll soon be on our way again.'

Suddenly there came a loud whooshing sound.

'Inebriated gentlemen in the Smoking Room letting off fireworks,' the steward said, a note of uncertainty entering his voice.

Robert Layard didn't wait to hear any more. He knew the sound of distress rockets when he heard them and he said urgently to Claudia, 'Go back to your stateroom and put on the warmest clothes you can find. I'm going to ensure Mama does the same. Then we will make our way to the Boat Deck.'

'The Boat Deck, Papa?' Claudia was incredulous. 'But why on earth?'

'To be near the lifeboats if it comes to having to take to one of them.'

Her father was not given to panicking and for a moment Claudia wondered if he had been drinking.

'A lifeboat?' There was disbelief in her voice. 'But Papa, the ship is unsinkable!'

'For once in your life, Claudia! *Do as I say!*' and, grim-faced, he strode back into his stateroom where he knew he was going to have the devil of a job persuading Celia to leave her bed in order to dress in warm clothes and go up onto a freezing cold deck, but if, for the first time in his life, it meant him losing his temper with her, then that was what he was going to do.

Back in her stateroom Claudia resignedly, but dutifully, did as her father had asked. She dressed, put on her fur coat and picked up the book she had been reading. If her night was going to be needlessly disturbed, she intended finding somewhere quiet where she could sit and read until the alarm was over.

'Would everyone please don life jackets and make their way to the Boat Deck,' a member of the ship's crew instructed as he passed down the wide corridor between the staterooms. 'If you need help in fastening them, please approach a member of the crew.'

In growing consternation, a mix of Britain's and America's crème de la crème emerged from their staterooms and into the corridor, some of them having hastily dressed, others in slippers and hurriedly donned dressing gowns.

The slight tilt of the ship to starboard which Robert had noticed shortly after they had set sail was now even more noticeable and Robert didn't like it. He didn't like it at all.

'But of *course* I'm not going to put a life jacket on in the middle of the night!' Claudia heard her mother protest. 'You are being ridiculous, Robert and—'

'And you are going to do as I say, Celia.'

Her father's voice was one that brooked no argument and a few short minutes later the Layards, along with a growing crush of other annoyed and bewildered people, were stepping out fully dressed onto the freezing cold First-class section of the Boat Deck.

An elderly lady standing near to Claudia asked plaintively, 'Is this a drill? I've sailed with White Star many, many times, on both the *Olympic* and the *Britannic*, and I have never experienced anything so bizarrely inconveniencing. I shall be complaining, of course. This kind of thing should never be allowed to happen. It's absolutely outrageous.'

'I told my lady-wife to stay put,' a gentleman a couple of feet away from Robert said to him. He was wearing a top hat and beaver-collared overcoat and smoking a cigar. 'I wasn't going to have her disturbed over something and nothing. A member of the crew told me the reason the ship juddered as she did was because the captain had had to veer hard to port to avoid an iceberg.'

'An iceberg?' Robert stamped his feet together to keep them warm. 'It must have been an impressive sight.'

'It was. Those who caught a glimpse of it judged it to be eighty-feet high. My brother-in-law said it hove into view, sheered the starboard side of the ship for quite a way – three hundred feet or so – and then disappeared into the darkness all in a matter of minutes. According to one of the stewards, the Second-Class deck is strewn with ice shards. The steward said some jokers were asking for slivers of it to put into their drinks.'

There came the whooshing sound and the bright light of more distress rockets being fired.

Robert's companion blew a wreath of cigar smoke into the frigid night air and said, 'My steward told me there are other liners quite close to us. The rockets will soon have them heading in our direction.'

'Do you think it's going to come to that?' Robert experienced a stab of shocked alarm. 'An order to abandon ship? Surely not.'

His informant nodded in the direction of crew members who were beginning to strip the canvas covers off the lifeboats.

'Those blighters wouldn't be preparing the boats if there wasn't a strong chance of them being needed.' He walked the few yards to the deck rail, tossed his lighted cigar overboard and as he by-passed Robert on his way back to the grand staircase, said, 'I'm going back to my stateroom to reassure my wife and make sure she has her life jacket on. She's a worrier. In my opinion most women are.'

Relieved that Celia had done as he had asked and was, like Claudia, wearing a life jacket over her fur coat, he decided that as a member of His Majesty's Government it was time he pulled rank and spoke to Captain Smith in order to find out what the level of danger really was, and just what ships were within easy reach of the *Titanic* if the worst came to the worst.

'I'm going to have a word with Captain Smith,' he said to Claudia.

And then, to Celia, he said, 'I won't be long, darling. I'm going to ask the Captain how long he thinks it will be before he has the engines running again.'

Before she could protest, he had kissed her on the cheek, squeezed her hand tightly and set off at a brisk pace in the direction of the bridge.

By now the sense of unease on the ship was palpable and Robert could well understand why, for what ten minutes ago had been a slight tilting of the deck was now far more pronounced. Twenty minutes ago there had only been a scattering of people on deck, but now the first-class promenade was rapidly filling with nervous, apprehensive passengers.

He took out his pocket-watch. It was a quarter past midnight. Half an hour since the ship's engines had so unnervingly stopped throbbing. As he continued making his way to the bridge at a fast pace, he saw that crew members were standing at the lifeboat davits, fitting in cranks and uncoiling the lines preparatory to lowering the boats over the side when, and if, the order came for them to do so.

A Philadelphian banker he had enjoyed a game of cards with only two evenings ago and who was wearing nothing but an overcoat thrown over winceyette pyjamas, waylaid him, saying, 'What the devil is going on, Layard? Do you have any idea?'

'None, other than that an iceberg sheered the starboard side of the ship and has damaged it in some way. I'm on my way to the bridge to have a word with Captain Smith and find out when we can expect to be on the move again.'

'If you get any sense out of him, let me know. I don't fancy freezing my balls off out here for a second longer than I have to.'

Other first-class passengers were also outlandishly dressed. One American lady, an eminent leader of New York society, was wearing slippers and what he took to be her husband's overcoat over a Japanese kimono. Others had simply thrown fur coats over their nightgowns. A fellow member of Britain's aristocracy had put lipstick on before leaving her stateroom, but had been too agitated to remember to remove her metal hair curlers.

As he neared the ladder leading to the bridge, a ship's officer barred his way, saying as he did so, 'Sorry, sir. Passengers are not allowed within the vicinity of the bridge.'

'I'm Lord Layard, an advisor to Prime Minister Asquith's government.'

'I'm afraid you are still not allowed on the bridge, sir.'

Robert was just about to argue the toss with him when he saw that the officer was armed with a pistol.

'You're armed!' he said, deeply shocked.

'Yes, sir. A precaution, sir. In case the order to take to the lifeboats is given and panic breaks out.'

Robert felt as if icy fingers were closing around his heart. 'Good God! Are things really so serious? There must be other ships in the vicinity. Are they coming to our aid? How long will it take them to reach us?'

'That I can't say, sir. If you have family on board then your best course of action is to be with them and to ensure they are near to a lifeboat. If the order to take to them is given it will be a case of women and children first. And don't delay,' he added grimly. 'It's my guess the *Titanic* will be at the bottom of the ocean in less than two hours.'

His blunt certainty rocked Robert back on his heels and

then, without more ado, he began heading as fast as he was able back to where he had left Celia and Claudia.

The deck that had been half empty when he had set off for the bridge was now rapidly filling with people all anxious to know why distress rockets were being fired and why lifeboats were being readied for lowering.

He squeezed, pushed, and side-stepped around them, the conversation he'd had with Claudia on the day they had sailed – that there were over two thousand people aboard the ship and sixteen lifeboats plus four collapsible lifeboats, each with a capacity for sixty people, which meant the total number of people who could be taken off the ship in the event of a disaster was less than half the number of people aboard – reverberating through his head.

Why hadn't such facts filled him with concern? Why hadn't he been alarmed at the lack of any boat drill on the days they had been at sea? He was an experienced yachtsman so why, in the Name of God, had he been so bloody, *bloody* complacent?

His first reaction at seeing that Celia and Claudia were exactly where he had left them was one of vast relief. His second reaction was that, for his own peace of mind, he needed them to be much nearer to one of the Boat Deck's lifeboats.

'I'm getting terribly cold, Robert.' Celia hugged his arm. 'I'm sure the hiccup with the engines will be sorted soon and even if it isn't, I see no reason why we should be standing on an open deck in the middle of the night and so, if you don't mind, I'm going back to our stateroom and bed.'

He clamped his free hand very firmly over hers. 'Captain Smith's orders are that we remain on deck until we are told otherwise and that we wear our life jackets. Pull the collar of your fur up to your chin and pull your fur hat down over your ears . . . there, that's better. And to help us keep warm, I think it would be a good idea if the three of us began walking circuits of the deck while we wait for the ship's engines to start up again and we can return to our beds.'

They began walking, the ocean surrounding the ship as flat and shiny as black glass; the sky a forest of stars. There was no sign of the iceberg that had collided with the ship, although other, smaller bergs, could be seen in the distance. The ship's eight-man orchestra had taken up a position at the top of the grand staircase and had begun playing a familiar show tune. Everything would have seemed reassuringly normal if it hadn't been for the tilt of the deck growing slowly, but surely, more pronounced.

'The ship is beginning to list quite noticeably,' Robert said with concern. Another rocket went off and crew members sprinted past them to the lifeboats.

'Wait here with Mama,' Robert said to Claudia. 'I'll find out it if this is precautionary, or if it is serious.'

Celia gave a cry of alarm, Claudia put a comforting arm around her and Robert strode across to where two crewmen were hurriedly putting lanterns and tins of biscuits into the boats.

'Excuse me, officer,' he said in a voice regularly taken notice of in the House of Lords. 'Is the situation catastrophic, or are you simply taking precautions?'

'It's catastrophic,' one of the men said, throwing in the last of the biscuit tins and straightening up. 'The berg we ran into has sliced the *Titanic* open below her waterline. She may not seem to be sinking, but she is. Captain Smith's orders are for women and children to take to the lifeboats.'

Even as he was speaking crew members were readying some of the lifeboats on their side of the Boat Deck and beginning to help life-jacketed women and children into them.

Celia turned a stricken face to Robert. 'I'm not getting into a boat without you, Robert! I'm not leaving you!'

She clung tenaciously to his arm, determined not to be separated from him.

Seeing Algy and his mother being helped into the lifeboat nearest to them, Claudia said urgently, 'Look, Mama! There's the little boy I told you about, the little boy who bowled his hoop into Papa's leg. Let's get into the lifeboat he and his mother are getting into.'

It was the distraction Celia needed and to Robert and Claudia's vast relief she allowed a member of the ship's crew to help her into the lifeboat. Claudia stepped into it after her and as there was a handful of male first-class passengers in the lifeboat as well as women and children, she fully expected her father to step into the boat after her, especially as she heard the crew member loading it say to him, 'At a squeeze there's room for you as well, sir.'

And then her father shook his head and she heard him say, 'No, officer. I think one more passenger would overload the boat and make lowering it down the ship's side to the sea far more dangerous than it need be.' And then to Claudia, he said, 'Don't worry about me, sweetheart. I'll meet up with you and Mama later.'

'But, Papa . . .!'

The lifeboat she and her mother were seated in had begun to be jerkily lowered foot by foot over the ship's side and Claudia watched helplessly and in mounting anguish as her father's beloved figure grew smaller and smaller and as the perfectly calm, ink-black sea drew nearer and nearer.

Brief minutes later the lifeboat hit the water with such force that it nearly overturned, and then the two-man crew unshipped the oars and began pulling strongly on them, desperate to put distance between the lifeboat and what they knew would be the suction caused by the *Titanic* when she disappeared beneath the waves.

There was no moon, only a mass of stars, an ocean that was perfectly still and the sound of the *Titanic*'s orchestra playing ragtime.

Celia covered her face with her hands, tears streaming between her gloved fingers, saying between sobs as the distance between the *Titanic* and the lifeboat grew gradually wider and wider, 'I thought Papa was coming with us, Claudia! I would never have got into this boat if I had known he wasn't going to follow us into it!'

'There are other lifeboats, Mama. Papa is very resourceful and he will be in one of the other boats.'

Somehow Claudia kept her voice from breaking, for she didn't believe for a moment that her brave, honourable father would be in a lifeboat if there was a woman or a child still in need of a place in one of them.

When the two crew members manning the oars judged they were far enough away from the stricken liner to no longer risk being sucked under with her when she sank, they stopped rowing, watching in dazed disbelief as the *Titanic*'s bow began dipping lower and lower towards the waiting sea, her lights still burning, her orchestra still playing.

A massive wave of water suddenly swept aft along the boat deck submerging everything and everyone in its path. Beneath its weight the bow sank beneath the surface and her two hundred and fifty-foot-high stern rose high into the air. As it did there came the sound of terrified screams and hundreds of ant-like figures could be seen scrabbling and falling as they tried to run up the ever-steepening deck, clutching at anything – deck rails, winches, ventilators, trailing ropes from the davits – anything at all that would halt their slide into the seething maelstrom of icy, hungry, death-dealing water.

And then, for a terrible moment, the mountainous black shape of the ship reared perpendicular in the darkness like a mammoth black sea monster and there came the deafening roar of engines tearing free and massive, heavy machinery breaking loose and crashing down through the ship, rending and smashing and crushing everything in its path and, along with the engines and machinery, huge boilers and massive anchor chains and tons upon tons of coal.

'She's going down!' someone shouted from the stern of the lifeboat as one of the *Titanic*'s massive funnels keeled over and there came the horrific, rending noise of metal being ripped and wrenched apart. '*Oh Sweet Christ! She's splitting into two and going down!*'

A woman who was squeezed hard against Claudia's left-hand side began feverishly running a rosary through her fingers.

Someone else began saying The Lord's Prayer.

A man said hoarsely, 'It's eighteen minutes past two. I give her a couple of minutes. Maybe less.'

And then slowly, inexorably, the two halves of the biggest, most luxurious liner ever built began to subside, sliding gradually under the water at a slant, bow first, and then gathering speed until the waves closed over her and all that was left was a night-black sea littered with deckchairs and crates and floating wicker furniture.

And people.

Hundreds and hundreds of people, all screaming and crying out for help as they began to freeze and drown in the icy ocean.

'We must go back!' Claudia cried out as the two crewmen manning the lifeboat's oars remained motionless, transfixed by the horror taking place. 'We can squeeze another ten people into this boat! Maybe more!'

The men snapped out of their trance, but not in the way Claudia had intended. Instead of rowing back to where people were desperately trying to stay afloat and alive in the sub-zero water, they began feverishly rowing away from them.

'Go back!' she shouted again, hysteria now in her voice. 'We can't just leave people to drown! We have to go back!'

'We ain't going back!' one of the rowers shouted savagely. 'We'll be swamped by people 'anging on to the boat if we go back, and the boat will capsize and we'll all be dead men!'

Panic-stricken agreement with his opinion came from everyone in the lifeboat other than herself and her semi-comatose mother and Claudia knew that she couldn't overrule them; that overruling them would put everyone on board at risk of drowning.

Sick at heart and fighting for self-control she bit her lip until it bled and dug her nails into her palms until the knuckles showed white.

All around them in the darkness were more of the *Titanic*'s lifeboats, the distance between them growing wider and wider. Very little noise was coming from any of them and all cries for help coming from the freezing sea turned very quickly to whimpers, until gradually, hideously, even the whimpers fell silent.

'May God have mercy on their souls,' a choked voice said from the stern end of the lifeboat.

Claudia looked down at her watch. Had it been only a little under three hours since she had been comfortably in bed in her stateroom, reading? How, since then, could so much unspeakable horror have taken place?

'Can someone take over from me?' the crew member manning the tiller asked suddenly, his voice taut. 'I injured myself helping to lower the boat into the water and I think I'm going to pass out.'

When there was no response from anyone, Claudia said, 'I've helped crew a yacht. I'll take over at the tiller.'

Taking care not to rock the boat any more than was absolutely necessary the two of them gingerly changed places.

'But w–w–where is R–R–Robert?' Celia asked dazedly, almost insensible with the freezing cold, her teeth chattering, 'R–Robert is a yachtsman. It should be R–Robert who is taking the t–tiller.'

'Papa is in another boat,' Claudia said, praying to God that what she so fiercely hoped would turn out to be true.

'Do us all a favour and ask your ma to keep her anxieties to 'erself,' a northern accent said from somewhere near the prow. 'We're all anxious about family members and friends. If your ma wants to do summat useful, ask 'er to pray – and when she does, for Gawd's sake ask 'er to do it silently.'

The rebuff – and a rebuff given by someone who, in Celia's opinion, must surely have been one of the *Titanic*'s steerage passengers – shocked her into stunned silence.

Algy left his mother's side and squeezed between Celia and a barely conscious woman seated on Celia's left.

'It's going to be all right,' he said to Celia comfortingly. 'I read in a book where people had to take to the lifeboats and they were all rescued and when they were, they were given huge mugs of hot milky cocoa.'

'Hot milky cocoa?' Never had Celia wanted anything in life quite so much.

Somehow, time passed. When not taking turns at the tiller Claudia was aware of dozing and waking and dozing again. When awake she thought of Xan and of her father, wondering if she was ever going to see either of them again; wondering if she was ever going to see Janna and Marietta ever again.

Eventually she became aware of the night sky slowly lightening. Dawn was beginning to break and the ghostly shapes of some of the *Titanic*'s other lifeboats could be seen in the distance. And then she saw something else. She saw a small and steady green light.

She blinked hard, praying she wasn't hallucinating. She

wasn't. And a green light signified the starboard light of a ship.

'Steer towards it, miss!' one of the crew members manning the oars said, his voice thick with urgency. 'Once her look-out sees us, we'll soon be aboard her!'

Claudia began doing so, but it wasn't easy for the distance between the lifeboat and the ship was littered with small bergs rising jaggedly two and three feet from the water.

'They're what we regulars on the North Atlantic crossing call growlers,' the crew member who had told her to steer towards the light said. 'And they're called that because, when an iceberg melts, air escapes from it and makes a sound like that of an animal growling.'

'Is that true, sir?' The thought of growling icebergs made Algy temporarily forget how agonizingly cold he was. 'You aren't joshing us?'

'What? At a time like this? No, I'm not joshing you. If you listen very carefully it sounds as if the bergs are having a conversation with each other. '

Algy's eyes rounded.

'It's the truth, young feller. As God is my witness.'

The ship they were tortuously making their way towards fired rockets into the air to let them know it had seen them and from their lifeboat, and from other lifeboats which in the early dawn could now be seen gravitating towards it, deeply thankful, exhausted cheers went up.

As they drew nearer to the ship the oarsman who had told Algy about the growlers said, 'She's a passenger liner. A Cunarder.'

Claudia didn't care what kind of a ship she was. As far as she and every other *Titanic* survivor was concerned, she was a ship that was about to save their lives and that was all that mattered. The name on her bow was *Carpathia* and as her crew began lowering rope ladders over her side, passengers who had been taking an early morning walk on her deck crowded the deck rails, staring down at them goggle-eyed.

As the lifeboat carrying Claudia and her mother bumped alongside the ship, lines were dropped and the lifeboat was made fast.

'Women and children first!' Algy's friend shouted authoritatively, catching hold of the first of the rope ladders. 'And no pushing and shoving! There's no need for panic. The *Carpathia* won't be going anywhere until everyone from our lifeboat, and all the other lifeboats, are safely aboard her.'

Those who, like her mother, were in no condition to climb a swaying ladder were hoisted in a bosun's chair up to an open gangway high on the ship's side. From there they were shepherded below deck to the main dining saloon where they were wrapped in blankets and plied with tea, hot soup and brandy.

No longer on a knife-edge of anxiety where her mother was concerned, Claudia climbed a rope ladder with fingers so frozen they barely felt part of her body.

'Here you are, miss,' a member of the *Carpathia*'s crew said, handing her a warm blanket and a mug of steaming tea as she stepped on the blessedly rock-steady deck. 'And there's hot soup and brandy being handed out in the dining saloon.'

'Thank you v-very much,' she said, her teeth chattering as she gratefully accepted the blanket and tea, 'but I'm g-going to stay on deck until I have n-news of my father.'

As dawn turned slowly into day other survivors came aboard in exhausted dribs and drabs, half a dozen of them having survived by clinging precariously to the slippery surface of an upturned lifeboat. Her father, however, was not one of their number, and nor was he one of the two dozen people who had survived the night huddled in one of the *Titanic*'s canvas collapsible lifeboats.

Six o'clock came and went and by then very few survivors were still being brought aboard. One of them was a young man who had been spotted clinging to a wooden crate wearing a life jacket over a waterlogged fur coat. Another was a *Titanic* crew member who had lashed himself to a door.

Just after seven o'clock another lifeboat hove into view. It was packed to capacity and as with agonizing slowness it drew alongside the *Carpathia*, Claudia leaned over the *Carpathia*'s deck rails, desperately searching for a glimpse of her father's face.

It wasn't there.

'Lord Robert Layard?' she asked survivor after survivor as they stumbled aboard the *Carpathia*. 'Have you any news of him? He's in his fifties. A well-built man with thick, silver-white hair.'

No one recognized her description of him. No one had seen him.

The crew member who, as she had kept her long vigil, had supplied her with endless mugs of hot tea, brought her yet another one.

Over the next hour other lifeboats from the *Titanic* nudged their way between the growlers and every time one of them did, Claudia was seized by the fierce, desperate hope that her father would be aboard one of them. It was hope cruelly dashed time and time again.

By a quarter past eight, all but one of the *Titanic*'s lifeboats was accounted for. Then the last one could be seen a hundred yards away, low in the water and packed to capacity.

As it drew nearer Claudia's eyes hurt with the effort of trying to find her father's face among the many faces aboard her, because he had to be aboard this boat. He *had* to be.

The sea which had been calm for so long, was now choppy. Painfully, inch by inch, the overloaded lifeboat neared the

Carpathia and still Claudia could see no sign of her father aboard her.

The boat made fast and began to unload and Claudia watched the arrivals with growing, numb acceptance. Her beloved papa wasn't aboard it – and there were no other lifeboats still to come.

At ten to nine the *Carpathia*'s engines throbbed into life again and as she began steaming in the direction of New York, Claudia knew all hope of finding her father alive was at an end.

She knew something else as well. With a breaking heart she knew that no one, not even Xan, would ever be able to replace him.

Chapter Nineteen

1913

It was 4 June, Derby Day. The hideous one-year anniversary in April of the sinking of the *Titanic* had come and gone and, accompanied by Kim, Claudia had joined Janna, Jasper, Marietta and a clutch of WSPU friends for a glorious day out at Epsom Racecourse. To Janna's relief Xan, whom Claudia had married a few months after her father's tragic death, was not with them, but was in Zurich, visiting someone Claudia described as being a distant relative of his. This meant that Janna would not have to pretend to like him. After the heart-wrenching loss of Lord Layard she had done her best to set aside her reservations about Xan, knowing how much her friend now relied upon him for everything. All the same, she knew it would be a much more pleasant occasion without his presence.

Normally at Epsom Kim would have had a reserved seat in the Grand Stand, but as Claudia had been emphatic that she wanted to be with her friends, he had chosen to join them at Tattenham Corner where he could keep a close eye on Marietta where Jasper Shilling was concerned. It never occurred to him that the person he should have been keeping an eye on was the WSPU friend Claudia had brought with her.

'Kim, I'd like to introduce you to one of my WSPU friends, Miss Emily Davison,' Claudia had said to him, and then, to Emily, 'Kim is my first cousin. He's a lieutenant in the Royal Navy.'

Civilities were exchanged and, for the first time in his life, Kim was aware that a rather plain female was not blushing with pleasure at being introduced to him. It was as if Miss Davison's mind was on things far more important than an introduction to a good-looking naval officer.

Making conversation, he said, 'This is a splendid spot to see the front runners as they thunder round the corner into the straight, Miss Davison. My money is on Anmer, the King's horse.'

'The King's horse?' Miss Davison was suddenly all interest. 'How will I know which horse that is?'

'By the number on the jockey's back and the colours he will be wearing.'

'And what will they be?'

He smiled down at her, amused by how indefatigably earnest she was. 'He will be wearing a purple jacket with scarlet sleeves and with gold-braid hoops sewn across the vest.'

'Then he'll be impossible to miss.'

'Yes, Miss Davison.' He had to struggle hard not to let his amusement at her intensity show. 'Quite impossible to miss.'

Among a sea of racegoers all decked out in their Derby Day finery Miss Davison was also impossible to miss because, unlike every other woman at Epsom that day, she wasn't wearing her summer Sunday-best, but a dark, serviceable coat and skirt and a no-nonsense black straw boater bereft of any kind of decoration.

Grateful that Claudia saw no reason to dress in a similarly austere manner just because she was a paid-up member of the Women's Social Political Union, Kim returned his attention to the race that was about to start. From where he and the rest of Oystertown's contingent were standing there was no clear view of the horses lining up, but they would have a first-class view of them as they rounded the huge horseshoe of Tattenham Corner and headed at full pelt down the straight towards the winning post.

Both he and Jasper had field-glasses slung around their necks and, as a deafening roar went up from the starting-post stands, they lifted the glasses to their eyes, ready for a first glimpse of the leading horse and rider.

Kim's money was on a horse called Aboyeur, and he was so euphoric at seeing Aboyeur in the lead that, as the horses pounded into the bend of the horseshoe, his usually fast reflexes weren't fast enough for him to restrain Emily as, quick as lightning, she ducked beneath the rails and sprinted onto the racecourse.

He had a blurred recollection of the world erupting around him in shouts and screams. Of seeing the horses bunched up against the rails and thundering towards Emily and of Emily, a WSPU flag in her hand, jumping up and trying to catch hold of Anmer's bridle. Of her failing to do so and of Anmer catching her with his shoulder, knocking her with terrific force clean off her feet before he, too, fell, sending his jockey catapulting to the ground.

He was aware of his and Jasper's shouts of horror; of Claudia clutching hold of his arm half-senseless with shock; of Janna's stunned, bloodless face; Marietta's cries of disbelief and of Emily rolling over and over until finally she lay face down, deathly still.

The rest of the riders swerved past her. Anmer's jockey rose unsteadily to his feet as Kim sprinted onto the race track towards Emily, Jasper and several policemen hard on his heels.

'Is she breathing?' Kim demanded, dropping to one knee beside her as two ambulance men sprinted up with a stretcher and Jasper and the policemen came to a breathless halt.

'Just about,' one of the men responded tersely. 'Are you a relative?'

'No. A friend.'

'Well, there's nothing we can do for her here. She's got a bad head injury as well as broken limbs. We're taking her to Epsom Cottage Hospital. Do you know where that is?'

'Yes.' It was a lie, but he would certainly find it.

While Jasper had shepherded a distressed Claudia and Marietta away from the scene Kim had taken a distraught and ashen-faced Janna with him and, for the four days that Emily remained unconscious before she died, he had taken her to the hospital every day to take turns with other members of the WSPU as they kept vigil by Emily's bedside.

Her death made the headlines of every national newspaper. *Suffragettes mourn the Derby martyr* was a typical headline. *Suffragettes plan official Day of Mourning for Emily* was another.

Emily's funeral wasn't easy to arrange. Her family lived in Morpeth, a small market town in Northumberland, and at their request Emily was to be laid to rest in the churchyard of St Mary the Virgin, a small church on Morpeth's outskirts.

Before a half-mile-long procession made its way to King's Cross Station where a train was waiting to take Emily's casket to Morpeth, a church service was held in St George's Church in Bloomsbury where the vicar, the Reverend Mr Baumgarten, was a suffragette supporter and sympathizer.

Like every other suffragette either packed like a sardine in the church, or thronging the steps and the street outside it, Janna and Claudia were wearing high-necked, ankle-skimming white dresses and WSPU purple, green and white sashes emblazoned with the words 'Votes For Women'.

'The press are claiming Emily wasn't trying to pin a WSPU flag to Anmer's bridle, but that she was trying to commit suicide by throwing herself beneath Anmer's hooves,' Claudia said to Janna beneath cover of one of the WSPU's anthems being sung to the tune of 'Men of Harlech'.

'It makes me so *angry*,' she continued, her voice unsteady with the force of her feelings. 'What is it going to take to make men realize how huge the injustice is in refusing to give women the vote? We have women doctors now. Women lawyers. And yet they are judged unfit to cast their vote as to who should represent them in Parliament!'

She was still incandescent with the unfairness of it all as the service came to an end and they followed Emily's casket out of the church.

There was a short flight of stone steps leading from the door of the church down to the pavement and fellow suffragettes in white dresses and sashes formed a guard of honour on either side of the steps, saluting in respect as the casket, covered with a purple, green and white pall and crowned with a laurel wreath, was carried past them and lifted onto a flower-laden, horse-drawn hearse.

Together with Emily's family, friends and officiating clergy and carrying a large banner that read *VOTES FOR WOMEN*, they led a funeral procession of thousands out of Bloomsbury Square and across Russell Square in the direction of the Euston Road.

The watching crowds were held back by lines of policemen and instead of the crowds thinning as the cortège neared King's Cross Station, the numbers increased, and although women in the crowds were in the majority, there were many men, some respectfully taking off top hats, the majority removing flat caps.

Behind them in the procession a band was playing a funeral march. Janna heard a woman in the crowd shout: 'God bless the little lady! She died a martyr to freedom! She died so that we women could get the vote!'

She felt her stomach muscles tighten. She had been one of Emily's closest friends, but not for a minute did she believe Emily had deliberately thrown herself in front of the King's horse as the nation's newspapers had sensationally stated. Emily was a practising Christian. Even to help women get the vote she wouldn't have committed an act Janna knew she would have regarded as suicidal, and therefore a sin. Knowing Emily as she had, she was certain that what Emily had been trying to do was to attach a WSPU flag to Anmer's bridle.

Backing that belief was indisputable evidence that Emily had not gone to Epsom with the intention of sacrificing her life for the WSPU cause, for at the hospital she, Janna, had been asked to verify the contents of Emily's drawstring bag.

It had contained three shillings and eight pence, two WSPU flags, a race-card, a ticket for a suffragette rally later on in the day and a return ticket to Victoria Station. And as Claudia had pointed out, a return ticket to Victoria Station was not something Emily would have bought if she had no intention of ever returning to it.

Janna had known there would be crowds lining the route of the funeral procession, but never in her wildest imagination had she imagined the crowds would approach the scale of those who had lined the streets three years ago when the late King's cortège had made its way to Paddington Station, en route for burial at Windsor.

When they reached King's Cross Station, the train Emily's body was to travel on was already standing at its platform and a special carriage had been set aside for her coffin. Under the watchful eyes of a top-hatted funeral director and his assistants the casket was carefully lifted into the carriage where a suffragette guard of honour was waiting to accompany Emily on her last journey north.

Only when that task had been carried out did Emily's family members, who had travelled to London to attend the service at St George's, board the train, as did hundreds of those who had attended the service and marched in the procession, Janna and Claudia included.

'We are going to win this fight to have equality of voting rights with men,' Janna said fiercely as the train left the grimy suburbs of inner London behind them and headed towards Peterborough and all points north. 'Emily may not have intended giving her life for the Cause, but her dying the way she did is going to be seen by future generations as a turning-point in women's fight for the vote. And we are going to win that fight.' Janna clasped her hands so tightly together her knuckles shone white. 'I've never been so certain of anything else in my life.'

Chapter Twenty

It was October and, as always happened when long summer days and pleasant evening strolls were fast becoming a memory, London's music halls were again playing to packed houses. Marietta was second on the bill at the Empire Theatre, New Cross, and not very pleased about it, her reason being that although New Cross was part of London, it was definitely unfashionable, being south of the river and nearer to what Marietta regarded as the wastelands of Kent than it was to London's West End.

She had been a music-hall artist for eighteen months now and the novelty and what had first seemed to be the glamour – and there was no glamour at all about New Cross – was wearing very thin. She missed the freedom of living in a windmill with views of steep grassland, the huddle of houses that was Oystertown and, beyond Oystertown, nothing but a vast expanse of sea and sky.

Most of all she missed Pascal and her two goats, Henri and Hortense. Was Tilly looking after them the way she, Marietta, had always looked after them? And what about the hens? One thing she was certain of was that Tilly wouldn't be calling them by name as she had always done.

And then there was Jasper. Compared to Kim, she found Jasper very uncomplicated. Kim expected things from her. He expected her to always look and behave like a lady – as Claudia always did. And although there were times when she very much enjoyed looking and behaving like a lady, she didn't enjoy looking and behaving like a lady all the time. It was too tiring. And Kim vehemently disapproved of her music-hall lifestyle. In his world ladies – unless they were ladies of the night – did not appear on the stage and live in disreputable theatrical digs.

There came a knock on her dressing-room door and it opened just wide enough for a young boy with a shock of tousled hair to put his head around it. 'There's a likely lookin' geezer 'ere to see yer. 'E sez 'e's a friend, but 'e looks more like a bookies runner ter me.'

'Cheeky young blighter,' Archie said affably, stepping into the cramped little room and just having time to give the boy a playful cuff around his ears before Marietta hurtled into his arms.

'Archie! How wonderful!' She hugged him enthusiastically. 'I was just in a deep mope about how much I'm missing Oystertown and everyone in it, and here you are! A little bit of Oystertown in London's New Cross!'

'Steady on with the "little bit of Oystertown", Marietta. I'll have you know I'm wearing my best togs.'

'Indeed you are!' She held him away from her, surveying him in genuine disbelief. 'Is that suit really made out of purple tweed?'

'It is, and I'll have you know that in purple tweed a Northerner can gain entry anywhere.'

'Well, as far as the New Cross Empire is concerned, you've certainly proved that.'

She sat down again on her dressing-table stool. 'Is Jasper with you?' she asked, trying to sound as if it was of little importance whether he was, or wasn't.

'No. He has a bare-knuckle fight tomorrow night and he's in last-minute training for it.'

Marietta's attempt to appear disinterested vanished. 'I thought he'd promised Tilly his bare-knuckle boxing days were behind him?'

'Aye, well. He's slept since then and had second thoughts.'

'And where is this fight going to take place? And who is he going to be fighting?'

As there was nowhere else to sit but the dressing-table stool Marietta was seated on, Archie leaned against the back of the closed door, his hands in his trouser pockets, one foot crossed negligently over the other at the ankle.

'It's going to take place in the usual place, the back room of the Duke. And he's going to be fighting some loud-mouth from London who says the reason Jasper doesn't fight anymore is because he's out of condition.'

Marietta could believe a lot of things of Jasper, but his being out of condition wasn't one of them.

'And will you be acting as his cornerman, just as you did in the old days?'

He shot her an impish grin. 'Of course. My corner-bag is already packed and ready to go. A bottle of water, two towels, a bucket, Vaseline, a sponge, a stool f Jasper needs it between bouts – which, knowing Jasper, is doubtful. Tilly is furious with him about it – and with the rest of Oystertown for encouraging it by already betting large sums of money on the outcome.'

'Tomorrow night, did you say?'

'Aye.' He eased himself away from the door and opened it. 'When I leave here, I'm heading off to Charing Cross Station for a train to Oystertown. Jasper has threatened that if I'm not there to act as his cornerman, he's going to have Smelly Bell stand in for me – and trust me, Marietta, he'll only ever do so over my dead body!'

Marietta chewed the corner of her lip. Jasper. Somehow, no one else had ever really replaced Jasper in her life. He was the one person she couldn't twist around her little finger; the one person who was as reckless and as unpredictable as herself. She hadn't been back to Oystertown since she had re-invented herself as a music-hall artist, but suddenly going back to Oystertown and seeing Jasper again seemed like a very good idea. There was also the chance that Claudia might be at Rose Mount. Most of all she suddenly, and very badly, wanted to see her father again and to wake up in the windmill instead of in shabby theatrical digs.

'And when you leave here, you're going straight to Charing Cross and a train to the coast?'

'I am. And if I want to be in time for the last train to Oystertown, I'd best be getting a move on.'

He opened the door he had been leaning against.

'Wait!' She sprang to her feet. 'I'm coming with you!'

He paused in the doorway. 'Where? To New Cross Station?'

'Yes, and then to Charing Cross and a train to Oystertown!'

He stared at her in exasperation. He had caught her as she was waiting to go on stage again after the interval and she was still wearing her glitzy stage costume and full stage make-up. How long it would take her to remove the make-up and change into street clothes he had no idea, but he reckoned the make-up alone would take an age to remove and he knew that if he wanted to catch the last train leaving Charing Cross for anywhere in the vicinity of Oystertown, he couldn't afford to wait for her.

He was just about to tell her so when she dragged a carpet-bag from out of a cupboard and began pulling open drawers, dragging whatever clothes were in them, out of them, and stuffing them into the bag.

'But I'm leaving *now*,' he protested, knowing he couldn't possibly put off leaving for the station until after she had finished her after-the-interval second performance, 'and by the time you finally come off stage and we get to Charing Cross, the last train to Oystertown will have gone!'

'Don't worry, Archie.' Still in her stage costume she slid her arms into a fake astrakhan coat and picked up the now bulging carpet-bag. 'I'm ready to leave now.'

'But you're due on stage again in five minutes!'

'Maybe I am,' Marietta acknowledged, making no move to put the carpet bag down again. 'And yet, somehow, I am certain my agent will cope. He does well enough out of me – he won't want to sack me. He'll no doubt forgive me and find me another booking before very long. But for now, when for the hundredth time I should be singing the yawningly boring "Maids of Cadiz", I shall instead be with you and hurtling by train to the little town by the sea I now have a feeling I should never have left.'

Chapter Twenty-one

4 August 1914

'War?' Archie said disbelievingly. He was standing at the bar in the taproom of the Duke, one foot on the bar rail, a hand clasped around a lunchtime pint of best bitter. 'Surely to God a bit of bother in the Balkans hasn't brought us to that?'

'It has.' Grimly Jasper slapped that morning's edition of the *Daily Mail* down on the bar so that Archie could see the giant-sized thick black headline: ENGLAND EXPECTS THAT EVERY MAN WILL DO HIS DUTY.

Slowly Archie pushed his pint of beer away from him. From the furore now coming from the saloon bar and from the street it was quite obvious that the news was spreading like wildfire.

From behind the bar a white-faced Tilly said unsteadily, thinking of Daniel and Archie and Jasper and all the other young men of Oystertown, 'Will it mean full mobilization?'

'I don't know.' A pulse throbbed at Jasper's jawline as he thought of the now uncertain future. 'But what I do know is that I'm not going to hang around to find out. I'm not going to wait for a public notice telling me where to report and risk finding myself in the army. The sea is my natural element and I'm going to serve as a merchant seaman.'

Tilly felt as if icy fingers were tightening around her heart. Five weeks ago, in Bosnia, the heir to the throne of Austria-

Hungary had been assassinated by a Serb nationalist, but as there was always trouble in the Balkans no one had paid it much attention, not even when Austria issued Serbia with a long list of demands, two of which Serbia failed to comply with. And then, on 28 July, Austria had declared war on Serbia. And then Germany's armies had massed threateningly on her border with Belgium.

It was enough to make anyone's head spin and now today the morning papers carried the news that Germany's armies had crossed the Belgian border and that as a consequence, in order to honour her long-standing treaty to protect Belgium's neutrality, Britain was now at war with Germany.

The prospect filled Tilly with horror, but the news wasn't having the same effect on the men crowding into the taproom, all of whom were passing copies of the newspaper from hand to hand and shouting for pints of beer with which to toast the news.

'So where is the nearest recruitment office?' Rosie Gibbs's husband, Moody, shouted over the general din. 'Because wherever it is, I'm off to it!'

'And I'm coming with you!' shouted Sparky Holden, who never liked to be left out of anything.

'Let's join up as a group!' someone else shouted from the centre of the crush. 'What a lark that'll be, all marching side by side with our rifles slung over our shoulders! We'll soon show those square-head Krauts what's what! Bleedin' 'ell, chaps! I can't bloody wait!'

And then, as she pulled a pint of Guinness for Tunny Boardman, Tilly saw Daniel squeeze into the taproom, his face set and pale as he pushed his way through to the bar.

'What's up with you?' Tunny said, slapping Daniel on the back as Daniel finally reached his objective. 'If you're worried about fighting, Lion, I wouldn't trouble yourself. It'll all be over by Christmas.'

'Idiot,' Daniel said through clenched teeth to Tilly as Tunny headed back into the centre of the crush, holding his pint of Guinness against his chest with both hands in order not to spill any of it. 'And what does he have to worry about? He's too old and fat to ever be called to the colours.'

'Is that what might happen?' Tilly's alarm deepened. Until now she had thought a war would involve only professional soldiers – young men who wanted to fight and had been trained to fight, but if there was a general call-up, it would mean young men who had no desire to find themselves on a battle-field – young men like Daniel – could very possibly find themselves on one.

The very thought gave her a sick sensation deep in the pit of her stomach. How could the murder of an elderly archduke – an archduke she had never heard of until he had been shot in a city and a country she had never heard of – be disrupting their lives in such a ghastly way? It was like being in a bad dream; a bad dream that, at the moment, showed no sign of coming to an end.

Not only did it show no sign of coming to an end, but over the next few days, for Tilly, it grew from a bad dream into a nightmare, for Daniel was the only young man in Oystertown not to stand in line at the local recruiting office and enlist or, like Jasper, to sign on as a crew member of a civilian cargo ship.

Oystertown was very small and in no time at all word spread that Daniel Picard had no intention of fighting and helping to give the Kaiser a bloody nose as every other red-blooded male in the town was vowing to do. Gertie Dadd said it was because he was half-French and that it was well known that all Frenchies were cowards.

The next day when Daniel approached the drapery shop to begin his working day he was puzzled by the number of people standing in little groups and staring at the shop's window. And then, as he neared them, he realized they weren't admiring his latest modest window display. Instead, they were looking at something written on the window; something that most certainly hadn't been written on it when he had locked up the previous evening. In white paint and in gigantic letters were the words: *FRENCHIE COWARD.*

He came to a disbelieving halt. *Frenchie* coward? Although his father was most certainly French, Daniel thought of himself as being English, and as Frenchmen weren't known for being copper-knobs, people unacquainted with his parentage always assumed him to be English, or sometimes, because of his red hair and light sprinkling of freckles, Scottish or Irish.

As the ugly words *FRENCHIE COWARD* danced in front of his eyes, he became aware of someone walking up to him from behind, and then a familiar voice said, 'Leave this to me, Lion. I've just been for some turps. I'll have those words off the window in no time.'

It was Harry the coal-man, grim-faced as well as grimy-faced.

At Harry's arrival the knot of people goggling at the window had quickly moved away, for with a job that entailed carrying heavy sacks of coal from his lorry to domestic coal holes, Harry was as fit and strong as Jasper and not someone to tangle with.

Deeply grateful, Daniel watched as Harry wiped the paint from the window with a turps-soaked cloth.

'Take no notice of it, Lion,' Harry said when the ugly words had disappeared leaving only smears on the glass. 'Some people are idiots and always will be. D'you fancy a morning pint on me in the Duke? Best to show you don't give a damn. It's a rule of life I've always gone by and it hasn't let me down yet. What d'you drink? Mild-and-bitter?'

* * *

To Daniel's vast relief there were no repeats of the window incident, but by mid-August, instead of the expected good news coming from the war front, all that came was bad news and his not being in uniform began drawing other kinds of hostile reaction. Men he had often hung out with before the announcement of war and who were now in uniform crossed to the other side of the street when they saw him coming. When he walked into the Duke, men he'd served with on lifeboat duty quickly finished whatever it was they were drinking and left to continue their drinking elsewhere. Children shouted, 'Ya boo, cowardy custard!' after him in the street. Women who had been regular customers in the shop he managed now took their custom elsewhere.

Before leaving to become a member of the crew of a merchant ship, Jasper had told him that he simply didn't understand him and he imagined that Kim's attitude towards him would be very similar, but as Kim had had no recent leave from the navy, he couldn't be sure. Daniel would have welcomed the chance to discuss his reasons, as once they had finally met, the two men had got along like a house on fire. Daniel valued Kim's opinions, even if there had been no talk of them collaborating on diving designs since Jonah's death. He had not been able to face the thought of going back to his technical plans. Yet he still counted Kim as a trusted friend, even if now he suspected they had very different attitudes towards the war.

Marietta had told him she was ashamed of him, but it wasn't something she admitted to anyone else. When anyone in Oystertown brought the subject up with her she simply said through gritted teeth that Daniel was a pacifist and that even if it meant him going to prison for his principles, he was going to stand by them. Of all his many friends in Oystertown only Janna truly understood his abhorrence of killing, even when that killing was in war-time. They had always been friends, but her understanding him, when no one else did, had drawn them closer and now when they walked the lower slopes of the Heights together they walked in such close, easy companionship that anyone seeing them from a distance would assume they were a courting couple.

'Turn Rose Mount into a recuperation home for injured officers?' Claudia stared at her mother so overcome by conflicting reactions she didn't know which was uppermost. It was a brilliantly patriotic idea, but it would also mean she would have no base in Oystertown to periodically return to and, as the war meant Xan working much longer hours at the Swiss Embassy, she had come to rely on the fact that whenever she became too lonesome, she could always stay at Rose Mount and enjoy a few days of Janna's company, and Marietta's too, if she was back home.

'It was Clementine Churchill's idea,' Celia Layard continued, steadily regarding her daughter's face as the afternoon light angled sharply across the Turkish carpet in the Belgrave Square drawing room. 'She says lots of people with country homes are aiding the war effort in this way.'

Clementine Churchill's rumbustious husband, Winston, was First Lord of the Admiralty.

'It will be staffed by an experienced live-in nursing sister whom Clementine has recommended, as many live-in junior nurses as the nursing sister in question thinks necessary and a local doctor who has agreed to visit whenever he is needed. Orderlies and inexperienced nursing staff will be recruited from local women whose husbands are fighting at the Front.'

It was a wonderfully ambitious project and pride that her mother had thought of it and was putting it into action all by herself, flooded through Claudia. She wondered if Xan would mind if she, too, came down to Rose Mount and helped out with basic nursing care. It would be something positive to do for soldiers who had been badly injured in the war against the hated Boche.

Now that the idea had entered her head, she was seized by the urge to act on it. She would go down to Oystertown on the afternoon train. First, though, she would have to let Xan know what it was she was going to do and she could do that en route to Charing Cross Station by leaving a message at the Swiss Embassy, telling him she would be in Oystertown for the next night or two.

Buoyantly she put on a flower-trimmed straw-boater, picked up a decoratively beaded handbag and, full of high spirits, left the house.

Fifteen minutes later, facing an official in the Swiss Embassy, her high spirits were no longer quite so high.

'Your husband left the building half an hour or so ago,' the smartly dressed young man behind the reception desk said apologetically. 'Would you like to leave a message for him, Mrs Keller?'

'No. That isn't necessary.' She shot him a disarming smile. 'And when he returns there is no need to tell him that I called. I was passing by and simply dropped in on the off-chance that he would be free to take me out to tea – which was very naughty of me, considering that it's still only mid-afternoon.'

Ten minutes later she was in a taxi-cab heading for Charing Cross Station. As the cabbie took a shortcut through the narrow streets of Soho she caught a glimpse of Xan and another tall, blond-haired man crossing the street and entering a restaurant which had broad strips of brown sticky tape criss-crossed against cracked and splintered windows.

Abruptly she leaned forward, about to rap on the glass divide and ask the cabbie to drop her off so that she could join them, and then common sense kicked in. Xan would hardly appreciate her descending on him when he was obviously about to have a business lunch.

Realizing that her curiosity would have to wait until evening before it could be satisfied, she sank back against the cracked-leather upholstery. As the cab emerged from Soho on its way to Charing Cross, she experienced a sudden stab of shock as she realized something else: the name of the restaurant Xan and his companion had entered had been *Der Goldene Vogel*, which, considering the fevered anti-German feeling which was now being very publicly expressed at the slightest opportunity, accounted for the restaurant having had its windows smashed in.

'And so,' Claudia said three hours later on the telephone to Kim, 'I'd rather like you to warn Xan that as he looks so very German it would be best if he avoided behaving as if he *was* German, otherwise the consequences are likely to be very unpleasant. If I told him, he would simply tell me not to fuss, but if you tell him, I know he will be more careful about the restaurants he patronizes.'

Kim had promised that he would and then the conversation had turned to Rose Mount and what a wonderfully large, comfortable recuperation home it was going to make for injured officers.

When they'd said goodbye to each other Kim had dialled the Swiss Embassy in order to speak to Xan, only to be told by the operator that the line was busy. After waiting ten minutes for it to clear his patience ran out and he told the operator who had been trying to connect him that he would try again in the morning. After all, it wasn't important. With war now a reality, what was important was the work he was engaged in at Portsmouth, helping to design a submarine that would be able to remain beneath the surface for far longer periods of time than anything the Germans had yet built.

And being privy to classified information as he was, he knew something the British population, complacent in their certainty that the Royal Navy was far superior to Germany's Imperial Navy, didn't know. He knew that not since English ships had faced the Spanish Armada in 1588 had the country faced such a daunting threat of invasion and that in the present conflict nothing, absolutely nothing, could be taken for granted.

Chapter Twenty-two

One month into the war and it was not going the way people had expected it to. There was no quick, crushing victory by British forces. On 16 August the town of Liège, in Belgium, had unexpectedly fallen to the Germans after resisting fiercely for several days. Janna, who was walking past Gertie Dadd's sweetshop when she read the newspaper-boy's placard headline, came to a sudden, stunned halt.

How on earth could the Germans already be gaining the upper hand? When war had been declared Sir John French, the Commander of the BEF, the British Expeditionary Force, had very firmly announced that the fighting would be over by Christmas, but Belgium was Britain's ally and if further Belgian towns came under German control the war was clearly going to last far longer than a few short months.

Jasper had already signed on as a crew member of a cargo ship that would soon be running the gauntlet of German submarines as it brought foodstuffs into British ports. Archie had taken notice of the posters on public buildings and railway and bus stations, all of which featured a picture of a fierce Lord Kitchener, the Secretary of State for War, beneath the words *Your King and Country Need You* in heavy black print and, together with Harry, the coal-man, had left Oystertown for an army training camp in deepest Hampshire.

Only Daniel was still in Oystertown and Oystertown men already in uniform blatantly cold-shouldered him and, even worse, sometimes hustled him into one of the many little alleyways that ran down to the harbour and gave him a knocking-about that left him battered and bruised. His employer at the draper's said he couldn't keep him on at the shop because there were now so few customers willing to be served by him and, for the same reason, Ozzie said he couldn't employ him at the Duke any longer.

'But as a conscientious objector you can still take an active part in the defence of the country,' Janna said to him fiercely when, after seeking him out at the windmill, she had found him seated on the grass a hundred yards or so away from it, his face badly bruised, his arms circling his knees, a half-smoked Woodbine held loosely between his fingers.

'And just how would I do that?' he asked bleakly.

She sat down beside him. 'Hundreds of conscientious object-ors are taking up non-combatant roles. There was an article about them doing so in this morning's *Daily Mail*. Here, I've brought the paper with me.'

She thrust it into his unwilling hand.

'In a non-combatant role you could be a medical orderly, a stretcher-bearer, or even an ambulance-driver. In any of those positions no one would be able to accuse you of cowardice and you would be helping to save lives, not take them.'

For a long moment Daniel remained silent and then he nipped his cigarette out. 'I'd need to do some pretty intensive First-Aid training in order to be a medical orderly.'

'The St John's Ambulance will give you training.'

'Will they?'

She nodded and Daniel felt a seed of hope spring into life. Giving medical aid to injured men would be a far different thing to shooting at the enemy with the intention of killing them and, with growing certainty, he became aware of what his role was to be in the ghastly fighting now taking place against the invading Germans on Belgium's border with France. After training with the St John Ambulance Brigade, he would be able to join a Voluntary Aid Detachment giving aid to the wounded at the Front.

Aware there wasn't a moment to lose before he put his intentions into action he jumped to his feet.

Startled, Janna rose to hers.

'Come on!' He grasped hold of her hand, well aware it was Janna who had led him to his present decision and that when he was treating the wounded in the horror that was Flanders it would be the thought of Janna that would keep him sane.

The realization of all she had come to mean to him overcame him with such unexpected power it left him breathless. Almost from their first meeting they had been chums, enjoying an effortlessly close camaraderie. This, though, was different, and as she stood so near to him that he could smell the fragrance of her freshly washed hair, his heart tightened in his chest.

'Janna . . .' For the first time in his life he was too crippled by nerves to continue with what he wanted to say, which was that she had become the most important person in his life.

'If you like, I'll come with you to the nearest St John Ambulance hall,' she said, certain it was the answer to the question he had been about to ask. 'Rose Mount is being turned into a Recuperation Home for injured officers and once I've gained some first aid training I'll be able to help out on the wards.'

Her dearly familiar face shone with good intent and he wondered how he could ever have thought her plain; even worse, how he could ever have taken her for granted. His doing so had been a huge mistake. A mistake he had no intention of repeating.

'Come on,' he said thickly, squeezing hold of her hand in a way that made her heart beat very fast indeed. 'If we set off now – and if we do so at a run – we can be signing on for medical training in less than half an hour.'

For Archie and Harry the initial excitement of training hard every day in readiness for enemy action against the Boche was fast wearing thin.

'There's a limit to the enthusiasm I can summon up for charging with a bayonet at swinging sandbags,' a perspiring Harry said to Archie after, in a long line of fellow recruits, they had charged for the twentieth time at what they had been told to imagine was the enemy. 'Why can't we just shoot the buggers?'

'Because although the top brass are dim, they're not so dim they don't realize the prospect of being bayonetted is more terrifying than the prospect of being shot. And,' he added, 'I reckon it's also because it saves on bullets.'

'Aim for the belly, not the ribs!' their sergeant-major bellowed as they sprinted yet again towards the sagging sandbags. 'And remember the three magic words when it comes to bayonets. IN! TWIST! PULL!'

That evening Archie retreated to the bell tent he shared with five other recruits and took a notepad and pencil from one of his uniform's many pockets in order to write the first of what he was determined would be a weekly letter to Tilly. He knew she would be looking forward to receiving it for it would reassure her that on the date it had been written he had still been in good health.

Dear Tilly, he wrote, resting his notepad on his knee, *Well, here I am, somewhere I'm not allowed to specify, for a couple of weeks' training. Training used to last for much longer but word is we are needed at the Front PDQ in order to give the Boche a kick up the rump as we show them the way back to Deutschland. The camp food isn't up to your standard, but then no food is. I go to sleep dreaming of your shepherd's pie and stew and dumplings, although that said, breakfast isn't too shabby; plenty of bacon and lashings of hot sweet tea.*

When it comes to what we do all day, life is pretty much all routine. A trumpet call at five-thirty in the morning followed by a swill down at a pump and a scramble into our heavy khaki uniforms (I feel, and look, like a postman in mine). Then it's breakfast and after that the day is split up into a series of drills. Bayonet drill, digging trenches drill, handling weapons drill, marksmanship drill. The first two drills are pretty tedious, but I enjoy the last two. I'm top in my platoon when it comes to marksmanship. Take care of yourself, Tilly. You're the only blood relation, other than Jasper and Janna, that I have. And give my best wishes to all the people in Oystertown who matter to me. Janna, of course, plus all the regulars in the Duke, especially Ozzie, Daniel, and that old rascal, Pascal. Also, Harry says will you make sure the bloke who has taken over his coal-round is looking after Bessie, his coal-cart horse properly and, if he isn't, get Ozzie to sort it double-quick. Bye for now and toodle pip, Archie.

As a member of the aristocracy Celia Layard had never in her life experienced anything that could be classed as physical labour, but she threw herself heart and soul into the mammoth task of converting Rose Mount into a recuperation home for badly injured and disabled officers and, helped by Claudia and a squad of local women, she did so in an admirably short space of time.

One of her first practical problems had been not only the lack of medical supplies, but also the lack of what she regarded as essential toiletries for the men, for none of them had so much as a toothbrush, shaving brush, razor or a flannel when, some on crutches and others on stretchers, they hobbled or were carried into large, airy rooms that had been turned into recovery wards smelling of carbolic soap. Once, in the peacetime that already felt like a distant memory, these had been the main bedrooms and reception rooms, but nearly all of that grand furniture had been hastily put into storage, replaced with iron bedsteads and sturdy wooden chairs. She was eagerly awaiting a consignment of bedside lockers, so important for the patients to retain a sense of privacy for their personal possessions.

Almost immediately Celia had set about making lists, some of them ambitious such as clothing lists, top of which had been long-johns (she had nearly fainted when she was first faced with the knowledge that even though they were all officers, only one in five of her patients possessed items of serviceable underwear), closely followed by pyjamas and dressing gowns.

'And while their bodies are healing their minds will need occupying,' Claudia had said with sensitive insight. 'We will need a book trolley, Mama. I'll ask Kim what sort of titles will be popular with the men. And for the recreation room we will need card-tables, packs of cards, jigsaws, Chinese chequers and chess.'

'And Ludo, Halma, and Snakes and Ladders,' Celia had said.

For the first time since her father's tragic death there had been animation in her mother's voice and Claudia had known that by transforming Rose Mount into a recuperation home her mother had at last found a way of dealing with her grief. She also knew that for the first couple of months and until her mother had grown in confidence in her new role at Rose Mount, her mother would be hoping she could rely on her, Claudia's, supportive presence there. And while she was giving her mother her supportive presence at Rose Mount, she wouldn't be able to spend as much time in London, with Xan, as she had been doing.

Her regret and disappointment that at least for a little while she would no longer be able to do so was intense, but not intense enough for her to change her mind about the decision she had made for she was quite certain it was the transforming of Rose Mount and giving support to her mother that was now of prime importance. And where Xan was concerned, he would always be there, waiting for her. It was something she would quite willingly have staked her life on.

Marietta was enjoying the war immensely for newspaper reports from the Front assured the public that everything was going the BEF's way and audiences in the music hall she was appearing at were packed to the rafters with men in uniform who had not yet been sent to the French–Belgium border to repel the invading Germans and who were itching to get there. Dolly had long ago forgiven her for deserting the stage in New Cross, as she had known he would. Now she had a lively new audience eating out of her hand every night, and she was relishing every moment.

And then, on 30 August, there was such a reversal of news from the Front that Marietta thought at first it was some kind of sick joke. News-boys were on every street corner, shouting: *'BEF retreat from Mons! Read all abaht it!'* And even more luridly, *'Bloodbath at Mons! Civilians caught in cross-fire! Women and children flee for their lives!'*

Photographs on the *Daily Mail*'s front page of long columns of terrified civilians pushing hay carts and wheelbarrows piled high with household possessions and children too young to walk was proof that the headlines were no joke.

Mons was a small town on the Belgian border with France and Marietta had never before been so conscious of the French blood that ran in her veins. Were the Germans on the point of invading the country of her father's birth? The thought filled her with fury and she was flooded with the desire to take physical action against them.

'And if I was a man I would do so!' she said passionately later that day to Dolly when he had walked into her dressing room as she was putting her make-up on before going on stage.

Dolly knew her well enough to believe her. Pushing her pots of stage make-up to one side he perched on a corner of her dressing table, one stubby leg swinging. 'How do you feel about singing for the troops as they leave for Flanders?' he said, enthusiasm for the idea thick in his voice. 'I'll make sure plenty of press photos are taken and it will make for good publicity. You don't want to let Marie Lloyd have it all her own way.'

Marie Lloyd was Marietta's bête-noire for Marie's popularity as a music hall artist was such that she'd earned herself the nickname 'Queen of the Music Halls', a nickname Marietta felt should have been hers.

She took a last look in the mirror, secured a wide-brimmed hat laden with peacock-feathers on her glorious upswept hair and said, 'And I shall go one better than Marie Lloyd, Dolly. I'm not only going to be singing patriotic songs for the troops here, in Blighty. I'm going to sing for them in Belgium as well – *et je vais le faire aussi près de la Ligne de Front que je peux obtenir* – and I'm going to be doing so as near to the front line as I can get!'

Chapter Twenty-three

April 1915

Eight months later the war was as far from being over as ever and the Prime Minister, Mr Asquith, had called for another five hundred thousand men to sign up for the army. The response had been immediate and all over the country queues at recruiting offices stretched for street after street and grim-faced women handed white feathers to any man of fighting age who wasn't in uniform, or about to be in uniform.

'We'll soon thrash the bloody Boche, pardon my language Miss,' Oystertown's milkman said to Claudia as he rolled a churn from his cart into Rose Mount's kitchen. 'The tide is turning, just you wait and see.'

Claudia was grateful for his optimism, even though she didn't share it. How could she when the newspapers were full of accounts of how the Germans had devised a hideous new weapon of war. Shells that screamed overhead and, when they exploded, filled the air with deadly chlorine gas.

Deeply grateful that Xan's Swiss nationality and his diplomatic position at the Swiss Embassy meant there was never going to be a situation where he would find himself being choked to death by chlorine gas and praying passionately that Archie and Harry and all the other Oystertown men who were fighting in Flanders would never be in such a situation either, she ran up Rose Mount's broad sweep of stairs in order to start her day's work on the wards.

Gone were most of the pictures which had once adorned the walls of the corridors. Robert Layard had been a keen amateur collector of fine art, but it was simply too difficult to keep dusting all the elaborate frames, time that could be so much better spent nursing the sick. A few remained – the most cheerful ones, and a new landscape Pascal himself had donated. Claudia smiled in appreciation as she passed it, but secretly hoped he would not give them too many more.

By the time she was back in what had once been a spacious master bedroom and now held six narrow beds, her mood had turned to dejection. It was over half a year since war had been declared and in all that time, although she had gone up to London several times in order to snatch a few hours with Xan, he had never once travelled down to Rose Mount to spend time with her.

'Much as I would like to, it just isn't possible for me to leave London when the situation on the Continent is so critical,' he'd said apologetically the last time he had met her off the train at Charing Cross. 'Once the war is won things will be very different,' he'd added, knowing she would think he was speaking of a victorious Britain, when what he'd really been doing was imagining a Britain crushed into servility beneath German jackboots.

Claudia was jolted from all thoughts of her husband by the need to check the dressings on the stumps of a twenty-one-year-old lieutenant who had lost both legs the first day he had gone into battle.

'I thought you'd abandoned me this morning,' Frank Colvin said, cheery despite the pain no amount of painkillers could ever completely deaden. 'Will you have time for a hand of gin rummy this afternoon?'

'I don't see why not.' She set her enamel dressing tray on top of his bedside locker. 'To distract you from what I'm about to do, why don't you start singing "It's a Long Way to Tipperary"? And I'd appreciate it if, just for once, you didn't add in any naughty bits of your own.'

He flashed her a cheeky grin. 'You're a cracker of a nurse, but you do spoil a bloke's fun. All right. Here goes: *It's a long way to Tipperary,*' he began singing in a fine tenor voice, '*It's a long way to go . . .*'

The patient in the next bed whipped a mouth organ out from under his pillow and began accompanying him.

'*It's a long way to Tipperary, To the sweetest girl I know,*' the other men in the ward sang, just as if they were at a university rugger match which, considering they were still in their late teens and early twenties, they could well have been. '*Goodbye, Piccadilly, Farewell, Leicester Square, It's a long, long way to Tipperary, But my heart's right there!*'

'Bravo!' a husky voice Claudia hadn't heard for several months called out from just beyond the open doorway as the song came to an end. '*Magnifique! Merveilleux!*'

'Heaven and all the saints!' Frank whispered as Marietta stepped into the room, a vision in a lemon-silk tunic-dress and a matching hat that sported a jauntily upright feather. 'It's one of the angels some of the lads said they saw in the sky at Mons!'

With a seductive sway of her hips Marietta walked up to his bed and shot him a dazzling smile. 'I'm afraid you are wrong.' She gave a dismissive, Gallic shrug of her shoulders. 'I've never performed at Mons. I have, however, been top of the bill more times than I can count at the Hackney Empire and the Shoreditch Alhambra. What is it you would like me to sing?'

Frank blushed a bright beetroot red. 'I'd like you to sing "Boys in Khaki, Boys in Blue", miss.'

'And after that can we have "Rule Britannia"?'

The speaker was Celia. Having been told of Marietta's arrival she had hurried to the ward all the shouts for a song were coming from and then, realizing what a tonic a visit such as Marietta's was for the men and not wanting her own presence to put too much of a damper on things, she had come to a halt in the doorway.

Marietta turned to face her. '*Mais oui!* But of course, Lady Layard! I always end any public performance with "Rule Britannia". And then,' she added, cat-green eyes flashing fire, 'to honour the French blood in my veins, I follow it with "*La Marseillaise*".'

'And so you should, for France is our very brave ally.' Celia was not about to be bested by someone she remembered as a young woman scarcely out of girlhood running about the Heights barefoot, her red-gold hair a torrent of tangles. 'I'd like everyone in Rose Mount to be able to enjoy this. Claudia, will you seek out Janna and then will the two of you help everyone in the other two wards who need assistance transferring from their bed to a wheelchair, and bring them in here.'

Within ten minutes every recuperating officer in Rose Mount had squeezed into the ward, either in a wheelchair, or on crutches. Crowding the doorway as tightly as pilchards in a tin were Rose Mount's handful of domestic and nursing staff – nursing staff which included Janna.

To thunderous handclapping, whistling, and for the men who hadn't had leg amputations the appreciative stamping of feet, Marietta followed 'It's a Long Way to Tipperary' with 'Nellie Dean' and 'After the Ball'.

Janna had never before seen Marietta give a public performance and she was overcome with pride that someone who could give such pleasure to so many people so effortlessly was, along with Claudia, her closest friend.

After singing 'Rule Britannia', in which everyone sang along with her as if their hearts would burst, Marietta brought her bravura performance to an end, the palm of her right hand patriotically over her left breast as she launched into the French national anthem.

The storm of applause as she reached the end of the last verse was so loud Celia thought it a miracle Rose Mount still had a roof on.

'I'm glad I didn't resist the impulse to visit Papa and then to come and say hello to you and Janna,' Marietta said as, with her hand tucked lightly in the crook of Claudia's arm, they took a turn around Rose Mount's terraced garden before it was time for her to leave for the railway station in the only taxicab Oystertown possessed. 'Always I think the war will soon be over and that life and friendships will return to normal, but nothing gets better. It only gets worse. In the last six months I have twice been to Flanders to sing for the troops and the front line was no further forward on my second visit than it was on the first.'

She ran her free hand over a bush of weigela, sending a cascade of tiny, wine-red petals onto the gravelled pathway.

'One of my admirers is a general and when I was singing for the troops in Belgium, he told me that our French allies suffered horrendous losses in order to take a wood covering only a quarter of a square mile. Nothing is as the newspapers would like us to believe. The British Expeditionary Force isn't advancing. It has simply dug in and is maintaining its position and the effort of maintaining it is costing the lives of thousands of British and French soldiers.'

Claudia came to a halt, her face draining white. 'But the field postcards Archie and Harry send Tilly are always optimistic!'

'If they weren't, I don't think she would receive them. I think you would find they had been conveniently lost in transit.'

Claudia gasped in disbelief and Marietta quickly said, 'Do you get postcards from Daniel? I occasionally get one, but the censor always inks out far more words than are left in so that the only sentence not totally obliterated is "*All for now, best love, Daniel*".'

'Yes, I do get postcards from him. At least the postcards let us know he is still alive and they make me aware of how lucky I am that Xan is Swiss and is safe as houses living in our London home and working at the Swiss Embassy. He hates it that I'm not in London with him. The poor darling must get very lonely and I hate the thought of how much he is missing me, but as long as I am needed here to help out with the nursing, it's something that has to be endured.'

Until now Marietta had never had a guilty conscience where any of her affairs were concerned, but as she thought of her careless sexual entanglement with Xan she came to a sudden halt, swamped for the first time in her life by regret and guilt. Admittedly it had been a one-off; once she had realized how close he was to announcing his engagement to her friend she had ended things immediately. No matter what the cost to her own relationship with Claudia, she couldn't allow Claudia to remain unaware of how faithless to her, her husband was.

'Claudia . . .' she began, and didn't get any further because Dolly was jumping up and down on the top terrace and waving his arms to attract her attention.

Cupping his hands around his mouth, he shouted, 'There is only one London train this morning and it departs in fifteen minutes' time! We have to leave for the train station, Marietta! We have to leave NOW!'

What Marietta had been about to say to Claudia wasn't something that could be said hurriedly for she very much doubted that Claudia would immediately believe her – and when she did believe her, it was impossible to tell what her reaction would be.

'I'm coming!' she shouted back to Dolly, knowing she couldn't drop a bombshell about Xan's infidelities and then, without even waiting for Claudia's reaction, cut and run.

Giving Claudia a swift bear-hug, she said with passionate sincerity, 'I'll be back in Oystertown and visiting Rose Mount again soon.' She lifted a skirt that was a fashionable three inches above her ankles a couple of inches even higher, then turned and, with sure-footed speed and grace, sprinted up the steps leading to the stone balustraded terrace.

Chapter Twenty-four

September 1915

Even though the war was still showing no sign of coming to an end Claudia was fizzing with happiness for she was spending the weekend with Xan in London and that evening they had tickets for Mozart's opera *Don Giovanni* at the Royal Opera House, Covent Garden. Xan's workload at the embassy was such that there weren't many opportunities for marital evening-outs together and, when one came along, for Claudia it was always a special occasion.

Instead of asking her maid to fasten her necklace for her, she asked Xan if he would do it.

As his fingers brushed the nape of her neck she trembled slightly.

'Are you cold?' he asked, trying to sound concerned.

'No. I'm simply looking forward to our evening together.' She turned to face him, her body brushing his, hoping he would put his arms around her.

He didn't, but he did make the effort to tell her she looked lovely, causing her to flush with pleasure. In the early days of their marriage his habitual Swiss coolness had caused her distress, but then she had become accustomed to it. After all, Xan being cool and intriguing was all part of his attraction and she comforted herself with the thought that if he were any different, he wouldn't be the person she had fallen in love with.

They went by taxicab to Covent Garden through streets crowded with uniformed Tommies, some strolling along in noisy groups; others arm in arm with a sweetheart or wife as they enjoyed a precious twenty-four- or forty-eight-hour leave. Even though it was not yet October, at the bottom-end of Pall Mall a barrow-boy with a red-hot brazier on his cart was selling roasted chestnuts, shovelling them into paper cones so that they could be eaten in the street. An elderly woman with a crocheted shawl around her shoulders was selling bunches of late-flowering carnations from a barrow.

The cabbie came to a halt outside the Royal Opera House. With excitement rippling down her spine and wearing a shimmering, gentian-blue evening-gown that flattered her blonde colouring and a white mink stole around her shoulders, Claudia stepped from the cab and onto the kerb.

As she entered the crowded, buzzing foyer of the Opera House on Xan's arm a silver-haired man caught sight of them. On seeing Xan his eyebrows rose in surprised recognition and he began threading his way through the crush towards them.

'Carl!' he said to Xan, coming to a halt in front of them. '*Wie geht es Ihnen?*' And then, aware that speaking in German would draw unwelcome attention to the two of them, he reverted quickly to English, but with an unmistakeable German accent. 'How strange to run into you here when I so seldom see you on the other side of the English Channel. How are things in Berlin?'

'I am afraid, sir, that you have mistaken me for someone else.' Xan's voice was ice-cold. 'My name is Keller, Alexander Keller, and I am Swiss.' And firmly taking hold of Claudia's arm he turned on his heel, forging a way for them through the crush in the direction of the auditorium.

From behind them Claudia heard the man say to a male companion, 'Isn't it strange how any German still not interned now claims to be Swiss?'

The unjustified calumny brought hot colour to Claudia's cheeks.

'Why didn't you tell that ghastly person that you were a diplomat attached to the embassy?' she asked, indignant on his behalf as they made their way upstairs to their seats in the front row of the Grand Tier.

'Because I don't engage in conversation with people who have mistaken me for someone else.'

His voice was curt and a pulse at the corner of his jawline had begun to throb.

She bit her lip, aware he was fighting hard to keep his temper.

As they reached their seats, he bought a programme and while he was doing so, she turned her attention to the people seated below them in the front stalls. It wasn't that she was truly interested in whether anyone they knew was also in the Royal Opera House that evening. It was simply a way of trying not to go over and over in her mind the scene in the theatre foyer when the German had so confidently approached Xan, greeting him with easy familiarity, and when Xan had said the man had mistaken him for someone else.

She had seen the look of recognition on the German's face as he had approached Xan, and she had also seen the look in his eyes when he met with Xan's reaction. The German had known Xan somehow, but had Xan known the German?

The lights dimmed and there was a ripple of applause as the orchestra filed into the pit and took up their instruments. Dutifully Claudia clapped along with everyone else, but her thoughts weren't on the coming performance. The man in the foyer quite obviously believed Xan's Christian name to be Carl. Yet this made no sense. Perhaps her handsome husband had a double. All the same, she wished he hadn't been spoken to in German, which could have provoked a very nasty incident indeed. It could have put him in danger, as the overall mood in the capital was so volatile.

Her mind was in such a whirl of what ifs and might be's that she felt giddy. On stage, and to increased applause, the curtain rose on Act 1, where the masked Don Giovanni was attempting to seduce Donna Anna. The wonderful music had its desired effect, reassuring her; whatever had just happened was annoying but could not compare with the enthralling drama about to unfold on stage.

In the low lights of the theatre she looked across at Xan's distinctive profile and slid her hand into his. Unlike thousands upon thousands of other young women she wasn't suffering the mental agony of having a husband serving at the Front – a husband who every day was at risk of death or hideous injury. She thought of Archie and Harry and of how, every evening when she said her prayers, she prayed for their continuing safety. She thought of Daniel who had become a conscientious objector. A conscientious objector who, as a horse-drawn ambulance driver, risked his life under fire day in and day out ferrying the wounded to field dressing stations and sometimes to military hospitals. And last, but by no means least, she thought of Jasper aboard a merchant ship – a ship constantly vulnerable to torpedo attack from German U-boats. Please God, she prayed, no harm would come to him; the very idea was unbearable.

An outburst of prolonged applause told her Act 1 had come to an end and, although her thoughts were far from what had just taken place on the stage, she again joined in the applause. Not to have done would have attracted Xan's attention and she couldn't very well tell him that her mind hadn't been on Don Giovanni's deception of Donna Anna, but rather on Archie, Harry, Daniel and Jasper.

She let out a sigh of relief that her friends had survived thus far.

Hearing it, and being irritated by it, Xan turned his head towards her. 'You're not bored, are you?'

'No,' she whispered back. 'I think the performance is quite magical.'

Xan returned his gaze to the stage. In his opinion opera was the highest of all art forms and he wanted to concentrate his entire attention on it and by doing so temporarily push the unfortunate episode in the foyer to the back of his mind. Running into someone he had been on nodding terms with in Berlin – and doing so when he had been accompanied by Claudia – had been potentially catastrophic. He had, however, extricated himself from the situation with possibly no harm done, for looking across at Claudia he saw by the rapt expression on her face that the only thing on her mind was Mozart's glorious music.

It was Kim, who, in a telephone conversation a few days later, unintentionally reminded her of the incident by politely asking, when she had told him of her and Xan's evening at Covent Garden, if they had enjoyed the performance.

'It was absolute heaven,' she said, adding wryly, 'and wasn't even spoiled by someone mistaking Xan for a German named Carl.'

'I can't imagine Xan being too pleased about that.' He tried hard not to let the shock he felt show. 'What on earth was his reaction?'

'He very politely – and in flawless English – corrected their error. German is, of course, one of Switzerland's four official languages and if he had wanted to, Xan could have replied in German, which would have confused matters more than ever. He sometimes even speaks German in his sleep.'

'That's not something to tell anyone else, Claudia. If you do, it will certainly be misinterpreted and cause Xan no end of trouble.'

'I won't. I promise.'

The pips went, indicating their time was up.

'Bye, Coz,' he said. 'Take care of yourself.'

'Bye, Kim.' Claudia's throat was tight as she said goodbye to him. Apart from her mother, he was her only close relation; she loved him dearly and worried about his safety as he and the rest of his submarine crew hunted down German U-boats and, in turn, were hunted by them.

As he severed their connection Kim was frowning. For some reason he'd never been able to fathom, it had always been assumed by those who knew both of them that he and Xan were close friends. They were certainly on civil terms with each other, which was just as well when Xan's marriage to Claudia had made Xan his cousin by marriage, but he wasn't close friends with Xan in the way he was close friends with Jasper and Daniel – and instinct told him that things were best left that way.

Archie and Harry were in Flanders, two of the thousands of British and French troops standing on wet duckboards in sand-bagged, foul-smelling, muddy trenches eight to nine feet deep somewhere to the west of Lille. The objective for their battalion was to take a village that, held by the Germans, was preventing British and French forces from re-taking Lille, a town of important strategic significance that was, for the second time in less than a year, in German hands.

Their unit had suffered a night of near non-stop bombardment and neither they, nor the rest of their battalion, had managed to get any shut-eye. Even now German field guns were periodically pounding away and anyone rash enough to climb the scaling ladders and poke his head over the rim of the trench they were in ran the risk of having it blown off.

'Bloody Huns!' Even though he was standing shoulder to shoulder with Archie, Harry had to bawl at the top of his voice for Archie to hear him over the sound of the guns. He felt in his mud-caked pockets for any dog-end he might have previously overlooked. 'I never hated 'em before – not even after they invaded poor little Belgium – but I hate 'em like the very devil now!'

A shell screamed over their heads, missing their trench by precious yards. Giant clods of earth, a helmet and a boot rained down on them. A rat ran over their feet. Harry gave vent to a string of blasphemies. Archie let out a stream of good old Yorkshire swear words.

Further down the trench their officer raised his arm preparatory to giving the order to advance.

Archie drew in a deep breath and gritted his teeth.

'*Stand ready!*' sergeants shouted all down the long British line.

Harry's hands tightened on the butt of his rifle. A Lee Enfield, its rate of fire in the hands of a highly trained man was impressive and Harry could shoot off thirty well-aimed bullets in under a minute.

Archie's eyes were fixed on the sergeant's upraised arm, his mouth dry, his heart pounding. In scenarios like this it was quite normal that only a quarter of the men setting out into enemy fire would be returning to camp when the day's objective had been achieved and, by the law of averages, the day had to come when he and Harry would no longer be among that lucky number. Fervently, and with every bone in his body, he was hoping that today would not be that day.

The officers about to lead them into no-man's-land, the hideous stretch of water-filled shell-holed desolation that separated them from the German lines – simultaneously blew hard on their whistles and lowered their arms and Archie and Harry and every other soldier in the Allied line erupted out of their trenches and, head-down, bent double and with bayonets fixed, sprinted yet again into a deafening, roaring, seething hell.

The machine-gun bombardment was remorseless. To the right of him and to the left of him Archie was aware of a sea of men spinning and falling like skittles under a merciless hail of bullets and knew that by some almighty miracle he wasn't yet among them. Instead, he was still running into the smoke, leaping over the dead and wounded as he fired and re-loaded and fired again at the solid wall of grey that was the oncoming enemy, his peripheral vision telling him that Harry was still upright; that his mate Harry was still at his side.

The noise was deafening, crippling, stupefying. It was a hell so hideous there were moments when he couldn't believe that it was real; when he thought he must be back home in Oystertown and in his small bedroom having the mother of all nightmares.

All around him and to the incessant noise of machine-gun fire, the men of his battalion were being mown down in huge swathes. No-man's-land was at least two hundred and fifty yards wide and they were now too far across it to make retreating a survivable option. He had to keep running. He had to keep firing his rifle. He had to keep believing that some way, somehow, the hell he was in, the hell he was plunging ever deeper into, was a hell he was going to survive.

Chapter Twenty-five

December 1915

The weather was bitterly cold and the war news did nothing to cheer people up. Eight months ago, ninety thousand British, Australian and New Zealand troops had stormed ashore at Gallipoli confident that they were about to give Germany's Turkish ally the mother-of-all-thrashings. Now, under cover of darkness and with only a week to go until Christmas, they were heading back to the beaches in full retreat, taking their horses and machine guns with them. Considering the thousands of men and horses involved it was a blessedly orderly retreat, but it was a retreat nevertheless and, as they read newspaper headline after newspaper headline telling them of it, the British public mood was grim.

Janna was blessed with a naturally sunny disposition and feeling dissatisfied with life, no matter how difficult the war now made things, was alien to her. However, as the year drew to a close, she was aware of a feeling of dissatisfaction so total it threatened to overwhelm her. That the war still showed no signs of coming to an end was, of course, reason enough for her to be feeling deeply out of sorts, but she knew that her own feeling of dissatisfaction was caused by something more than simply war fatigue.

As she trundled the afternoon tea trolley around Rose Mount's Christmas-decorated recovery wards she was acutely aware of how little genuine nursing care at Rose Mount was ever demanded of her. Changing an amputee's stump dressing was as near to real nursing as she ever got. Yet only a few miles away, on the other side of the English Channel, thousands of wounded soldiers were in dire need of experienced nursing care and were dying in agony for the lack of it.

Mechanically she began handing out mugs of hot tea. She knew there were military hospitals in London, but she doubted that London hospitals would be short of nurses. The only other military hospitals that she knew of were clustered on the French coast at Étaples, where, according to newspaper reports, there was a transit camp of huts and khaki-brown bell tents as big as a town.

'And Étaples,' she said to herself as she handed out the last mug of tea and wheeled the tea trolley back into the kitchen, 'is where, with my St John Ambulance qualifications, I am going to go – and not any time in the distant future, but just as soon as I possibly can.'

And instead of refreshing her tea urn with freshly boiled water she went in search of Celia in order to tell her of the decision she had come to; to thank her for all her many kindnesses to her; and to say goodbye to her.

'You are leaving Rose Mount? Immediately?' Celia pushed her chair away from her desk, bewilderment both on her face and in her voice. 'But why, Janna?'

'I want to nurse the badly wounded, not men who are well on their way to recovery and who are no longer in need of urgent nursing care. There's a piece in today's *Daily Mail* saying that the big clearing hospitals on the Channel coast are desperate for more qualified nurses, as, at the Front, are advance dressing-posts and casualty clearing stations. I'm going to join a St John Ambulance VAD Unit and then go wherever my nursing skills are most needed.'

'Join a Voluntary Aid Detachment? But surely after you apply there will be a waiting period until you are accepted?' Celia struggled to imagine Rose Mount without Janna's cheery, capable presence and found it impossible.

'There may be a waiting period, but even if there is, I don't believe it will be a long one. I think it will be just the opposite. I think nurses with St John Ambulance Nursing certificates will be in such demand at the Front that I could well find myself in Boulogne by tomorrow night.'

Celia didn't know if Janna's assumption was correct or not, but she did know that no argument she could drum up was likely to change Janna's mind. And Janna travelling alone to the French coast under war conditions didn't bear thinking about.

Suddenly her legs felt so weak that she had to put a hand on the back of the nearest chair in order to steady herself. It occurred to her that hard as she found it to like her son-in-law, at least Xan having married Claudia meant that Claudia was not preparing to leave England for the war-torn, blood-soaked fields of Flanders.

With a great effort she pulled herself together, saying, 'If you are utterly set on going to France, I have something I would like you to take with you.'

She pulled open one of her desk drawers, took out something not much bigger than a ring-box and lifted from it a small silver crucifix on a fine chain. The cross bore the figure of Christ and the silver was old and dull from generations of being lovingly worn and held and prayed over.

As she placed the cross and chain in the palm of Janna's hand, she said with an emotional break in her voice, 'It belonged to my grandfather. My grandmother gave it to him thirty-five years ago when he left for the Transvaal to fight in the First Boer War. She believed that if he always carried it on him he would come home safely, which he did. Many years later, just before he died, he gave it to me and said a day might come when it would also keep me safe and I was wearing it when Jasper rescued me from the sinking *Sprite*. I would now like you to carry it with you all the time you are in Flanders.'

'I will. I promise.' Janna couldn't say any more because her voice was too unsteady.

Soon she would be leaving all that was familiar to her and crossing the English Channel, maybe even on the night ferry to Boulogne. She didn't speak French and there would be no one to meet her there. For a brief second, she was overcome by the enormity of the task she had set herself and then she thought of Jasper and Kim who, although serving on different types of ship, had already exchanged fierce, prolonged fire with the ships of the German Navy and then last, but by no means least, she thought of Daniel who, she had to admit, she loved with all her heart and who was risking his life daily as a stretcher-bearer under constant enemy fire.

Digging her nails into her palms she took a deep steadying breath and squared her shoulders. She couldn't let Jasper, Kim, Daniel and Archie down and, in order not to let them down, she was going to support her country's war effort with the only skills she possessed, which were her nursing skills – and she was going to do so where it really mattered, which was in a hospital or a medical clearing centre as near to the front line as it was possible for her to get.

Chapter Twenty-six

June 1916

Marietta was on a stage in Étaples for a weekend of entertaining the troops and, never short of a man in uniform to buy flowers and champagne for her, was having a wonderful war, although Étaples itself left a lot to be desired. Situated on the flat and bleak French north coast behind dunes thick with marram grass it was a town that had given itself entirely over to accommodating British and French soldiers who were on leave or, if not on leave, were either waiting to go up to the front line, or were recovering from debilitating wounds. The plus side of this was that audiences for visiting entertainers were always huge and always noisily appreciative.

Accompanied by Dolly and squired by a French general who had fallen for her charms earlier in the year when she had been appearing on stage in Paris and who, whenever he could, had become something of a camp follower, Marietta had just finished a glorious rendering of '*Au Revoir* But Not Goodbye, Soldier Boy' when, with a stab of delight, she caught sight of Archie and Harry in her audience.

When she left the stage for the first of what she knew would be several curtain calls, she said to the nearest stagehand, 'On the fifth row, left-hand side, fifth and sixth in, are two friends of mine. Would you invite them round to my dressing room?'

And then she stepped back on stage to a frenzied storm of applause and in her sexily husky voice launched into an emotive rendition of the always popular, 'I'm Always Chasing Rainbows'.

As she was singing, the stagehand threaded his way towards Harry and Archie. He tapped Harry on the shoulder and said, '*Mademoiselle Picard aimerait que vous la rejoigniez dans sa loge.*'

'Sorry, mate,' Harry said, 'we don't speak the lingo.'

'You may not,' Archie said, 'but I've managed to pick it up a bit. He said Marietta would like us to meet up with her in her dressing room.' And then to the stagehand he said, '*Merci, mon ami. Il n'y a rien que je voudrais mieux que d'avoir une conversation avec Marietta à nouveau.*'

The stagehand gave a toothless grin and signalling for them to follow him led the way backstage to Marietta's dressing room, saying chummily as he ushered them into it, '*L'Oiseau Chanteur d'Or sera bientôt avec vous.*'

'What did he say?' Harry demanded, frustrated at his inability to understand French.

'He said Marietta will be with us as soon as possible – which I take to mean as soon as she comes off stage.'

The stagehand closed the door behind him and Harry said, 'All right, you've made your point, you did learn to speak the lingo after all.'

Archie grinned. 'Put a beret on my head and give me a Gauloises to smoke and you wouldn't be able to tell the difference between me and a born-and-bred Frenchman.'

'I believe you because you're certainly not your average Kentish-born oysterman.'

'Ah, but my father was, so you can't disown me.'

Archie's complacency was annoying and Harry said with deep sincerity, 'Believe me, Archie, there are times when I'd like to give disowning you a damn good try.'

Archie was just about to make a suitably quelling riposte when the door flew open and Marietta burst in on them.

'Archie! Harry!' She ran up to them and threw her arms around Archie's neck, kissing him on both cheeks and then greeted Harry in the same way. 'How wonderful! *Comme c'est merveilleux!*'

As they breathed in the scent of her Evening-in-Paris perfume Archie grinned and Harry blushed as if he was an adolescent and not six foot tall and impressively broad-shouldered from years of ferrying sacks of coal on his back.

'We must celebrate with a fine meal and champagne, and Dolly and Vidal must come with us!' Marietta seated herself at her dressing table and began removing her stage make-up.

'Dolly and Vidal?' Archie wasn't overly keen on the thought of sharing the precious little time they would have with her, with a couple of people he didn't know.

'*Mais oui!* Dolly is my agent and also my friend, and Vidal is my . . .' Marietta tilted her head to one side, Titian-red waves and curls rippling waist-length as she paused in what she was doing. 'Vidal is my very gallant protector and you will come to like him very much.'

Harry, who had a huge capacity for taking things in his stride, said that he was sure he would. Archie, aware of how Marietta had always played fast and loose with whomever she was having an affair with – and in his experience she was always having an affair with someone – thought the chances of his liking Vidal were fairly remote, but that he would give the bloke a fair chance.

With her heavy stage make-up removed Marietta applied a light dusting of powder to her cheeks, fresh kohl to her eyes and ran the merest fingertip of Vaseline to gloss lips Harry had always thought were the most kissable he had ever seen.

'And now in a moment Vidal will be here and so you must tell me Oystertown news while I change out of my stage costume and into something far more suitable for the wonderful evening on the town the five of us are about to have.'

Rising to her feet she stepped behind an Edwardian clothes-screen that had seen better days. Seconds later a black corset that was a recognizable part of her stage costume was flung to rest over the top of it.

'Have you news of Jasper? News of Kim?' she asked as a pair of black fishnet stockings followed the corset. 'And how about Janna and Claudia? Is Janna still a nurse at Rose Mount, or is she back at the bakery slaving away for that old witch, Mrs Keam?'

'Neither. She is now a qualified St John's Ambulance VAD nurse and about six months ago she left for France under her own steam in order to begin working at a Voluntary Aid Detachment clearing station close to the Front, or as a nurse in a military hospital.'

From behind the screen there came a rustle of silk which Harry assumed to be an intimate item of lingerie being removed. Immediately the blood flooded his cheeks and also a more private part of his anatomy. He shot Archie a swift glance to see how a bloke who had never been known to have a romantic relationship was coping with the present situation, expecting him to be deeply uncomfortable.

To his surprise, if Archie was uncomfortable, his discomfort didn't show.

'And what about Jasper?' Marietta stepped out from behind the screen half in and half out of a low-backed, emerald-green evening dress. She turned so that Archie could zip it up for her. 'Is he still in the Merchant Service?'

'Last heard of he was on a Merchant Service ship regularly crossing the Atlantic and dodging U-boats in order to bring much-needed foodstuffs into Britain from America.'

He dutifully zipped her into her shimmering evening gown, wondering where she was expecting to be taken to by Dolly and Vidal; wondering if the three of them often went out on the town in a threesome.

Marietta seated herself at her dressing table again and scooped up her flame-red mane of hair, twisting it into a glossy figure-of-eight chignon that sat elegantly in the nape of her neck and which finished her transformation from a sexually provocative stage artist into a stunningly elegant young woman. Watching the transformation Archie realized Marietta had always had the ability to be anyone she wanted to be, the only common denominator being that she was always unpredictable and exciting.

The dressing-room door opened and a giant-sized, portly figure wearing the uniform of a French Army general squeezed into the already over-crowded dressing room. He was sporting an impressive handle-bar moustache and there was an equally impressive array of medals decorating his chest.

With a happy cry of, 'Vidal! Please allow me to introduce my friends from England!' Marietta ran towards him, hugging his arm, saying as she did so, 'Archie, Harry, my very, *very* good friend, General Vidal Favreau. Vidal, Archie and Harry. When I lived in England, Archie and Harry were always very kind to me.'

Had they been? Neither Archie nor Harry could remember a specific circumstance, but the name General Favreau was a name highly respected by all British soldiers and they were more than happy to be viewed by him in an admirable light.

'Then they must both accept my deepest thanks.' General Favreau's handshake was bone-crushingly strong, his voice a no-nonsense deep bass. 'I am here in order to invite Marietta to dine with me at The Trocadero. As I would like her friends to become my friends I would very much like it if you were to be my guests also.'

Although, like the general, Archie and Harry were in uniform, Archie's uniform was that of an army sergeant and Harry's was that of a lowly lance-corporal. They were going to make an odd-looking group at The Trocadero. However, as General Favreau was obviously uncaring of how odd they might look, Archie and Harry had no intention of worrying about it and, minutes later, the four of them set off for The Trocadero, Marietta with a white fur stole around her shoulders and her arm tucked into the crook of General Favreau's arm; Archie and Harry strolling nonchalantly along behind them.

Chapter Twenty-seven

It was the last day of June and Harry and Archie were no longer living the high life in Étaples with Marietta and General Favreau. Instead, they were two of several thousand British and French soldiers, all of whom were heading on trains to somewhere in northern France known as the Somme.

'And the Somme is where, together with our French allies, we are going to turn the tide of this damnable war for once and for all!' a British general had roared at them an hour earlier as they had assembled at the railway station, lining up platoon by platoon. 'Much of the hard work has already been done for you, for there has already been a week-long artillery bombardment of the German positions; a bombardment that will most certainly have worn down any morale and nerves the enemy may still be in possession of. You are about to take part in the biggest Allied offensive of the war so far, the long-awaited Big Push, the decisive engagement that will almost certainly bring the war to an end. May God go with you, and may you win a mighty victory!'

'What's the betting he isn't coming to the Somme with us?' Harry asked as, with difficulty, he and Archie eased themselves and their heavy packs into a compartment that still, at a pinch, had room for two more passengers.

There was much good-natured shuffling up and re-adjusting of packs in order to make room for them and the first thing

Archie noticed when, finally, he was seated and could look around at his and Harry's travelling companions, was how young they all were. He would have staked a week's wages that none of them had as yet reached their twenty-first birthday. An eager-looking, spotty youth who was seated opposite him and didn't look a day over sixteen said, reading Archie's thoughts, 'Wotcha, mate. I'm Charlie Brewer. I don't look eighteen, but I am. The bloke seated on your left is my older brother, Barney. He can't wait to get to the Front and biff the Boche, but he ain't too bright and so Ma wanted me to come along with him, so that I could keep an eye on him.'

It would have been easier to believe that elephants were pink than that Charlie was eighteen, but Archie thought it politic not to say so.

Instead, he said, 'Archie Wilkinson. Before I joined up, I was a barman.'

'Harry Slater,' Harry said, always happy to widen his social circle. 'Me and Archie are from Oystertown, on the south coast. We go back a long way and when we enlisted, we enlisted together.'

'And what were you in Civvie Street, Harry?' a freckle-faced boy who looked young enough to still be in school, asked.

'Me? I was a coal-man.'

Someone said his name was Colin Duggan and that in Civvie Street he had been a milkman. Others pitched in with their names and occupations. There was Bob Wallis, a farmhand from West Burton in the Yorkshire Dales. Joe Fletcher, a carpenter from Manchester. Alan Rycroft, a Bradford mill worker. Ernie Balfour, a postman from the Isle of Sheppey.

By the time the train finally began edging slowly out of the station they were on such easy, bantering terms with each other it was as if they had all gone to the same school. Harry got out the pack of well-used playing cards he never went anywhere without and embarked on a game of three-card brag with Colin Duggan. Bob and Ernie took the opportunity to have a little shut-eye. Joe took a small notepad with an attached pencil out of one of his breast pockets and resting it precariously on his knee began slowly and painstakingly to write a letter home.

Archie looked out of the window. The countryside they were now travelling through was lushly green, gently rolling and dotted with small woods. There was no sign here that France was fighting tooth and nail to keep herself free of German domination. All this would change, though, the nearer they got to their destination. He knew enough about French geography to know that the large area known as the Somme had been named after the river running through it. He wondered if they would be going as far as the river and, if they did, if they would stay this side of it, or cross over it. And, whatever their destination, he wondered how long it would be before they reached it.

Although the distance to where they were going was not far – Archie judged it to be only a matter of seventy or eighty miles – it was several hours before their agonizingly slow-moving, stop-and-start-for-no-reason train ground steamily to a halt.

'Where the heck are we?' Joe Fletcher asked as, fighting cramp in one of his legs, Bob Wilkinson struggled to his feet and lowered the window down.

From what sounded to be a distance of only two or three miles away came the unmistakeable roar and thump of artillery fire.

Bob squinted at the nearest signpost, shouting back over his shoulder, 'We're at somewhere called Albert.'

Down the length of the very long train the order came for them to prepare to disembark.

They stood up, heaving their packs onto their backs and stretching out cramped muscles.

'By the sound of that little lot we can only be a short march from the Front,' Alan Rycroft said as there came another earth-shattering roar of artillery fire. There was tension in his voice as well as excitement. 'I can't wait to engage with the Hun and give 'em the devil of a thrashing.'

He was eighteen and his innocence – for it was obvious he didn't know the reputation the Boche had when it came to warfare – was obvious. At twenty-nine, Archie felt almost paternal towards him but knew he couldn't allow such a feeling to show.

Instead, as they stepped off the train, he punched Alan matily on his upper arm, saying in the last seconds before Alan disappeared in the crush to rejoin his platoon, 'Be brave, but don't be rash. Live to fight another day.'

'Will do, Archie.' And with a jaunty grin Alan turned away to be immediately lost in a sea of khaki.

They were billeted that night in the small town of Albert which, they were told, was just shy of three miles from the Front; they would be leaving for the Front in the early hours of the morning.

Field kitchens put in an appearance. Welcoming hot tea was brewed. Tins of beef and vegetable stew were heated and spooned into mess tins. Cigarettes were lit and passed around. There were rumours that heavy artillery and mortars were going to be used for the destruction of enemy trenches and machine-gun and observation posts and that, as a consequence, going into battle next day was going to be a breeze.

Someone began playing 'Mademoiselle from Armentières' on a mouth-organ. Harry got out his pack of cards and, aware that if he didn't take prompt action he was about to be coerced into yet another game of three-card brag, Archie rose to his feet. 'I'm going for a mooch around town, Harry,' he said. 'I need to stretch my legs after so many hours sitting on a barely moving train.'

'Rubbish,' a member of their squad said good-naturedly. 'You're off to find a knocking-shop.'

There were many lewd shouts as to what he could do on their behalf when he found one. Archie, who had no intention of going anywhere near a brothel, said that he would do his best to oblige.

The town's shattered and destroyed streets teemed with British and French soldiers and, threading his way through a sea of British khaki and French slate-blue uniforms, he headed instinctively for the centre of the town and what remained of the town's square. Though he was crowded in on every side he was also, for the first time in as long as he could remember, alone, and being alone meant that he had the luxury of being able to think without having his thoughts disturbed.

He thought of Tilly and of how, by accepting him as family, albeit an illegitimate member of it, she had transformed his life. He couldn't imagine life now without her and without his half-siblings, Jasper and Janna. And Janna had brought so many other people into his life, people like Claudia and Marietta.

Thinking of Claudia and Marietta he shook his head in perplexity. He couldn't think of two girls more dissimilar and yet, together with Janna, the three of them were the best of friends, just as he was the best of friends with Jasper and Harry.

He wasn't a churchgoer, but as an insurance policy he always said a prayer for their safety every night before settling down to sleep. He turned a corner, narrowly avoiding being mown down by a lorry full of kilted Scots Highlanders. In front of him was what remained of the town square. It was dominated by a basilica that had been heavily shelled but, together with its tower, was still standing. On top of the tower, and a victim of the shelling, a gilded statue of the Virgin Mary hung precariously, head down.

A gnarled old man dug him in the ribs, saying, in French,

'Legend is, young man, that when the Virgin falls, the war will end.'

Archie grinned and responded in French, saying, 'Then I'm surprised no one has helped her on her way.'

As a flood of army vehicles roared into the square at one end and out of it at the other the old man cackled with laughter, and he was still cackling with laughter when he disappeared down one of the narrow crowded side streets.

Archie was suddenly filled with a sense of calm and well-being. Everything was going to be all right. How could it not be when so many thousands upon thousands of British and French troops would, in another twelve hours, be going over the top in crushing waves to put paid to the enemy once and for all?

There was the gleam of a small river at the end of one of the streets and he began making his way towards it, whistling as he went, hoping it was a tributary of the River Somme.

Later that evening, back with his platoon of twenty-five men, he was met by the news that they would be leaving for their positions at the Front at 0400 hours ready to be in position to go into the attack by 0730 hours and that he should get what shut-eye he could.

'And while you were out on the town,' Harry said, 'word came round that once we have engaged with the enemy, we are not to help any comrade who is wounded. It's the job of the stretcher-bearers to bring casualties back to the British lines.'

'Then you will just have to see that you jolly well don't get wounded,' Archie said, unbuttoning his army jacket and making himself comfortable for the night. 'Tomorrow may well be the most decisive day of the war. Best get your head down and get what beauty sleep you can.'

* * *

At 0500 hours they handed in their personal effects and were issued with steel helmets.

'Bleedin' 'ell,' Harry said graphically, 'I thought that this time we were going into battle with less to carry, not more!'

At 0600 and after each man had had a tot of rum poured into their mess tins – which they immediately knocked back – they started for the line, leaving Albert in artillery formation, platoons marching at fifty-yard intervals along pre-prepared routes.

Archie gritted his teeth, full of white-hot determination that when battle commenced, he would reach and cross the German lines, helping to push the enemy back in the direction of their homeland, a place he passionately felt they should never have left.

Harry suddenly said, 'The racket of British artillery fire we heard when our train pulled into Albert, was to wipe out Boche barbed wire and attack posts, wasn't it?'

Archie nodded.

'That should make things a bit easier, then, don't you think?'

'The only thing that would make things easier,' Archie said through gritted teeth as they began marching out of Albert, 'is for this bloody senseless war to be over.'

In less than an hour and along with thousands of other British and French troops they were directed company by company into previously dug front-line trenches that stretched for a daunting fifteen miles, with only 250 yards of no-man's-land separating them from heavily fortified German positions.

'What I hate most about this war is the perishing waiting,' Harry said with deep feeling. 'It gives you too much time to think.'

That Harry spent much time thinking had never previously occurred to Archie. He took out his pocket-watch. It was ten minutes past seven. Twenty minutes still to go until they once again faced rifle and artillery fire and anything else the demented Boche chose to hurl at them.

'And what do you think about, Harry?' he asked, vaguely curious.

'I think about Bessie, my old horse.'

To his horror Archie heard a definite break in Harry's voice.

'But isn't Pascal taking care of her?'

'He's *supposed* to be taking care of her, but you know Pascal. He's drunk more often than he's sober.'

'He isn't now he's married to Tilly.'

Archie looked at his watch again. It was now a quarter past seven. In another fifteen minutes they would, yet again, be facing the might of the most militant nation in the world and here the two of them were, possibly, having the last conversation they would ever have with each other, or with anyone else come to that, and all they were talking about was Harry's elderly cart-horse.

It wasn't a subject Harry had finished with. 'Promise me, Archie.' The wobble was still in his voice. 'You have to promise me.'

'If I survive and you don't, I promise I'll look after Bessie for you.'

He looked down at his watch again. The minutes were fast ticking away and it was now twenty past seven. A family of rats scuttled along the rear of the trench. Further down the trench someone was unsteadily saying the Lord's Prayer.

Silently Archie joined in with it, his stomach muscles tightening into crippling knots. As he mentally said the Amen, he felt a moment of sheer panic and clamped down on it hard. He had schooled himself to have no more feelings than a machine when he went over the top and it was a survival strategy he wasn't about to abandon.

At 7.30 a.m., true to form in being predictable, the German guns opened up. Along fifteen miles of British trenches whistles blew and under the roaring, deafening, pulverizing sound of German guns and artillery the order came from British high command that eleven divisions were to now begin walking at a steady pace towards the enemy with their rifles held in front of them, bayonets fixed and pointing upwards.

Under a deluge of shrapnel, rifle and machine-gun fire they obeyed orders and, never breaking ranks, were mown down in their thousands.

Harry saw Archie spin like a top and then fall as he was hit by enemy fire. He saw him lie perfectly still as men of their battalion either sprinted around him or leapt across him, and then, knowing he couldn't possibly return to Oystertown without Archie – that not in a million years could he tell Tilly that he had left Archie behind on a foreign field – he was seizing Archie by the shoulders, shouting his name like a banshee, willing him not to die with every ounce of strength that he possessed.

Chapter Twenty-eight

Christmas 1916

It was the bleakest Christmas Claudia could ever remember. It had been a grim, harrowing year and Christmas 1916, for thousands of families, would not be a joyous one. How could it be when husbands, fathers, sons, brothers and sweethearts would not be home for Christmas and, when the war finally ground to an end, as it surely had to do eventually, thousands upon thousands of firesides would be permanently without a beloved family member?

Claudia spent Christmas Day with her mother in the small and elegant apartment her mother lived in when acting in a supervisory capacity at what was now The Rose Mount Recuperation Centre for Wounded Officers. Where Xan spent it, Claudia didn't know and the fib she told her mother, that he was on emergency duty at the Swiss Embassy and that he sent his apologies and hoped to see her early in the New Year, just about covered his absence.

Celia said: 'Are you meeting up with Tilly and Pascal later? I forgot to tell you, when a few days ago I went up to London on the train to do some Christmas shopping, I visited the Royal Academy and one of Pascal's paintings was on display. It gave me such a funny sensation to see it. It was being very much admired and I had to fight the urge not to tell the little group standing in front of it that the artist was a family friend.'

Claudia smiled, glad that at least Pascal was doing well despite the war. How typical of her mother to be up to date with the art world. Then again Celia was always acquainted with the latest national news, such as that about the fiery, white-haired, dapper little Welshman, David Lloyd George, who, for nearly three weeks now, had been their prime minister.

As if reading her thoughts, Celia said: 'David is going to make a most volatile and interesting Head of State.'

Claudia had forgotten what a huge circle of her late father's political and titled friends had kept up a friendship with her mother. It suddenly occurred to her that if her mother wanted to marry again it would be very easy for her to do so. One of her father's closest friends had been Sir Edward Grey, who had been widowed ten years ago and had recently left the House of Commons after accepting a peerage. As Viscount Grey of Fallodon, he now sat in the House of Lords. If her mother had it in her mind to marry again, she rather thought Viscount Grey of Fallodon might well be at the top of any list of suitable second husbands her mother might be making.

An hour and a half later, Claudia was in Tilly's little cottage on Harbour Row catching up on Oystertown gossip before she ventured up to London on an afternoon train.

'Pascal is at the windmill,' Tilly said as, sitting at either side of a table covered with a fringed chenille tablecloth they waited for a pot of tea to brew. 'This cottage is too small and cramped for him to paint in and, even if it wasn't, the light here, at the bottom of the hill, isn't the same as the light at the top of the hill – and light is of prime importance to an artist, especially in the short, dark days of winter.

Her voice was filled with loving affection and Claudia felt a pang of envy, wishing she could truthfully talk to her friends and family about Xan in the same loving way Tilly so effortlessly spoke about Pascal.

'What is the latest news, Tilly?' she asked, changing the subject. 'I came from Rose Mount in a taxi – I couldn't face the thought of the long walk down the hill – and for such a small town I saw a frightening number of women wearing black armbands.'

By now the tea had brewed and Tilly poured it into two of her best china mugs, saying unsteadily, 'For a town as small as Oystertown we've lost far too many brave young men. Sparky Holden's mother received a black-edged telegram only a month ago – and I can remember when she proudly waved him off, his kit-bag over his shoulder. Rosie Gibbs is a widow now. A nephew of Ozzie's will never be coming home again. Mr and Mrs Keam's only son died in a military hospital at Étaples. The same military hospital Archie is in.'

Claudia sucked in her breath. Her mother hadn't said a word about Archie having been wounded, but then she wouldn't have wanted to darken what little Christmas spirit the two of them had managed to summon up.

With her stomach muscles cramping into knots, terrified of what the answer was going to be, she said, 'How badly was Archie injured, Tilly?'

'Not as badly as some poor blighters.' Tilly's voice was unsteady and her hand trembled as she added milk to her tea, for her relatively recently acquired half-brother had come to mean a great deal to her. 'He's lost an eye, and he's lost a leg from the knee down. What he hasn't lost, as far as I can tell from the letters he somehow manages to send home, is his optimistic disposition and, by the sounds of things, his ability to keep a room – although in this case, a hospital ward – effortlessly entertained.'

The two of them fell silent, aware of how fortunate they were that in a war being described in the newspapers as the most terrible in the whole of human history, the menfolk who mattered most to them, Jasper, Kim, Daniel, Archie and Harry, were all still alive and that of the five of them only Archie had been so severely wounded as to have lost a limb.

Fervently counting her blessings, Tilly said, 'No one I know imagined at the start of this war that it would go on for so long. We all thought it would be over in three months – perhaps even less – and yet here we are, two years and nearly six months later, and not a jot nearer to celebrating the end of it.'

As she waited for Claudia to pick up the conversational ball and bat it back to her – and as Claudia failed to do so – it occurred to Tilly that their conversation had become a little one-sided.

'Is anything the matter, Claudia?' she asked, suddenly concerned. 'You're very quiet. There's nothing wrong at the Nursing Home, is there?'

'No. Nothing.'

'Then what is it? Something is obviously wrong. When I had a glass of sherry and a slice of Christmas cake with Celia, she told me how very disappointed you were that Xan had been one of the diplomats detailed to man the Swiss Embassy's desk on Christmas Day and Boxing Day.'

'No, Tilly. It's nothing to do with Xan's Christmas duty rota.' Claudia's hands were clasped together so tightly her knuckles shone. After the merest beat of hesitation, she added, 'Although you are right in thinking it is to do with Xan.'

She hadn't intended confiding in Tilly. She hadn't intended confiding in anyone, but her marriage had become such a bleak, loveless wasteland she knew if she didn't confide in someone, she would go mad.

She took a deep, steadying breath and then crossed her self-imposed Rubicon by saying in a rush, 'Xan doesn't love me. I sometimes wonder if he ever has. He spends very little time with me and, when he does spend time with me, he shows no interest in me, is so curt and indifferent towards me, it breaks my heart.' Her voice was choked with tears she was holding back only with great difficulty.

With a pair of tongs Tilly put another lump of coal on the already glowing fire. She had never counted Xan Keller as being a friend, or even of his being an acquaintance, but now didn't seem the right time and place to say so.

Replacing the tongs on their stand in the hearth she said in deep concern, 'How do you see your future, Claudia? Although Xan isn't aristocracy, you are. And aristocracy doesn't divorce, although they do, of course, often lead separate lives.'

'Until the war is over and peace finally comes, I shall do some kind of war work and afterwards . . .' Claudia paused, deep in thought, and then said, 'Afterwards I shan't distress Mama by seeking a divorce, but I will never live with Xan again.'

The coals in the grate collapsed down a little, glowing red-hot.

'Who else have you confided in, or are thinking of confiding in? Will you be writing to Janna? She is still nursing at the Military Hospital in Étaples. I have her Nursing Home postal address.'

Tilly rose to her feet, walked across to a mahogany sideboard that served as a storage space for all kinds of miscellaneous items and retrieved her address-book, a pencil and a piece of notepaper. She wrote down Janna's Nursing Home postal address and handed it to Claudia. 'While I'm here, why don't I give you Jasper's address, or at least one that will find him. You never know when it will come in useful.'

'Yes, I'd like that. I believe he has a PO Box in Portsmouth. Kim mentioned it some time ago.' Claudia sighed. 'Time for me to go, Tilly. I don't really want to but needs must.'

When Claudia had kissed her goodbye and left for the train station in the same taxi that had ferried her from Rose Mount to Harbour Row, Tilly refreshed the tea in the teapot and sat down in order to think about what she'd just been told.

Claudia was lonely, anyone could see that. To think that she'd once assumed that the rich were shielded from such things by virtue of their wealth. Now she could see how much the young woman was suffering, and wished that she could come up with a ready-made solution for her. She smiled to herself. In a different world, Claudia's pale beauty would be perfectly complemented by Jasper's dark, handsome good looks.

But her nephew and the daughter of Lady Layard and the late Lord Layard? Even though Jasper and his lifeboat crew had, six and a half years ago, saved the lives of Lord and Lady Layard when the *Sprite* had capsized in heavy seas, she still didn't think such an aristocratic family would look kindly on a liaison between Claudia and an oysterman. She wondered if, when the war was over, class differences would no longer be so set in stone and doubted it. When it came to marriage and the fathering of children it would take more than a world war to change public opinion in the matter of crossing the age-old class divides.

Three hours after saying goodbye to Tilly, Claudia was walking up the steps of the Layard town house in Belgrave Square.

The familiar figure of Beamish was no longer there to greet her for conscription had caught up with him and, according to a postcard she had received from him some time ago, he was biffing the Boche on the French–German border.

His temporary, much older, replacement gave her a polite nod and said stiffly, 'Good morning, My Lady,' as she entered the house.

Seconds later she was walking up the wide curving staircase to the bedroom she still slept in when staying overnight in London. So much of her time was now spent at Rose Mount that she needed to have more clothes there, especially more warm winter clothes.

Declining the help of any of the maids she dragged a suitcase from the top of a wardrobe and began packing it with the kind of winter clothes that wouldn't look embarrassingly stylish and out of place at The Rose Mount Recuperation Home, or in Oystertown's high street. When she had packed all she thought she would need to get through the rest of the cold season it occurred to her that although she had selected half a dozen lace-edged handkerchiefs, she hadn't found any plain, larger-sized handkerchiefs. The kind of handkerchiefs it would be useful to have when she was working long hours helping out on one of Rose Mount's recuperation wards.

Serviceable-sized handkerchiefs meant men's handkerchiefs and she opened the dividing door that separated her bedroom from Xan's. It occurred to her that even in the early days of their marriage it was a room she had rarely entered. The top two adjacent drawers of the rosewood bedroom suite were the smallest in the room and the likeliest home for small items such as handkerchiefs.

She opened one of the drawers. It was full of immaculately paired socks and sock suspenders. Closing it, she opened the drawer next to it and was rewarded by the sight of crisply ironed, neatly folded Irish linen handkerchiefs. As she scooped them up the paper lining came out of the bottom of the drawer with them. Beneath it was a large white envelope.

Slowly she dropped her armful of handkerchiefs onto the bed and stood looking down at the envelope, her heart beating fast and light. The envelope was large for an ordinary-sized letter, and it wasn't bulky. Could it be a Will? But if Xan had made a Will without telling her, surely he would have left it with a solicitor for safe-keeping? Was there something inside the envelope that Xan didn't even want his solicitor to see?

She picked it up, surprised at how stiff its contents were. Not paper, then. And if it wasn't paper, then the other probability was an invitation card, or possibly a photograph.

Still with it in her hand she sat down on the edge of the bed. If it was a photograph – and she now felt certain that it was – then who was it a photograph of, that Xan had hidden it in such a way?

Convinced it could only be a picture of someone who meant a great deal to him; someone who meant so much to him that he had gone to the extraordinary lengths of keeping that person's photograph secreted away in a drawer that she, Claudia, would never normally have opened, she slid the contents from the envelope and, taking a deep steadying breath, looked down.

And what she saw made her heart slam hard against her rib-cage for it wasn't, as she had been expecting, a photograph of a woman. It was a photograph of a detailed drawing of the interior of a submarine, every feature highlighted and meticulously labelled.

For a few seconds she stopped breathing. Why would Xan be in possession of such a drawing? It made no sense. In her confusion she rose from the bed and went over to the window, the photograph still between her trembling fingers. This had to mean something, and in her heart she began to suspect it could be far, far worse than a casual infidelity. That would have been bad enough. But this was potentially of another order.

Why hide such a diagram? What had he been going to do

with it? Had he been going to pass it on to someone, and if so, who was that person? And, more to the point, what was their nationality and what were they going to do with it?

Trembling with shock and anger, she recalled the incident at the opera house. Now she saw those brief seconds in a whole new light. She'd dismissed the encounter as a mistake, but it all began to make a horrible kind of sense. Carl from Berlin would have every reason to hide plans of a submarine beneath the lining of a drawer – and Xan the Swiss diplomat was nothing but a sham.

Nausea rose in her throat. She needed to speak with someone she could trust and who knew about naval matters, which meant she needed to speak with Kim. The drawback to that plan of action was that Kim was currently on naval manoeuvres some-where off the coast of Norway, as far as she knew, and not contactable. Which left Jasper. And according to what Tilly had told her while searching for his address earlier that very day, Jasper was Second Officer on a cargo ship ferrying food from Canada to Britain across an Atlantic thick with German sub-marines. A letter to the Portsmouth PO address would take far too long in this case. There were, however, such things as telegrams. She could send Jasper a telegram asking him to meet up with her as a matter of urgency the next time he was in port – and asking him to tell her which port that would be.

With that decision made she felt as if a load had been lifted from her shoulders. Carefully she slid the photograph back in its envelope and replaced it beneath the drawer's lining paper.

That done, and the handkerchiefs replaced, she took a deep steadying breath and, with legs that were still unsteady with shock, left the house and flagged down a taxicab.

'The main post office, Trafalgar Square,' she said, stepping inside it, aware that the most important thing now was for her to send a telegram and to correctly remember the name of Jasper's ship.

Chapter Twenty-nine

May 1917

It had been a bitterly cold spring. Snow had fallen on and off in Northern France all through March and April and even though it was now the first week of May there were still patches of countryside lying beneath a light, but stubborn covering of it. In Étaples, on a hospital ward that was at the sharp end of things as both motor-ambulances and horse-drawn ambulances delivered horrendously wounded men, and men who needed 'patching up' in order to withstand the journey back to a hospital in Blighty, Janna was two hours into a long ten-hour shift.

She was on the point of snatching a precious five-minute break when two stretcher-bearers came to a halt in front of her and one of them said, indicating the dead body on their stretcher, 'Where do we take this poor sod, nurse?'

'To the mortuary. The entrance is at the back of the building.'

She was just about to turn away in order to enjoy what was left of her far too short tea break when she became aware that the stretcher-bearer who hadn't spoken, was a stretcher-bearer she knew – and knew well.

She sucked in her breath and Daniel said, 'You've recognized me? Sometimes people don't when I'm in my St John Ambulance uniform and on duty.'

She nearly said it would be impossible not to recognize him when they had been so close to one another, but realizing that now was not the time and place for such a reminder, said instead, 'The tin helmet you have acquired may hide your distinctive spiky ginger hair, but your freckles will always be a giveaway.'

He grinned. She looked very trim and neat in her grey and white nurse's uniform and he said impulsively, 'What time are you off duty, Janna? Whatever time it is I'll swop duties so that I'm off at the same time and we can go for a drink and something to eat. I know a bistro that serves omelettes round the clock.'

'Omelettes with real eggs?'

He pretended to be deeply indignant. 'Of course with real eggs! If we should run out of conversation – which I think extremely unlikely – we will be able to listen to the soothing sound of the bistro's hens as they happily root around in a yard at the back. It's a sound that reminds me of home and the windmill.'

At the thought of Oystertown and her own harbour-side home a lump formed in Janna's throat and it was all she could do to keep her voice from wobbling as she said, 'I'm not off-duty until eight o'clock.'

'Then from eight o'clock onwards I'll be waiting for you at the hospital gate.'

As he turned away from her, she saw for the first time the chevrons of a full sergeant on the sleeves of his jacket.

Her jaw dropped. How had Daniel who, as a conscientious objector, had seen his name, followed by the words *Frenchie Coward* scrawled in foot-high letters across the window of the shop he worked in, earned such a military promotion?

'Stop wool-gathering, Nurse Shilling,' her Ward Sister said, breaking abruptly into her thoughts. 'And I wouldn't have allowed your minute's chat time with Sergeant Picard if it wasn't that he is a highly decorated officer, having been awarded the Military Medal for conspicuous gallantry and devotion to duty under heavy fire, and as it is obvious from your conversation with him that he is also a long-time friend of your family.'

Janna stared at her. How could Daniel be a highly decorated officer when he was a conscientious objector who had opted for being a stretcher-bearer rather than a fighting soldier?

'And when you have finished dressing wounds, I'd like you to relieve one of the nurses presently on theatre duty.'

'Until what time, sister?' Janna's heart sank as she saw her evening with Daniel slide into a world of what-if and might-have-been.

'Until the sister on theatre duty decides she has no further need of you, or until the night staff come on duty. Now no more pointless questions. You are needed in Theatre Three.'

'Yes, sister.'

She headed for the sweep of stairs that led upwards to two more floors of wards and downwards to the operating theatres. As she scrubbed-up in the scrub room adjacent to operating Theatre Three she wondered again what the bravery had been that had earned Daniel such a prestigious medal for gallantry – and of how typical it was of him not to have told her about it.

The theatre sister broke into Janna's thoughts by asking her, now she was fully prepared, if she was ready to step into the operating theatre.

Janna nodded. For the next few hours Daniel wouldn't fill her thoughts, for all her attention would be focussed on the soldiers, nearly all of them in their teens or early twenties, who would be wheeled into the theatre on a trolley and then, after undergoing the amputation of a shell-shattered limb, or limbs, be wheeled out of theatre and into a recovery ward where they would begin the agonizing process of coming to terms with a life spent on crutches or in a wheelchair.

Étaples was a small working port sited on the estuary of the River Canche and the smell of fish hung over it in a way that reminded Janna of Oystertown. To her relief Daniel splurged on a taxicab to save them walking through its narrow streets, saying as the taxi trundled them at a sedate pace from the three-mile stretch of army hospitals and into Étaples proper, 'I've booked a table at an old and very respected bistro Napoléon is said to have dined in, although I wouldn't put money on it as it's hard to find any kind of a French hostelry he isn't said to have patronized.'

Janna laughed, happier and more carefree than she could remember being for a long time. She had expected to be taken to a halfway respectable wine bar, or even to a not-very-respectable wine bar, but it had never entered her head that she would be on her way to where once Napoléon Bonaparte was said to have dined.

When she was working long hours on the wards, she wore her hair coiled in a knot in the nape of her neck and she hadn't had the time to do anything different with it, other than pretty it up at each side with a tortoiseshell comb. She was in her very seldom worn 'best' dress, the dress that, ever since she had arrived in Étaples, had never seen the light of day. Made of midnight-blue crêpe de Chine it had a prettily scalloped neckline, short cap sleeves, an undefined waistline and a flounced hem that came to a halt a fashionable length above her ankles and over it she was wearing her warm St John Ambulance Brigade cloak.

It was almost dark in the back seat of the taxicab and Daniel's thigh was pressed hard against hers. She wondered if he was as aware of it as she was. If he was he gave no sign of remedying it by putting more space between them, and she had no desire to pointedly edge away.

As if reading her thoughts he turned to her with that wonderfully familiar expression, saying, 'I'd better warn you that the French Government has issued a directive to restaurants saying they can only serve two courses, only one of them meat.'

'I can survive that restriction just as long as one of the two courses is an omelette served with a green salad and thin French chips.'

He shot her his easy smile that, whenever he was with her, was never far away. 'I imagine that can be managed and, if it isn't, we'll find somewhere where it can be.'

For a reason she couldn't satisfactorily define their physical proximity in the darkness of the taxicab had been making her feel tense. Now she felt the tenseness vanishing. This was Daniel she was with. Daniel, who she had known for over seven years. Daniel, who she had once dreamed of having a romantic relationship with but had come to realize that was an adolescent's dream. Then they'd become proper friends, growing ever closer as they shared their commitment to their VAD training. She knew that closeness was undoubtedly more real than her girlish dreams. Now here they were, going for an evening meal together, and she loved the sensation of his hand being so very close to hers. Would this finally be the time that they would take their friendship a step further?

She wondered how she felt about that and, as the answer was she didn't know, shrugged the dilemma away. There would be time later to come to conclusions about what the evening they were enjoying together signified. For the moment, as the taxi came to a halt on the cobbles outside the bistro, she was simply going to enjoy to the full the evening that lay ahead.

Like nearly all the bistros in Étaples, Daniel's carefully chosen one had plain white-washed walls, a tiled floor and a handful of tables covered by gay red-and-white chequered tablecloths. There was a choice of two dishes chalked up on a blackboard. Neither was the promised omelette. There was, however, *Ragoût de lapin* and *Carbonnade*.

'So which is it to be?' he asked. 'Rabbit stew or beef and onions cooked in beer?'

'Beef and onions,' she said, adding, 'I had forgotten that being half-French a menu in French is no mystery to you.'

The waiter approached and Daniel ordered the *Carbonnade* and a pitcher of red wine. When that task was taken care of and a basket of bread still warm from the oven had been placed on the table, he said, 'Have you any news of Archie and how he's managing the desk job he wangled for himself in Boulogne? I understood he was there in order that, along with thousands of other disabled soldiers, he could board a hospital ship back to Blighty. How come he got himself a desk job and is still there?'

Laughter rose in her throat. 'Can you imagine Archie returning to Britain when the entire German army is rumoured to be lining up all along the French–German frontier and likely to pour over it at any moment?'

'No, I don't suppose I can, and especially not after the latest news.'

'Which is?'

'Which is that President Wilson has announced that in order to make the world safe for democracy, America is to take up arms.'

'Oh, thank God!' Her voice was unsteady. 'I know it was rumoured America was about to enter the war, but are you telling me it has actually done so?'

'According to news filtering through on today's grapevine it has. It will take time, though, to ship an American army across the Atlantic and when they finally arrive they will be arriving without any previous large-scale battle experience.'

'But even so, Daniel – Americans!' Janna's eyes shone with elation. 'They're going to make a huge difference. How can the Germans even *think* they can win this ghastly war if a country as huge as America is now batting in our corner?'

'I don't have an answer for you. In my limited experience, square-head Germans keep things so close to their chests it's impossible to know what they are thinking. However, I know what I'm thinking, and it's this. Do we stay with red wine for all of our meal, or do we switch to something lighter when it comes to the dessert?'

It wasn't what he was really thinking. What he was really thinking was that it was time he finally told Janna what he had been so close to confessing that day back home in Oystertown. He wasn't sure how long he could sit at the same table as her without blurting out that he loved her, and not just as a friend; he was actually in love with her, and in truth had been for a long while. Now here they were, both stationed in Étaples, hell on earth in so many ways – except for the most important one, her presence.

'Let's keep to red wine,' Janna said in answer to his question and then, seeing how pale he had suddenly become, she added anxiously, 'Do you need a little air, Daniel? If so, we could hold off on the meal for twenty minutes and go for a short walk.'

'No.' He was more clear-headed than he could ever remember being. Without a shadow of doubt he knew now what it was he needed in order to make his life full and complete. It was Janna. Why hadn't he realized he would never find deep, fulfilling happiness without her? The realization was so enormous, it dazed him.

'I'd like to have been able to give you news of Jasper,' Janna was saying, happily heedless that at the present moment Jasper was the furthest thought from Daniel's mind, 'but news from Jasper is always catch-as-catch-can. He's only ever conscientious about letting Tilly know he's still alive and then he leaves it up to her to pass the news on.'

'Janna –' His pulse was pounding and the roof of his mouth was dry. 'Janna, I . . .'

'And I haven't had an evening out like this since I can't remember when,' she continued as a steaming-hot casserole dish was placed in the middle of the table accompanied by a ladle indicating that they were to serve themselves from it.

Neither of them made the attempt, Janna because she wasn't sure if it was down to her to do so and Daniel because tucking into the beef and onion stew was the last thing now on his mind.

'Janna,' he began again, determined that as he had finally psyched himself up to tell her everything, nothing was going to deflect him. He reached across the table, taking her hands in his. 'Janna, I –'

The bistro's door rocked back on its hinges and a local man sporting a matted beard and wearing a fisherman's jersey and greasy trousers tucked into equally greasy boots strode in, waving a newspaper and bellowing, '*Il va y avoir des ennuis au Front! Nos alliés Russes ont déposé leur tsar!*'

There was a split second of stunned incredulity and then the bistro erupted in deafening speculation as to where the Russian action in deposing the Tsar might lead. The only person who didn't know what the fierce excitement was about was Janna, and Daniel had to bite back his urgent confession to say, having to shout to make herself heard, 'Word on the street is that there's going to be trouble at the Front! That our Russian allies have deposed their tsar!'

Someone began singing the '*Marseillaise*' and Janna had to remind herself that France had led the way where republicanism in Europe was concerned.

Determined not to be side-tracked by the clamour going on around them, Daniel embarked on his declaration for the third time.

'I love you, Janna!' He had to raise his voice to make it heard above the general clamour. 'I can't bear the thought of going through life without you. I've waited far too long to say it. Tell me you feel the same, please tell me.'

Janna drew in a deep, unsteady breath. The present moment was one that had indeed been a long time in coming and she had often wondered what her answer would be when, and if, it did. It wasn't that she didn't love Daniel. The problem in her head and in her heart was that she had also loved Jonah, and that there was a corner of her heart that Jonah would always occupy.

Daniel's hands tightened on hers and in a moment of wonderful clarity she realized she didn't have to stop loving Jonah's memory just because she now loved, and was loved by, Daniel. Jonah would always be a part of her just as, from now on, Daniel would always be a part of her.

Her hands were still trapped willingly in his. 'Yes!' She, too, had to raise her voice in order that he could hear her over the general din and shouts from the street of 'Long Live the Russian Republic!' followed by the deafening singing of the '*Marseillaise*'. 'Of course I feel the same! I love you with all my heart!'

'Truly?' He looked as if he couldn't believe such a blessing in life could possibly exist.

'Truly.'

Oblivious of the mayhem in the now packed-to-capacity bistro he rose swiftly to his feet and, narrowly avoiding a waiter, drew her to her feet and into his arms.

As he kissed her cheers and whistles from their fellow diners augmented those that were still, for a different reason, coming from the street. Daniel, who suffered from a redhead's ability to flush easily with embarrassment, didn't even blush. It had taken him an absurd amount of time to realize how very necessary Janna was to his happiness and the one thing now at the forefront of his mind was that he wanted to marry her as soon as possible.

Chapter Thirty

In Portsmouth a sombre-faced Kim strode in the direction of the harbour-side cafe where he had arranged to meet Jasper. Both of them were on a precious twenty-four-hour pass and Kim was certain Jasper would have preferred to be spending his time in a far more enjoyable manner than meeting up with him to discuss what, on the telephone, Jasper had described as being an urgent family matter best handled by the two of them face to face.

It had taken what felt like an eternity to coordinate their leave but Jasper had been determinedly elusive about the actual subject of their meeting.

When Kim entered the cafe, he saw that Jasper was already seated at a table in a quiet corner and that he was in uniform and had almost as much gold braid circling the cuffs of his Merchant Service jacket as he, Kim, had circling the cuffs of his Royal Navy jacket.

His stomach muscles tightened. Their lunchtime meeting was both necessary and, because they both had past history and not-so-past-history with Marietta, tricky.

Jasper was uncharacteristically cautious, checking all around them before he started to speak. 'You'd better sit down, Kim. This is as bad as it gets. Claudia's sent me a telegram and it's a matter of national security.'

Kim remained stony-faced. 'I was under the impression it was a family matter.'

Jasper nodded briefly. 'When you hear what I have to say you'll realize why this could not be done over the phone. The truth is, it's both. It's Xan. He's betrayed us – he's betrayed his supposed neutrality because he's about as Swiss as you or me. And, unforgivably, he's betrayed Claudia's trust.' A vein throbbed in his neck.

Kim swallowed hard and took the blow. He realized he was actually far from surprised. 'I believe you,' he said simply.

Jasper gave him a long look. 'I imagined you would protest his innocence. You were his friend, I understand?'

Kim pulled a face. 'Not as much as everyone assumed. But, in fact, this makes sense of something that happened a long time ago; in fact, it's been almost two years. Claudia convinced me it was nothing but now I see what must have been behind it.'

Jasper stared at him. 'What do you mean?'

Kim understood that he would have to recount the full tale. 'It was when Xan and Claudia went to the opera. They were in the theatre's foyer and a middle-aged man made a bee-line for Xan. Addressing him as Carl, he greeted him with the German phrase for "how are you?" Claudia told me that Xan's response was to say to the man – in English – that he had mistaken him for someone else. That he was Swiss, and that his name was Alexander Keller.'

'And?'

'And Claudia said there had been such a look of disbelief on the man's face that it took her all her self-control not to giggle. Her reading of the incident was that Xan had a double and she told me about it because she thought I would be as amused by it as she had been.'

'And were you?'

'No. Far from it.'

He took a silver cigarette case from his jacket pocket and flicked it open. After they had both taken a cigarette and lit them, he said, 'Xan has always claimed to have no living family other than Claudia and her mother, and those are relationships by marriage, not blood relationships. When he and Claudia married the only guests on his side of the church were his colleagues from the Swiss Embassy.'

Kim blew a plume of blue smoke into the air and then said, 'I think the person who goes by the name of Alexander Keller is duplicitous enough to get away with any subterfuge.'

'You could well be right. He's been smuggling photographs of detailed technical drawings of submarines to the enemy – and God only knows how long it has been going on for.'

They were silent for several minutes as they pondered the enormity of what it was they were on the brink of having to accept.

Finally, Jasper said, 'A very long time ago, even before their engagement was announced, Janna told me that when she had been visiting Claudia in Belgrave Square she had walked in on Xan searching through Lord Layard's desk drawers. His explanation was that Lord Layard wasn't at home and that he, Xan, had lost his pocket-watch. Since then, Janna has never fully trusted him, and neither have I.'

A pulse throbbed at the corner of Kim's jaw. 'I've come to believe Xan married Claudia in order to be accepted into the government circles her father moved in and to eavesdrop socially on the conversations of very highly placed government ministers. When my uncle was alive and a member of the Prime Minister's inner circle, he and Celia regularly gave dinner parties that were attended by highly placed government ministers and, as by then Xan was well on his way to becoming his son-in-law, by Xan as well. I was once a fellow guest with Xan when the Prime Minister was the Layards' guest of honour and, as you know, Asquith could be dangerously garrulous when relaxing in the company of people he believed were loyal and trustworthy.'

Never having been a guest at a dinner party, much less a dinner party graced by the presence of the Prime Minister, Jasper didn't know, but knew it would be distracting to say so.

Instead, he said, 'I'm assuming Xan went to great efforts to make your uncle's powerful friends, his friends?'

'Knowing what we now know about him, I think we can take that for granted. No one would imagine they had to mind every word they said when Lord Robert Layard's Swiss soon-to-be son-in-law was in their company – especially when that young man was a diplomat attached to his country's embassy.'

Deep in thought Jasper flicked ash from the end of his cigarette into a conveniently placed ashtray. That Xan Keller needed stopping in his tracks fast before he passed on yet more top-secret information than he undoubtedly already had was something that went without saying.

What also went without saying was that normal channels, such as walking into the nearest police station and making a statement as to Xan's activities, were not, in this case, viable. For one thing he, Jasper, was an oysterman-turned-merchant seaman, and an oysterman-turned-merchant seaman making allegations about a Swiss diplomat would be given very short shrift.

He explained his thoughts to Kim. 'And when – after God knows how long a time – eventually I was believed and Xan was arrested and charged with spying every daily newspaper would carry a banner headline announcing to the world that the supposedly Swiss son-in-law of the late Lord Layard was in fact a German spy. At one fell stroke Claudia and her mother would be ostracized, their lives ruined, and any action you were to take in their defence would mean you being tainted by association and your naval career being as good as over.'

Kim clenched his hands so tightly his knuckles were white. 'And no doubt he knows this. He's got us snookered.'

'Let's see. I won't let their good name be tarnished. It can't and won't happen.' Abruptly Jasper pushed his chair away from the table and rose to his feet. 'Let's continue this conversation out in the street. So far no one has been seated near enough to us to overhear what we are saying, but it's only a matter of time until they are.'

Out on the cobbled and crowded dockside and as seagulls screeched above their heads, Kim said tersely, 'Why won't it happen?'

'It won't happen because I know a way of not allowing it to happen.' There was grim certainty in Jasper's voice. 'And trust me, Kim. You're better off – and safer – not knowing what that way is.'

Daniel spent all his spare moments wondering if Janna would want a church wedding, or if she would be happy for his army chaplain to marry them or perhaps, as this was France, if the local mayor would agree to perform a civil ceremony. Then he would remember that he had not formally asked her, and that he had better do so as soon as possible. They had wasted enough time as it was.

He'd imagined revisiting the bistro, and this time they would have the rabbit, or perhaps there would be omelette on the menu after all. As it turned out, the occasion had nothing like such a romantic setting. The war was to blame, of course. Each time they arranged to spend the evening together there would be a new consignment of injured troops and he would be run off his feet, while Janna worked back-to-back shifts.

Finally, they grabbed a moment together by the side door to the medical supplies hut, and shared a welcome cigarette. 'This tastes disgusting,' he'd said with a broad grin, and Janna had agreed, even while exhaling the smoke.

'Shall we get married soon?' he asked, as if simply following on the same conversation.

'Of course,' she answered at once – and then they looked at one another, and burst into uproarious laughter.

When the laughter had ended, they carried on holding one another's gaze and then they were kissing passionately, the cigarette and everything else forgotten. Nothing else mattered except them being together.

'Do you very much want to be married in church?' he asked as, with arms still around her he looked down into her face, a face he knew he would never tire of looking at. 'Because I think that in an Anglican church banns have to be read for three consecutive Sundays before the wedding day, and I'm not even sure there is an Anglican church in Étaples.'

It suddenly occurred to him that there was a puzzled expression in her eyes. Had he come to a wrong assumption? Was she perhaps not an Anglican, but a Roman Catholic? And didn't Roman Catholics only marry Roman Catholics?

He could feel beads of sweat breaking out on his forehead. If that was the case, and as he doubted if he had even been baptized, he wondered if it was an omission he would have to remedy.

Reading his thoughts she said, 'I think as your father is French and you have a French surname, the most uncomplicated way for us to be married would be to go to the town hall and ask if the Lord Mayor will join us together as man and wife in a civil ceremony.'

'And if he will, will you be happy for him to do so? You won't miss not having a church ceremony with a best man and bridesmaids and being showered with confetti?'

'Absolutely not.' Her heart had begun racing like a steam train. 'It's being married to each other and the promises we will make to each other that are important and, for that, all that is needed is a wedding ring.'

'And I'm going to buy one when, first thing tomorrow morning, we are en route to the town hall to speak with the Lord Mayor.'

It was a plan of action Janna could find no fault with and as he held her close against his chest, she counted herself the most fortunate young woman in the world.

Chapter Thirty-one

October 1917

The fighting in Flanders continued unrelentingly. All through August and September it had rained almost non-stop and the ground was churned into a knee-deep – and often thigh-deep – sea of mud by flailing hooves and thousands of booted feet. It was mud that struggling horses suffocated in. It was mud that, if help couldn't get to them, wounded men choked to death in. And it was mud that made stretcher-bearers' jobs near impossible. In good conditions four men could carry a wounded man on a stretcher. After heavy rain –and it had rained solidly now for weeks – the resulting mud took a minimum of ten men, and sometimes twelve or fourteen men, to bring a critically wounded man to the nearest advanced aid post. And it was a task which, more often than not, took place under heavy enemy shellfire.

Since Archie had lost a leg below the knee and, on being discharged from hospital, had wangled himself an army desk job in Boulogne, Harry hadn't formed another close friendship. Something deep within him recoiled at getting to know a stranger and then losing them to the random chance of war. All those young men – boys, really, that he and Archie had befriended just before the Somme – where were they? He'd heard that Rycroft was killed, but knew nothing about the rest. He didn't fancy their chances.

All his concentration had been on decimating the enemy, which he did with spectacular and furious tenacity. To no one's surprise but his own he had by now received swift promotions through the ranks, becoming first a lance-corporal, then a corporal, and finally a sergeant in charge of a platoon of twenty-five men.

He didn't have a family he could let know about his promotions. Tilly was the nearest thing to family that he had, and so it was to Tilly that he sent a postcard with a sentence he hoped would not be blacked out by the censor: *TRUST YOU AND PASCAL ARE BOTH WELL. I'M STILL FINE AND DANDY AND BIFFING THE BOCHE EVERY CHANCE I GET.* He then signed it with a flourish, underlining the word sergeant and adding a jaunty exclamation mark for good measure.

Never, in all his life, had he so longed for home, for if the sea of drowning mud sucked injured men down into it to their deaths it did the same, and in far greater number, to the horses. And it was the suffering of the horses that tore at Harry's heart. The thought of Bessie, his old, gentle coal-cart horse ever suffering in such a way was a constant nightmare to him and he had sent a three-line letter to Pascal about the necessity of his keeping her well-hidden if the army's local horse procurer paid Oystertown a surprise visit.

For the last three years he had survived the battlefield hell he had been plunged into by, in his imagination, walking the streets of Oystertown. He would start off outside the windmill, where, in his mind's eye, he would exchange pleasantries with Pascal and Tilly, and ask after Marietta. Then, with eyes closed, he would in his imagination walk the short rough path that led from the windmill to his favourite viewpoint at the top of the Heights.

There, for the length of time he judged it would take him to smoke a Woodbine, he would visualize himself sitting with his arms hugging his knees, imagining the world was still at peace and there were no such obscenities as wars and eighteen-pounder field artillery guns capable of cutting down hundreds of men in mere minutes.

Another favourite method of escape from the present grim reality was to remember Janna's and Daniel's wedding which had taken place a couple of months earlier. Daniel's army chaplain had performed the ceremony, Étaples' Registrar had been there to legalize it, and he, Harry, had acted as Daniel's best man. The thought of marriage had never previously tempted him, but as Janna and Daniel had exchanged vows their faces had been so radiant with the love they felt for each other he had, for the first time, wondered if, in opting for life as a bachelor, he was seriously missing out on something and if it was time he, too, found someone to share his life with.

Perhaps, when the war was over, Janna and Daniel would invite him to be a godfather when their first baby put in an appearance. This last thought always cheered him, for he was fairly sure it was customary for a baby to have, as one of its names, the name of its godfather. It didn't look as if he was going to marry and have children of his own, but he would drop the nod to Daniel and Janna and make sure their firstborn son's second name was Harry. Daniel Harry Picard had, he thought, a fine, noble ring to it.

In many respects married life didn't make a great deal of difference to Janna's and Daniel's lifestyle. All nurses were expected to avail themselves of accommodation in one of the nursing home blocks that had been built within walking distance of the vast complex of army hospitals in Étaples and similar single-sex arrangements applied to male nursing staff. Their only opportunity for lovemaking was when they managed to synchronize their rotas so that they both had a two-day off-duty pass on the same two days. When that happened – and it happened far too rarely – Daniel borrowed a motorbike that one of his fellow stretcher-bearers had acquired and, with Janna on the pillion, they would head to a village seven miles behind the front line that the war had seemingly forgotten about. There they would book into a small guest house where they were always the only guests and where, in an overgrown garden, there was a tree-shaded pond on which several ducks glided and goldfish swam.

Their old-fashioned, brass-headed bed faced a casement window with diamond-leaded panes down which heavy rain now streamed. Daniel regarded the teeming downpour with his jaw clenched, knowing what a murderous swamp the front line was being turned into. Even worse, the ground that wasn't swamp was pockmarked with deep shell holes which the relentless downpour would be fast turning into death traps and where, if a man fell into one of them, the more he struggled to regain anything resembling solid ground, the more the sea of mud would hold him fast, sucking him further down into it.

For stretcher-bearers the added weight of the body on the stretcher – a stretcher which had to be carried shoulder-high across ground on which enemy shells continually rained – ensured that every stage of retrieving a wounded man was a death-defying one.

It wasn't, however, a risk he was running today. Today he was a precious few miles behind the front line – a front line that after three years of bloody, agonizing, senseless war had barely moved – and he and Janna were in each other's arms and about to make love yet again.

He was just about to roll her lovingly beneath him when he heard the familiar sound of an army motorbike skidding to a halt on the cobbles below their bedroom window. The rider didn't turn the bike's engine off. He simply shouted loud enough for Daniel – and anyone else who happened to be in the guest house – to hear him, 'All leave cancelled, Picard! You and every other Conchie medic is needed at your allocated front-line dressing-station with a fully packed medical pannier! And make sure your pannier is packed to the gunnels with dressings. According to the rumours coming down the line you're going to need every one of them!'

He slewed his motorbike around, shouting as a parting shot: 'And if the lady you're with is a nurse you need to get her back to her hospital in Eat Apples PDQ. She's going to be needed there just as urgently as you are needed at your front-line dressing-station.' And with a loud revving of his engine, he sped out of the yard leaving a plume of blue smoke hanging in the air behind him.

By the time Daniel had turned away from the window Janna was halfway to being fully dressed.

'Is Étaples often referred to as Eat Apples?' he asked as she zipped herself into a navy serge skirt and he began hurriedly pulling on his stretcher-bearer uniform.

'I don't know if it's widely referred to as Eat Apples.' She pulled a Fair Isle sweater over her head, adding as she pushed her arms into its prickly, but comfortingly warm, sleeves, 'But I do know it is how the medical staff on the wards refer to it.'

She pulled on a French army jacket she had bought cheaply in an Étaples flea market, hauled on a pair of sturdy second-hand boots that had come from the same place and entered Daniel's arms for the longest, deepest, most passionate parting kiss imaginable.

For Marietta, General Favreau and Étaples was a distant memory as, by now, was the French colonel who had provided her with a spacious, light and airy apartment in one of the smart houses to be found on the tree-lined Place Denfert in the fourteenth arrondissement of Paris and who had then been posted to the French–Belgian border, leaving Marietta with a year's rent conveniently fully paid.

The elegant apartment was on the hugely sought-after second floor and possessed herringbone parquet floors, a vast marble fireplace, double doors and floor-length windows that opened onto a narrow balcony. There was also a *chambre de bonne* on the building's top floor – a maid's room with a dormer window in which Marietta had speedily installed a pretty seventeen-year-old French girl, Léonie, as an all-purpose maid. To Léonie's delight Marietta had given her a smart black dress to wear, plus a pretty lace apron and cap and, from that moment on, Léonie had thought Marietta the most wonderful woman in the world.

The war had ensured there was no one from what Marietta thought of as being her old life who was still a part of her life. A little over three years ago German troops had crossed the Belgian border in the narrow gap between Holland and France. As they were clearly intent on occupying Paris, Dolly had high-tailed it for the nearest port. There he had paid an exorbitant sum of money to a French fishing-boat skipper who, reassuringly indifferent to the risk of attack from German U-boats, had promised he could land him on the blessedly English side of the English Channel.

Marietta hadn't blamed him, but neither had she been tempted to emulate him. She had never run from danger and wasn't about to start doing so now, especially when the last time she had heard from Daniel he was still in Flanders working as a stretcher-bearer, something that meant he was constantly under enemy shell-fire.

She wondered if he had thought to name her as his next of kin if, as was only too likely, he was blown to smithereens by Boche artillery shells as he sprinted into no-man's-land, retrieving wounded men from the crucifying barbed wire of the front line. Or would he have named their father, in faraway Oystertown, as his next of kin? There was simply no way of knowing and so speculating about it was pointless. All she could do was pray he was still alive.

It had taken Jasper what he felt was far too long to wangle some more leave, but as soon as he was back on British shores he could put his plan into action. His overwhelming instinct was to somehow make his way to Oystertown, for a long overdue reunion with Tilly, but a different kind of duty called. So he boarded a crowded train into London and, on his arrival at Waterloo and from a public telephone on the station's concourse he dialled the Layards' familiar Belgrave Square number.

'It's Jasper Shilling,' he said when Beamish's replacement answered the telephone's ring. 'I'd like to speak with Mrs Keller, please.'

Before Celia's new and relatively inexperienced butler could reply that Mrs Keller was not at home, there came the click of an extension receiver being lifted and Xan said, blatant curiosity in his voice, 'Can I perhaps pass a message on to Claudia, Jasper?'

'Yes. Would you tell her I have a few days' leave and Kim has phoned me suggesting I might like to spend a day of it down at Portsmouth. There's a technical problem with the submarine whose design he is largely responsible for and as the submarine is in dry dock there will never be a better time for Claudia to have a close-up view of it.'

Xan frowned. To be shown around a submarine wasn't a desire Claudia had ever expressed to him. However, that was neither here nor there if there was a possibility that he could talk himself into being invited in her stead. Whether, unseen by Kim or anyone else, he would then be able to take any photographs of the submarine was another thing entirely, but it was certainly a possibility worth pursuing.

'I'm afraid Claudia is out on what she anticipates being a day-long shopping jaunt with a woman-friend. Is there any chance I could have a close-up view of the submarine instead?' he added, trying to make it sound as if such a request was only natural curiosity.

Jasper hesitated, but his hesitation was minimal for there was nothing he wanted more than to be on his own with the man he knew for a certainty was a German spy and now, at last, he was being given the perfect opportunity.

'If you want to keep me company down to Pompey and back you are very welcome.' His voice was lazily casual.

'Pompey?'

'Pompey has been Portsmouth's nickname from time out of mind. As I don't fancy the drive I'm going down by train. If you are up for joining me – and as I always have a pack of cards on me – we can have a few hands of poker on the way.'

'It sounds a good idea.' Xan, who suspected that Jasper was a highly skilled poker player, privately thought the idea was ghastly but had no intention of saying anything that would scupper their new-found chumminess.

'There are trains departing from Waterloo to Portsmouth on the hour, every hour, and the journey only takes just under two hours, sometimes a fraction less.' Jasper glanced down at his watch. 'The next train is due to leave in forty-five minutes. Forty-five minutes will give you plenty of time to get from Belgrave Square to Waterloo. I suggest we meet beneath the station's clock. With luck, when we board the train, we will be able to get seats facing across a table suitable for a game of cards.'

And without waiting for Xan to either agree, or disagree, he replaced the telephone receiver on its rest in the reassuring certainty that wild horses wouldn't prevent Xan Keller from being seated opposite him on the next train bound for Portsmouth.

Chapter Thirty-two

Harry was in a deafening, thundering hell somewhere to the west of a village – or what was left of a village – called Poelcappelle. Its villagers had had no other choice but to abandon it, taking with them, on carts and prams, what household possessions they had been able to rescue and with the family goat, or cow, tethered and trailing along behind them.

Harry neither knew, nor cared, just whereabouts Poelcappelle was. He only knew he didn't want to be there. There hadn't been a day in October when rain hadn't fallen in sheets and the ground that he and his men were now struggling across was a jelly-like, voracious swamp interspersed with six- and seven-foot-deep shell holes filled to the rim with polluted water. Making the nightmare even worse was the way that taking a step was to sink to the knees in the mud and the effort of dragging a leg out of the mud in order to take a further step needed super-human willpower and determination.

On his right-hand side and through the heavy sheets of rain a farmhouse loomed. Fifty yards or so away from it a rain-drenched elderly woman was struggling to make a loop in a long length of stout rope in order to retrieve someone, or something, that had fallen into one of the shell holes. There was no sign of anyone coming to help her. And then Harry heard the sound of desperate, terrified whinnying. Realizing it was a horse the woman was trying to ease out of the shell hole before it broke its legs struggling to get out, or pulled her down into the shell hole with it, he asked his lieutenant to cover for him while, under the pretence of answering a call of nature, he broke ranks.

As the mud-soaked ground shuddered beneath his approaching feet the woman whirled round to face him.

Seeing the alarm in her eyes Harry came to a halt several yards away from her and raised both hands to signal that he meant her no harm.

'I've come to help with the horse,' he said, trying to get over the shock of discovering that far from being elderly, the woman he was facing looked as if she was somewhere in her mid-thirties. 'Not to take him away from you,' he added in swift reassurance as the alarm in her eyes deepened, 'but to help you get him out of the shell hole before he fatally injures himself and has to be shot.'

Instead of being reassured she backed away from him and it suddenly occurred to Harry that she had no English and hadn't understood a word he had said. As he had no French, other than ordering a beer in one of the many local taverns, it seemed that unless he resorted to sign language the two of them were at an impasse – and all the while they were at an impasse the terrified horse was rolling its eyes and growing more and more agitated.

He indicated that he needed her to hand him the rope she was holding and, apprehensively, she did so.

Praying he would be able to summon up the necessary strength to help the horse out of the shell hole Harry swiftly made a loop at one end of the rope, finished it with a bowline knot and then, murmuring softly and reassuringly to the horse as he did so, he hooked the loop over the head of the terrified animal.

'It's a knot that won't tighten when we pull on it,' he said reassuringly to the watching woman, hoping the tone of his voice would compensate for her not understanding English. 'Now all we have to do is use our combined strength to help the horse help itself. All right?'

'*Il s'appelle Napoléon!*'

It was so out of context of the present situation that for a moment he wondered if she was quite right in the head.

Seeing he hadn't understood, she indicated the horse. '*Napoléon!*' she shouted again. '*Il s'appelle Napoléon!*'

Realization that she was referring to the horse, and not to Napoléon Bonaparte, finally dawned and, together, they began the difficult task of easing the horse out of the shell hole and once more into the land of the living where immediately it collapsed, lying on its side, panting heavily and rolling its eyes.

Harry, who as well as being saturated with rain was also panting, hunkered down on his heels beside it. At last, when he judged himself capable of speech, he said, 'At home in England I have an elderly mare called Bessie. A friend of mine is taking care of her while I'm here, in Flanders.'

With a great deal of effort Napoléon struggled up on his legs and Harry didn't add that he doubted if Bessie would still be alive by the time the war was over and he was back home in dear old Oystertown. His only consolation where Bessie was concerned was that she would never suffer as thousands of horses at the Front suffered, bleeding and dying in unspeakable agony for reasons they couldn't possibly understand.

She squatted down beside him and, as if it was the most natural thing in the world, took hold of his hand.

Harry wasn't accustomed to unsolicited expressions of female compassion and quite suddenly – and embarrassingly – he knew himself to be on the brink of tears. Blinking them away before she should be aware of them, he clumsily rose to his feet, saying awkwardly, 'I have to go. I have to catch up with my platoon before I'm missed.'

He didn't add that if he couldn't catch up with his platoon he might eventually be shot for desertion, although it occurred to him that it was an unpleasant possibility. He added in a rush, 'My name is Harry. I come from a small English town called Oystertown, and I'm a coal-man.'

He could tell that apart from his name she hadn't understood anything he had said, and then she said with a shy smile, '*Je m'appelle Juliette.*'

Juliette. It was a beautiful name. A name Harry knew he would never tire of hearing, or saying. Minutes were ticking by and with every minute it became more likely that his absence from his platoon would be noticed and that he would be put on a charge, or worse. He had to leave her, and he had to do so immediately.

'I'll be back, Juliette!' His throat was so tight it hurt. 'I promise.'

And then, before she should see how close to tears he was, he turned on his heel and broke into a sprint to catch up with his platoon, hoping with all his heart that the promise he had made to her was a promise he would be able to keep.

Once out of Portsmouth Harbour railway station Jasper said to Xan, 'The harbour complex is gigantic and according to Kim the submarine is in a dry dock a couple of headlands away.'

'Then how do we get to it?'

Important as it was for Xan to get all the information possible about any of Britain's shipping, whether Royal Navy or Merchant Service, he didn't relish hiking over what, in October, would be windswept headlands in order to get a close-up view of them and, even more importantly, photograph them.

'We hire a small boat with a motor. I'm a First-mate in the Merchant Service, and I'm in uniform. There won't be any problems. You're not afraid of the open sea, are you?'

'Not in the slightest.' It was a lie. Xan had never previously gone out on the open sea in anything as small as a motorboat and, if the truth were told, he didn't particularly want to do so now.

He was wearing a heavy tweed coat and he dug a hand into one of its deep pockets, closing it around a camera so small its main selling point was that it could, if necessary, fit into a waistcoat pocket. Small as it was there was still no way that, in front of Jasper, he could take the kind of photographs he was determined to take of the submarine. It was something that didn't matter, for in another of his large coat pockets was a German Army Service pistol complete with a silencer and Jasper, once he had steered the motorboat within sight of the dry dock, would be superfluous to requirements.

Jasper could imagine what was going through Xan's head only too well, and that Xan had a weapon somewhere about his person was something he took for granted. He, Jasper, didn't have a weapon, and nor did he think that after all the years he had spent successfully taking on all-comers in back-room boxing rings he would need one now.

His First Mate Merchant Service uniform enabled them to leave the harbour without being boarded and searched by harbour officials and once out in the open sea they began heading towards the nearest of the headlands.

As they rounded the headland the waves grew bigger, sea-spray stinging their faces, and Xan became fidgety.

'You're taking the boat too far out to sea.' There was an unmistakeable edge of panic in his voice. 'When Kim told you about the submarine, he said it was in a dry dock.'

The harbour was now hidden from sight by the headland they had rounded and Jasper cut the engine saying as, without power, the boat dipped and rolled, 'I'm afraid I've not been straight with you, Xan. I would no more enable you to have access to British naval information – information I know you would immediately pass on to Britain's enemies – than I would fly to the moon.'

Xan sucked in his breath, his nostrils whitening, his hand tightening on whatever it was that he had in another of his overcoat pockets. Jasper saw the movement and, taking no chances as to what it signified, sprang towards him.

The boat rocked perilously. Xan cried out in alarm and dropped the pistol in order to grab something solid and steady himself, only there was nothing there to grab. As Jasper clenched his fist intending to punch Xan hard on his jaw, Xan took a hasty step backwards, lost his balance, tottered and, with a cry of alarm, fell over the side of the boat.

Jasper swore. Neither of them were wearing a life jacket and although he was a strong swimmer, he had no way of knowing how strong a swimmer Xan was. He looked towards the shore. There were no other small boats to be seen, and nor were there any groups of spectators on the cliff-top following the drama with binoculars.

The pistol Xan had been holding was now sliding from side to side in the bottom of the boat and Jasper scooped it up and tossed it overboard. As it immediately sank from sight, he cupped his hands around his mouth.

'Make up your mind what it is you are going to do!' he shouted. 'Sink, or swim back to the boat! And if you choose to swim back to the boat, I'll knock you into oblivion with a left hook that will render you senseless and hand you over to the Portsmouth Naval Police who will throw you into a cell until you stand trial on the grounds of being an enemy agent. After which you will no doubt be sentenced to death by hanging!'

'*Geh zum Teufel!*'

Jasper didn't have a word of German, but correctly assumed that Xan was telling him to go to the devil.

He shrugged. It wasn't the first time he had been given that instruction, but what those giving it didn't appreciate was that he was totally indifferent to it.

As Xan continued to tread water and hurl what were no doubt more insulting suggestions to him in German Jasper thought of the consequences if Xan were to return to the boat and if he was to haul him back into it. Knowing how precise and slow the law could be, it wasn't a foregone conclusion that Xan would be swiftly arrested and thrown into a cell until he could stand trial. Xan had cultivated many influential people as friends during his marriage to Claudia, friends who no doubt would be totally disbelieving of his being a spy and who would give him glowing character references in court. And the likeliest outcome of that would be his being given bail.

If that happened, before you could snap your fingers, Xan could obtain a passport and identity papers under another name – a very Swiss name – and would continue with his duplicitous life as a German spy.

It would then be Claudia and Celia the press would hound, for they would be seen as being guilty by association. Overnight, where the high society circles they had always moved in were concerned, they would become pariahs, their names and photographs on the front pages of the more lurid tabloid newspapers and, in responsible newspapers such as *The Times*, there would be veiled speculation as to whether the late, previously highly respected Lord Robert Layard had been criminally lax in not realizing the true nationality and loyalties of his son-in-law. The very scenario that he and Kim had discussed, and which they were so keen to avoid at all costs.

By now the heavy tweeds Xan was wearing were not doing him any favours. Jasper would have laid bets on Xan being a strong swimmer, but it was obvious that Xan's water-saturated clothing was hampering his efforts to stay afloat and, gritting his teeth, he threw one of the motorboat's lifebuoys towards him. He had to give the man a chance. What Xan did with that chance was up to him.

'And what are you going to do if I grab hold of it?' Xan shouted, hysteria in his voice as the lifebuoy fell so near to him he had only to stretch out his hand to take hold of it.

'I'm going to see you stand trial as a spy, you traitorous bastard!' Jasper shouted, grateful there were no other boats within earshot. 'I'm going to have the satisfaction of knowing you will hang!'

'Like hell I will!'

And ignoring the lifebuoy Xan turned clumsily around in the water and began to swim. He swam away from the lifebuoy; away from the boat; away from the land and away from a death that wouldn't be of his own choosing.

Jasper continued to watch him until his blond hair could no longer be seen and until there was no likelihood of someone on the cliff-top, or on the shore-line, alerting the coastguard of a swimmer in difficulties far out at sea.

Only when Xan had been lost to sight for over half an hour did Jasper rev the motorboat's engine into life, retrieve the lifebuoy and begin heading back in the direction of the harbour. If the harbourmaster, or anyone else, remembered that there had been two men aboard the boat when it had left harbour he would say Xan had become violently seasick once they had reached the open sea and that he had insisted on being put ashore at the first available opportunity, further along the coast.

He would then telephone Claudia, telling her the same thing. If, and when, Xan's body was washed ashore, there would be no marks on it to indicate foul play and, with luck, when the coroner gave his verdict, it would be one of death by misadventure.

Chapter Thirty-three

December 1917

The war was now well into its fourth year and to universal dismay was showing no signs of coming to an end. Coal rationing, in a winter where snow had fallen particularly early in many areas, was causing great hardship and the entire country was war-weary for just as fighting died down in one area of northern France, it would break out in another.

In late November it had done so on a mammoth scale in and around the French town of Cambrai when, in the half-light of a bitterly cold dawn and backed up by both British and Canadian troops, three hundred and seventy-eight British tanks had rolled across no-man's-land. The subsequent battle with German forces had raged for nearly a week and the lists of men who had fallen now topped a horrendous forty-five thousand.

'It seems as if there will be no end to it,' Janna said to a fellow staff nurse as, in the kitchen of the nurses' home in Étaples, she checked on a Christmas plum pudding that was taking an unconscionably long time to cook through. 'Word is that despite our soldiers having the benefit of being backed up by several battalions of the Tank Corps – and I got that information from a wounded colonel being loaded into an ambulance en route for the docks and a hospital ship to Blighty – tanks aren't manoeuvrable enough to cross ground riddled with trenches seven feet deep and six feet wide. And the result,' she continued, judging that the pudding needed at least thirty minutes more steaming time, 'is every hospital corridor is lined head to tail with tank crews on stretchers awaiting urgent surgery. If I take a twenty-minute break, will you keep an eye on the water in this pan and make sure it doesn't boil dry?'

'Yes, just as long as you do the same for me when you get back.'

Five minutes later Janna was seated on an otherwise empty bench in the hospital's grounds. Time on her own in which to think was hard to come by for she shared a room with three other girls and there were nearly always two or more of them in the room, chattering like a mob of starlings when she would have preferred a little time on her own. Even opting for an empty bench in the grounds had its risks for if anyone saw her seated there alone, they would assume she was in need of company and would sit down next to her in order to have a friendly chat.

Today, though, she was left in peace to enjoy a cigarette – a bad habit she had picked up and was determined she would knock on the head the day the Allies emerged victorious and the world was mercifully free again.

She closed her eyes, thinking back over the last turbulent year, praying it would be the last full year of the war.

In March, the Russian Tsar had abdicated and had also abdicated on his haemophiliac son's behalf. The next heir in line for the Russian throne, the Tsar's brother, Grand Duke Michael, had then refused the crown and, as a consequence, three hundred years of Romanov rule had come to an abrupt and bloody end and a republic had been born.

In April, provoked by German U-boat attacks on American merchant ships in the North Atlantic, America had entered the war.

In July, Russia's provisional government had crushed a Bolshevik uprising and there were bizarre rumours that the leader, Lenin, had escaped across the border into Finland disguised as a fireman.

In September rumours had come from out of Russia that the Tsar and his family had been sent to Tobolsk in Siberia to protect them from the Bolsheviks.

In October Lenin had returned to Petersburg, or Petrograd, as it had been re-christened, and within days the Bolshevik Central Committee had voted for an armed uprising against the Provisional Government.

In November, under the slogan, 'Peace, Bread and Land', the uprising had overthrown the Provisional Government, and had declared Russia a socialist republic.

'Phew!' was the general response as the world had waited to see what the Russkies – the nickname the Russians were now generally known by – would do before the year was out, desperately short as they were of bullets, boots and bread. As if in an answer to prayer vile weather became the saviour of the Russians as, day after day, icy rain fell in sheets and was followed by heavy falls of snow, all of which brought a short, but very welcome temporary halt to the fighting.

Janna wondered if snow had also fallen early in Oystertown. The Heights and the windmill always looked picture-postcard pretty when under snow. Claudia's family kept a toboggan in what had once served Rose Mount as a coach-house and before the war, whenever a similarly heavy snowfall coincided with Kim being at Rose Mount on leave, she had happily joined him and Claudia in tobogganing down the steep, snow-covered track that ran from the top to the bottom of the Heights, shrieking every inch of the way in a mixture of terror and glee.

She wondered if, and when, such carefree days would ever come again, and she wondered where Kim was now. Knowing how much she liked to receive them he was in the habit of regularly sending her a postcard from each of his various, more exotic ports of call. One postcard had been posted in Portsmouth – somewhere not very exotic at all – but in a sentence that the censor had missed he had written that when the ship he was serving on set sail it would be doing so heading north towards the Arctic Circle.

What he hadn't specified was whereabouts in the Arctic Circle it would be heading, and why it would be heading there. There was a small library in the nurse's home and among the books on its shelves was an encyclopaedia. There were maps on nearly every page and it had taken only minutes for her to discover the ports that lay within the Arctic Circle. As it had snowed early in northern Europe, she wondered what the snowfall would be like, and if Kim's ship would have dangerous ice floes to contend with.

From behind her someone dropped a hand onto her shoulder.

'You should have been back on duty ten minutes ago,' a fellow staff-nurse said, sitting down next to her. 'If I was you, I'd head back to the ward before I was seriously missed. And don't stub out a gasper you've only half smoked,' she added as Janna rose to her feet. 'I'll finish it off for you.'

And she removed the Wild Woodbine from between Janna's fingers and, with a sigh of satisfaction, put it to her own mouth, inhaling deeply.

Janna wrapped her nurse's cloak more tightly around herself and began heading in the direction of her hospital ward. When she would next see Daniel, who had volunteered to be on duty over Christmas, she didn't know. What she did know, though, was that he would be thinking about her just as often and just as longingly as she was thinking about him.

* * *

Over the previous few days and under Celia's direction Rose Mount's recuperation wards and her own small apartment had never looked so festive. Holly wreaths graced every possible door. Garlands of colourful paper-chains hung from corner to corner in each recuperation ward and, to top everything, three days before Christmas, Billy Gann and Pascal arrived with two magnificent ceiling-high fir trees planted in tubs covered in red crêpe paper.

'One fer the part o' Rose Mount that's a recuperation 'ospital, and one fer your drawin' room,' Billy said kindly to Celia, wiping his nose with the back of a hand that hadn't seen soap and water for many a day. 'And if yer don't 'ave any decorations ter put on 'em,' he added, 'yer don't 'ave to worry còs Tilly's bin makin' lots o' tree decorations out o' beads and fevvers and bits o' wire and Pascal's got 'em all in the box 'e's carryin' under 'is arm.'

Tears of appreciation pricked the backs of Celia's eyes. When she had lived in Belgrave Square, she had always been on good terms with the neighbours who had lived in close proximity to her, but with none of them had she enjoyed the kind of deep, genuine friendship her Oystertown friends gave so unstintingly.

'There now,' Pascal said gruffly. 'No need for tears at a time like Christmas.'

'No, indeed.' Celia gave him a grateful smile. 'And now you must both have a glass of something to keep the winter chill out. What is your tipple, Billy? And yours, Pascal?'

'A tot o' whisky if you 'ave it,' Billy said hopefully.

'I do. I have both Macallan and Johnnie Walker.'

Billy stared at her, baffled. He'd always been too grateful for any glass of whisky put in front of him to worry about what the label said on the bottle it had been poured from.

Before Celia came to the erroneous assumption that Billy

might prefer a cup of tea, Pascal said helpfully, 'I think Billy's tipple would be a glass of Macallan.'

'Aye, that's the ticket,' Billy added swiftly, knowing that the result of any prolonged dithering could end up with him being offered nothing stronger than a cup of Darjeeling that for some reason he couldn't fathom Celia always served without milk. 'A tot o' Macallan will go down the little red lane just fine.'

'And if you make mine the same, I'd be monstrously grateful,' Pascal said, hardly able to believe that in the middle of the afternoon he and Billy were in Celia Layard's small apartment at Rose Mount and about to enjoy a glass of what was, in his opinion, the king of single malt whiskies.

To show her appreciation for all her Oystertown friends Celia had arranged a come-one and come-all Christmas party for them, throwing it on 23 December so that it wouldn't clash with any family Christmas Eve arrangements any of them might have made.

Although she had no intention of letting anyone know it, her party had an ulterior motive. She had never entertained any fond feelings for her late son-in-law, but Xan Keller had bizarrely drowned three months ago, and no real explanation had been forthcoming. The coroner had duly recorded the death as being by misadventure. Knowing how unlikely it was that Claudia would be accepting any Christmas party invitations she might be sent, Celia decided she would take matters into her own hands and would throw a Christmas party in her now very festive-looking small apartment. A party at which she, Celia, was the hostess, was a party her daughter wouldn't easily be able to avoid attending, and it would be within the bounds of propriety.

As she made preparations Celia thought back to how different the party was going to be to those she had once held in her Belgrave Square home. In those days – days that now seemed very far off – waiters had been hired from a London agency. Fresh flower arrangements had been delivered from Harrods. Extra staff had been engaged, some to ensure that no one was standing with an empty glass, others to help with kitchen and cloakroom duties.

At this party everyone helping was a personal friend. Pascal was in charge of a cider, rum and cinnamon punch bowl, something Tilly had told her she was bound to live to regret.

Rosie Gibbs had asked if she could be put in charge of seeing to everyone's coats and Gertie Dadd had brought along paper sweetie-bags, some full of dolly mixtures and others full of jelly babies, and all of which, tied at the neck with festive red ribbon, she was handing out with great largesse.

Celia had been quite right in assuming that the twenty-third was a more convenient date for many people to accept a Christmas party invitation than Christmas Eve would have been. Ozzie Dadd told her Christmas Eve would have been a no-no for him as he would be serving behind the bar at the Duke of Connaught from opening time to closing time. Celia also knew it would be the first Christmas he would be spending with his new wife. Against all odds, he'd left behind his lifetime of bachelorhood when he'd met and married Annie, who'd arrived in Oystertown from Dover, to care for an ailing aunt. Instead of returning to her home town when the aunt had died, she'd been swept off her feet by the landlord of the Duke, much to everyone's surprise but, after they'd become used to the idea, delight. Olivia Pettman said that if it had been a Christmas Eve party, she wouldn't have been able to attend it because, as the minister's wife, her presence at the Christmas Eve carol service was obligatory. Gertie said that Christmas Eve was the one evening in the year when she attended a church service.

'Reverend Pettman always sets up such a lovely candle-lit Nativity scene,' she said to Celia as she and Mrs Pettman both arrived at her Rose Mount apartment at the same time, but from different directions, 'and I like the carol singing. I'd sing carols all year round given the chance.'

They were far from being the first guests to arrive and Rosie relieved them of their coats and hand-knitted scarves and hats. Mrs Pettman was persuaded to have a glass of ginger beer, the strongest drink she permitted to pass her lips, while Gertie accepted the punch, drained it in one go and happily took another.

It was then that the doorbell rang.

Celia's forehead creased in a puzzled frown for everyone she had hoped would be celebrating Christmas with her was already doing so.

'Leave it to me, Celia,' Ozzie said masterfully. 'It will be Mummers. I don't expect you get many of them in London, but around here they are a local tradition at Christmas time. They paint their faces and dress up outlandishly and go from door to door. When the householder opens the door to them, they generally sing a song, or tell a rhyme and then it is customary for the householder to give them a little money, to wish them a very happy Christmas and to send them on their way.'

'Have you some money on you, Ozzie?' Celia was all for keeping local traditions alive.

Ozzie obligingly plunged a hand into his trouser pocket.

It was then Celia heard a voice she hadn't heard for a long time and her eyes widened. 'Forget about the money, Ozzie! Those aren't Mummers at the door! It's Marietta!'

And she ran out of the drawing room and into the hall before anyone could get there before her, flinging the front door back on its hinges and then opening her arms in order to take Marietta into them.

'*Un très Joyeux Noël!*' Marietta cried as the taxicab that had brought her from the station edged cautiously away into the snowy night. 'Isn't this beyond marvellous, Celia? And is Janna here? And Claudia?'

'I'm afraid Janna is still in France but not only is Claudia here, so also is your papa!'

And with perfect timing Pascal strode from the further reaches of the crowded drawing room and into the small hallway, his mane of silver-white hair, moustache and thick curly beard giving him the appearance of an Old Testament prophet.

At the sight of his daughter he gave a bellowing shout of joy, wrapping his arms around her and, as she squealed in pretended protest, lifting her off her feet and swinging her round and round until, dizzy and laughing helplessly, they half fell through the drawing-room's open doorway, collapsing in a happy heap on the nearest unoccupied sofa.

Chapter Thirty-four

January 1918

It was New Year's Day and the coldest winter anyone could remember. The announcement of a new government policy which was to come into place on 11 February did not help people's spirits. By then everyone would have been issued with ration books and, when they received them, they were to register with their local grocer, for it wasn't only meat that was now to be rationed. Sugar, tea, coffee, butter, cheese and margarine were now to be included as well.

'I never thought I'd live to see the day when I'd be told what I could and couldn't buy at the butcher's and the grocer's.' Gertie Dadd was standing next-but-one to Tilly in a queue at the butcher's, a queue so long it reached out onto the pavement and nearly as far as the Fox and Firkin. 'Are we living in a free country, or ain't we?' She wasn't addressing Tilly, or anyone else in particular; simply the world at large. She stamped her feet in order to keep the blood moving around in them. 'Helen Nettles says things are even worse in Russia,' she continued, 'although 'ow she knows what's going on in Russia, I can't imagine.'

'She 'as a nephew who 'as a posh job in the Foreign Office,' the woman immediately in front of Tilly said. 'I expect 'e's let slip that the Russkies are no longer up to snuff and can't be depended on.'

'And what are we going to do if the Reds fall by the wayside? That's what I want to know,' Gertie said as the queue shuffled a couple of feet further forward. 'My sister's bin telling everyone fer weeks that the Russkies can't be trusted and no one's taken a blind bit o' notice of 'er.'

'Why should they, Gertie? You don't,' someone joshed from a little further down in the queue and, despite the freezing cold and the knowledge that when they did get to the front of the queue there would only be mince, pigs' trotters and tripe on offer, everyone near enough to have heard chuckled with good-humoured laughter.

Times were hard – an horrendously high number of black-edged telegrams from the Front never seemed to stop arriving in Oystertown – but the bottom line was that they were British and, full of British bulldog spirit, were utterly determined that no damned Huns were going to get the better of them.

'It isn't the Russian people who can't be trusted.' The speaker was a teacher in the local junior school and there was educated certainty in her voice. 'It's the Bolshevik leaders, men like Trotsky and Lenin, who are the problem.'

The queue edged up another couple of feet.

'Oh, aye. Trotsky and Lenin.' Gertie was in full flow again. 'Both little chaps, ain't they? I don't think little chaps should govern a country. They nearly always turn out to be bullies tryin' to make up for their lack o' size. You need a big, tall, imposin'-lookin' bloke to govern a country.'

'I'd remind you that our prime minister is a little on the short side,' someone else said tartly from a yard or so further back in the queue as a fresh flurry of snowflakes began to fall. 'I doubt Lloyd George is an inch over five feet five and so if I were you, Gertie, I'd watch my mouth. You don't want people to think you're being disloyal in a time of war.'

Gertie opened her mouth to make a rude riposte and then, much to Tilly's relief, thought better of it and shut it again. An altercation in the street over David Lloyd George's suitability to govern merely because he wasn't a smidgeon over five feet five was the very last thing that was needed when there was finally an edge of hope that the war might be on its way to coming to a close, for if the latest newspaper reports were to be trusted Germany was rumoured to be on the back foot. On Kim's most recent telephone call to Claudia, he had told her that the talk among his fellow Royal Naval officers was that Germany was on the edge of over-extending itself and that if, and when, it did, the British military would be ready with something Kim referred to as being 'the Big Push'.

'And when that happens,' Kim had said, 'I think I can guarantee you that the war will be as good as over.'

The butcher's boy, concave-chested and wearing a blood-spattered apron that reached down to Wellington boots that were far too big for him, stepped out onto the pavement.

'There's no more pigs' trotters left!' he hollered to the queue with his hands cupped around his mouth, 'and we've nearly run out 'o mince. There's still some tripe though, for them that want it.'

Tilly wasn't keen but they had to eat something. The queue edged up a further couple of feet. Frozen to the marrow and gritting her teeth she moved up with it, her mind not on her own physical discomfort, but on Janna and Daniel.

Every letter she received from her niece spoke of their happiness, even if they were rarely together and only in extremely squalid conditions when they could manage to co-ordinate a snatched moment of leave. How Tilly longed to see them, finally married, and to witness their joy. The war was now entering its fifth year and ever since its outbreak Daniel had served as a stretcher-bearer, braving enemy shell-fire in order, together with fellow conchies, to retrieve wounded men from the battlefield and ferry them to one of the many St John Ambulance Brigade Hospitals in Étaples. They were the largest voluntary hospitals serving the British Expeditionary Force in Flanders and were considered to be the best-equipped hospitals in northern France. She could only begin to imagine the dangers he faced, and did not want to contemplate what would happen to Janna if one of those enemy shells found him as a target.

Tilly was brought out of her reverie by the woman behind her poking her rudely in the middle of her back and saying, 'You're holding the queue up with your daydreaming, and my time is precious even if yours isn't. Don't you know there's a war on?'

In the small apartment she and her mother had retained for their own use when converting Rose Mount into a Recuperation Home Claudia was staring at Jasper in stunned disbelief. 'I can hardly credit it! Is this some kind of joke?'

They were facing each other, Claudia pale as death in her mourning black, and Jasper – wearing his Merchant Service uniform – grim-faced, a pulse pounding at a corner of his jaw.

She had just shown him a letter from the Swiss Embassy informing her, as Xan's next of kin, that although Switzerland didn't have an honours system, either military or civilian, as a long-serving Swiss diplomat Xan was to be awarded a post-humous medal in recognition of the outstanding service he had given to his country.

'Xan wasn't even Swiss!' The words were out of Jasper's mouth before he could stop them. He took a breath. 'He was a German! A German spy who, under cover of being a Swiss diplomat, gave as many Allied war secrets to the enemy as his position gave him access to!'

Claudia shook her head, her lip quivering. 'And here he is, being honoured as if he were a hero. When you think of all those who must have died because of his treachery . . . they are the ones who deserve this honour, not him.'

Even when in such great distress she was still radiantly beautiful and her pain was like a dagger to his heart.

Running a hand through his thatch of black curls he said quietly, 'Xan wasn't the person you, and we all, believed him to be, Claudia. He was an expert at disguising who he really was. You are not to blame. You must not think that you are.'

Without turning round she took a couple of steps backwards until her legs came into contact with a chair and then, trembling violently, she half fell down onto it.

'I only wish that I had realized much sooner.' Her voice was hoarse as her eyes held his. 'What am I to tell the embassy?'

He hunkered down in front of her and took her hands in his, deeply relieved that she trusted him so fully.

His honey-brown, gold-flecked eyes held hers. 'You must respond by expressing appreciation for the way the embassy intends marking Xan's long service with them. Not to do so would seem odd.'

Knowing he was right she bit her lip and then, with great reluctance, broke their handhold, rose to her feet and crossed the room to where a leather-inlaid desk stood in one of the room's two alcoves. Seating herself on the chair that partnered it she withdrew a sheet of Rose Mount's headed notepaper from its central drawer and picked up an elegant-looking fountain pen.

He stood with his back to the deep bay window and its view of snow-covered garden, sombre heaving sea and leaden sky, watching her as she began writing and pondering on both the ease of their friendship and also the oddness of it. He was a Merchant Service seaman. She was a member of the upper classes. Under normal circumstances there would never have been the remotest social interaction between the two of them, much less firm friendship, but they hadn't met in normal circumstances.

It had been the terrible storm that had brought them together. He had been the skipper of the lifeboat who, with his crew, had set out in the worst weather in living memory in order to pluck her parents to safety in the seconds before their yacht keeled over and disappeared beneath mountainous waves.

He was brought out of his thoughts of the past by Claudia signing the letter, blotting it and placing it in an envelope embossed on its flap with Rose Mount's address. Then she sealed it, stamped it, addressed it to the Swiss official who had written to her and rose to her feet and faced him.

'I'm not going to ask a member of the household staff to post it, Jasper. I'm going to walk into Oystertown and post it myself.'

There was nobody to object to her plan, as Celia had left for London and the family house in Belgrave Square in order to attend a New Year Eve's party being given by the Foreign Secretary's wife who was a long-time friend.

'Then I'll walk there and back with you,' Jasper said, well aware of how treacherous the ground was. 'If you slip on the ice and twist or break an ankle, chances are you will freeze to death before anyone comes across you and is able to go for help.'

She opened her mouth to protest and then closed it again as she became aware of how close to each other they were standing. It was a situation she could easily rectify. All it needed was for her to step away from him, but putting further space between them was the very last thing she wanted to do. What she wanted was to feel his arms around her, hugging her so close she would be able to hear his heart beating.

'Claudia . . .' His voice was thick with the desire he had recently come to realize he felt for her and which, aware of the social gulf that lay between them, and the apparent success of the marriage he now knew to be a sham, he had thus far kept firmly under control.

It wasn't under control now, though. It was naked not only in his voice, but also in his eyes, and as he lowered his head to hers she lifted her face to his, her eyes closing, her lips parting as she received, and gave, the most passionate, sweetest and most satisfying of kisses.

When at last he raised his head from hers, he said, still holding her in his arms and his voice thick with emotion, 'Unless you've changed your mind about walking into Oystertown to post the letter to the embassy you need to wear not only your thickest coat and a woolly hat, but also sturdy boots and fleece-lined gloves as well.'

'I promise you I shall dress as if setting off for the North Pole.'

'I've got a much better idea.'

With one arm still holding her close he released his other arm from around her waist and placing his forefinger beneath her chin he gently tilted her face upwards so that she couldn't evade his eyes.

'Let me post the letter for you.'

She shook her head. 'No. Posting this letter is something I need to do for myself.'

A sixth sense warned him that arguing with her would achieve nothing and so he settled for saying, 'Then if you are really determined on posting it yourself, let's set off for the post-box now, together, before there is a further fall of snow.'

She opened her mouth to say she didn't need chaperoning, and then decided she had no objections at all to being chaperoned just as long as it was Jasper who was her chaperone.

With her heart beginning to beat fast and light, she said, 'Give me five minutes in which to change my shoes for Wellingtons and to put on my warmest coat and hat.'

When, a handful of minutes later, she re-entered the room wearing an ankle-skimming black Astrakhan coat, a Russian-looking matching hat and, rather spoiling the overall dramatic effect, green gardening Wellingtons, he could see no sign of the letter that was to be posted.

Reading his thoughts, she said, 'I haven't forgotten my letter to the Ambassador. It's tucked in an inside pocket of my coat.'

He took hold of her gloved hand and tucked it into one of the deep pockets of his naval overcoat.

The ground was treacherously icy on the little-used cliff-top path between Rose Mount and Oystertown and Claudia had to keep tight hold of Jasper's arm in order to prevent herself from slipping and falling. Like the rest of Oystertown's female population she had always thought Jasper heart-stoppingly handsome, and yet had never considered anything might come of it. The social divide between them was so impossibly deep. Also, during the relatively long period of time the two of them had known each other, an occasion like today, when it was just the two of them and there was no one else in sight, was rare.

As they trudged through the snow together she said, genuinely curious, 'Have you wanted to be a merchant sailor ever since you were a small boy?' She could not yet think about what that kiss might mean. Was it just a product of their heightened emotions at such a difficult time? Or dared she hope that there was something more? She strove to regain an air of friendship.

'No. As a small boy all I ever wanted to be was an oysterman, but when war with Germany broke out, I knew there would soon be conscription and that I'd find myself in the army if I didn't take decisive action myself, and so that is what I did.

Opting for my natural environment – which is the sea – I joined the Merchant Service. And the Merchant Service,' he added, shooting her a down-slanting smile that made her tummy turn a dizzying somersault, 'is where I intend staying even after this insane war is over.'

As Oystertown came into sight and the ground began to gently slope down towards it, he asked her something he had long been curious about. 'As you and your family are aristocracy, have you grown up hob-nobbing with royalty?'

'It means I've grown up being respectful of their rank, but not intimidated by them. King George is painfully shy and he's cultivated a gruff manner in order to try and cover it up. Queen Mary is also shy. She doesn't make friends easily, but even though there are quite a few years difference in age between them she has long counted my mother a close friend and is very fond of her.'

Jasper tried to get to grips with the fact that Lady Layard who, because of his having saved her life at sea he had long been on respectfully easy terms with was, in her turn, on respectfully easy terms with Queen Mary, and couldn't. In the photographs of Queen Mary that appeared in newspapers when she was launching a battleship, something that since the beginning of the war she now seemed to do on a weekly basis, or cutting a scarlet ribbon in order to open a children's home, or a hospital, she looked so fiercely formidable he thought she was capable of intimidating even him.

Once they had reached Oystertown's high street, walking became a lot less perilous as the majority of shopkeepers had shovelled the snow from off the pavement in front of their shops and into the street's gutters and then scattered cooking salt on the cleared pavement to prevent fresh ice from forming.

The post-box was situated halfway down the cobbled street close to Oystertown's butcher's and as Claudia dropped her letter to the Swiss Embassy into it there came the sound of a noisy altercation taking place from inside the butcher's shop. Seconds later a small rough-coated terrier, so thin its ribs were showing, shot out of the open shop doorway with the butcher chasing after it, shaking his fist. 'Thieving little hound!' he roared, his face flushed beetroot red as he came to a halt only feet away from where Claudia and Jasper were standing. 'I'll teach you to try and thieve from my shop counter!'

He was a man of wide girth and as the dog had disappeared in order to presumably cause havoc elsewhere, he staggered to a halt, panting from his unaccustomed exertion and then, glaring at Claudia and Jasper as if they were personally responsible for the dog's behaviour and uttering a string of profanities, he stumped back into his shop.

'Let's hope the little mutt meets with more success elsewhere,' Jasper said wryly. 'He's vanished from sight fast enough.'

'Yes, he has, hasn't he?'

Claudia could only agree with him for beneath her ankle-length coat the little dog was cowering against her legs for warmth and protection.

She said, 'Would you step inside the shop and ask the butcher for a pound weight of his best sausages, Jasper?'

Jasper was about to say that even for her he wasn't going to demean his Merchant Service uniform by shopping for sausages when wearing it but, gritting his teeth, did as she asked.

A little further down on the snow-covered pavement Billy Gann, inebriated and unsteady on his feet at the best of times and now seriously challenged by the perilous conditions underfoot, was weaving his way unsteadily towards her.

'Why are you 'angin' about catchin' your death in this weather?' he asked as he paused on his erratic progress to the nearest public house. 'A pretty young lady like yerself should 'ave someone escortin' 'er,' he added, hiccupping and wiping his nose on a grubby, well-worn sleeve.

From the unseen shelter of Claudia's ankle-length coat there came the sound of a warning growl.

Alarmed, Billy looked swiftly both up and down the high street, but could see no likely culprit. There came another growl and unnervingly it seemed to be coming from somewhere very close to him. He wondered if some joker in the Duke had laced his pint of bitter with something that was making him hallucinate and, as the growling had now been followed by the sound of heavy panting, he decided it was high time he played safe and headed off in the direction of the nearest hostelry.

With relief Claudia watched him disappear into the Fox and Firkin at the same time as Jasper stepped out of the butcher's, a parcel wrapped in a sheet of out-of-date newspaper tucked beneath his right arm.

'The butcher says the dog is a stray. He says he's done his best to keep him from starving, but as customers fight shy of having to walk past him to enter the shop, he'd be very grateful if we would find him and take responsibility for him, and move him either further down the high street or further up it.'

'But of course we'll take responsibility for him!' Claudia's tender heart was outraged at such blatant callousness. 'How could we not?'

The temptation to tell her a score of reasons why not were nearly too much for Jasper.

He took a deep breath, apologized to an elderly gentleman for the fact that they were blocking the pavement, and said, 'It would actually be you taking over responsibility for him if you do find him, as my New Year's leave comes to an end in a week's time and if there is one thing that is a certainty in all this, it is that I can't take him to sea with me.'

As if realizing that the conversation taking place was one that would determine his entire future the terrier edged out from beneath the shelter of Claudia's coat and sat, looking from one of them to the other, one ear up and one ear down, brown eyes fiercely hopeful that his luck was about to change and that, instead of the callous treatment he had endured for so long, he was about to receive an act of kindness.

'The poor little chap quite obviously hasn't had a decent meal or enjoyed any kind of affection for a long time.' Claudia's voice was full of compassion. 'Would you give him a sausage, Jasper? And then I'm going to take him home with me.'

Jasper's eyebrows rose. 'Home to Rose Mount?'

'Of course I mean home to Rose Mount!'

He was about to ask what the probable outcome would be when her mother returned to Rose Mount, but the moment the thought came he jettisoned it. If Claudia had given a stray dog a home, one thing was certain. Celia Layard would be the last person in the world to eject him from it.

He said, resigning himself to the inevitable, 'Beneath your coat are you wearing a belt you can manage without for a little while and that you wouldn't mind if, when I return it, there was an extra hole punched in it?'

'Yes,' she said, immediately guessing the use Jasper intended putting it to. 'I am. And no, I wouldn't mind if, when you returned it, it had an extra hole punched in it.'

She unbuttoned her coat just enough to be able to undo, and remove, her skirt's narrow leather belt, handing it to Jasper and trying not to wince as Jasper took a penknife from one of the inside pockets of his Merchant Navy overcoat and skewered a hole in the expensive leather.

'You two young people are a danger to life and limb!' an elderly woman whose cheeks were raw with the biting cold said as, on the slippery pavement, she cautiously navigated her way around them. 'If you want to do a bit o' courtin', act like a couple o' Christians and find somewhere decently sheltered to do it in!'

Claudia fought down a giggle as she realized that the emotions fizzing between herself and Jasper were now clear for all to see. Jasper simply ignored the advice and strode back into the butcher's to beg a couple of yards of the string the butcher used when parcelling up meat for his customers.

'If my giving it to you means the two of you remove yourselves and that sorry-looking animal from outside o' my shop, you can have a whole bally ball of it,' he said equably to Jasper.

'A couple of yards long enough to serve as a dog-lead will be quite enough.'

The butcher cocked an eye to where, through the shop's large window, Claudia could be seen, the dog's nose poking out from the shelter of her coat as it sat as close to her legs as it could get.

'Your lady-friend bears a strong resemblance to Lady Layard's daughter,' he said speculatively, 'although I don't recognize her from her coming into my shop. In my limited experience, single young women who are aristocracy don't tend to shop for their own meat. Meat is something they always have delivered.'

He rummaged on the shelf beneath his wood-block counter, withdrew a ball of string, chopped off a length a couple of yards long and handed it to Jasper, saying as he did so, 'I don't reckon yon dog's ever seen sight of a lead. You might find that carryin' a parcel o' sausages and gettin' 'im to walk to 'eel all at the same time is going to be near-on impossible.'

Jasper bit back a not very polite retort.

'And what name are yer goin' to give 'im?' the butcher called out after him as Jasper headed out of the shop. ''E looks as if he'll be a lively little rascal once he has a good meal inside him.

It's my belief that in taking him on you might find you've bitten off more than you can chew.'

Still tight-lipped Jasper stepped out onto the pavement. The second he did so the dog rushed up to him, kicking up flurries of freshly fallen snow as he ran in excited circles around him as if the two of them were experiencing the reunion of a lifetime.

'Try and keep still, little dog,' Claudia said, trying to calm him down as, with a pocket penknife, Jasper fashioned a make-shift dog collar from the belt of her skirt and then threaded the string through it to act as a lead. 'You are covering Jasper's uniform in wet snowy paw prints.'

'The butcher referred to him as being a lively little rascal,' Jasper said as, once on the makeshift lead, the dog jumped fearsomely high in order to try and reach his face and lick it, 'and I think the name Rascal suits him.'

They began walking back up the high street, Rascal trotting in a very well-behaved manner at Jasper's heels, and Claudia said hesitantly, 'Should we perhaps have asked the butcher to put a notice in his shop window asking if anyone has lost a small dog and, if they have, if they would leave their name and address with him?' There was a distinct wobble in her voice. 'It isn't that I *want* Rascal to be found – and certainly not by someone who half-starved him – but a person like that is very likely to prefer money to being reunited with him and then Mamma and I won't run the risk of being accused of having stolen him.'

Privately Jasper thought it highly unlikely that anyone would accept money – or anything else – for Rascal's return.

What he was going to do, when he had walked Claudia and Rascal back to Rose Mount, was to return to the high street, buy a dog-collar and an identity disc from the local ironmonger's and then have Rascal's name engraved on one side of the dog-tag and Claudia's name and address engraved on the other side of it.

What Celia's reaction would be when she returned from London and found an under-nourished mongrel happily installed at Rose Mount he had no way of knowing, but he would stake good money that Rascal would never be hungry, homeless, or friendless ever again.

And, if he ever needed to make use of it, the little dog had given him even more of an excuse to make a beeline for Claudia's door as soon as he had his next period of leave. Though, gazing at her now, he doubted he would need such an excuse.

Chapter Thirty-five

Celia's reaction was one of surprise that soon turned to delight, as Rascal quickly became adept at winning over the heart of whoever happened to be nearby. This included plenty of the wounded officers venturing into the chilly gardens at Rose Mount, to avail themselves of the fresh air with its beneficial salty tang. Rascal was strictly banned from the wards, as he presented a risk to hygiene, but to see his energetic capers around the wintry lawns was as restorative as many of the medical interventions on offer.

It was not long before he began to show the effects of a proper diet, and his small ribs were no longer visible. Not only was he enjoying regular meals courtesy of Claudia, but plenty of the patients took to slipping him treats. It would have taken a heart of stone to resist his brown eyes gazing upwards, ever hopeful.

Celia was soon as enchanted as the rest of the inhabitants of Rose Mount, and had taken to allowing the little dog to sit by her feet when she was at the desk in the apartment, even providing a special cushion for him. He was perfectly content to lie there as she tackled the never-ending pile of correspondence which came from running the recuperation home, springing into action when she rose to take the letters to whoever was next venturing into Oystertown to post them.

His favourite person in the world was Claudia, but she was

busy on the wards for much of the day. However, when she finished her shift and returned to the apartment, he would be beside himself with joy, leaping up to shower her with all the affection and gratitude he felt for her having rescued him.

Today, though, as the daylight was fading and the soft light from the desk lamp bathed the room, Claudia's thoughts were for once not on the little dog. Nor were they on Jasper, back on board his merchant ship and with no idea when his next leave might be. Rather, she gazed at the newspaper that her mother had deliberately left on the chair, one headline uppermost.

'So they've passed it.' Claudia could not help the bittersweet tone creeping into her voice.

'They have.' Celia rose as her daughter came across the room towards her. 'I'm so sorry it isn't everything you wanted, my dear. But it's a start. You know they would never have got it through if they included all your points. It simply wouldn't have washed.'

Claudia wandered to the big bay window and gazed out at the darkening skies, to where the waves would be pounding the beach in their familiar insistent rhythm. Some things never changed. This was a big step forward, she knew, as she also knew that her mother was right – but she had wanted this to be a triumph, not a work of compromise. Still, she assured herself, it was the start – and for years it had felt as if it would never happen.

Yet it had happened. There it was in black and white: the Representation of the People Act had gone through. After the years of protest, the marches, the deliberately provocative acts of vandalism, the unspeakable sufferings of abuse and force-feeding, women had finally won the right to vote.

Except, it was not all women. It was only for those over thirty and who met a property qualification – and the latter alone would rule out most of the women of Oystertown.

Claudia gritted her teeth. The same new law made it possible for all men over twenty-one to vote, whether or not they had property.

Celia could guess only too well what her daughter was thinking.

'They had to alter the law for young men otherwise all those who've been fighting abroad for so long would be disqualified,' she pointed out. 'The old system said they had to be resident at home for twelve months – impossible in wartime. It's to recognize their service.'

Claudia nodded. Then she turned, fired with the injustice of it. 'But they won't recognize the way that women have risen to the challenge, working in munitions, taking over the jobs when their menfolk have gone to the front. Or at least, the younger ones. Women like me.'

Celia dipped her head in sober acknowledgement.

'Because otherwise, with so many younger men dying, women would actually outnumber the male voters, wouldn't they? And we can't have that. Oh no. That would never do.'

Again Celia recognized that her daughter was right. 'Yes, that is the way it is, my darling. But it is an immense step forward. And,' she crossed to her daughter and placed her hands on her shoulders, 'I know I disapproved of what you did. Your methods. I thought it was terrible, so unladylike. That you were damaging your prospects, putting your future at risk. Yet now I see that you had right on your side – and I'm proud of you.'

Claudia could not help but gasp, knowing what an admission this was. 'Really? Honestly, do you think that?'

Celia gave a low chuckle. 'Well, I can't deny that I wish you hadn't taken part in that demonstration in Downing Street. But the bravery many of you showed, for your principles . . . yes, you made a difference and changed the minds of many in government. And then when your Mrs Pankhurst said that she would set aside the campaign in order to back the war effort – that won over many who'd been suspicious of her motives before. It has taken a long time but finally the wheels have been set in motion.'

Claudia smiled into her mother's eyes but then felt a chill envelop her, at the thought of those who had not lived to see this moment. First and foremost, Emily, who had hoped so fervently for their campaign to succeed. And then her mind flew to Janna, somewhere over in France, probably unaware of history being made. Probably too exhausted to follow the news, when the papers eventually made it that far.

Rascal decided that enough time had been spent talking and jumped up at her, his small paws resting against her knees, his little face eager for attention.

'Oh, come on, then.' Claudia bent and picked him up, resting her nose in his wiry coat. 'You don't mind either way, do you? As long as you get your scraps, you're happy. Maybe you're right.' She gave a sigh and looked across to her mother. 'At least you'll be able to vote next time, whenever that may be. I'll just have to wait a few more years.'

'That's the spirit, darling.' Celia was relieved to hear the determination in her daughter's voice. 'And rest assured, I shall make the very most of it – because I know everything that you and your friends went through to lead us to this point. Nobody will forget it.'

Chapter Thirty-six

The winter seemed endless. Even though it was now nearing the end of March there were still occasional falls of snow and by the time one fall had melted into dirty, discoloured slush, another had replaced it. Making the general discomfort worse as it wasn't only basic foodstuffs that were still being rationed, but coal was now being rationed as well. Just at a time when everyone had well-nigh forgotten what it was to be warm, they had to think twice about every lump of coal they put on their pathetically meagre fires. It was even rumoured that in order to save fuel, King George had had a line drawn around the inside of his bathtub over which the water was not allowed to rise.

''E's lucky 'e can 'ave a bath at all, no matter 'ow deep or not the water,' Smelly Bell said disparagingly when the rumour eventually reached him. 'I 'aven't 'ad a bath since I was a nipper. A bit of 'onest muck nivver 'urt anyone, that's what my old mam used to say. And it must be true, because it's nivver 'urt me.'

And having in his own mind set the world to rights he continued shuffling unsteadily through the latest fall of snow, happily wearing an overcoat Gertie Dadd had given him and which had once belonged to her late, not-very-much-missed, husband.

* * *

Tilly had been doing her best to follow the train of events abroad, reckoning that doing so might help her work out when her loved ones would most likely come home. However, it was not straightforward and she struggled to understand what was going on, poring over the newspaper every day, her chair pulled up close to the scanty fire in the little cottage in Harbour Row.

On 15 February, Russia had officially cut loose from its former Entente Allies. On 20 February, at noon, what had been a fleeting armistice on the Eastern Front came to an end and the Germans had immediately put pressure on the Bolsheviks to accept their terms.

On 24 February, the German army had marched virtually unopposed into Estonia and Petrograd was threatened.

On 3 March, the Bolshevik regime which was now governing Russia had not only signed a peace treaty under which Russia surrendered Poland, Lithuania, Riga and part of Belarus to Germany, but they had also agreed to pay a staggering 3,000 million gold marks in reparation.

And it hadn't ended there.

Two days later, the Bolsheviks had declared that Moscow, not Petrograd, was now Russia's capital city, and two days after that had renamed themselves the Russian Communist Party and the country, the Russian Socialist Federative Soviet Republic.

'And so is Russia now out of the war?' Tilly asked Pascal and then, without waiting for an answer, added, 'And whereabouts are the Russian royal family? The Tsar and Tsarina and all five of their children can't just have vanished into thin air!'

'Yes to your first question, Tilly my love,' Pascal said. 'As for where the Tsar and Tsarina and their children are now, we will just have to wait and see. In a situation like the one they are in, no news is probably good news. As Tsar Nicholas and King George are first cousins – and are as physically alike as peas in a pod – my guess is the Romanovs will be arriving at Buckingham Palace or Windsor Castle any day now to sit this hideous war out as guests of King George and Queen Mary.'

He didn't add that something they should both be worrying about was an even larger headline in that morning's newspaper. In times gone by Tilly's interest only ever centred on the *Oystertown Gazette*'s Births, Marriages and Deaths announcements, but ever since Britain had been at war with Germany, anything to do with Russia had also been added to the list of things she liked to try and keep up with and she quite obviously hadn't yet read the latest news regarding it.

Tilly turned the page.

A few seconds went by and then he heard her say in stunned incredulity, 'It says here that under a New Military Service Bill the maximum conscription age is now fifty-one. Fifty-one! What earthly use will men of that age be to the forces? Thank God I married an older man . . .'

Pascal was saved from replying by someone hammering heavily on his and Tilly's street door. Heaving himself from his comfortable fireside chair he had only taken a couple of steps across their small sitting room in order to answer the urgent knocking when the door was flung back on its hinges and Ozzie strode into the room with something that looked suspiciously like army call-up papers clutched in his fist.

'I thought, being a publican, I'd be exempt from the draft! I'm essential to the war effort!' he said explosively, coming to a halt in the centre of the little room and shedding snow from his boots at every step. 'I don't mind being called to the colours! I've been itching to give the Boche a good thrashing ever since the buggers invaded poor little Belgium, but I don't like leaving the trouble and strife on her own. The cellar-man we have is next to useless and Annie will do herself an injury if she starts trying to manoeuvre huge barrels of beer around and so what

I'm wondering, Pascal, is would you be willing to give her a bit of help while I'm away?'

'I would be happy to, Ozzie.' There was deep sincerity in Pascal's voice.

There was a brief silence and then Tilly said, 'Maybe I can be of help as well. You both seem to have forgotten that I've earned a living working behind the bar in the Duke ever since I left school. It's my second home. And if it will make Annie feel less isolated, I'll happily move into the Duke to keep her company, and you might care to join me, Pascal. Have a word with her, will you, Ozzie?'

'I'll tell her of your offer the minute I get home.' Ozzie felt as if a tremendous weight had been taken off his shoulders, knowing Tilly would make sure Annie came to no harm while he was away in Flanders, decimating the hated Boche.

He chewed the corner of his lip, wondering how many other Oystertown men in late middle age were now in receipt of call-up papers, or if his receiving them was simply an anomaly.

He said hesitantly, 'There can't be many local men of my age who have received call-up papers today. What d'you say we seek them out with the object of our all sticking together when we arrive at Boot Camp? Forming a tight-knit group in order not to become separated? I read in *The Gazette* some weeks ago that a small group in Yorkshire have done just that and have called themselves the Northern Tykes. We could do something similar, only instead of going under the name Northern Tykes we could call ourselves the Oystertown Pals.'

Pascal, who was more well-read than Ozzie, said, 'You mean as in the book *The Three Musketeers*? All for one and one for all?'

Ozzie had no idea what a musketeer was, but he liked the sound of all for one and one for all.

'That's exactly what I mean!' he said, his enthusiasm for the project growing at the rate of knots now it had been dignified with a name. 'This is the fifth year of the fighting and we are no nearer to celebrating a peace than we were the day war broke out.'

'We will be once the Yanks arrive.' Pascal's voice was full of certainty.

Tilly's eyes held his. 'And when is that likely to be? By the end of April? The beginning of May? Or sometime never?'

Pascal reached for his pipe and tobacco pouch, saying as he tamped loose-cut flakes into the bowl of his pipe, 'Lord help me, Tilly love. I'm not a soothsayer! But what I do know is that once they arrive, they'll be so full of vim, vigour and bulging wallets we'll wonder how we managed without them.'

Chapter Thirty-seven

Janna lay on her narrow bed in her comfortless room and stared at the ceiling in a rare moment when she had the space to herself. Rust and splinters had been flaking off for as long as she had lived here and nobody was likely to come to mend it any time soon. Idly she wondered if the whole thing would come down before the war ended – whenever that might be.

Word was that the Germans had had great success with their spring offensive and that the new front was only seventy-five miles from Paris. That didn't sound very far, for an army on a winning streak. She wondered if Marietta was there or if she'd gone on yet another tour, bolstering the morale of the allied troops, distracting them with an evening of rousing entertainment from their grim daily task of keeping possession of their trenches and acres of mud.

Reaching out to her rickety bedside table, her hand fell upon a sheet of paper. Letters took longer and longer to reach the field hospital but that meant they were even more precious when they finally arrived. Claudia's immaculate handwriting filled the page, and the sight of it made Janna smile despite herself. She could picture the weighty fountain pen that her friend would have used, and how she would have sat at the desk with the view of their beloved sea. The little bottle of purple-blue ink. The blotter, its edges aligned just so.

And now, apparently, she had a new companion, a four-legged one. Claudia had described the little dog's antics, making Janna smile even more widely. Her friend deserved some happiness, after the misery of Xan's betrayal and the ongoing privations of the war, which even her family's privilege could not fully guard against. Not that Claudia complained; Janna knew her well enough by now to read between the lines, however.

She wished they could have been together when the news came through about women winning the right to vote, even if neither of them were yet eligible. Nor was Janna herself likely to be if that property qualification remained. All the same she felt it was a vindication of everything they'd done, not only the exhilaration of marching with a band of similar-minded suffragettes, but also the hours of tedium filling envelopes and fielding telephone enquiries. Claudia had introduced her to a whole new way of looking at the world and life would never be the same.

Janna had had reason to be grateful for the chance to mix with women from such different backgrounds when tensions erupted among the nurses. From the day she'd arrived she had been aware of it. Some of the professional nurses had felt threatened by the volunteers, most of whom were from families not unlike Claudia's. They spoke in a certain way, dressed and often thought in a certain way. If Janna hadn't had experience of this from the WSPU offices she might well have felt intimidated, retreating into silence. But her time there had stood her in good stead and she now knew she could cope with just about anybody.

Turning over with a sigh, she reflected that by now they were all so exhausted they didn't have the energy to argue between their factions. Every last drop was channelled into getting the job done.

Then came the noise that always revived her, no matter how low she was feeling – the sound of Daniel's motorbike pulling up nearby. In a trice she was on her feet, smoothing the creases out of her old cotton dress, tugging her hair into shape. Of course he wouldn't mind what she looked like – but she wanted to feel at her best, to show him that he was special, that she'd put in some effort, no matter how hasty.

Rushing out to meet him she barely noticed the cold breeze, the shouts from the busy camp all around, the ever-present mud. All that mattered was not to waste one precious second of time with him, so rare was it for them to have a moment together.

He sat astride the bike, his helmet and goggles tucked under his arm, and gave her his easy, familiar smile, his freckles pale after the long winter and cold spring. In that one moment all was suddenly right in her world. Never mind the chaos, the damp, the smell of the huge field hospital complex of Étaples. There was Daniel, and he was hers – and she was his.

She ran to hug him, laughing as she did so. 'I never know when you're going to be here!' she exclaimed. 'Lucky it wasn't yesterday, I had to do extra shifts. More shrapnel injuries than ever, you wouldn't believe.'

'Oh, I would.' His eyes crinkled in humour but also in recognition of what she must have seen.

Janna nodded, knowing that this was true. There wouldn't be many other people from her old life in Oystertown who would understand, but Daniel surely did. It was one more element in the strong bond between them – the brutal reality of what war did to human bodies, the blood and the gore. She wouldn't be telling the others about that if she returned. No, she corrected herself swiftly, when she returned. They had to hang on to hope.

'I haven't got long,' he went on apologetically. 'No time for a visit to our favourite guest house, sorry.'

'That's a pity.' Janna's eyes roved over him hungrily, as his did the same to her.

'I thought we could find a quiet spot – down by that old bridge maybe.' A few weeks ago, they'd happened upon an ancient track through the fields, which ended in a semi-collapsed stone bridge, maybe once a thoroughfare for local farmers. It was as secluded a spot as they could hope for, without travelling far from the hospital.

'Lovely.' Janna swung herself onto the bike to ride pillion. She'd long since got over her fears – there was no time to wonder if it was safe, or respectable, or anything like that. It was their only way of spending time away from the hectic camp and the random gaze of others, and that was what mattered.

Daniel needed no further encouragement and in a moment they were off, with him skilfully weaving between the worst of the muddied ruts that lined the rough roads around the massive camp of tents and makeshift buildings of the hospital.

Negotiating the puddles and other vehicles, he steered them towards a small side road and then onto the old track, weaving between fields. Slowly the landscape became less sodden and grew greener, a clue to how this place must have looked before the war rolled in to ruin it. There were gentle undulations and birdsong flooded the air, heralding the hope of summer. As if on cue, the sun broke through the clouds which had obscured it up until now.

Reaching the old bridge, they drew up beside the rough stone wall that marked one end of it, and Daniel propped up the bike as well as he could, since some of the stones had been dislodged and the remainder were decidedly shaky. Jana reached into the saddle bag and brought out a tarpaulin, dusting off the dried mud that still clung to the edge.

'Should have brought a picnic,' she said, grinning.

Daniel stuck one hand in his jacket pocket. 'Well, I've got these. They aren't too bad.' He produced two apples, a little wrinkled but certainly edible, and Janna's face lit up.

They sat on the tarpaulin, leaning their backs against the wall, the sun warming them as they munched on their apples. A blackbird trilled its call across the neighbouring field and for a moment they could have been home, on the path above Oystertown, the light breeze on their faces. All that was missing was the sharp salty scent and sound of the sea.

Janna rested her head on Daniel's shoulder and he drew her closer, and for a while they were lost in each other. It was not until the sun fell behind another cloud that they broke reluctantly away.

She gave a slight shiver as she sat upright, pulling her jacket more tightly around her. 'Do you ever think about what you'll do when we get back to Oystertown?' she asked after a moment. 'Will you try to go back to the shop? Or even move away? Back to London, maybe?'

Daniel leaned back against the wall and put his arms behind his head, taking his time to answer. 'I've been wondering about that,' he said eventually, gazing up at the sky as if to focus his ideas. The clouds were moving more swiftly now and a shaft of sunlight spread across the field. 'I shan't go back to the shop, Janna. Not after the way they treated me. Even if they'd have me – and that's by no means certain.' He drew a breath. 'Pascal doesn't need me – Tilly's no doubt looking after him far better than anyone else could. So in theory we could go anywhere. But you want to go home to Oystertown, don't you?'

Janna didn't have to think about that one. 'Of course.' Then she shifted a little. 'If you'd be happy there, I mean. If you think everyone is still going to call you a conchie even after all you've done, then we can go somewhere else. I shan't mind.'

'You would,' Daniel predicted acutely. 'Anyway, I don't think I'd want to work in the high street again. I'd rather do something for myself. I'd rather . . .' He frowned, as if the idea was still forming in his mind. 'Well, I keep going back to when I first came. Before we really knew anyone and settled in – how I loved designing the diving suit. Sorry, I don't want to upset you by reminding you of what happened.'

Janna shook her head. 'You won't upset me. It's not as if I ever forget.' It was true. Her feelings for Jonah, her grief at his loss, might have changed as she had matured but they had never left her. Their short time together had marked her deeply. Even in the joy of her marriage to Daniel, there was always that bittersweet note from the past. The one slight comfort was that at least Jonah had not lived to see the destruction of war. He would have volunteered for something rash, no doubt; he had been spared that.

'Of course, I couldn't even begin to think about going back to designing, after he died. I set all that aside.' Daniel was growing more certain now. 'Now, though, I keep wondering about what I could do. I still love the idea of coming up with something new, improvements, the technical side of it all. I'm not in a position to do much about it here. But when we get home . . .'

Janna quietly thrilled at the way he said it, as if, despite being a relative newcomer, Oystertown was truly his home too. It gave her confidence. 'You must talk to Kim about it,' she said decisively. 'I bet you any money he stays in the navy. I bet they have come up with all sorts of things as the fighting has gone on, and they'll need to take time to tie it all together, to make sure they're ready for whatever the future throws at them. You'd be just the person, Daniel. You have to do it. Say you will.'

Daniel looked momentarily taken aback, as if he had expected her to object, or at least to be more reluctant. The memory of Jonah could have put her off the plan. Now he sat up, more resolute.

'All right. I will. I promise.'

Tilly was doing her best to look after Pascal but there were times when it was far from easy. Now that she was at the Duke for much of the week, he was back at the windmill, painting until the light had faded away. Now the days were getting longer, that meant very late.

'*Mais c'est nécessaire*,' he assured her. 'This war, it seems it makes people want to buy my paintings. I must strike while the iron is hot – that is what you say, *n'est-ce pas?*'

Tilly had to acknowledge that this was true. Even without Marietta to act on her father's behalf, taking the finished works to London and making all the arrangements with the galleries, Pascal's pictures were in as much demand as ever – perhaps more. Every now and again he would announce that he feared his happy marriage would destroy his inner fire, but if anything the reverse was the case. He himself now reluctantly made his way up to town, dressed in his brightest colours as if to counterbalance the dull tones of the service uniforms all around, to conduct business for himself. Tilly was always wary when he went, not putting it past him to take his earnings into the nearest tavern and remain there until the purse was once again empty.

So far, though, he had mostly resisted temptation, declaring that he had no need when his favourite tavern was but a stroll down the hill, presided over by the country's finest bar woman.

Tilly always breathed a quiet sigh of relief when he re-appeared, although she took care not to show it – to Pascal or anyone else. For a start, Annie needed no encouragement in the anxiety stakes. She had never believed that Ozzie would be called up and so had been completely unprepared when he'd had to leave so abruptly. Tilly also suspected that she was far from happy at having to share the bar work with a woman known to have had past history with her husband.

Nothing to be done about it, Tilly thought now as she polished the glasses, holding each one up to check for thumb-prints or other smears. Her relationship with Ozzie had ended as soon as she'd agreed to marry Pascal. Annie had come along well after that, so it wasn't as if she'd had to share him. Nevertheless, the atmosphere could be fraught or frosty, depending on Annie's mood.

Tilly shook her head to dislodge the uncomfortable thought, and her magnificent hair tumbled around her shoulders.

'Penny for 'em!'

Tilly looked around and was unsurprised to find that it was Billy Gann, ready for his first drink of the day – or, at least, his first in a recognized hostelry. What he had had for break-fast was anyone's guess. The number of male voices heard around the premises was shrinking still further, now that some of the middle-aged clientele had been forced to follow their landlord and head to France. Tilly smiled, thinking that nobody in their right mind would admit Billy to active service – he would not be safe with a gun.

'The usual?'

'I won't say no, Tilly.' Billy settled himself a little unsteadily on a stool and gripped the edge of the bar. 'Any news of Ozzie? Or anyone else?'

Tilly was glad he'd asked before Annie showed her face, as even such a general question could set her off. 'Don't think so, Billy.' She set the pint glass in front of him. 'No, I tell a lie. We've had a short note from Harry. He says the march on Paris has run out of steam. Even though the Germans made good progress over the spring, they've lost heart and can't make the most of it. Something about being overstretched, the supplies not getting through.'

Billy sipped his beer and raised his eyebrows. 'Still got his foreign lady friend, has he? Bet that makes him happy if he's got more time to spend with her.'

Tilly gave a little shrug. 'I think so. He says he's picked up a bit of French at last.'

'I bet 'e 'as. Best way to learn,' Billy declared, before taking another sip. 'Good job they never got no closer to Paris. That must be nice for Pascal – isn't his girl there? Her what does the singing and dancing on stage?'

Before Tilly could answer, the door from the street opened again and none other than Pascal himself strode through it, as vigorous as ever, never a concession to growing older. 'What is this? You are speaking of me, Billy, my friend?' He leaned across the bar to plant a big kiss on Tilly's lips before turning again to his longtime drinking companion.

Billy swayed a little on his seat. 'I was just saying, you must be glad the Germans didn't get no further towards Paris, if your Marietta's still there. Must be nice to know she's safe for the time being.' He glanced at his friend, who immediately set back his shoulders and laughed.

'Marietta, she can cope with anything. If she gets into trouble she will talk her way out of it somehow. I never worry about her.' He smiled at Tilly and she took his meaning, reaching for another glass. 'Now we will drink a toast to my successful trip. Three more pictures sold since the last time! Yes, I know it is early in the day but we must not pass up the chance to celebrate. Who knows when we shall have such fine news again!'

Tilly poured him a whisky just how he liked it, but she was not fooled for a minute. Pascal might come across as hale-fellow-well-met and without a concern in the world, but deep down she knew he worried about Marietta, so far away and so nearly behind enemy lines. He might convince everyone else – but not her. Heaven forbid the rest of the world should realize it, but Pascal had a soft heart as much as any other father.

Chapter Thirty-eight

It simply wasn't worth it, Harry told himself. Nice to have a bit of leave, yes, he wasn't going to turn that down, thank you very much. But it didn't give him enough time to go where he really wanted to. Fat chance of making it to Oystertown and back. He could rule that out. Sadly, he also had to discount the chance of travelling the much shorter distance to Juliette's home, given the state of the countryside in between her and the camp where he was now stationed. How he longed to see her – and also the handsome Napoléon, now long recovered from his near-disaster in the shell hole. Harry quietly blessed the animal for otherwise he and Juliette would never have met, never have realized their common love of horses which had led to so much more.

Harry's platoon had been drafted west of Flanders, bedded in to halt the German attack over the spring, knowing that at all costs the enemy must not reach the Channel and the all-important ports along the coast. It had been a relentless task all through the spring and early summer, but now it looked as if the Allies had succeeded in keeping the Germans out of the strategically significant areas. Now the rewards came: small periods of leave for the exhausted troops.

Harry made up his mind. Archie was in Boulogne, busy at his desk job as he was no longer able to perform active service. He'd go and catch up with his old friend and comrade. It might still be France and a military setting, but it would at least be a different one. With little time to send word of his arrival, Harry prepared his pack, figuring that Archie was unlikely to stray far from his post.

He'd hitched a ride on a supplies truck, not much faster than walking but solid, able to cope with the state of what passed for roads. The last few miles, he'd agreed to walk, as the truck headed off to its final destination further south. Harry took in the devastation all around as he strode along, but he couldn't feel down for long. The day was warm and the air became fresher the closer he got to the sea. It might not be Oystertown but it was on the coast – and there were the cries of the seagulls, unconcerned by the progress of the war, and no doubt happy at the influx of troops which meant more scraps to feed on.

After a couple of wrong turns, Harry finally found somebody who could direct him to Archie's place of work. He'd assumed it would be easy to find but hadn't reckoned on the sheer numbers of troops all around. The place was huge, and he reminded himself he was not used to towns of any size, in peacetime or wartime. The voices were from all over the British Isles, with lots of French as well, plus the Anzac battalions – and, if he wasn't very much mistaken, the distinctive sound of the occasional American. At last, the Yankees might have arrived.

Then, he came to what looked as if it had once been the home of somebody important – a merchant, perhaps. It stood a little apart from the neighbouring buildings and would have been an impressive sight, had it not been for the overall air of disrepair. Roof tiles had slipped, windows had cracked and been hastily repaired with brown tape, as if there was something else far more vital to be done. It most certainly had not been designed as an office or headquarters. Yet now this was what it had become.

Harry made a guess that Archie would most likely be based on the ground floor, as losing a leg would have made stairs tricky. He stepped into what once must have been a grand entrance hall, looking for any signs – but there were none. So he set about finding him by the simple expedient of knocking on all the doors – some more rickety than others – and sticking his head round them. After the fifth or sixth attempt, an irritable corporal told him to try at the end of the corridor and dismissed him.

Harry thanked him, glad he didn't have to work in that particular room. As he raised his hand to knock on the final door, he caught the sound of cheerful whistling and he gave a wide smile. It was a tune he knew well – one that he and Archie had often heard Marietta sing. This was beyond a shadow of a doubt the right spot. He flung open the door and there was Archie, piles of paper stacked on the desk before him, a patch over where he'd lost the eye, but giving his all to the popular song.

Instantly he looked up from where he was sitting and did a double take. Then his face broke into a broad grin. 'Harry,' he said simply. Then he roared with laughter. 'What the hell are you doing here?'

'Came to see you, of course.' Harry set down his pack. Even for a well-muscled former coal-man, it was a heavy weight. 'Thought I'd better check to see that you were doing all right. That you haven't been messing up all that paperwork.'

'Oh, I'm keeping on top of it.' Archie pushed himself up to standing and picked up a crutch. Expertly he swung himself round the corner of the desk and used his spare arm to clap his old friend on the back. 'Time for a cuppa? Care to inspect our mess?'

'I won't say no,' said Harry, suddenly aware that he'd had nothing to eat or drink since emptying his water flask while on the truck.

Archie led him out of the main house and round to the back, to what perhaps had been stabling. Now the single-storey building had been turned into a makeshift canteen, with the familiar aroma of stewing tea floating to greet them. Flies buzzed around the open door but Archie swatted them away, ushering Harry to the end of a long well-scrubbed deal table, with benches to either side. 'Wait here – I'll fetch us something.'

'But how will you manage . . .' Harry began, but Archie dismissively waved away the question. 'I've learned,' he said shortly, before smiling again to take away the edge.

Harry presumed he must have, and was convinced a couple of minutes later as Archie returned with a tray in his free hand on which were balanced two mugs of tea and a plate of roughly cut cheese sandwiches.

'Here. It makes a change from bully beef, I'll tell you that much.'

Harry's hunger got the better of him and he tucked in, without pausing to reply. Archie looked on with an expression of satisfaction. Evidently, he was not letting his disability get in his way.

Finally, Harry had finished every last crumb and allowed himself to meet his friend's gaze. 'That's better,' he stated, leaning back. 'Hadn't realized just how famished I was.'

'So I can see.' Archie grinned. 'So, what news do you have? Anything I might be interested in?'

Harry shrugged and shook his head. 'Everything I get is so old, you probably heard it weeks, if not months, ago. The only thing I do apart from trying to keep my head down in action is manage the very occasional dash up to Flanders to see Juliette. It's never long enough but at least I can say a bit more now. Not just inky-pinky-*parlez-vous*.'

Archie nodded sagely. 'Just as well; you've been over here for long enough. She'll appreciate that, you know. I enjoy trying to speak with the locals – passes the time. Takes my mind off wondering what's going on along the Front.'

Harry agreed. 'Not that we need words,' he admitted, with the closest he ever got to a blush. Then he hastily sought to hide it by changing the subject. 'Now if I was not mistaken, I caught some new voices as I was coming through town. Sounds as if the Americans have finally got here.'

Archie set down his mug. 'You're right. I mean, you might not have heard, but they have been fighting already. There was a to-do somewhere much further south, couple of months back – that was their first real piece of the action. But now, they're here and they're growing in numbers. Took them ages to get across the Atlantic, that was the trouble. Or part of it. No doubt some argy-bargy about who was going to be in command, them or us, or all together or separate. I didn't pay much attention to all that. All that really matters is that they're here and they're ready. Won't be long before we start pushing back in earnest, you mark my words.'

Harry blew on his tea, not because it was still too warm, but to buy a little time to take that in. It was the news they had all been waiting for ever since the announcement had come through that the United States would be joining the war. About time, he thought privately, but he didn't want to say so aloud, not knowing who might be listening. Archie had to work here, after all. He didn't want to make trouble for his old friend.

'Well, let's hope it's soon,' he said slowly. 'Because I've had enough, Archie, I don't mind saying. Weeks upon months upon years of it – and all I really want is to take Juliette back to Oystertown, to meet my Bessie. They'll get on like a house on fire, I just know it.'

Archie's eyes crinkled at the edges in amusement. Trust Harry's first priority to be getting his girlfriend to meet his horse. But then, from what he'd heard about Juliette, it would suit her down to the ground. 'Hope you don't have to wait too long, then.' He glanced up as a slight young woman in civvies approached.

'This is where you are!' she exclaimed, in perfect English but with a distinct French accent. 'I went to your desk but you were not there. I thought, what does he like more than to work on the forms I give him? Oh, I know, like every British man, he will have gone to find some tea. And I was right.' Her vivacious face showed her amusement and Harry noticed, with dawning understanding, how Archie's face lit up in return.

In all the years he'd known him, the other man had shown not the slightest interest in the opposite sex – indeed in anybody, or not in that way. He was possibly the only man in Oystertown and beyond who had purely feelings of friendship for Marietta. Not a flicker of physical interest had he ever displayed. And now here, after Archie had lost an eye and a leg, and was miles from home in a crowded, noisy, makeshift HQ, something was going on.

'Ah, Harry – Sergeant Slater. May I, ahem, introduce you to Mademoiselle Leclerc. Well, Louise. She, ah, works in the office for our captain. Louise, Harry is an old mate of mine from back home. He was the one who saved me when I got these.' He indicated his injuries.

Louise's deep indigo eyes grew wide. 'Oh! That Harry! *Vraiment, Monsieur*, I must thank you. I do not believe that Archie would be here today if you had not done what you did then.'

Harry almost blushed again. 'Well, I don't know about that . . .'

'It's true, Harry, you know it as well as I do.' Archie's tone brooked no argument. 'It's a simple statement of fact. And of course I'm very grateful. And I'm pleased to say that now, well, Louise is grateful too. We've spent quite a bit of time together recently, Louise and me.'

The young woman nodded and her bobbed chestnut hair glinted in the sunlight coming through the windows set high up in the walls.

Harry blinked. 'Well, yes, so I see. I mean, that's nice. Nice for you both.' He was blathering, he could tell.

Archie's smile grew wider and wider. 'There you are, you see,' he said cheerfully. 'You aren't the only one to have found a way of improving your French, Harry.'

Chapter Thirty-nine

Marietta stretched in her seat, observing the other members of the audience in the dim light. There were not many of them. Most people preferred the later showings in the picture palace, but of course some had to work in the evenings. Shift workers, be it in factories or hospitals. Soldiers on night duties. And, of course, entertainers, of whom Marietta was one.

The place was not a patch on the plush cinema houses she had enjoyed in Paris, or even back in London, but her work had brought her to Amiens and she had to make do with what was available. At least it gave her a chance to catch up with films she had missed. Social life in Paris had been cut short when the enemy had started to shell the French capital in March and had gone on doing so. Even Marietta's latest conquest had been less inclined to venture out for entertainment's sake. She'd thought he would not mind, being a senior military man, but it turned out that he did.

She was looking forward to two episodes of *The Count of Monte Cristo*. That was the trouble with working her irregular hours – she'd seen the first ones, and then the last, but not the ones in the middle. This afternoon she was determined to put that right. She'd have to let the adventure wash over her, and not try to recall all the details. Perhaps she should have chosen a comedy – the new Charlie Chaplin was doing the rounds, popular with the locals and military of all nationalities alike – but somehow the historical drama was what she craved. It would take her mind off everything that had happened in the war so far.

Before that, though, there would be the newsreels. She had become accustomed to tuning them out; it was always so depressing, even if they were extremely patriotic and presented every defeat as a victory. She took everything with a big pinch of salt these days. She sat back a little, noticing how the plush fabric on the armrests had grown worn and scratchy, a shadow of its former glory. The seat was not very comfortable either – rather lumpy. Never mind, she told herself, it really was the least of her worries.

It frustrated her that every time she met an interesting officer, it was only a matter of time before they assumed she would give up her career to marry them. Kim had been the first in a long line and at least the time spent with him had been worth it. She could count upon him as a friend, she was sure. The latest proposal had come from a French army colonel at least twice her age, who had hinted that she should not allow herself to be left on the shelf. He had strongly implied that he would be doing her a favour. Marietta had set him straight in very direct terms and then left the table of what passed for the best restaurant in town. She'd enjoyed his company up to a point, but why would she want to be tied to him for ever?

Sighing a little at the memory, she tried sitting at a different angle. It was better, but only marginally. There was nothing for it but to watch the newsreel and hope it provided distraction.

First came the familiar opening to the Pathé bulletins. Marietta felt her concentration drifting off. Then what came next brought her attention back, and she sat more upright.

The Americans had arrived and begun actively to join the fighting – well, she had known that. It was hard to miss them as they were all over town, full of energy for the battles to come, and so well-fed and healthy too. Several had approached her, of course, but she had not been inclined to take up their offers. The gulf between their enthusiasm and her weariness after years of war had seemed unbridgeable.

Now they were making a genuine difference, fighting alongside the Allies in a successful offensive. Even given the usual bias of the newsreels, Marietta could tell that the tide had changed. For years it seemed all the fighting had been to win, and then lose, and then maybe win again, the same miserable few feet of mud. This was on a whole grander scale. For the first time in the entire desperate conflict, something decisive was going on and it was in their favour.

In the front row, a group of three off-duty soldiers cheered and one began to sing '*La Marseillaise*'. His companions nudged him, laughing, and he piped down, but the atmosphere in the tired old picture house had altered. It was as if for the first time in a very, very long while, there was hope of victory.

Marietta found that she had a lump in her throat. She gave herself a mental shake. She never cried. No matter what assailed her, she carried on and did not give in to tears. It was a point of pride and she was not going to surrender to emotion now.

All the same, as the newsreel ended and the credits rolled, she could not help but wonder about the future. She had had to change her plans so many times, thanks to the war, that she had all but given up trying. Everything was focussed upon getting through it, waiting for peace to arrive. What if it was on the horizon at last? What might she do?

The drama that she had come for began, as the Count of Monte Cristo took to the screen. Marietta's imagination ranged far and wide, loving the passion, the glamorous clothes, the powerful gestures. Some people said that soon there would be sound as well as pictures in films, that it was only a matter of time. Marietta had no way of knowing if that was true or not.

Yet it was an enticing idea. As the lead characters gesticulated on screen, the possibilities began to take shape in her mind. She knew she looked good; there was no point in false modesty. She knew how to use those looks to full advantage – little room for modesty there, either. It would be criminal not to make full use of the talents she had been born with. Another of which was her voice. How many of those people up there on the screen right now sounded as good as they looked? In the future an aspiring star would have to have both looks and voice.

Marietta shivered. She was fed up with always being on the move, travelling in often terrible conditions to lousy lodgings, rarely seeing her family and friends. While there was a war on, it had been her duty, and so she had done it. But after it ended, there was no good reason not to follow her dream. She could reach far bigger audiences, and all without having to change venues every few days.

The final scene played out and at last the show was over. The scattered members of the audience started to pick up their jackets and bags, readying themselves for whatever awaited in the real world beyond the picture palace's doors. Marietta slowly got to her feet, in their worn but still smart summer heels. There would be plenty of other aspiring actresses, she was under no illusions about that. She put her shoulders back and pursed her lips. They might well be as good-looking as her and be able to sing – but she doubted any could do it better.

Claudia never knew whether to be pleased or full of dread when the telephone rang. For so long it had usually brought bad news. From time to time, it meant a call for her mother, frequently from Sir Edward Grey, her father's old friend. Claudia had held out hopes for a romance there. But recently Celia had played down the idea, hinting that things had cooled.

Claudia had tried to probe further but her mother had clammed up. She'd cornered Kim on one of his rare visits and demanded that he confess if he had heard anything. He'd dodged the question as well as he could, but Claudia knew him too well. In the end he'd muttered something about past affairs, and that Celia was better off making a clean break if she didn't want to suffer the same indignities. Claudia was not sure how involved her mother had been, but could see that this was the right course of action. It saddened her to think that it had come to nothing – but Celia seemed resolute and not at all broken-hearted.

So the caller was unlikely to be Sir Edward. Taking a deep breath, Claudia reached for the earpiece. 'Oystertown two five –' she began but a voice down the crackly line cut her short.

'Claudia! Is that you?'

'Kim!' It was hard to make out what he was saying but she'd recognize those tones anywhere. 'Yes, of course it's me. Mama's out trying to raise more funds for burns dressings. I'm manning the fort.'

'Listen, I haven't got long.' Kim spoke quickly, almost as if he was out of breath from running. 'You'll see it in the newspapers but I wanted to tell you as soon as I heard. It's confirmed. It's over.'

For a moment Claudia couldn't work out what he meant. 'What is? What are you talking about, Kim?'

There was a huff of impatience. 'The war, silly. The Kaiser has abdicated. They're going to sign the armistice tomorrow morning first thing and announce it before lunch. It's true, Claudia. Get your best champagne flutes ready, or polish the tankards down at the Duke, or whatever you want to do, but it's true. Look, I can't stay, I'm wanted at the Admiralty, but I'll try to come down as soon as I can. Tell the others. Got to go.' And the line went dead.

Claudia sat at the little chair by the desk, staring out at the sea as she had done so often for the past four years. It was grey, the horizon obscured by autumn mist, but the familiar cries of the seagulls penetrated the foggy air. She could hardly believe it. It seemed impossible that this grinding deadly conflict could finally be over. Yet she also knew that Kim was the last person who would play a cruel joke; she trusted him implicitly. In fact, most likely he had taken a big risk, breaking off from whatever official business he was on to let her know the tremendous news.

She stood up and found she was shaking.

She could not bear to be alone, not now she was in possession of such news. Hastily she scribbled a note for her mother and propped it on the desk. Then she ran for her coat, protection against the insistent mizzle. They were short-staffed at Rose Mount, they had been for some while, and she saw nobody as she rushed along the corridor to the still-imposing front door.

Then it was a scrabble along the path, the quickest way into town, along the high street and into the Duke. Stopping at the entrance of the main bar to catch her breath, she looked around. It was quiet; most of the regulars had of course been called up by now, and those who remained were no longer able to come here every day. Poverty and rationing had seen to that.

However, the noise of the door shutting brought Tilly around the bar from the kitchen, wiping her hands on her apron, her magnificent hair tumbling around her shoulders.

Before she could speak Claudia recovered her breath. 'Tilly! Oh, Tilly! I've got the best news ever!'

Tilly looked at her dubiously. 'Are you all right, Claudia? Only your coat's buttoned all wrong, you're only wearing one glove and your scarf's fallen off behind you.'

'Doesn't matter, none of it matters.' Claudia felt the full weight of what she was about to announce and she could not stop smiling. 'It's over, Tilly, it really is. They're signing the peace tomorrow. Better get those beer barrels ready.'

Tilly looked at her as if she was mad. 'You been working around the clock again? Sounds like you need more sleep. You're talking nonsense.'

Claudia shook her head, understanding that it was too much to take in, the news they'd all longed for and for so very long. 'It's true. Kim rang. It'll be official tomorrow morning. The Kaiser has stood down. We've won, Tilly, we've won.'

Tilly was lost for words, for the first time ever. She blinked furiously and then came around the bar to where Claudia was standing. For a moment she seemed to freeze on the spot and then she pulled her into a tight hug. Wordlessly, the two women embraced and then Claudia began to cry, not with sadness as much as in relief. Finally, finally, the killing would stop. Finally, their loved ones would come home.

'Pascal! Pascal! Where are you? Whatever you are doing, stop it, you've got to come with me.'

Tilly flung open the door to the windmill, not knowing if her husband had heard her or not. She doubted it but she couldn't keep the urgency from spilling out. Even painting would have to take second place to this news.

From Pascal's face she could tell she had some convincing to do. 'What is this? Why do you interrupt my concentration? You know very well that when the spirit of creation is moving it is madness, folly, to get in its way!' He waved a paintbrush like a furious wand.

Tilly stood her ground. 'You're needed down the Duke today and even more so tomorrow,' she told him. 'We're going to be busier than we've ever been. The war's over. Just like that. They'll announce it tomorrow. Then all of Oystertown will be in need of a drink, and you and me are going to serve it to them.'

Pascal looked at her as if she was mad. 'And how do you know about this?' he demanded suspiciously, as if it was too good to be true.

'Claudia came to tell me. She heard it from Kim, who's up at the Admiralty right this minute. It's no lie, Pascal. It's a fact.' She paused and a sob escaped. 'Janna and Daniel, they'll come home. They'll be safe. They'll come back.' She sank down onto a stool, careless of whether it had splodges of wet paint on it or not.

Pascal was transfixed for a moment, brush still in hand. Then he sprang into action. 'But there is no time to lose! Come, Tilly, we must hurry back to the Duke and start to prepare!' He swiftly threw the brush into a jam jar of turps and cast about for his coat, all thought of finishing his painting forgotten. 'Come, *ma chérie*, we must celebrate, as you say. You are right, *comme toujours*.' He planted an enormous kiss on her cheek and she turned her face up to him to continue it. For a brief second they relished the moment. Then they were off, down the hill, the path slippery from the fog, and back into town, where the few people out and about regarded them with amazement, if not alarm.

'It'll be over tomorrow!' Tilly cried, not stopping to explain, and Mrs Pettman the minister's wife paused in her conversation with her neighbour, before commenting on the dreadful power of drink, and so early in the day too.

Chapter Forty

To Tilly it might well have seemed that the war had ended just like that. Yet the events leading up to the decisive moment had been nothing like as instant.

The offensive that had begun in the summer following the arrival of the US soldiers was, as Marietta saw on the newsreels, the first piece of genuine good news for the Allies. This had led to the big push following the Battle of Amiens, at which point the German leaders realized the war could not be won. The Allies advanced further, all the way to the Hindenburg Line, as Germany's own allies abandoned the fight.

Morale had slumped among the German forces and eventually many sailors rebelled and refused to carry on. This led to the Kaiser recognizing the inevitable and standing down, ending the power of the royal family. Two days later, the Armistice was signed: at the eleventh hour of the eleventh day of the eleventh month. Or, strictly speaking, several hours before that, as Kim had known, in order that the news could spread in time for the official announcement.

The news took some time to make its way from the offices of Whitehall and Westminster out into the streets, into cities across the land, to the soldiers still fighting on the front lines, and into the smaller towns and villages across Britain, France and Belgium. But in Oystertown, where they had

had prior knowledge of what was to come, the glasses and tankards were lined up in readiness, the ales and spirits ready to pour.

'To victory! Cheers! *Santé*!' Pascal had procured a bottle of champagne from somewhere and had popped it open with great enthusiasm, meaning it showered everybody within reach and missed half of the glasses it was intended for.

Nobody cared. Billy was quite content to drink brandy instead. He'd shoved up from his usual place to allow Smelly to stand there, enjoying the unfamiliar sensation of being permitted inside the pub. He raised his beer and cheered, his breath as rank as ever.

Celia smiled gamely, having been warned by Claudia what it would be like in the Duke. She had never ventured inside before, and could not quite believe that she was marking the end of the war in such a place, rather than in the company of members of the cabinet or the royal family. Yet much had changed over the past four years, and running Rose Mount as a hospital had opened her eyes to a whole different side of the society of which she was a part. She would return there soon and share the good news with the recuperating officers but for now she wanted to be with her daughter – and Claudia wanted to be with Tilly, and Pascal, and the other inhabitants of Oystertown who had gathered in the place where they'd done all their celebrating: of weddings, christenings, birthdays and wakes.

Annie looked on, happy for her customers, but gritting her teeth and trying to hide her sorrow that Ozzie was not here to join them. 'Don't you worry, love, he'll be back soon!' Billy shouted, but Annie knew that might not be the case for a long while yet. It stood to reason. There were so many troops stationed abroad – they couldn't exactly fit them all onto one boat and bring them home straight away.

Meanwhile, she was grateful that Pascal was there, marking the occasion in colours even more outlandish than usual, helping to heft the barrels from the cellar, talking to twenty separate people all at once. They would have been lost without him. Tilly could manage a lot of the heavy lifting but not at the same time as joking with regulars, acquaintances and those who never normally set foot inside a tavern. Besides, he had insisted on resurrecting the old bunting and flags, hanging them up to add to the air of festivity.

'There's tea and biscuits up at the manse if anyone fancies those instead!' Tilly called now, just in case anybody should feel the need to give the alcohol a rest.

Nobody took her up on the offer. Leaving the Methodists to their more sober form of celebration, everyone continued to show their delight by raising their glasses time after time, depleting the stocks already curtailed by rationing. Annie tried not to think about tomorrow. She ought to rejoice today along with all the rest of them.

Claudia threw herself into the party, not giving a jot that this was the last place she would have imagined herself at the start of the war – indeed, she could admit to herself, until a relatively short time ago. It had been so important to Xan to maintain their position in society, to attend the correct functions, the suitable engagements. Now she knew why. He had been forever on the lookout for possible contacts, snippets of gossip, revealing details which he could pass to the enemy. His side.

This made her all the happier to drink warm beer from a battered half-pint tankard, washing down one of the pickled eggs that Tilly had discovered in a huge jar behind the bar. 'Might as well finish them off,' she suggested, and so Claudia accepted another. She might even come to enjoy them after a while, she decided.

'Good lord. What on earth is that smell?' said a well-known voice and she spun around on her heel to find herself face to face with her cousin, who was reeling backwards at the sulphurous stink of the egg.

She grinned with no shame. 'Don't tell me you have never had one of these, Kim? And you must have smelt far worse things on board those ships you love.' She shook her head in amazement. 'I thought you had to be at the Admiralty? How come you have managed to be here? How did you know where we would be? Even Mama is here, you know.'

'I do know. I went to Rose Mount first but soon realized my mistake.' He shrugged out of his uniform jacket, on which the gold braid sparkled. 'Of course you're all here. That's what I said to you yesterday, wasn't it!' He paused as Tilly passed him a beer, reaching over Billy's shoulder. 'Yes, well, they needed me yesterday. It's all a bit bonkers today. People are dancing in the streets, that sort of carry-on. Not a lot of work being done. So we thought we'd come down here, join the rest of you.'

'We?' Claudia was momentarily baffled but Rascal was ahead of her. Slipping his lead, barking with joy, he scampered across to the main door leading to the street, and jumped up at the figure standing there.

Claudia followed his progress and almost dropped her drink.

It was Jasper.

Claudia hadn't realized how the beer had affected her until the cold air hit her. It seemed that drinking beer in the daytime was very different to sipping cocktails in the evening. She reeled a little and Jasper immediately put out an arm to steady her, and used it as an excuse to pull her close.

'What – what are you doing here?' she gasped. 'Weren't you meant to be on a ship out in the Atlantic or something like that? How did you get leave?'

359

Jasper laughed and tipped her face up so that he could look into her blue eyes. 'Anyone would think you weren't pleased to see me,' he teased, and she tapped him firmly on the chest.

'You know very well what I mean.'

'All right. I do.' He laughed again. 'You can blame your cousin. He had me called down to the Admiralty when he heard that my ship had come into port, over near Bristol. It's a coincidence that it's also the armistice. I was meant to go to a meeting with him but it's all postponed now. So I joined him when he said we could get down here and back before anyone high up got around to noticing.'

'I'm glad,' Claudia said simply, and then he was kissing her and she was kissing him back, and she didn't care if anyone was looking out through the windows of the Duke or not. The only thing that could break their passion was Rascal, who eventually grew fed up of not being the centre of attention. Clearly, he assumed that these two, of all the people in the world, should make him their priority, and so he barked and jumped up until they did.

'All right, boy.' Jasper bent down to pat the little dog, ruffling the fur on his neck until the creature calmed again. 'You'd rather be inside, wouldn't you? Your coat's all wet. And so is yours,' he added, registering that beads of moisture were clinging to Claudia's once-fine tweed. 'Come on, we should join the fun.'

Claudia nodded and smiled, now in the knowledge that he was safe, and unlikely to have to face the dangers of the Atlantic run again. 'We should. Oh, Jasper. We've got so much to cele-brate. To be grateful for.' For a moment her voice was choked.

He took her hand and squeezed it. 'We have.' He looked at her with great intensity, drinking her in. Then he took a step towards the tavern door. 'Another half, then?'

Claudia threw caution to the winds. 'Half be damned. I'll have a pint and worry about it later.'

Epilogue

1928

Marietta strolled into the Verandah Cafe and thought how it felt like a home away from home. She'd had plenty of occasion to travel on the RMS *Mauretania* over the past few years, always preferring this luxury liner to its rivals. The American vessels were out of the question – they had to adhere to their government's laws forbidding alcohol, and that did not suit Marietta's style at all. Besides, the *Mauretania* had held the record for the Atlantic's fastest crossings for many years, only recently outpaced by a newcomer.

The word was that the liner's latest refit had seen this room modelled upon the Orangery at Hampton Court, back in England, the country to where she was now headed once more. Some people also pointed out that when this gorgeous room had first been designed the open side had meant that passengers sitting near that edge would find themselves drenched in wet weather or rough seas. Never mind, she thought, whisking her bias-cut satin frock neatly on a path through the wicker armchairs, they'd solved that problem now.

Sitting at her favourite table she quickly glanced in the small mirror she always carried in her beaded bag. That was the price of fame; she always had to look the part. It was a full-time job to keep her skin fashionably pale when she spent so much time on America's West Coast, with its glorious sunshine. She wore a hat or carried a parasol for much of the year, but she still had to be on her guard.

She wound her hair carefully away from the back of the chair. Even though she was now approaching forty she was proud that it still showed no traces of grey. She employed the best hairdressers and knew that they would take care of that particular problem when it finally arose. Her success had given her the freedom to spend as much as was necessary on maintaining her appearance. She knew some critics called it vanity, but she regarded it as a good investment in her career. She'd worked hard to get to this point; she wasn't going to let them goad her into making a mistake.

Any minute now her manager would come to join her, so that they could work through her forthcoming schedule. The studio back in Hollywood had at first objected when she told them she was going to return to England for a period, but then decided it would serve their purpose well. She would go on a grand promotional tour for her latest movie, and this would build on her carefully honed image as an English rose.

Marietta had laughed at that, wondering if they had forgotten that she was half-French, but the studio boss had reminded her that the public didn't care about the detail. It was all about appearance. Marietta had smiled and nodded but was glad she could make the journey without a major argument. The fact was, nothing on earth was going to keep her from being back on home soil for a very special event. If they had decided to cancel her contract, well, so be it. Happily, it had not come to that.

Stan Sidwell waved as he came through the entrance, turning heads with the cut of his velvet jacket. Stan was always immaculately turned out, but that wasn't why he was Marietta's manager. He could spot a tiny change in a contract from a thousand paces and he never, ever failed to point that out to whoever was trying to pull a fast one. He more than earned his percentage. He also had no interest in Marietta's physical charms whatsoever, and in fact he reminded her of a more worldly, more flamboyant version of Archie. Of course Archie now had his French wife, and she would see them both soon enough. Stan's preferences lay elsewhere – which bothered her not at all.

'So,' he said now, settling himself opposite her in one of the comfortable chairs, 'here is your itinerary.' He handed her a foolscap folder. 'Day One: we dock at Southampton. Then, you said you had personal business. Don't suppose you're going to let me know what that might be?' He pushed his hand through his very slightly receding hair.

'It's no secret really.' Marietta rested the folder on her lap as she elegantly raised one hand to attract the attention of a waiter. She knew many of them, thanks to her frequent trips. 'James, would you be so good as to fetch me a Bee's Knees – and you'll have the same, won't you, Stan?'

'Don't mind if I do.' Stan was used to Marietta making such decisions. He generally went along with it – she could choose what she liked from the cocktail menu as long as she left the big matters up to him.

James turned neatly away, hindered only slightly by the swell of the ocean.

'Well, then. You were saying.' Stan raised an eyebrow.

Marietta turned her fabulous cat-like eyes on him and Stan did not react at all. She took a breath. 'Bet you didn't have me down as someone who followed British politics, Stan.'

Stan paused as James returned with two delicate glasses full of chilled honey-coloured liquid, little twists of lemon perched on the sides. Marietta thanked him charmingly and raised her glass by its elegant stem. 'Cheers, Stan.'

Stan raised his too. 'To success,' he said succinctly. 'Now. Tell me. You know you can't surprise or shock me.'

Marietta took a sip. 'It's not shocking,' she said, setting the glass down on the little table between them. 'Or rather, it's shocking that this hasn't happened earlier.'

Stan sat forward. 'What hasn't? Spill the beans, Marietta.'

She smiled a little. 'It's not personal. It's more a matter of history. There, I have surprised you after all.'

'Not a bit,' replied Stan staunchly.

'Well, you know that after the war they changed the law and all men over twenty-one could vote, and also women for the first time – as long as they were over thirty and had the right amount of property.'

'Think I'd heard something along those lines,' Stan drawled. He himself came from the north of England although he'd worked hard for years to remove any trace of that from his voice.

'Now it so happens my two best friends – apart from you of course – were very active before the war, marching as suffragettes, getting arrested, working behind the scenes doing the boring administration: you name it, they did it. They knew that poor woman who died at the races.' Marietta paused for a moment, remembering how upset Janna and Claudia had been. 'Anyway. They've carried on, writing to members of parliament, campaigning, doing whatever they could think of. Finally, they're passing a bill to make the conditions the same for both men and women. They'll all be able to vote once they turn twenty-one. It won't matter if they live in a cottage or a castle.'

Stan nodded. 'Well, since you put it like that, it does seem pretty unfair that it's taken so long.'

'I should say so.' Marietta's eyes lit up. 'I didn't think about such things when I was younger but now I see why they fought so hard. Look at how I'm treated in Hollywood – they assume I'm just a silly sausage who likes to dance and sing a bit, but as long as the audience wants to watch and listen to me, they're happy. They wouldn't dream of taking my opinions seriously – about politics or history or anything like that. Not you, Stan, I know you're different.' She reached across and briefly put a hand on his arm. 'The thing is, my friends are having the biggest party ever to celebrate when the bill goes through. It'll be the first week of July. We've got a bit of time to keep the bosses happy first. And then there is no power on earth that will make me miss that party. You can come, they'll love you.' Or at least most of them will, she thought. Time enough to think about that. 'But there's not a chance that I'd be anywhere else. So now you know.'

Stan looked up as a young couple approached, the woman clutching a magazine. 'Excuse me, but aren't you . . . aren't you Marina Makepeace? From *Adventures in Paradise*?' She was scarcely more than a girl, very nervous but excited. Her beau spoke up.

'Yes, we saw it in New York and now they're showing it on the big screen in the dining saloon after dinner.'

'May we . . . may we have your autograph?'

Marietta sighed inwardly, knowing she must play her part. The two fans were quite sweet, not pushy like some. All the same she was glad she had arranged to dine privately in her stateroom, rather than risk being mobbed at a public table.

'Why of course.' She dipped into her little bag and drew out a pen. 'Give me your magazine. There.' She signed with a flourish and Stan gave a nod of approval.

And then, thought Marietta, I shall keep my assignation with the ship's surgeon. Such an attentive man – he'd helped to pass the long hours on several previous voyages. If she was to be working hard on her promotional tour, she deserved a little play beforehand.

* * *

Rose Mount was at its best in July, Claudia thought, pausing for a moment in between carrying trays of plates and cutlery to the big table, covered in a white linen cloth, which had been set up on the top lawn. The flower borders were radiant with roses in deep reds and vivid pinks, attracting bees and butterflies alike.

Thank God it hadn't rained. Yes, there was more than enough room inside, now the house had resumed its life as their private home and not a hospital. That transformation had taken longer than they'd imagined and Celia was still making minor adjustments to the fine furnishings. However, it would not have had the same air of celebration, the sheer joy of everyone mingling on the lawns, the terraces, the cliff path. The sun was out and it was as if the heavens were giving their blessing to what had finally come to pass.

Claudia halted in her train of thought. It hadn't simply happened out of the blue, a matter of inevitability. The suffragettes and the suffragists had done this – herself and Janna and all the rest. Their great inspiration, Emily Pankhurst, had died last month, but the leader of the suffragists, Millicent Fawcett – less radical than the women of the WSPU but just as indefatigable – still lived, and had seen the passing of the bill. She and all the others had brought about this long-overdue moment of justice.

Claudia laughed under her breath when she remembered that protest in Downing Street, how unthinkingly she'd gone into the fray. Perhaps she would be more moderate now, but she'd never regretted doing what she'd done. Although, she acknowledged ruefully, if it had been Janna who'd done it, she wouldn't have had an influential family to get her out of prison.

There was Janna now, partially backlit in the golden sunshine, for a moment not so very different from how she'd appeared when they'd first met all those years ago. As she came closer Claudia could recognize the changes – not so slim now, after bearing two children, and with her hair a little more tidily cut. Her clothes were still practical, even if her days of working on the oyster perches were over. Now she was waving at her friend and hurrying across the verdant grass.

'Did you manage to order more fruit cake?' Janna asked, her face a little pink from rushing everywhere all morning. 'I'm afraid we'll run out.'

'Not to worry, it's all in hand.' Claudia grinned, thinking that there had been years when either of them would have rejoiced at the thought of just one cake to share between everyone. But now they were back in times of relative plenty, and they had no intention of scrimping, today of all days.

'Where's Daniel?' she asked, casting her eyes over the lawn and back to the house for a glimpse of Janna's husband.

Janna shaded her face with her hand and turned around. 'He was over there a moment ago – I bet he's gone into the office with Jasper.' She sighed in mock-exasperation.

'Probably. Even on a day like today, they'll have some kind of technical problem to sort out,' Claudia shrugged.

Everything had changed for Daniel and Jasper after the war, and it was Kim who could be blamed for most of it. It had been his idea – and why he had summoned Jasper to the Admiralty meeting the day before the armistice, almost ten years ago. Kim had never forgotten the ideas he'd heard were being mooted around Oystertown before the fighting all started, putting paid to their part-time attempts at developing designs. As soon as Daniel had made it home from Étaples, he had been included as well. It had been just what he'd dreamed of doing, but had been unsure of how to go about it.

Kim's contacts in the Navy had ensured that whatever ideas they could come up with would be listened to – and now Kim had risen through the ranks, his word of recommendation carried considerable weight. Jasper and Daniel had gone into business together, Jasper bringing his years of nautical experience of boats small and large, and Daniel his ingenuity and love of a technical challenge. They were the perfect combination, and now they had Archie helping behind the scenes. At first Kim had expressed concern, knowing that Archie had little direct experience of the sea, but Archie had laughed him off. 'I organized the logistics for most of the troops in Amiens,' he pointed out. 'I reckon I can sort out an office, especially one that doesn't get shelled several times a week. It'll be a walk in the park in comparison.'

So Archie had moved back into the cottage on Harbour Row, bringing Louise home with him, and Louise's little girl, who had been little more than a toddler during the Battle of Amiens. Now Violette was a vibrant teenager, and of all things had decided that she would love nothing more than to work on the oyster perches. Janna had warned her it would be cold, wet work, but the girl was not put off. She'd embraced life in Oystertown as if she'd been born there. Janna was secretly glad that there would be a new oyster girl to take on her mantle.

Of course Louise was not the only foreign bride to arrive after the war. It had taken many months for Harry to be brought back and demobbed, and by that time he'd mastered enough French to ask Juliette to come with him. They had married in a civil ceremony in her home town in Flanders and then had a joyous church blessing in Kent, putting aside any conflict of her being Catholic and Harry being decidedly agnostic at best. They'd wanted an occasion for everyone to join in, and that is what had happened. Totally in character, they had arrived at the church in a cart festooned with blossoms and pulled by two magnificent horses, their manes and tails braided, their coats glossy from brushing. Nobody who had seen the emaciated Bessie and Napoléon in the war years would have recognized them but the happy couple would have had it no other way.

Claudia snapped herself out of her reminiscences and together with Janna set about arranging the plates on the pristine cloth, firmly secured in case of a rising sea breeze. Celia had brought out several crystal vases filled with artfully cut garden flowers, deep blue irises set against pale sweet peas in pink and lilac. As she placed one at the end of the table Claudia caught sight of Jasper emerging through the big French windows, their fine lace curtains billowing behind him. She had to smile – she still felt her pulse race each time she saw him, even after years together.

It had been quite the scandal to begin with. Some of her society friends had dropped her at once, but she now knew them to be mere acquaintances and not true friends. Those who knew her best could only approve. The select few knew the truth about her marriage to Xan, and wanted her to be happy in whatever way she chose after that debacle. Her mother, the staunch bastion of respectability, supported her completely – that was the measure of how the war had changed Celia.

Then once people had accepted Jasper as a successful man of business, adviser to Kim at the Admiralty, objections faded away. It made Claudia secretly grin to think that the buttoned-up matrons at high-powered events shaking his hand and admiring his still-unruly dark hair had no idea he'd once been a fisherman with a sideline in bare-knuckle fighting. But she herself never forgot. It was what had made him who he was – and she'd realized some time ago that she had no real interest in respectability. The stone-throwing suffragette and the daring lifeboat captain – not such a mismatch after all.

They too had had a quiet civil ceremony, once she'd completed a conventionally acceptable period of apparent mourning for Xan. She had not been inclined to follow it with a big party; her relationship with Jasper seemed too important and unique to subject it to a reception such as she had had with Xan. Jasper had not objected. Money behind the bar at the Duke for all their family and friends was perfectly fine and he'd enjoyed himself far more than he would have done in a stuffy room at the Savoy.

Of course everything had been far from plain sailing in the years since the war had ended. There had been the terrible outbreak of flu that swept through the forces and civilians alike, sparing nowhere. Oystertown had seen its share of casualties. Celia herself had had a narrow escape, as had Billy Gann, proving that the disease was no respecter of social position. Poor Ozzie had been home for only a month when Annie succumbed, a woman apparently in her prime but powerless against the virus. He'd never quite got over it, despite the passage of time.

Jasper came over to the table and swept his wife into a hug, which would have scandalized the matrons even now had they been present. 'How is it all going?' he asked when he'd released her. 'Not still running around managing every detail, I hope? You are meant to be enjoying this, you know. It's your party.'

Claudia shot him a look. 'I will, and I am, but not before everyone's here. You were with Daniel, I take it? All the children are inside? Good, that's one less thing to think about. What time is Kim arriving – did he say? He kept changing his mind yesterday, not being sure of when he could get away.'

'He'll be here, don't worry,' Jasper assured her. 'Amelia would kill him if he missed this.'

Claudia flashed him another look. 'I should jolly well hope so.' She liked Kim's bride, knowing he had finally bowed to the inevitable and picked someone from their own circle, eminently suitable as a high-ranking naval wife. She was ten years younger than him, fair of skin and hair, and delicate of build. She had a core of steel, though, which Claudia thought was good for her cousin. He might have had a yearning to throw over the traces during his affair with Marietta but this existence suited him much better deep down. And Amelia was determined to make the most of their life – so perhaps not so very different to Marietta after all.

And there she was.

Nobody could miss the arrival of Marietta, now known internationally as Marina Makepeace. She didn't have to wear her screen make-up or costumes to turn heads; she had lost none of that allure she'd had aged twenty. In truth, the man accompanying her was more flamboyantly attired – but there was no doubt who was the centre of attention.

She waved at Jasper and also at Kim, who'd just got out of his own car. Her real focus though was on Claudia and Janna, whom she rushed to hug. For a moment it was as if they were young women again, fresh out of girlhood, full of hopes and dreams and with no idea of what awaited them, and just as well. Then she belatedly introduced Stan, and turned to greet Celia, and many of the other guests whom she'd known for so long. Finally, she came face to face with Pascal and Tilly.

There was no doubt that age was catching up with her father, no matter how he battled against it, never ceasing in his hectic routine of painting whenever the light was right and inspiration struck. Marietta noticed he moved more slowly, more stiffly. But his face, although more lined, and his moustache less outrageous, bore the same expression she'd always recognized: love of life and love for his only daughter, and such pride in what she'd achieved. Tilly was still striking, even if grey was creeping into her luxuriant hair – it didn't seem that she minded overmuch.

Marietta hugged them and was hugged in return, under-standing how much she missed them. It was knowing they were still here, ready to turn to in times of crisis, that gave her the impetus to strike out in her career, to take on Hollywood in all its glamour and seediness. It was a world that dealt in dreams and fantasies; here was the real world, her own flesh and blood, the land, the sea.

Daniel appeared over Tilly's shoulder and smiled at his sister. 'Good to have you back,' he said simply.

'It's good to be back.' Her gaze skimmed the groups of people, checking that Stan was all right, but he could make himself at home anywhere. There he was, chatting with Archie. 'So, what happens now? When do we start to eat? I'm always starving,' she added, her eyes twinkling so he would know it was a joke – and in the knowledge that, for both of them and many more of the assembled company, being short of food was an all-too-real memory.

Pascal overheard. '*Mais bien sûr.* However, there are to be speeches.' He laughed as Marietta rolled her eyes. 'Do not fear, they will not be long. Meanwhile, let me pass you a glass of champagne. That will revive you.' Marietta nodded enthu-siastically as her father magicked a bottle from somewhere and topped them all up.

Claudia was making her way to the top of the terrace steps. Her hair broke free of its casual bun and a corn-coloured tress was caught by the sea breeze before she tucked it behind one ear. If she was nervous, she showed no trace of it, as she came to a halt and clapped her hands.

'I won't keep you long!' she called to everyone as they stilled their chatter, all eyes now on her. 'We just wanted to mark this occasion, to celebrate the passing of the bill through parliament. I know some of you will think that this is a very dull reason for a party but it's anything but.' She paused to take a breath, to stand fully straight. 'To some of us it's a big event. Well, come to think of it, for any woman over twenty-one but as yet still under thirty, and for any woman at all who wouldn't have met the property barrier, it's a very big day indeed. We now have the means to decide our own future, for ourselves. So I'd say it's the best reason to have a party. Let's raise our glasses!' Nobody needed encouragement to do that.

'And now, I just want to stand aside for one of my fellow campaigners – and one of my best friends. Janna, will you come up?'

Janna gasped. 'What, me?'

Claudia nodded, knowing that if she had given her friend any warning in advance she would have found some means of slipping away. 'Of course. It's your day every bit as much as mine.'

Janna took a big sip of Daniel's champagne for courage, and to give her blush a couple of moments to fade. Then she squared her shoulders. Claudia was right. Some of this was down to her. She'd faced worse in France than a crowd of well-wishers. Handing Daniel back his glass, she stepped forward.

'Thank you, Claudia, and thank you, everybody, for being here today.' She gazed around at all the faces turned up to look at her. 'Especially those of you who have come a very long way.' Her eyes sought out Marietta's. 'Claudia has said how much this means. I'd never have got involved without her – but I'm so glad I did. I won't bore you with all the matters that went on behind the scenes for so many years, but they all helped to bring us here. Now every one of us can help to build a better future. Let's raise our glasses to that.' She smiled encouragingly and everybody murmured, or shouted, 'The future!' Janna nodded in satisfaction. 'And if I, an oyster girl from Oystertown, can travel up to London, and to France, and be part of shaping what's to come – then that means that anyone can. Every single one of you.' She nodded again to show that she was finished, and stepped down to where Daniel was waiting, to a round of applause.

'You were marvellous,' he said, his hazel eyes warming with pride at the sight of her at his side. 'Will we see you standing for parliament, then? There's no reason why not.'

Janna shook her head. 'I think we might leave that to my sister-in-law.' She tipped her head back to gaze properly at him, at his peppering of freckles that she loved. 'We've travelled all over but I think we know this is our place in the world. There's no better view than the one over this bay, is there?'

Jasper had overheard her. 'None in the world,' he agreed. 'No matter where we've been and where we're yet to go, we'll always come back to where we know best.'

They stood there, amid the chatter, the cries of the sea birds, the ceaseless sound of waves on the beach, the happy humming of bees in the roses and wild flowers beyond reaching down to the start of the sand. Down the hill was the harbour, its waters today a sparkling blue, with none of the dark menace they all knew the bay could contain. There were the boats, many moored up as their crew were at this very party. Oystertown had come through the war and survived to see another day, another decade – and it was where they all belonged.

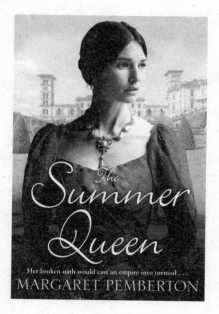

The Summer Queen

MARGARET PEMBERTON

Sweeping across Europe from Britain to Russia at the turn of the twentieth century, *The Summer Queen* explores the lives of a royal family united by love, yet divided by war.

'This engrossing saga follows Victoria's grandchildren – including Kaiser Wilhelm II, the Tsarina of Russia and the future Queen Mary – over forty turbulent years before their dreams end in war and revolution' *S Magazine*

OUT NOW

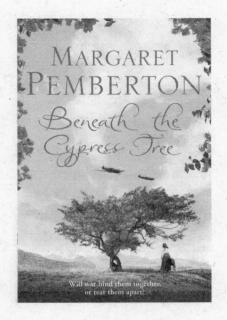

Beneath the Cypress Tree

MARGARET PEMBERTON

A sweeping saga of friends and lovers, set in Crete during the Second World War.

'Margaret Pemberton is one of the best saga writers around, writing gritty, gutsy tales'   *The Bookseller*

OUT NOW

A Season of Secrets

MARGARET PEMBERTON

Sweeping from the Great War through the Jazz Age to the 1940s, this unforgettable tale follows the entwined lives of the Fentons, an aristocratic family from Yorkshire.

OUT NOW